Colin P Brown

The Surgeon

All rights reserved. No part of this book may be reproduced, stored in a retrieval system, or transmitted, in any form or by any means without the prior permission of the author, nor be otherwise circulated in any form of binding other than that in which it is published and without a similar condition being imposed on the subject purchaser. Trademarked names appear throughout this book. Rather than use a trademark symbol with every occurrence of a trademarked name, names are used in an editorial fashion, with no intention of infringement of the respective owner's trademark. The information in this book is distributed on an "as is" basis, without warranty. Although every precaution has been taken in the preparation of this work, neither the author nor the publisher shall have any liability to any person or entity with respect to any loss or damage caused or alleged to be caused directly or indirectly by the information contained in this book.

This is a work of fiction. Names, characters, places, and incidents either are the product of the author's imagination or are used fictitiously, and any resemblance to actual persons, living or dead, events, or locales is entirely coincidental.

For Al who opened my eyes to the world of detecting.

1

'Call Heather.'

Jason's pronunciation was unusually loud and precise; as though instructing a secretary; hard of hearing and possibly of foreign extraction.

Confirming the car had heard correctly, a well-educated female voice responded with calm serenity.

'Calling Heather.'

From the speakers, the sound of a phone ringing filled the enclosed space.

'Hello.'

Heather's voice was unmistakeable – friendly, bright and feminine; the sort of voice that raised the spirits, whatever she chose to say.

'Hello darling. Just leaving. I should be home in twenty-five minutes, tops.'

'Okay Sweetie. I'll be waiting up…and I'm not tired.'

Jason experienced an involuntary twitch in his trousers.

'Blimey, make that ten. Bye. Love you.'

'Love you too.'

The call may have ended, but Jason's smile lingered; an expression and a feeling born of contentment. The day had already provided much to be thankful for: happy customers; a team that never failed to do their bit to achieve that degree of happiness; convivial conversation with his staff, his manager, and a certain lady whose young son had managed to open, then drop a tub of dragees, the small silver sugar balls spreading further than anyone would have thought possible, transforming the shop floor's surface, designed for shoes of all descriptions, and trollies, into something more familiar to ice skaters. All this and yet there were still two hours before the clocks announced midnight. Charlie and Lily would be asleep, but still he would take pleasure in placing a gentle kiss on their cheeks, hoping their dreams would register the act. Only then would he sink into his wife's embrace; warm, soft and loving.

The fleeting glimpse of an owl, swooping through the headlight beams, changed the subject as effectively as switching channels on the TV. As delightful as this unexpected gift of nature was, at this hour thoughts were transient and it held his attention for no time at all, this being grabbed by the radio, his mind questioning the entertainment value of a faceless man inviting listeners to phone in on such subjects as the rights of railway workers to strike, and the problem of unleashed dogs fouling public footpaths.

Jason's eyes shifted towards the centre of the dashboard. His finger prodded one of the pre-select buttons; the station instantly changing from the mutterings of Dave - a first-time caller - to the music of Jason's formative years – the mid-nineties. His attention then returned to the road, just as a white van came out of nowhere to overtake at speed, the driver choosing to complete the manoeuvre far too soon. Startled, Jason's hands gripped the wheel a great deal tighter, his foot instinctively pivoting from accelerator to brake. The van's arc became sharper, forcing evasive action, Jason steering to the left without giving thought to what might be in his path. Adrenalin stretched the moment, permitting Jason's mind to consider the inevitable collision – but it did not come. Against all odds, miraculously, both car and van came to an abrupt halt in a darkened lay-by, both seemingly avoiding any sort of damage.

With Jason's foot off the pedals, the engine cut, bringing relative quiet, the most noticeable ambient sound being the Macarena, playing at mid-volume, oblivious to the occasion.

Jason remained behind the wheel, too shaken to leave the vehicle to challenge the other driver. His hands continued to grip the leather as his brain absorbed and stored details of the event. Someone had the right to be angry; someone had questions to answer; someone had most definitely been in the wrong. Jason knew his position, but strangely the other party seemed reluctant to express theirs.

As the seconds pulsed by, Jason became increasingly aware that neither party had emerged to remonstrate, or else say sorry. If the driver of the van was drunk, he could be expected to stagger from the scene; if he felt aggrieved, or was some ignorant Neanderthal, he might be expected to throw open his door, haul himself from the cab and move aggressively in Jason's direction – but there was nothing.

The vehicles had come to a halt in a narrow lay-by, parallel to each other, but with the van set far forward, so the rear nearside corner of the van almost touched the front offside wing of the car. The headlights of Jason's vehicle illuminated one side of the featureless van, a small patch of tarmacadam, and an embankment beyond, planted with bushes, decorated with litter casually discarded by passing motorists. The van's engine was still running, its rear lights still shining. Blank panels indicated a privately owned vehicle. A dirty sweatshirt, or similar item of clothing, was trapped in the rear doors and hung down over the number plate; proof of a driver who was cavalier about the rules of the road, or was keen to disguise his identity.

As time continued to pass, Jason came to wonder whether he might have misread the situation. Had he allowed himself to be governed by stereotypical beliefs with regard to the character of *white van man*? Perhaps, without warning, the driver had become unwell and without intending to cut anyone up, had bolted for the sanctuary of the lay-by from where he might call for assistance. At that very moment he might be in desperate measure, slumped over the steering wheel, clutching his tightening chest, his heart sending shooting pains down his left arm, too distracting to allow him to make that vital call.

Tired of waiting in economy mode, the car's engine re-started suddenly, jolting Jason from a state of torpor, urging him to act. With practised movements that required no conscious thought, he removed the key from the ignition, folded it into the fob, killed the lights, opened the door, swung his legs to the right, and stood up. It was then he realised the rear quarter of his car projected into the road; a perilous position as not even the reflectors faced the oncoming traffic. Leaning back into the vehicle, his fingertip jabbed the illuminated triangle in the centre of the dashboard, activating the hazard warning lights. Withdrawing from the interior, he slammed the door shut, before popping the bunch of keys into his pocket. Despite this activity, still there was no reaction from the other party.

Four orange lights flashed rhythmically; two red lights shone from the rear of the van; a pair of headlights directed forwards, towards a leafless hedgerow, but these were not the only sources of light, the glow of a full moon in a cloudless night sky, providing ample light to navigate by, improving with each moment as Jason's eyes grew accustomed to the conditions.

The corner of Jason's vehicle being so close to the van, the natural route to the other driver's door caused him to step across the broken white line, into the empty road. There he froze to the spot, convinced something was lurking in the shadow of the van. His eyes widened, peering into the darkness, his feet refusing to take another step until whatever it was had identified itself.

A lone car sped towards him, coming from the direction both halted vehicles had just driven; an expensive car with Christmas decorations for headlights. Wishing to avoid life changing injury, the nervous pedestrian stepped nimbly from the road into the shadows. The lights were soon upon him, reflecting green off the eyes of a startled fox which scuttled quickly to the other side of the carriageway, narrowly avoiding ending the day as road kill. The excessive speed of the passing vehicle took it from the scene in a flash, returning silence, broken only by the sound of a diesel engine idling.

Relieved, but feeling rather foolish, Jason continued towards the other driver's door, half expecting an extremely drunk person to come to consciousness at any second and growl at him in an incomprehensible fashion. Stepping up to the door, Jason readied himself to leap backwards at the first hint of aggression. The window was wound down; the cab was empty.

For a moment, Jason stood motionless in the cool autumn air, confused as to what he should do next.

In an atmosphere of inactivity, the sound of the van's diesel engine grew in prominence; enough to mask the careful footsteps of a hooded man - dressed from head to foot in black - who approached from behind. The grab was made with practised professionalism, one hand muffling the victim's mouth with a pre-cut length of gaffer tape, the free arm clenching the victim's shoulders so he became unbalanced, causing him to fall back. Simultaneously, two similarly attired men pounced; one strapping the victim's wrists with cable ties, before pinioning Jason's elbows to his sides; the other binding Jason's ankles together tightly. A hood, smelling heavily of fabric softener, was placed over the victim's head, drawstrings ensuring it could not be dislodged easily; the odour ensuring he could not detect smells which he might otherwise remember and later report to the police.

Being of average build, Jason was bundled out of sight of the road with ease, where latex-clad hands conducted a thorough search of his clothing, discovering a bunch of keys in his right trouser pocket; half a packet of mints and a crumpled, but unused, man-sized tissue in the left. These having been cast to one side, the next task was for the assailants to drag their prey to the back of the featureless van, to be hauled inside. Here they were at their most exposed, the doors facing the empty carriageway. However, this stretch of road having been chosen for its qualities - dark and quiet - potential witnesses were few and gave ample warning of their approach. Two vehicles passed, one tailgating the other, the follower becoming the leader in one swift manoeuvre. In all likelihood, the boy racer was concentrating so much on the obstacle in his way, he failed to notice the lay-by, the car, or the white van that occupied it, never mind the small group of men, masked by the night, whose hands kept a vice-like grip on their captive's arms. Likewise, the driver of the car being overtaken was fully occupied with his rear-view mirror.

Relocation was achieved as soon as the coast was clear, after which the rear doors slammed shut. Through them, Jason heard a car door open, assuming it must be his own. The sound of it shutting again was followed closely by the sound of the van's passenger door opening and closing with force – the man certainly had a heavy hand.

The noise of the engine under acceleration was quickly drowned out by a looped soundtrack, played through a stereo system – random sounds: ducks quacking; construction work; bygone steam trains; water flowing; a lion roaring. Not a word had been spoken since Jason had issued a single expletive at the moment the van had so abruptly come into view. Now, not even a muffled cry was to be tolerated. On the first occasion he released a groan, it was met with a 'Shhh!' The second earned him a firm kick to his side. There was to be no third, and no sounds to report to the police, other than those which the kidnappers wanted him to hear.

The abducted man had expected to be home in less than half an hour. Despite minor discomfort, he had chosen to pass the work's toilet by, preferring to wait for the comfort and familiarity of his own facilities. That swift decision now came to haunt him as his bladder began passing ever stronger signals to his brain, advising it would soon have to empty, or risk bursting. As though reading his thoughts, whoever shared the floor of the van with him, rolled him onto his back, unfastened his trousers, reached into his underpants, pulled out his penis, and fed it into some kind of plastic bag with a stiffened neck. This was taped in place.

Adding to the fear induced by finding himself the target of abduction, the victim was left feeling violated as he had never been before. However, the act also served to strengthen his resolve. This was where he would draw the line. No matter how uncomfortable it became, he would not urinate into a bag. That was for pets; he was a man; a man with principles and honour.

In films, Jason had often seen the hero bundled into the boot of a car, from where he listened intently to changing road noise and ambient sounds, later enabling the authorities to retrace the route to the abductors' lair. In reality, other than detecting vague changes of direction, he would have nothing to recall. Besides, the journeys in films were relatively short. This felt as though it continued for many hours. For all he knew, though, this might be another layer of disguise. The kidnappers already controlled three of his senses: what he smelled; what he saw; what he heard. Perhaps they also sought to control his perception of time, the driver directing them round and round in circles, so his passenger would come to confuse minutes with hours, hours with days. If this was his intention, he had performed his task admirably.

Jason's thoughts turned to his family – to his children who would sleep unaware, but awaken to the absence of their Daddy; to his darling wife who would come to realise her husband was missing, not knowing whether he was alive or dead.

Masked by the soundtrack, a trickle of water became a steady flow. A tear rolled down a beaten man's cheek.

2

There was no reason for Jason to call home every evening; his wife knew the routine only too well and could normally expect to see him in person twenty-five minutes later. So regular was his routine, if he thought to capture an image of the wall clock each time he walked out through the staff entrance, the photo album on his smart phone would be choked with dozens of identical images – the little hand pointing to the ten; the big hand at three minutes past the hour. Nevertheless, he called without fail, to exchange words so familiar to both parties they might have been scripted.

This brief contact meant a lot to him. Working from lunchtime until ten in the evening, five nights per week, straddling every single weekend, his wife holding down a regular job of her own, Jason's opportunities to speak with Heather were all too infrequent.

The phone calls meant a lot to Heather too, and for her they served an additional purpose.

To maximise her opportunity for sleep, Heather had developed a routine of her own. Once the children had been read to and put to bed, she would make packed lunches for the morning, de-clutter the house of all the things Charlie and Lily had left lying about, slip into her fleecy pyjamas, and curl up at one end of the sofa with a crime thriller; preferably Scandinavian. Then would come the call; her cue to conduct her night time ablutions, before retiring to the bedroom, there to catch up on the world of social media while awaiting her husband's return.

This night was different. This night being a Friday, Heather did not need to get to sleep with such precision, their only alarm on a Saturday morning being the children, and they usually slept in until nine. That meant, mood permitting, Jason was more likely to get lucky than on any other night of the week.

By ten-thirty, anticipation was beginning to build, requiring several video clips of playful kittens behaving badly to keep her mind from becoming overwhelmed by desire. By ten-forty-five, Heather's eyes began wandering repeatedly to the top of the screen, keeping a track of the time. At ten-fifty, she fired off a text, 'Where are you? I'm getting worried.' She supplemented her words with a pair of emojis – a yellow face with a worried frown; a second blowing a kiss.

To this there was no reply.

Her finger swiped the screen, right to left, then tapped once. An app opened, revealing two cursors: one – a flattering image of Heather - representing her position on a map; the other – a clown's face - identifying the position of her husband. He was only half way home. Strange. She jabbed Jason's cursor with the tip of her finger, opening a window containing his contact details. Another tap and his phone was ringing. If he was in his car, he would hear the tone in surround sound. If he was out of the car, in all likelihood he would hear his phone ring, feel the vibration in his pocket and, or see the screen illuminate his surroundings. There was not a defence lawyer in the kingdom who could later claim Jason was not aware his wife had tried to contact him, but still there was no response.

Desires of the body having abandoned her, all Heather wanted now was to know the whereabouts of her husband. She tapped the refresh icon, hoping to find the clown's face had progressed on its journey, but Jason's car, or at least his phone, remained unmoved. Her finger and thumb stretched the screen, magnifying the map to such an extent she could see his cursor in line with an isolated lay-by. She sent another text.

'Are you all right? Have you broken down? xxx'

Forcing herself to remain calm, Heather awarded her husband a further five minutes to answer.

The moment arrived and passed, at which point Heather realised that setting an ultimatum was a waste of time unless the person making such a demand had a plan of action ready to enforce; and she had none.

Heather's thumb danced across the screen of her phone. After a pause, a drowsy voice responded to the vibration of plastic against bedside cabinet.

'Hello, dear. Is everything okay? You don't normally call this late.'

'Hello, Mum. I'm really worried. Jason rang to tell me he'd just left work over an hour ago and he's still not in. I've tracked him on the phone and he appears to have stopped at a lay-by. I've tried texting and ringing several times, but he's just not answering.'

'Oh dear, I hope he's all right. We'd come over, but Dad's taken his pills. There's no way he can drive tonight. He's out for the count. Have you phoned the Police?'

'No, Mum. Do you really think I should? Isn't it being a bit premature?'

'I don't know, dear. God forbid something's happened to him and there's a delay coming to his rescue.'

'I know, but…'

Heather's mother understood her daughter's reluctance.

'Here's an idea. If you're worried about wasting Police time, why not ring their non-emergency number? At least they could give you advice.'

'Okay, Mum, maybe I will. Love you. Bye.'

'Bye, dear. Keep me informed.'

Far from reassuring her, the call served only to feed Heather's anxiety. She was left torn between the advice of her mother - something she normally trusted implicitly - and her reluctance to bother the Police unnecessarily. Heather was well aware of the trivial matters members of the public would seek to address through the use of the 999 emergency number: asking whether it was safe to eat food that had passed its sell-by date; reporting a garden bird, killed by a neighbour's cat; forgetting where the car was parked – and she did not want her name added to the list of anecdotes maintained by the Force Control Room, which in an attempt to cut down misuse of the system, occasionally reported to the media the sins of their public.

In the end, Heather accepted her mother's compromise, and her thumb danced across her smart phone once more.

'Police non-emergency line.'

'Oh, hello. I...I think my husband's gone missing.'

Despite her desire to sound confident, Heather's voice was shaking.

'Why do you think that?'

'Well, he rang me at ten o'clock as he was leaving work. It normally takes him about twenty-five minutes to get home and he's still not here. I've sent him several texts and rung him twice, but I've had no response.'

'Perhaps he was driving.'

'No, his car reads the texts to him. He loves it. Anyway, I checked his whereabouts and he appears to be in a lay-by on the Old Felworth Road. I thought he might have broken down and was away from the car, but it doesn't explain him not answering.'

'Madam, I really think it's too early to be getting worried. I'm sure there's a simple explanation. This lay-by, is it far from you? Are you able to travel there?'

'It's only about five miles away,' Heather confessed, 'but I don't drive.'

'I see. Well, I'm sorry but we have no patrol cars available at the moment. It might be a couple of hours before we can send one.'

'I can't wait that long. I'll ask my neighbour if she can take me. If not, I'll get a taxi.'

'Okay, if you find anything untoward, call again.'

The operator had been let off the hook. She had handled the call politely, dealt with the issue swiftly, and by suggesting the caller do her own investigation had avoided committing dwindling resources.

Heather sent another text, but could not wait for a reply. Discarding her dressing gown on the hall floor, she exchanged it for a long coat, wearing it both to keep out the cold and to disguise the fact she was wearing pyjamas. Leaving the front door ajar, she padded along the connecting path to her adjoining neighbours, at number 52.

It took a while for them to answer. The couple were retired and chose to lock out the world early every evening, preferring a cup of tea in bed and a few chapters of a good book to repeats and imports on the television. Given their ages, not only did Irene and her husband fall outside the target TV audience, but whatever programme was aired, they had both seen some version of it before – *Jack the Ripper - the True Story* lacked novelty, as did most documentaries.

A second press of the doorbell was required before the hall light came on, shining through the frosted glass panes of the door. The lock turned and soon after a suspicious face peered through the narrow opening. Fortunately for both parties, Heather was instantly recognisable, an ornate porch lamp bathing the unexpected caller in the cool light of an energy efficient bulb.

'Oh, Hello Heather. We thought you might be burglars. Although I don't suppose burglars would ring the doorbell first, would they.'

She smiled; a friendly smile.

It occurred to Heather, given the circumstances, it had been the lady of the household who had taken the brave decision to come to the door; a role more traditionally reserved for the husband and his golf club, testing its weight and balance before leaving the room. What must have been the hastened conversation which resulted in Irene throwing back the bedclothes, leaving her husband curious but safe beneath a double layer of duvet?

'Sorry to bother you, Irene. Jason's not arrived home and I'm worried. I phoned the police but they can't do anything for another couple of hours. I know it's a lot to ask; I've tracked his phone to a lay-by on the Old Felworth Road. Is there any chance you could give me a lift there? I'm really worried.'

'Don't be so silly, dear, of course I can.'

'One more problem - the kids are in bed.'

'Don't worry, I'll send Bob round. Give me five minutes to throw something on and raise the old man from the dead and I'll be right with you.'

Heather padded back to the glow of her own hall. If Irene and Bob had time to make themselves decent, so too did she. However, to her mind, worrying what the world thought of her, amid such a crisis, seemed trivial. The time was better spent gathering the necessities: her phone; her keys; her spectacles.

In quick time, Irene and Bob appeared on the doorstep, the former pushing the door open before stepping through onto the mat. Neither looked in the least bit inconvenienced.

'Thanks Bob. I'm sorry to drag you out of bed.'

'Think nothing of it,' he replied, cheerily.

He had in his hand a newspaper, folded to the puzzle page, and a pen.

'The kids are asleep. With any luck you won't hear a peep out of either of them.'

Settled in the passenger seat of Irene's Citroen, her seatbelt freshly clicked into place, Heather's feelings of concern for her husband were temporarily trumped by those of awkwardness and guilt for having disturbed her neighbours at such an hour. Although she knew her chauffeur genuinely did not mind, she being the kind of person who would do anything for anyone, expecting nothing in return, Heather felt the need to excuse her untimely intrusion.

'This is so good of you, Irene. At times like this it's a real pain I can no longer drive.'

'That's all right, dear. You both do so much for us; it's lovely to be able to do something in return.'

'It's nice of you to say, Irene, but we don't do any more than you've done for us.'

The engine sprang to life. Irene turned towards her passenger and issued a friendly smile.

'Okay, let's just agree that we're both good neighbours and leave it at that.'

Once under way, Heather related to Irene the events that had led them to be in the car, punctuating the end of her every sentence with another text or another failed attempt to call her husband.

'I'm sure he'll be all right. He's probably just broken down,' Irene reassured, as her passenger's thumbs became frantic once more.

Her natural and honest positivity did little to calm Heather's nerves.

'If that was the case, he could have broken down anywhere,' Heather replied, resting her phone in her lap, clutching the case tightly in the hope she might feel it vibrate a response. 'What are the chances he'd break down just as he passed the lay-by? Besides, he'd have rung me.'

Judging further platitudes might serve only to exacerbate the situation, Irene decided not to offer a counter argument, or further opinion, but instead issued some sound advice.

'Worrying like this isn't going to help. We're only a few minutes away so try to stay calm and keep an eye out in case we pass him.'

Much to the frustration of the passenger, the journey continued at a leisurely pace, the speed partly determined by Irene's night myopia, partly to ensure neither occupants of the car missed anything of importance.

Approaching the lay-by, Heather and Irene immediately spotted Jason's vehicle. Despite the area being otherwise empty, with plenty of room for Jason to park parallel to the road, they found his car left at an absurd angle, almost at a tangent to the direction of passing traffic, its rear end projecting into the carriageway, its hazard warning lights blinking.

Irene pulled in, bringing her vehicle to a halt, a car's length from Jason's.

Heather was quick to get out, swiftly followed by Irene who left the car's headlights on to illuminate the scene. By the time Irene had walked round to the other side of the Citroen to close the door that had been left wide open and abandoned, a frantic Heather had reached her husband's car and determined a number of things: it was empty; it had been left unlocked; Jason's blazer remained on the hook in the rear; and he was nowhere to be seen. She called out repeatedly, each time with greater force, until her voice became hoarse and silent. At the same time, her eyes peered into the hedgerow. There came no response. All the while, Irene stood still, feeling helpless. Her voice was old and weak and could not compete with Heather's. Neither could her eyes, which no longer had the keenness of youth.

Desperate, Heather called her husband's number again. It was not answered, but she could hear it 'ring' - the sound of a cricket chirping loudly. The tone emanated from the pocket of the driver's door. There, Heather found her husband's phone, its screen indicating missed calls and many unread texts – kisses she had sent, but had gone unseen.

Questions threatened to overload Heather's mind, two of which dominated all others. Why would he not take his phone, whether he had left the scene to seek assistance, or to relieve himself? Secondly, he was obsessed with security, often deadlocking the front door as soon as he had passed through it, much to the annoyance of his wife when she later came to answer the doorbell. Why then had he left his car unlocked? Without explaining her actions, she began to walk the length and breadth of the lay-by; peering beneath her husband's car in the unlikely event he had somehow become trapped beneath it; setting her gaze upon the ground and to the boundaries. Only when she had exhausted her search, she came to a halt, let her chin fall to her chest, her hands to her sides, closed her eyes, and began sobbing. Irene came to her, engulfing her body in a warm embrace. After a short while, seeing no change in her neighbour's demeanour, her arms broke away, permitting her to take her own phone from her coat pocket.

Irene did not share her neighbour's concern about inconveniencing the police.

Having completed her call, she wrapped her arm around her neighbour's back, clutching Heather's shoulder for a second time.

'They've promised to send a patrol car straight away. Now, let's sit in my car and wait for them in the warm.'

Heather allowed herself to be led like a lamb.

With the engine idling, the Citroen provided an oasis of heat, light and a comfortable place to sit. Through sniffles, Heather asked question after question, none of which Irene could answer. All she could do was offer weak possibilities and a packet of soft tissues, kept in the glove box for emergencies. Whatever she truly believed, she was not letting on.

Only one topic filled Heather's mind, so intensely that it quickly became too exhausting to speak of further. However, the seconds it took for her to check the time on her phone was all the rest she needed, before new questions and fears spewed from her mouth. Time check after time check; pauses and unanswerable questions; so the regime continued for what felt like eternity.

Finally, no more than twenty minutes after the call had been placed, a car pulled up behind the Citroen, making itself known as a police patrol by flashing its blue and red lights silently but manically; a strange mixture of stealth and aggressively overt.

The lights triggered Heather to bail from the car and run towards the first officer she saw, who leapt from his seat to corral her to safety, narrowly avoiding her being swept to oblivion by a passing articulated lorry. At first she made no sense, the young officer appearing overwhelmed by the onslaught, but a few experienced words, spoken by the driver, an older officer, brought Heather to her senses.

She breathed. She paused. She blew her nose.

'Right, Ma'am, I am Police Constable Billinge and this is PC Semmens. Can I ask your name?'

It was only as the introductions were made Heather realised how young the second officer looked – painfully young; not having lived long enough for his body to fill his uniform. The distraction calmed her.

Heather returned her attention to the older man.

'Er, Mrs Ressler.'

'And your first name?'

'Heather.'

He turned to her companion.

'And who might you be, Ma'am?'

'Oh, my name's Irene Spillman. I'm Heather's neighbour. I made the call.'

'Okay, Heather, Irene,' PC Billinge responded, looking to each of the ladies in turn, 'let's see if we can get to the root of the problem.'

The group remained close-knit while Heather related the events leading up to the moment, and explained why she was convinced something untoward had befallen her husband. It was no longer possible for her to panic, such was the calming influence of the older man who, when Heather was finished, looked to his colleague.

'Dave, how about you take a look at Jason's car while I get some of this stuff down before I forget it.'

The young officer nodded, took a torch from his belt and made his way over to the abandoned vehicle. Having circled it, Dave Semmens found no obvious mechanical damage that might have caused the driver to pull over in an emergency, or at the first suitable spot: the tyres were all in good condition and facing the way the manufacture intended; there were no dents or scuff marks that might indicate he had been involved in a collision; with another vehicle, an animal, or a human.

He turned his attention to the interior. In the driver's door pocket, he found Jason's phone, returned there on the advice of Irene who thought the crime scene should remain untouched. A pair of booster seats occupied much of the rear. A uniform blazer hung from a hook above the door, directly behind the driver. Pinned to the outside, a badge informed customers the wearer's name was Jason Ressler; manager. Semmens checked the jacket thoroughly, finding Jason's wallet in the inside breast pocket. It contained debit and credit cards, a small wad of notes, and a photograph of his family – Heather and their two kids.

Next, accepting not many cars had spare wheels these days, he thought it nevertheless prudent to check the boot. This car did have one; it and the equipment needed to replace it being found beneath the floor, seemingly never before having seen the light of day. A flat tyre was not the answer, or any part of it.

Heather and Irene were advised to return to the Citroen while the two officers extended the search to the lay-by and the immediate surrounding area. The older man was very much in charge, not only giving his colleague instruction, but advice. It seemed likely the younger of the two was in probation; it also seemed possible to Heather this might be a bring-your-son-to-work-day. However, whatever disparaging thoughts she harboured, it turned out to be the boy who made the first discovery, catching a glint of metal in the beam of his torch – car keys.

There was no need for Heather to identify them as belonging to her husband. PC Semmens simply pressed the buttons to lock and unlock the car, establishing it as fact. He then went one further, using the keys to start the car and reposition it to a less dangerous spot. The two officers then appeared to hold a brief discussion as to the pros and cons of moving evidence, the teacher letting the pupil make up his own mind. The two men then walked towards Irene's car, the women getting out to meet them half way, keen to hear the officers' conclusion, and what they intended as their next step. However, before PC Billinge could report his findings, he had first to explore other possibilities.

'Heather, can I ask, has your husband spoken of having problems at work?'

'No,' Heather replied in a curious tone, wondering what might lead the officer to ask such a question.

'Is there any reason he might suddenly decide to run off?'

'No... I'm sure I'd know. Everything's been fine – normal.'

Steve Billinge's eyes bored into her, challenging Heather to think hard and disclose anything he had said or done to suggest he wished to disappear.

Genuine effort caused Heather to frown.

'No. I mean he rang at the normal time and sounded fine. It was his idea we should take the kids to the zoo tomorrow afternoon, not mine. He bought me home flowers the other night....He was excited that we might have a cuddle tonight.'

'Does Jason suffer from depression?'

At this, Heather realised the officer was implying her husband might have taken his own life. She became angry.

'My husband has never thought of hurting himself,' she responded, delivering the words deliberately; with force. 'Besides, he has everything to live for: his kids; me; his job. I'll show you how close we are. Check his phone.'

'I'm afraid it's not as simple as that. Even if I had access to his phone, without a warrant, I'd be in breach of the Interception of Communications act. I could land up in prison.'

'But that's mad. If you can't, I certainly can. His PIN's the same as mine.'

PC Billinge looked awkward, struggling with the idea of being given access to data, confidential to a man who was not there to give him permission.

'If it helps, both our phones are registered to me as I set up the accounts. Jason finds it a bit of a pain. I tend to deal with all the finances – bills, insurance et cetera – so when he wants to contact the company they won't talk to him until I've been on the line to confirm it's okay.'

Heather's explanation was sufficient to stop the officer denying her access, but still he felt unable to scroll through the content of the phone without authorisation from his superiors.

Heather opened a page of conversations her husband had recently had by text. Being lazy, these exchange of words were rarely deleted, merely added too. Hence, conversations on entirely different subjects merged together seamlessly. None came as any surprise to Heather as she opened every string in turn. Only one was to a woman – a person known to the entire Ressler family. Heather turned the screen towards the police officer, ensuring both had equal view.

'You see?

We're going to the zoo on Sunday. Do your kids want to come too? Of course the invite includes you.'

Satisfied the officer had absorbed the meaning of the text, Heather worked her way systematically through every social media app on her husband's phone, and more, quickly demonstrating there were no secrets in their marriage; he had things planned for the near future, all of which involved his family; and that he was a family man. The texts between the couple were loving; his posts on Facebook attempted humour; they shared an e-mail address; they shared the same app that could locate each other's phone, at any time; they shared their calendar; his photo album was liberally punctuated with images of his family, including some of a smiling Heather, posing for him at various landmarks and dinners. Jason kept notes: shopping lists; DIY projects; suggestions for things he might buy his wife for their wedding anniversary. If there were secrets between them, they were buried deep; if he intended to run off, it did not appear he had intended to do so when he left work. What could possibly have happened in the ten minutes between Jason making the call to his wife and him reaching the lay-by, just five miles down the road, to warrant him abandoning his phone and wallet in an unsecured car, without offering a single word of explanation to anyone?

PC Billinge stepped to one side, as if to afford himself privacy. However, it did nothing to prevent Heather and Irene overhearing the officer requesting an ANPR check. Heather knew this stood for Automatic Number Plate Recognition and explained this to Irene who was looking mystified. What Heather could not fathom was the relevance. The answer was soon to come.

'Thanks.'

PC Billinge re-joined the little group to explain his actions and his discovery.

'We have an image of Jason's vehicle, leaving town, just at the time you said. Although fuzzy, my colleagues can see a man in the driving seat; no one beside him.'

As much for the benefit of the younger officer as the civilians, Steven Billinge explained the significance.

'Certainly when he left work, Jason didn't have anyone in the car with him. Of course, if he was being sneaky, he might have had someone tucked away in the back seat, but hardly anyone realises we capture an image as well as read the number plate, so that's unlikely. Of course, he could have rendezvoused with someone here, but that still doesn't explain why he left his valuables, why his car was unlocked, why he parked so haphazardly, or why he threw his keys into the bushes. I'm beginning to not like this.'

There were still a few more questions the well-seasoned officer had for the missing man's wife. They had to be asked, but he doubted they would provide a solution.

'Are there any friends he might have gone to?'

Heather answered but was beginning to sound exasperated.

'No, Jason doesn't have any close friends of his own. Not that he's unsociable. It's just that we share our friends and he mostly met them through me. The nearest - Jen and Aaron – they live only a few roads up from us. His parents are about twenty miles away. If he had needed to see them, he would have driven there, wouldn't he – he'd have needed the car. Even if it was an emergency and he had to find an alternative way of getting there, he'd have rung me, wouldn't he?'

PC Semmens did not hear a word Heather had spoken, his focus having suddenly been shifted by the notion he had missed something. Assuming it would lead to nothing, but wishing to put his mind at ease, he sidled away from the group, in the direction of Jason's abandoned car.

His colleague stayed put, fishing for clues.

David Semmens stepped round to the vehicle's passenger side, opened the door and leant in. He had already checked the door pocket on his first sweep, but had neglected the glove box. Operating the catch caused the door to spring downward with greater force than gravity alone would have produced, the contents having put strain upon it, exceeding the manufacturer's specifications. The officer hastily removed a bulb replacement kit, a pair of woollen gloves and a zipped folder, containing the owner's manual and other car-related documents. Towards the bottom of the storage compartment, a folded magazine ate up much of the remaining capacity, proving to be a current season holiday brochure to which was stuck a post-it note. Upon it, in a female hand, in purple ink, were written the words 'Hi Sexy. Can't wait to be alone with you, love Anna.' The message was accompanied by a large love heart encompassing the letters J and A, and no less than half a dozen kisses.

It seemed Jason might have had good reason to disappear after all.

David beckoned his mentor to him. Steven Billinge patted his colleague on the shoulder for a job well done, but his face showed no satisfaction. Potentially what was worse than finding that a man had disappeared, with the possibility of his safe return, was a man who had deceived his wife and family to run off with another woman.

He returned to speak with Heather. She saw the look on his face and assumed the younger officer had found something to confirm her initial fears.

'Aren't you going to put a tape round the area and take photos?'

'I'm sorry Heather, but from what I can tell, this isn't a crime scene.'

'What do you mean? Where is he then?'

'Look, there's no evidence your husband is a victim. There are no signs of blood or a struggle, and nothing is missing. At this moment in time, your husband has simply failed to come home…and… there's this…'

Constable Billinge produced his key piece of evidence, handing it to Heather for her to draw her own conclusion, undoubtedly the same as his own.

'This can't be.'

Heather began sobbing again and was immediately engulfed in Irene's arms, who looked towards the magazine held in her neighbour's hands, and to the note attached to it.

'Oh!'

'Look, Heather, I feel I must tailor your expectations. People go missing all the time. We'll add you husband's details to our system, but you have to remember, anyone over the age of eighteen who is not suffering mental incapacity may be absent through their own choice and may not want to be found. If we do find him and he doesn't want anyone to know, we have to respect that. My Inspector will do a risk assessment and is likely to conclude that, for the present at least, Jason is not missing, as such, just absent.'

Through her sniffles, Heather responded.

'There's a difference?'

'There's a big difference with regard to resources. He'll look at the risk. There doesn't appear to be substantial grounds to believe Jason is in danger. In fact, in light of what my colleague found in the glove box, there appears to be no apparent threat at all.

'It's not like in the movies. We'll broadcast to all local officers to keep an eye out and if we find anything, and he wants you to know, we'll keep you informed.'

In shock, Heather buried her thoughts in the practical implications.

'How do I get my husband's car back?'

'Don't worry', Irene interjected, 'I'll take you home now. Bob and I will collect the car in the morning. He's insured to drive anyone's vehicle.'

PC Billinge had the last words.

'I'm sorry Ma'am, I truly am. Now I suggest you remove any valuables from the vehicle and lock it.'

He touched Heather's elbow, hoping it offered her comfort. He looked to Irene and gave her a sombre smile. He then beckoned his apprentice to the patrol car to write up his notes, leaving Heather to return home to continue her sleepless night.

3

Following a journey of indeterminable length, but long enough for the floor to tenderise Jason's hips, shoulders and any other part of his body in contact with the irregular floor of the cargo bay, the van finally came to a halt. He guessed it to be well after midnight. The fear that had subsided over many hours, Jason's mind being unable to maintain its initial intensity for such a prolonged period, was instantly rekindled – like bellows forcing air through dormant embers. The sudden cessation of animal and train noises cleared his mind to expect nothing but the worst.

The unseen guard pinched his thigh, feeling for the corner of the heavy-duty tape that held the now heavy plastic bag to Jason's groin. There had been no spillages, suggesting they had used something designed for the purpose.

Anticipation turned to short-lived agony as several sharp tugs tore hairs from his skin. Then came the indignity of having his penis tucked back into his underpants before his trousers were re-fastened.

Without a word of communication passing between his kidnappers, or directed toward him, Jason experienced the vice-like grip of two hands on his bound ankles, dragging him partially from the vehicle. Without any say in the matter, he found himself sitting up, his legs hanging downwards. Well-developed forearms thrust between Jason's ribcage and his under-exercised biceps. The hand of a third person took hold of the binding at his ankles - three men; something Jason would tell the police on his release; assuming he ever got to give evidence.

Not a single grunt, or a single, strained puff of breath was to be heard. Clearly these were extremely fit specimens of man; something else he would pass on to the authorities; that and the fact the surface on which they had parked was laid to pea shingle, it revealing its unique note, compressed beneath burdened feet that bore the additional weight of a very average man.

There came an awkward manoeuvre and a change of sound – that of heavy gauge plastic sheeting, crumpling beneath the shuffling, shifting weight of kidnappers and their prey. That lone sound was short lived, the looped soundtrack of diggers and waterfalls returning as swiftly as it had departed, but this time coming from multiple sources – not multiple speakers of a single hi-fi; rather multiple portable devices, arranged about the property. Someone was passing from room to room, turning them on, each out of synch with the others, each adding to the cacophony. However, the sum of the parts, although discordant, was at least set to a moderate level, unlikely to disturb the neighbours, if indeed there were any.

Another awkward manoeuvre and then the sensation of being dumped unceremoniously on a padded surface. Jason could only assume he had reached his final destination. Whatever his abductors had in mind, in all likelihood, it would happen here and perhaps sooner rather than later. At least he might get some answers.

His mind worked fast. Of course, he hoped for the best; to be well-treated until he was released, and not be subjected to any form of pain during the interim. He had now experienced humiliation and felt he coped with it well. However, the mere thought of torture, or ill-treatment - however mild it might be - filled him with dread.

The fact he did not know why he had been taken added to his concern. If they had taken him for his money, they had got the wrong man. How would that go down when they realised his family could raise little more than a few hundred pounds, and that being on credit cards? He did not mix with the criminal fraternity; he had never been near a loan shark; and he had never strayed to be with another woman, so could not be accused of wandering into another man's territory; nor did he know the code to the safe at work. Were there any other reasons a man might be kidnapped? Serial killers looking to wear his skin perhaps, but surely they worked alone. The sex trade, but surely they wanted females and boys.

Jason breathed deeply through his nose and allowed himself to speculate the worst scenario. If he was to die, he hoped it would be quick; he hoped he would go with dignity, denying his captors their perverted pleasure.

In the weeks leading to his final day on Earth, a condemned man of the Victorian age could put to the back of his mind his fate until the bell began to toll, fifteen minutes before the drop. Then he would have to brace for the certainty of an unpleasant end. Would Jason walk to the gallows with a firm step, or would his legs buckle, causing him to be carried?

The anticipation brought him knowledge of fear such as he had never experienced before. He felt helpless; filled with frustration at not being able to move freely, or resist the things that were being forced upon him. Beneath the hood, he produced an ugly smile, restricted by the tape that held his lips fast. Tears pooled in his eyes.

Pairs of hands held him down while his bindings were re-arranged, strapping him to the 'bed', feet spread apart, arms to his sides. Only his covered head was permitted the luxury of mobility.

Then came the sound of men retreating from the room, but Jason could sense one remained. He was right. The drawstring about his neck loosened, allowing the third man to lift the hood clear of Jason's mouth, nose and ears, leaving it positioned so it still covered his tear sodden eyes. The tape was torn from his mouth. Jason winced.

'Shhh!'

This simple instruction, to remain silent, was accompanied by a gentle double-slap across the captive's cheek. Jason understood its meaning, nodding briefly but frantically, willing his captor to know he would obey without question.

The relief of being able to inhale fresh air for the first time in hours, was tempered somewhat by the fear of what was to come. A hand took grip of the top of the hood, and in one swift movement, jerked the item from Jason's head, the third man performing his task at arm's length, in his captive's blind spot, so he could disappear from the room without being seen.

Jason knew he must remain silent, but that did not prevent him looking about the room in which he had been abandoned; at least as much as his restricted movement would permit. Whatever he lay on, he had been left in the centre of the room, his feet directed towards a window, carefully fitted with a large sheet of plywood, or similar, a notch having been cut so it fitted snuggly around the windowsill. The board pinned a pair of closed curtains in place, presumably to give the impression to passers-by the occupants were sleeping, were on holiday, or were simply too lazy to open and close them. The thin material acted as a gasket, sealing the board tight against the wall, barring all light from the outside world.

The ceiling was that of a domestic building: low, in comparison with any commercial structure; and textured, suggesting a handyman had followed the latest fashion in the 1980s, but had not returned since. From it, a single light pendant hung down. Freestanding false walls of studwork had been erected inward from the decorated walls of the original room, rising to a height just short of the ceiling. The timbers were sparse, the carpenter using only what was required to support large sheets of heavy duty green polythene. Evidently, from the sound of plastic under foot, and the preparedness of the room in which he now lay, a lot of time and effort had been ploughed into the project – but for what purpose? Was the plastic there to ease the task of removing forensic evidence, once the victim had been released, or, more alarmingly, was it there simply to contain the spill of blood?

The wallpaper, visible beyond the polythene shroud, suggested a bedroom; its size downgrading it from master to perhaps second, or even third. He had not been carried up any stairs, so it seemed reasonable to surmise he was being held in a bungalow.

Whatever other clues there were to discover, they would have to wait, the visual examination being cut short abruptly with the arrival of an extraordinary figure who moved from Jason's blind spot, through his peripheral vision, to full view. The person was tall - very tall – and of questionable gender. It appeared to be a man, disguised as a woman – perhaps transgender. Of more concern, he or she was wearing the garb of a surgeon.

A white, enamelled, tin baking dish was placed between Jason's ankles. With intense interest, the captive followed his captor's every movement.

Without making a sound, and with gloved hands, the man who wore a combination of surgeon's pyjamas and an ill-fitting wig, topped with a disposal blue bandanna, removed the novelty cufflink from Jason's shirt. His left arm, having been strapped to the bed with cable ties, was powerless to prevent his sleeve being rolled back as far as the ties would allow. The cross-dressing surgeon took something from the dish – a paper-backed blister pack. Jason baulked when he recognised it as a cannula; his back arched in an attempt to withdraw from the area; his arms tensed in a fruitless effort to break free; his breathing became shallow and fast, his brain believing it might somehow help the body it served to flee. None of it made a difference. Jason winced as the needle dimpled his skin and slipped into his vein; he panicked as the surgeon introduced an unknown substance to the cannula, applying steady pressure to a syringe. Seconds later he no longer cared. The room in which he lay was just another room; a transgender surgeon was of no interest; the bindings no longer restrained him, but simply prevented his arms flopping over the sides of the bed on which he felt so comfortable. The sedative did not insist he sleep, but it suggested it might be a good idea, given the hour. To help him on his way, the overhead light was extinguished, leaving only borrowed light from the hall passage to illuminate the room. Before long, another sound added to the looped tape; that of Jason snoring loudly, the perpetual soundtrack, and the occasional beam of a torch, conducting his dreams.

It was natural for the captive to want to sit up as he returned to consciousness. The fact he could not came as a startling reminder of his situation. It was also natural he would want to call out, but the best he could manage was a desperate hum, his mouth having been gagged with a bandage and wadding. Fear took hold, causing him to writhe like a pinned snake; the plastic ties that held him to cut into his skin; his muscles to burn. His effort remained constant until his reserves finally ran dry. Even then, his body continued to spasm, over and over, until eventually he lay perfectly still, exhausted.

At that moment, Jason reminded himself of a prayer he learned as a child. His faith had been taught to him at Sunday school and remained with him, present but fading, until gradually he determined he was agnostic. By the age of twenty-seven he had become a devout atheist.

> *God, grant me the serenity to accept the things I cannot change,*
> *Courage to change the things I can,*
> *And wisdom to know the difference.*

No longer a believer, but believing this to be very good advice, Jason accepted the futility of resisting his bindings and looked instead to discovering the full extent of his predicament.

Someone had placed a clean white sheet across him, covering from his ankles to beneath his chin. He could not see his groin, but felt discomfort and surmised a catheter had been inserted into his bladder. He had schoolboy memories of visiting his grandfather and how unpleasant it had been, seeing a yellow tube, one end diving beneath the bedding, the other terminating at a bulging see-through bag on a hook. Strangely he could not remember where his grandfather had been at the time; nor could he see his face. He wondered if his own bag was empty or full and whether he would scare his own son, Charlie, in the same way, if he had been present.

Traces of the unknown substance still coursed through his veins, causing his thoughts to drift towards sleep, and to the place in his head he normally retreated to when he became bored. Determined to overcome the sedative's effect, Jason tensed his hands, hoping this would somehow help. It worked...to a degree, his mind returning to a muffled reality of his situation.

He was still fully clothed, although his waistband and flies had been loosened. The fact they remained at all was comforting; the thin layers of fabric forming an armour of sorts.

He turned his attention to his surroundings. This was clearly not the same room he had been dumped in on his arrival. It was much larger; perhaps a converted living room. A larger window was blocked in much the same way as in the other room, allowing no trace of day or night to penetrate. Yet there was light – a lot of light.

In all likelihood, the single, naked bulb exceeded the recommended maximum wattage, it producing a light too bright for comfort, although infinitely preferable to being locked in the dark. If that was not enough, a directional standard lamp was positioned close by.

Although his movement was limited, Jason was nevertheless able to scan the room for features: freestanding false walls of studwork and green polythene, similar to those he had seen in the reception room; more sheeting covering the floor, there being evidence of something firmer – linoleum perhaps – laying beneath, presumably to prevent heels stretching the plastic into soft carpet. Thanks to the over-specified bulb, Jason's eyes were able to overcome the opacity of the plastic, to see details beyond: a selection of bookshelves and storage units, rendered unreachable by the temporary wall; and dated and valueless framed oil paintings, hanging from chains, themselves hooked to a continuous picture rail that circuited the room.

The furniture within the confines of the membrane barrier was sparse: the bed to which James was now secured; the standard lamp; a pair of chromed trollies, each shelf supporting a number of small storage boxes of various dimensions and colours; a tall kitchen bin with a foot-operated lid. Jason had seen something similar in a hospital examination room, when Lily was being treated for a suspected broken wrist, but which turned out to be just a nasty bruise. Electronic Monitoring equipment was absent, and the furniture would clearly not meet National Health Service standards, but somehow the room still shared the same ambiance. The perceived connection caused sensations that he could not put aside. His head and eyes moved to the extremes of their arc, his brain working hard to translate the images they brought to it – vague outlines of items only partially visible through the thin sides of the storage boxes. To his relief, he saw no implements; no torturer's roll, ready to be unfurled to reveal an assortment of truth-extracting pliers and knives; no electrodes; no drills. Nevertheless, the presence of the trollies and their cargo would have continued to own his attention were it not for his ears detecting the sound of someone else in the room, moaning, audible above the looped soundtrack. Jason looked down the length of his body, pivoting his right foot sideways to reveal the source of the murmur.

As an additional shock to an already shocking situation, Jason discovered the presence of an adult figure, occupying a wheelchair in the opposite corner of the room, positioned so that it faced the bed. The person was, the captive thought, probably a woman, based on the fact he or she was diminutive. It was impossible to be sure, however, as she wore something over her head and entire body – perhaps a burka; perhaps something inspired by one. Fashioned from black material, it covered the face, other than the eyes and surrounding skin, visible through a slit in the head covering. Even at this distance and angle, Jason believed he could make out eyes of blue, surrounded by the pale skin of a Caucasian. They were fixed to the middle distance, and untroubled. Whatever had caused *her* to moan, it seemed to have passed.

The room had a door. Although Jason was unable to see it, a turning key gave away its position.

The cross-dressing surgeon re-appeared, sporting a well-developed chest, and high heeled shoes. There was little to identify the person beneath. The figure held an iPad and a stylus in gloved hands. Through the surgeon's protective goggles, Jason saw the figure's eyes – not wide open and excited, but professional, self-assured; distinguished.

The surgeon tapped the screen with the stylus, activating a pre-prepared audible message, spoken in a synthetic female voice; well educated; plummy; calming.

'I am sorry for the gag, but I suspected you might call out inadvertently when you woke, before you realised it is against the rules.'

Having delivered the message, the surgeon placed the iPad and stylus down on one of the trollies, before gently removing the tape and wadding from his patient's mouth. Jason made no attempt to call out. His eyes spoke for him – terror.

In silence, the surgeon administered a measured quantity of something to the cannula, still embedded in Jason's vein. He then took up the iPad for a second time, tapped the screen several times, and released a second pre-prepared piece.

'I would prefer to have administered a general anaesthetic. Unfortunately, I do not have the luxury of an anaesthetist, so my hand is forced. I have given you a sedative to avoid you being traumatised by the procedure, and I shall numb the area of the surgery so you will not feel pain.'

Confused, Jason struggled to understand what was happening to him. Forgetting the instructions of the first message, words tumbled from his mouth.

'Why am I here? Who are you!? Why are...'

The surgeon made no effort to respond, but proceeded to tilt his patient's head to one side and strap it to the bed. For the second time in less than twelve hours, Jason did not care. Nor was he curious about the sound of hair clippers vibrating against his skin; nor the sharp prick of a local anaesthetic being injected close to his right ear.

4

PC Billinge reported Jason Ressler's disappearance to the duty Inspector. A man of experience, Billinge's opinion mattered. The inspector ran his eyes over the documentation presented to him. It was as it should be, but before he made his assessment, the inspector wanted to hear from the officer in person, anticipating he would add meat to the bone.

Steven Billinge was a master of brevity, able to summarise succinctly without notes or preparation.

'It's a bit weird. Not the usual scenario. Jason Ressler, thirty-six, a married man with two young children, was driving home at the end of his shift at a supermarket where he's a manager. He called his wife, Heather, to let her know he was on his way home, but then appears to have brought his Ford Fiesta motor vehicle to a sudden stop in a lay-by, along the Old Felworth Road, abandoning it with its arse end sticking out into the carriageway. We found it unlocked. His phone was in the driver's door; his blazer was hanging in the back with his wallet, containing cards and cash, in the inside pocket. No signs of a breakdown, an accident, or a struggle. Mrs Ressler unlocked her husband's phone and demonstrated no apparent reason for his disappearance. In fact, nothing we saw pointed to a motive...that is, until PC Dave Semmens found a holiday brochure in the glove box which gives a strong indication he's run off with another woman.'

'Dave Semmens? Do I know him?'

'No Boss, he's a newbie. I've been holding his hand while he finds his feet. Good lad, but fresh as they come.'

'Could the brochure belong to someone else?'

'I don't think so. It's the current season, so it's not as though it's been in there for more than a few months, tops, and it had a note stuck to it - *Hi Sexy. Can't wait to be alone with you, love Anna.*'

Recalling the exact phrase, the constable's eyes looked up and to the left as though he was reading the words from pages displayed inside his head.

'So it wasn't actually addressed to this Jason Ressler?'

'No, but the note included a love heart with the letters J and A written inside it. Not to mention all the kisses.'

'How very sweet. So, Steve, what do you think?'

'Well, Boss, I reckon he'll show up again in a few weeks, either with his tail between his legs, or he'll be missing the kids. He clearly doesn't want to be found at the moment as he's left anything traceable behind. This Anna must be a rich bitch with enough money for both of them.'

'Thanks, Steve. I'm inclined to agree. I'll put this one down as *absent*. Do me a favour though, call the local A&E and make sure he hasn't been run over. We'd look pretty silly if he'd been admitted and we didn't know about it.'

'No worries, Boss. I've completed all the necessary paperwork. If he turns up, we'll know about it.'

***

The car journey home was accompanied by an awkward silence. Heather sat in the front passenger seat, her husband's blazer on her lap, clutched to her stomach. On top of the jacket, the glossy cover of a holiday brochure suffered between gripped fingers. Heather looked at its outline, the details obscured by the lack of light. She could make out a lighter patch – the sticky note upon which she knew damning evidence was written. Unable to read the words, her mind's eye could still see the rounded female hand. Purple ink – a woman's choice; 'I's dotted with circles – a woman's touch; a heart – more intimate than kisses; a free hand – the hand of someone who was relaxed. She tried to convince herself the note was meant for another, but the two initials, protected by a love heart, forbade her. The brochure advertised cottages – the choice of mature adults. The nature of the note, however, indicated someone much younger – a giggling child, not long out of school. Jason was an attractive man but, approaching forty, he was certainly past his prime. Surely, for a young girl to become smitten she would have to be overwhelmed by his charm, or excited by his company. Heather considered her husband had many positive attributes, but he was never going to be the life and soul of the party, or be kissing the hands of flocking debutantes. Perhaps, then, Anna was older and expressed herself like a lovesick teenager, her youth rekindled by the excitement of stealing another woman's husband.

A careful driver, Irene was in no greater hurry to get home than she had been to reach the lay-by. Heather could almost feel each revolution of the tyres against the smooth road surface. More creases appeared in the literature between her fingers.

Irene pulled up at a roundabout. There was no need to because very few other people were on the roads at this time of night, but this is what she had been taught many, many years ago, and those lessons had stood her in good stead for more than half a century.

Much to her surprise, given the ambient temperature outside, her passenger chose this moment to operate the electric window, lowering it fully into the door. With only a delay sufficient for Irene to raise her eyebrows and no more, Heather cast the brochure into the night, accompanying her action with a short but visceral scream that immediately collapsed into floods of tears.

Irene checked her mirrors, applied the handbrake, took the vehicle out of gear and turned on the interior light.

'Are you okay, dear? Do you want me to stop here for a while?'

Her finger was already moving towards the hazard warning switch.

Heather recovered quickly, her sobbing becoming a sniffle. Her expression was calm; calculating.

'Yes please,' she replied, turning to her neighbour. 'I might need that glossy love note after all if I'm going to find that whore and kill her.'

Before Irene could become the voice of reason, the door was open and Heather was out. Given the time of night, trying to save the council a little money, the majority of street lamps had extinguished. However, for safety, those illuminating the roundabout still shone bright. Spreading pages had prevented the launch taking the brochure far from the vehicle and so it was soon retrieved. In fact, it took longer for Heather to make herself comfortable in the passenger seat once more than it had to recover the booklet. As she clicked her seatbelt home, bitterness and anger deserted her, to be replaced by overwhelming confusion, leaving her feeling numb; as though shouting for help in a vacuum.

The journey continued. Silence returned. Irene was out of her depth. Her foot pressed a little harder on the accelerator.

As both ladies exited the vehicle, Irene offered to stay with her neighbour, but was relieved to hear Heather decline politely, she needing time alone to think. Heather found the strength to thank Bob for baby sitting at such short notice and at such an hour. He smiled, told her he was a fraud because neither child has stirred, and was about to ask what had happened when he spotted his wife over Heather's shoulder, frantically making signs not to go there and to come away.

Irene suggested her neighbour should try to get some sleep and told her not to worry about Jason's car.

'I'll knock in the morning for the keys. No need for you to come. Bob and I will take care of everything. You'll need to stay here with the kids.'

'Thanks Irene. You're a star. Here, you might as well take them now.'

Heather fished into her coat pocket and handed her neighbour the whole bunch.

'Come on Bob, let's get you home.'

Bob stepped past Heather and followed his wife through the front door, turning at the threshold to say goodnight.

'Don't worry love. Whatever's happened, I'm sure it will be fine. I'll drop the keys back late morning, if that's okay. I'd better go. Don't want to upset the missus. Besides, I gotta catch up on my beauty sleep if I'm gonna stand a chance with the ladies.'

Heather produced a pained smile. Irene gave her husband a dig, not because he had made a bad joke, but because the insensitivity of his remark triggered an automatic response, causing her elbow to jar against his ribs. He had no idea what he had done, but this was not unusual.

Heather was relieved to hear the click of the door latch, the disappearance of witnesses allowing her to run to the living room to bury her face in a cushion, unobserved, and there to wail until exhausted, without fear of waking her children. She was prepared to test her capacity to cry to destruction and would have done so had something not fallen to the floor with a thump, directly above her head. Creeping upstairs, she found Charlie asleep on the floor. So sound was he that she was able to lift him back onto the mattress and cover him with his duvet without him stirring.

For Heather there was no chance of burying her emotions in slumber, her mind being expanded by so many questions, all of which were too frightening to consider. Tea seemed the obvious solution. It had triumphed over adversity during the wars and could be called upon in peacetime also.

The wait for the kettle to boil organised her mind, filtering through only one thought at a time. She considered whether she truly believed that her husband of nine years - father of their two young children – had run off with another woman. The evidence supporting that scenario lay on the kitchen table, crumpled by her own hand; dirtied by the pavement it had fallen upon. It had not been in the car when she retrieved her spare pair of glasses from the glovebox the other evening, indicating someone – possibly a marriage-wrecking whore – had placed it there recently. Countering this single, damning clue, Heather had her husband's phone. She had already surfed the apps at the lay-by, demonstrating their content to the police officer there, but that did not mean she could not do so again; at her own pace and in the privacy of her own home.

Heather knew she was a plot writer's dream, never seeing the twist in the tale until the big reveal, but when she later watched a film for the second time, she had no problem noticing the clues that had been there all along. When she had revealed the content of her husband's phone to the officer, she had no inkling Jason might have been unfaithful to her. Now that was a distinct possibility, she wondered if she might see clues that had been there all along. Heather read her husband's texts, Facebook statuses, and e-mails, expecting to see them in a fresh light, but this was not a script and the clues she sought were absent. Thinking hard, she recalled conversations they had engaged in; their plans together as a family; plans he instigated and enthused about. Nothing pointed towards infidelity. As always, he had rung her as he left work, and sounded fine. He had made plans for them all to visit the zoo on Sunday and wanted to try out his new bridge camera on the elephants and giraffes.

Who was Anna?

The sound of boiled water pouring onto a teabag triggered a new set of questions; practical questions. How would she cope on her own? Could she survive without Jason's income? Would she have to move? What was she supposed to tell everyone? Her parents!? Charlie and Lily!? Other people would have to know: Jason's employer – his next shift started at lunchtime; her employer – she could not go back to work with such a crisis hanging over her head.

Soon the floor was open to questions.

Heather sat on the sofa in near darkness, damp tissues strewn about, a cold mug of tea in one hand, her phone laying on the armrest, trapped beneath her spare palm. Other than Irene and Bob, the county's police service, Jason and his bitch, the only other people aware he was missing were her parents. They would want an update, but something in her head prevented her picking up her phone and pressing that little green button.

Her emotional state was fluid, but in an instant it became fixed by a vibration passing through her resting hand. It lifted autonomously, revealing a picture of her mother. For the briefest moment, Heather considered not answering, but almost against her conscious will, she found the device pressed to her ear.

'Hello Mum,' Heather said in a flattened voice. 'It's not good news.'

Lynn Truman suspected the worst.

'What's wrong?'

The caller's voice was trembling.

'Jason has gone missing. We found his car abandoned.'

'What are the police doing?'

'To be honest, not much. They took some details and told me I could phone them in the morning for an update.'

'This is outrageous. He could be anywhere. He could be hurt.'

'Mum, it's not like that.'

'What do you mean?'

'Mum, the police believe Jason's run off with another woman.'

The disclosure was too much. Tears began to cascade down Heather's cheeks. Another tissue was whipped from the box to staunch the flow of mucus that ran from her nose.

'Mum, how can he have done this to me? I feel so stupid. How he and his slut must have laughed when they were making their dirty little plans. It's bad enough he's done this to me, but what about the kids?'

With some coaxing and reassurance, Lynn drew the full story from her daughter's lips. Unlike Heather, she professed to have suspected something all along. The conflict in Heather's mind as to whether or not to think the worst of her husband was shifting towards the declaration of a winner, and where Jason was concerned, the decision did not look favourable.

'As soon as your father wakes up, we're coming straight over. Do you want me to get a taxi?'

'No, Mum. You're miles away. It would cost a fortune. Besides, I'm not sure I want to see anyone at the moment.'

'Nonsense, child. As soon as Dad comes to, we're on our way. I'll bring you breakfast. I bet you're not eating.'

By the time her parents arrived, Heather had already phoned the police. They confirmed Jason had not been admitted to the local A&E and that the inspector had marked the file 'absent'. Nevertheless, the details would remain on their system until he was found.

Lynn was outraged.

'Do you want me to phone them?'

'No, Mum. It wouldn't be any use.'

The unexpected arrival of their grandparents brought Charlie and Lily downstairs. Avoiding awkward questions, Granddad took them into the kitchen to prepare a breakfast fit for a sleepover – full of all things unhealthy. Then they were to get dressed and go to the park.

Feeling she was there to be useful, Lynn began cleaning the house from top to bottom while Heather began working her way through her contact list, ringing round all their friends. No one could shed light on Jason's whereabouts, but at least one suggested she put something on Facebook. If it went viral, it could be in Timbuktu by teatime. Everyone offered their help. Too many of them offered to come round.

Having exhausted the list, Heather's attention was once more drawn to the battered brochure. She examined each of its pages, hoping for an indication as to which hotel or cottage they might be staying at. None were ringed; no corners of the pages were folded over. She considered ringing them all, but quickly realised it was pointless. Even if she could conceive a way of making them disclose the information, there were too many numbers to phone and the booking was just as likely to be in the name of the husband-stealing cum-slut as it would be in Jason's; more so, as he had deliberately chosen not to take his bank cards with him.

Her next step was to call Jason's manager.

Martin Feller was a name known to Heather, although she had never before met him, or spoken with him. He had the business coursing through his veins, but Jason always had a good word to say about him.

Martin was not without experience of the crises that sometimes befell the family of employees. He had not experienced a missing person before, but he had dealt with death. Hence, he was well practised in saying the right things. Heather neglected to mention the most likely reason for her husband's disappearance.

'Surely, if he has been kidnapped and they're after a ransom, they must know he's not a wealthy man.'

'There's no suggestion of a ransom. No demands have been made.'

'Then why else might he have gone missing?'

No sooner had the words parted his lips, he regretted saying them. He had dealt with death, but not suicide; not murder.

'I'm sure he'll be fine. Please let me know if there's anything I or the company can do for you.'

Having made his blunder, Martin Feller was clearly looking for an early end to the conversation. Heather had no intention of making him squirm, but there was one question she had to ask.

'One more thing, Martin, does a woman called Anna work there?'

'Yes, we have an Anna Richardson. She's part of Jason's team. Why?'

'Is there any chance I can have a word with her. She might be able to help me with something.'

'I'm sorry, Anna's on leave at the minute.'

'Do you know when she'll be back?'

'Well, she left yesterday evening and said she'd be away for a fortnight.'

The words crushed Heather's heart. It was all she could do to end the call politely.

'I see. Well, thanks Martin. I'll let you know of any developments.'

The phone returned to the home screen.

'Fucking wanker! He's run off with one of his staff.'

Heather's mother replaced the toilet brush in its holder and rushed to the lounge. Her daughter was not crying; she was apoplectic with rage; her eyes wide; her empty fist pounding the cushions.

'What makes you so sure?'

'Because his manager told me that some tart called Anna Richardson works under Jason and surprise, surprise, she went on holiday for a fortnight on the very night he went missing.'

'I see. Well, I did say, didn't I?'

'I feel so fucking stupid. What I don't understand is what is going to happen two weeks from now? Is she just going to go back to work as though nothing's happened, or did she say that to give them a head start? And another thing, why a brochure for English getaways?'

'That I can answer – no passport required, so one less means of tracking them.'

'No money; no phone; no cards; no car. Why?'

'As I say, no trace. She may be loaded.'

'Working under Jason? *He* doesn't earn much, so what must she be on?'

'Perhaps she's just had a windfall.'

Lynn allowed a moment for the truth to sink in.

'Listen, Heather, your father and I were discussing this on the way over. Regardless what happens, we thing it best we have kids for a while. It wouldn't be good for them to hear you crying. It will become obvious their dad is absent. This way they'll be distracted.'

Heather did not want to lose her children, but they were too young to be of support. Her mother was right – as always. She had been right to phone the police; she had been right to conclude Jason had been unfaithful, long before Heather was prepared to accept it; now she was right in suggesting what was best for the children.

On their return from the park, it did not take any persuasion for Charlie or Lily to pack their bags. Soon after, they were gone, with the promise of ringing every night. And then the house was empty, all bar Heather and a bottle of wine.

***

Some hours later, the sound of the doorbell startled Heather from a restless slumber on the couch. Saliva had pooled beneath her cheek, dampening the cushion on which she rested her head. She rose clumsily and shuffled out into the hall with all the grace of an elderly lady wearing open-backed slippers. There she caught a glimpse of her tousled hair in the mirror; puffy eyes betraying an evening of tears and alcohol abuse. It was enough for her to consider pivoting on the spot and returning immediately to her safe haven in the lounge, leaving the unknown caller to stand on the doorstep until they realised they were not welcome. However, the option of retreat was denied by the presence of her husband's keys on the doormat, suggesting it was Irene, or her husband, who stood the other side of the door. If so, Heather felt it incumbent upon herself to express thanks for them retrieving Jason's car. Besides, given their level of involvement and knowledge of Heather's weakened emotional state, it was unlikely either would return next door without first satisfying themselves their neighbour was all right.

The doorbell chimed for a second time. Given the circumstances, it sounded too cheery, suggesting the batteries would have to go.

The door swung inwards with false confidence. Heather's face wore a smile, but her eyes betrayed its true nature – a falsehood. The deception was soon revealed when the intended recipient turned out to be someone unexpected, causing the muscles in Heather's face to release their tension; the muscles of her shoulders and back to allow her upper body to slump.

'John?'

Expecting to see the prim and trim figure of her very lovely second mum from next door, or Irene's portly but equally lovely husband, when faced with the familiar but unexpected figure of an old friend, Heather failed to welcome her visitor with anything but a confused scowl.

John had anticipated Heather might be in need of emotional support, and having previous experience of her in times of crisis, knew the state he might find her in, but even by her standards, she looked to be in a bad way.

'Hello,' John said, producing a smile intended to put Heather at ease.

'Hi.'

The homeowner could not have produced a less engaging response, short of remaining mute.

Heather made no effort to turn her visitor away, or invite him in.

Seeing the need for positive action, John stepped forward. Heather moved to one side as one might make way for someone leaving a shop, giving it no greater thought. As he stepped across the threshold, the visitor removed his jacket, before hanging it over the newel post. To have asked Heather's permission would have given her the option of denying him, and she needed him, even though he suspected she might not know it.

Heather closed the door, her hand lingering on the handle as if she could not decide what to do next.

John took her hands in his and looked into her reddened, emotionally empty eyes.

'Is there anyone else in? Are you alone?'

Heather shook her head with effort, but remained silent.

'What about the kids?'

'At my mum's.'

Her answers were delivered without power; almost at a whisper.

Frustrated at the lack of interaction, desperate for her to open up, John released his grip on her hands, guiding them to her sides, before cupping his own hands, one on either of her damp, reddened cheeks. His head moved towards her face; a subtle change of attitude. His eyes looked deep into hers.

'Okay,' he said gently, 'so I've been reading stuff on Facebook and you're going to fill me in, but first I want you to go upstairs and have a shower. Then we'll talk.'

A spark of life returned to Heather's features. In her visitor she saw a good man and wondered why she had ever let him go. She had loved him. She believed he still loved her. To her knowledge he had always been faithful, but perhaps back then she had wanted something more. Perhaps they had wanted different things out of life, but she could not remember, her mind clouded by the thick fog of alcohol, fatigue and tears.

John's hand reached round to apply firm pressure to her shoulder blade, encouraging Heather to do as he instructed.

'Okay, I'll have a shower, but you need to make yourself comfortable. I'm not pouring my heart out if you're sober. You know where everything is.'

'It's a deal. I'll be in the lounge.'

He smiled, his hand sliding from her shoulder, his palm feeling the texture of the material and the warm firmness of her form beneath.

John was a patient man and knew, at least where women were concerned, there was no such thing as a quick shower. In all likelihood, she would let it run to warm up longer than he would normally take start to finish. She had been that way when they had lived together; there was no reason to think things had changed.

The visitor's phone and a perpetually replenished wine glass kept him occupied for a very long time. When Heather eventually joined him in the living room, he could not moan; she needed comforting, not chastising. Besides, there was a reward for his patience and understanding. Heather appeared wearing nothing but a bathrobe, looking fresh, her hair styled; and she smelled heavenly.

She sat beside him, accepting from him a large glass, filled almost to the brim.

'So, what the fuck's going on?'

John considered a fresh mood warranted a fresh approach; direct and lively. He was right.

'Well, look at you, you smooth talking bastard.'

The strength in her voice had returned and there was a smile, albeit fleeting. The calm before the storm. Her eyes fixed on his, her strangely shifting lips indicating she had something to say, but was unsure how to put it into words.

Her eyes dropped, her mouth latched onto the glass. She took a generous sip, leaving freshly applied lipstick on the rim.

'It's Jason. The cheating bastard has run off with another woman.'

'Wow. But I thought he'd just gone missing and everyone was wondering what might have happened to him. Are you sure? I mean, we're talking Jason here. He dotes on you.'

'Apparently not. I was frantic when he didn't arrive home. I waited and waited. Then I rang the police, who weren't much use. Eventually it was getting silly so I asked Irene if she could give me a lift.'

'The old lady next door?'

'Yes, she's so good to us. She'd do anything. Anyway, we found his car unlocked and abandoned in a lay-by half way home. His wallet and his phone were still inside. You can image, we were both so scared, we called the police. Well, Irene did. I mean, I couldn't talk I was trembling so much. When they arrived it was all very routine to them, but after they'd searched the scene and asked us loads of questions, even they began to sound worried…until one of them…could have been a school kid wearing fancy dress, he looked so young…took a look in the glovebox.'

'Oh, yes?'

The next part was harder to recount. Heather loosened her lips with another gulp of wine.

'Well, the young officer found a holiday brochure with a sticky note attached to the front, written by some whore called Anna. I rang his boss. Turns out one of Jason's team is called Anna too. And she left on her holidays the very same evening my husband disappeared. Now there's a coincidence.'

'Fuck.'

Heather took a quick sip.

'Fuck, indeed. Fuckety, fuck, fuck, fuck.'

Her teeth pressed into her bottom lip, hardening the Fs.

She took another gulp of wine, emptying the glass.

It was John's turn to fall silent, staring at his own glass, held in both hands upon his lap.

Heather took the bottle, inspected the level of wine within it, put the neck to her lips and drank until it was empty. Only then did she speak again.

'I know what you're thinking.'

'Hmm,' John replied, dragging himself back into the conversation. 'What? No you don't.'

'I think you're thinking how things could have been different.'

Her body language was smug, her head lolling back on her shoulders, her smile displaying the utmost confidence in what she alleged.

Her drunken visitor chose to play dumb. Heather was having none of it.

'Don't give me that. You and I were an item for nearly three years before I ended it for no damned reason I can think of right now. I met Jason. You met Ingrid. We made a lovely foursome until she got fed up with you.'

'Ouch,' John responded, feigning hurt, his free hand miming a dagger plunging into his heart.

Heather could see he was not serious, but even in her drunken state realised she had spoken insensitively.

'Sorry, I didn't mean that. She was a lovely girl, but you two were never meant for each other.'

The visitor looked sad.

'Maybe she just didn't live up to my expectations. I mean, after I'd had you, how could there be anyone else?'

'Soppy git.'

Heather could see he intended to speak again and allowed him the opportunity.

'I've always wondered, does Jason know about our past? I mean, you introduced us at my wedding, but I don't suppose you told him how we knew each other.'

When Heather replied, she appeared and sounded to be reflecting upon her past.

'No. I mean, he knew we were best of friends, but nothing more than that.'

'Do you ever think about us back then? How it might have been?'

'Sometimes, but up until he ran off with that tart, I honestly believed Jason was the one for me...forever. We seemed so good together. There was a time, in the days before Jason and I got serious, I thought you might try and win me back, and I might have let you. Maybe you let me off too easily. I dumped you and you just took it on the chin, and then you carried on being my best friend, as if that was enough for you. You seemed so cool about it; reverting to friends mode. Truth be known, I fought my feelings every time we all met up. More so since you became single again. But there was never any chance of me giving up what I had, for you. Why would I? I thought it was perfect. But in an alternative universe, it would be nice to think you and I never drifted apart.'

There was silence as both parties considered their positions; what was and what might have been.

John was first to speak, deciding it best to re-route the conversation.

'Has no one offered to come round?'

'I asked them not to. You obviously didn't get the message.'

'Sorry.'

'Don't be. I'm glad you're here.'

'Well, I'm glad I came, although I doubt my head will thank me in the morning.'

Jason expected to see a polite smile, responding to his weak attempt at humour, but instead he saw the face of a business woman ready to propose a deal.

'I've been thinking.'

'Oh, yes?'

'You know you're the closest Jason has to a friend of his own, don't you?'

'I guess.'

'When I was waiting for him to come home, do you know what I was doing?'

'No.'

The short word closed with an upward drift.

'I was in bed waiting for him to come in and fuck me.'

John chose to gulp rather than spit his mouthful of wine. Having never heard Heather use language so crude; not the word itself - she had already used that during the course of the evening - but the context, the openness, the subject.

His reaction did nothing to staunch her confession.

'It's our routine on a Friday night, you see. If it's going to happen at all, Friday night is when we do it. Neither of us have to get up for work in the morning. I don't work Saturdays and he doesn't go in until lunchtime. Truth be told, the anticipation was getting me so wet, I was watching YouTube videos just to keep distracted.'

John looked awkward. Even if she said nothing else, her revelations so far would surely come back to haunt her as she sobered up. This was now about damage limitation.

'Should you be telling me this?'

'I think I should because what I'm trying to say is that I have unfinished business. You said, if there's anything I can do...well, there is.'

Heather rocked forward, placed her glass down on the table, stood up and slipped the bathrobe from her shoulders. It fell to the floor, revealing the same well-honed figure the visitor had intimate knowledge of a decade before. Bearing two children had done nothing to spoil its contours.

'Are you sure you want to do this?'

John's attempt at remaining the perfect gentleman was not working. The crotch of a gentlemen's jeans would never bulge in such an obvious fashion.

'You clearly want to. At least a part of you does.'

The visitor wriggled in his seat, trying to disguise the subject of her remark.

'Don't get me wrong. I'd be bonkers if I didn't want to, but I've never cheated on anyone, and as far as I know, nor have you.'

'Is it cheating on someone to have sex with another man when the relationship is over? Especially when it's over because that utter bastard has been sleeping with some whore of a work colleague.'

It was only right that John should make her see sense. Even if he was to succumb, at least he could say he tried.

'But you might forgive him. It might all turn out to be a terrible mistake.'

A new determination spread across Heather's face.

'The way he ran off with *her*. He didn't just leave. He chose to humiliate me. As to it being a terrible mistake, don't forget, I've seen the evidence. There was a holiday brochure in his car. It had a note on the front... from her. And don't forget, she went on holiday the same evening he went missing. There's been no mistake and there certainly won't be any forgiveness.'

'But if there was. Where would that leave me?'

Heather's dull mind took its time to understand what her prey was suggesting.

'Ah, I see where you're coming from.'

With that she sat down beside him, picked up his phone, activated the video mode and made a short recording.

'For the record, this isn't rape, it's revenge.'

The phone captured her nakedness and her hand cupping her friend's groin.

'There, no backlash.'

Heather led John to the marital bed.

'You're in for a treat. Jason has always complained I'm not very *experimental*. There are certain things I've never done for him. Well, you should know. I never did them for you either.'

She sat on the edge of the bed, John standing in front of her. As her bewildered lover removed his top, she opened his jeans and pulled down his Calvin Klein's. He sprung forward.

'I want him to know you know you're bigger than him. I want him to know I've done things with you I would never dream of doing with him. I want to humiliate him, as he has humiliated me.'

She took charge – something she had never done with her husband – pushing her friend to the bed. She climbed on top, guiding the revenge inside her. Her enjoyment was exaggerated. John's, however, was real. She studied his face, judging when he was getting near. Then she climbed off. John rose up on his elbows, looking for clues as to what he should do next. Heather was still in charge.

'I'm going to treat you to something I would never do to Jason.'

Overcoming her revulsion, her mouth formed round the end of her lover's erection. After a short time, she paused.

'Tell me when you're about to...you know.'

Being a gentleman of sorts, John gave fair warning at which point Heather finished the job by hand. The final moment took her by surprise; not the when – that was quite obvious – rather the quantity and the distance it travelled. Far more than she remembered.

She lied that she had reached orgasm. She was glad it was over and that her friend enjoyed it; his reward for helping her get her own back.

'I was going to cut up his clothes. Now I want him to collect them. I want to tell him what I've done.'

John considered the enormity of the situation. There was no going back for either of them.

'So, what happens next? Does this mean we're going to be an item again?'

'I think not.'

'Okay, I'll get dressed and then I'll be off.'

Heather was grateful when her one night stand declined the offer to stay the night, instead saying he would walk, or something, and come back for his car as soon as he had sobered up. Already pangs of guilt were breaking through the anaesthetising properties of alcohol, so it was best he was gone. Perhaps this was no way to treat a friend, but he had done her a favour and been paid handsomely for it.

John left soon afterwards, carrying with him mixed emotions. Heather returned to the sofa, curled up and began sobbing afresh.

5

Experiencing a far ruder awakening than if triggered by a bedside clock radio, accidentally tuned to a Rock Classics station, Jason was raised from his drug-induced slumber by the sound of a micro pump inflating an arm cuff, the blood pressure monitor clenching his bicep so tightly, it caused him to wince. Although woozy, he still recognised the room as that in which he had first been dumped on his arrival at this nightmarish hospital. His mouth was parched, but at least he was able to breathe, his captors no longer feeling the need to gag him.

His strength having not yet returned, Jason wriggled half-heartedly, bracing against numerous cable ties that held his legs, torso and upper arms firm. Instinctively his forearms lifted, revealing a cannula, piercing the flesh just below the elbow of his right arm, and a steel cable, clamped about his left wrist. The latter captured his attention more than the stoppered needle, but before he could determine what was at the other end of the cable, the surgeon came into focus, now wearing an open white lab coat over women's clothing - a tweed skirt and flouncy pale blue blouse – his head disguised by a wig, styled in the fashion of a 1980s US soap actress. Skin-hugging rubber gloves failed to hide masculine hands.

'What do you want from me?' Jason asked hoarsely.

The surgeon ignored him.

'Are you allergic to any medicine – pains killers? Antibiotics?'

The words were detached from the surgeon's mouth; the same posh but synthetic electronic voice that had been used in the makeshift operating theatre, speaking for him, on his command.

'No?'

Jason was confused.

'Good, I can administer an analgesic for the pain.'

A prolonged squirt of something was added to Jason's bloodstream.

'What's happened to me?'

The question had been anticipated, a pre-prepared answer having been stored within the memory of the iPad, ready to be played at short notice. The surgeon took a moment to retrieve the appropriate audio file before responding by proxy.

'I have removed your right ear, but do not worry, it will heal.'

The statement caused the patient to jolt violently, his right hand arcing from the resting position at his side, to his shoulder. Horrified, he lifted and twisted his bandaged head, presenting it to the tips of his fingers, confirming nothing more substantial than padding lay beneath the crepe.

Jason's face distorted in disbelief; his muscles tensed against his bindings.

'Why have you brought me here? Why have you done this to me?'

His voice was raised, the pace quickened.

The surgeon first lifted a finger to his lips as a reminder to his captive he must remain silent, before, with stylus in hand, he began composing a new message.

The wait was horrible. Jason could not speak, he was not allowed to; he could not move; he could not anticipate what the surgeon was writing; he could not rush a process over which he had no control.

The stylus struck the play icon. Instinctively the surgeon lifted his chin, the natural desire being to present an open face when speaking with his patient, despite, on this occasion, the words being delivered by a synthetic woman's voice, detached from that of the masked and decorated captor.

'There are lessons to be learned and this is where we start. Maybe, when you die, I shall return all the missing pieces – so you can be buried together. For now, I will keep them here.'

A shiver passed through the patient's body, leaving weakness in its wake.

With the sweep of his hand, the presumably-male captor indicated a glass jar sitting upon a wheeled, chromed trolley. It contained an ear, buoyant in a clear fluid - presumably formaldehyde, or similar. Jason could not swear it was his own, but assumed it was. The crazed surgeon seemed to enjoy shocking his patient, having placed the jar among a collection of many others, all of which were empty. Some were of quite a size, ready to accept who knew what. Were they all meant for him? Was he to be chopped up, bit by bit until he became a human jigsaw, divided up among so many screw-top pots? The surgeon had mentioned missing pieces – plural; he had mentioned death.

Jason began crying quietly; the whimpers of a defeated man.

Ignoring his captive's torment, the surgeon slapped gently on his cheek, ensuring he had the victim's undivided attention. Only then did the stylus tap the screen once more.

'I have some business to attend to so I shall be leaving you alone. Do not try to escape. I have a habit of punishing those who do wrong, whether or not they are directly to blame.'

The surgeon's words were few and far between. Information being so scarce, Jason hung off every syllable.

The message was pre-prepared. Therefore, every word was meant to be said and heard. Did it have a deeper meaning? If the surgeon believed Jason had done wrong, if he failed to comply, would someone else pay the consequence, or, was Jason being punished for the wrongdoings of others?

The electronic voice advised him not to make any undue noise. In this, the surgeon was nothing more than cabin crew, demonstrating the donning of a buoyancy aid while a pre-recorded message instructed what to do should the aeroplane plough into the ocean. His free hand directed Jason's attention towards two opposing CCTV cameras that, together, covered the useable areas of the room. If that was not sufficient to deter Jason from any idea of non-compliance, his captor brushed his white coat to one side, revealing an automatic pistol, wedged in the waistband of his skirt, and if that was not enough, he then produced three photographs from his pocket – candid shots of Heather, Charlie and Lily.

It was then Jason discovered his bed had wheels, the surgeon pushing it against one wall. Sturdy cable ties were then applied to the patient's wrist, binding him to a metal loop which was firmly bolted to the studwork barrier. Jason doubted, even if he possessed a pair of scissors, he would be able to sever the plastic ties.

'I shall leave the catheter in place. On my return I shall grant you more freedom. Your leash will permit you access to the bathroom, next door, as and when you wish.'

It was then that Jason returned his attention to the metal cable, one end looped round his wrist, secured in place with bolts. Only a pair of spanners, bolt cutters, or an angle grinder would grant him freedom. The other end was looped and bolted, attaching him to a much longer cable that formed a continuous line, fixed at one end to the studwork within the room, the other end disappearing from view, presumably anchored to a wall in the bathroom. When cut free of the cable ties, his metal tether, attached to his wrist, would slide along the fixed cable, allowing him the freedom to move from the recovery room to the bathroom without straying. To this end, the room had been relieved of its door.

The surgeon left the room, wheeling before him the trolley laden with jars, the glass vessels chinking frantically against each other. Attached directly to the studwork, Jason's field of vision was restricted, leaving him to rely heavily on his sense of hearing. Although he could not be sure, he believed the trolley was taken no further than the room adjacent to the one in which he was incarcerated.

Soon after, the perpetual audio loop changed from men in battle, to a menagerie – to the sound of countless animals excited for their supper. Hidden among the roar of lions, the caw of birds and the howl of wolves, Jason heard other sounds, leading him to believe the surgeon was wheeling the laden wheelchair, seen earlier in the operating theatre, from the property. The front door closed. Locks were applied. The unnatural ambient sounds continued.

The lecture he had received prior to the surgeon's departure only made sense if Jason had been left in the property alone. Certainly there were no sounds to indicate the presence of anyone else. Perhaps the men in black had only one responsibility – to abduct and deliver – their services then dispensed with until called upon again at the appropriate time. Jason considered what those services might be: to transport him home; to abduct someone else; to dispose of his body!?

Much as had been the case during the journey to the surgeon, Jason's panic subsided gradually, the emotion being too tiring to sustain. The void was naturally filled with thought. Foremost on his mind was the present situation; the loss of his ear; the one-sided conversation, spelled out letter by letter. With regard to what had been said, Jason had detected something of interest. Granted, he was a supermarket manager, not a university lecturer, but still he cared very much about the way people spoke. His subconscious jarred every time an aitch was dropped, or the common digraph, th, was substituted with a double f. It was perhaps, for this reason, he noticed something strange about the way the surgeon had crafted his sentences - his captor never abbreviated anything. It was as though the English language was too precious to him. Perhaps it was a sign of his education. Perhaps it was a clue to his identity; at least to his psychological makeup.

The captive made a conscious decision to remember his observation, hoping it might be of importance to the authorities when he was finally able to report his ordeal to them. Thinking what he would tell the police, he tried to fix his mind upon reviewing every scrap of information he had gathered so far, but for all that his senses drew him to moment and to the place, his thoughts were pulled in the direction of home, wherever that might be. Dominant were images of his beautiful wife and their two adorable children, so innocent and uncorrupted by the world about them. He spoke aloud to each, reassuring them he would return, and that he would be a better husband and a better father for his ordeal, a trial that had taught him to appreciate the things he already thought he did, but now knew he had not. Without complaint, he would work through the list of chores he had deferred for so many months; if he was to be at work at their bedtime, he would instead read to Charlie and Lily in the mornings; he would take them to the zoo as promised, letting them buy from the gift shop whatever their hearts desired; he would kiss and cuddle his wife twice as often, if not more, and let her know he loved her a hundred times a day, whether by word or by deed. With his eyes closed he could picture them. His lips pursed as he planted a kiss on each. A smile crept across his face, fading reluctantly.

The boarded window; multiple, asynchronous versions of the same tape, playing continuously throughout the property; the absence of timepieces; and drug-induced sleep; all conspired to warp time, rendering any sense of its passing hopelessly inaccurate. The only thing Jason could say was that the surgeon seemed to be alone on his return, and it felt he had been away less time than Jason had been in the back of the van. If he were to be pressured to make a guess, he would reluctantly settle on approximately an hour. Given the person being transported was confined to a wheelchair, requiring time to load and unload him or her into a vehicle of some description, and allowing for a return journey, it stood to reason the veiled spectator lived nearby. The fact the unresponsive voyeur had remained at the property for little more than the duration of the operation, suggested the severing of Jason's ear and his suffering were for that person's benefit. That, in turn, suggested revenge for something Jason had done to his spectator, but what? As hard as he might, he could not recall ever having wronged someone so grievously they would desire to kidnap and mutilate him. In fact, he could not recall a time when someone had become so irate they wanted to hit him. Customers could be awkward, but none had ever threatened atrocities such as this.

As promised, the transgender surgeon returned to Jason's bedside, removed the sheet that had covered him, and in doing so revealed the reason the victim had felt somehow different since waking from the operation – other than, of course, the fact his ear had been taken. He was now dressed in striped flannel pyjama bottoms with an opening at the front through which the catheter had passed; and a sweatshirt, curiously adapted to permit its removal without disturbing the tether. One sleeve had been shortened, to above his elbow, explaining why he had not noticed when he first awoke and lifted his forearms from beneath the sheet; the other had been removed at the shoulder and the side had been cut from the waist to the neckline, fastened with lengths of Velcro. The work was that of an amateur - probably one who had never attended even an introduction to sewing. Indeed, it was the work of a car mechanic. Nevertheless, the adaptation was practical, allowing for the removal of the captive's clothing without the need to interfere with the steel cable.

Without a word being said, the surgeon removed the catheter and snipped all but one of the cable ties with wire cutters.

Before severing the last, the surgeon took up the iPad once more.

'I punish non-compliance. If you cause me problems, my men have instructions to act on my behalf, if I am unable. Even if that means others suffer.'

The lady's soft voice did not convey threat well, but the words would have been sufficient, even had they been spoken by an innocent child. Jason understood them well. He was to be afforded certain freedoms, but if he abused the opportunity by attempting to overpower his captor, even if he was successful, the men in black would then turn their attention to his family, and he would be powerless to stop them.

'I'm not going to try anything. Just let me off this bed.'

Moments later, Jason felt relief as the last cable tie was snipped free and collected in gloved hands. He waited for the surgeon to step back, not wishing his actions to be mistaken as hostile. Only then did he swing his legs sideways and sit up, avoiding sudden movements.

'How long are you going to keep me here?'

The surgeon tapped the screen. The plummy voice replied.

'Just until I am happy with your recovery. You may now use the bathroom. Do not tamper with the dressing. Do not get it wet. I suggest you seek counselling through your GP. I know your wife, Heather, is a therapist, but it would be wise for you to see someone to whom you are not so emotionally attached. I am sure the police will help you find someone suitable.'

There was no build-up to the captive's anger. One moment he sat listening passively, the next his emotions exploded, overriding his intention to remain calm, whatever the provocation. His feet dropped to the floor, his body stood erect, the index finger of his right hand jabbing the air in the direction of his enemy.

'You crazy fuck! You've cut off my ear for no good reason and now you're trying to show concern. What sort of freak are you?'

The surgeon stood his ground, unflinching, composed and composing, his stance reminding the captive who was in charge.

His finger having fallen limp at his side, all Jason could do was look on and wait. Finally the response came, split into two parts, the first being a warning.

'Do you think it wise to antagonise your kidnapper? Behave yourself, for your sake and for the sake of your family; Heather; Charlie; Lily.'

The surgeon left a pause; a moment in which to judge his patient's reaction. It was subtle, but it was undoubtedly present – a sudden increase in intensity in his captive's stare. The realisation things were known about him; details that added weight to what otherwise might be misconstrued as an empty threat. The surgeon had photographs; he knew names, not just of his wife, but of his children too.

Satisfied, the posh lady conveyed the second paragraph.

'You have been through a lot and you still have so much more hardship to experience. Even the strongest man might buckle, given your circumstances. I urge you to accept my help. You will need it."

Having delivered his warning, the surgeon looked to his victim, subtle facial movements challenging him to comment further.

'Please forgive me. I spoke out of turn. I...I'm grateful for your help. There is no need to punish my family for my outburst. I am truly sorry.'

Jason's head tilted forwards, his line of sight dropping to the floor. In this position he could not see how his plea for clemency had been received; could not hear the tap of stylus against glass, drowned out, as it was, by the surgeon's endless soundtrack or random noises.

'You should wash your hands. I will bring food.'

The consultation was over; the surgeon removing himself to another part of the property to which Jason had no access.

Afforded unprecedented freedom, Jason was keen to use the few minutes he believed he had to test the solidity of the barrier at the window - to pick and scratch with his fingernails in search of any weakness - but he was not alone, reminded of that fact by the two, small, red LED lights that indicated the all-seeing CCTV cameras were in operation. Even if the surgeon was not looking on in real time, any misdemeanour on the part of the captive might later be revealed, in slow motion if needed.

To this end, Jason instead heeded his captor's advice and slid his tether along the fixed line, heading for the bathroom with the intention of washing his hands. It brought him first into the hall along which he had been manoeuvred on his arrival. There was no question he might linger there as it risked provoking the surgeon's displeasure. Nevertheless, his eyes absorbed the scene in a second. The hallway was not long, turning through ninety degrees after perhaps four metres, plastic sheeting covering its every surface, bar the ceiling. The passage lacked a studwork wall, perhaps because it was of insufficient width to accommodate one on either side, perhaps because it would be too complicated, it feeding the front entrance, three closed internal doors, and two doorless openings, the latter being portals to the recovery room and bathroom.

The bathroom was of a modest size, containing a toilet, a wash basin and a bath, with shower over, its rubber hose pushed over the spouts of both hot and cold taps. The tiles and the suite were of the 1970s; the former being garishly patterned; the latter of pea green enamelled steal and porcelain. The floor was laid to linoleum, so old it had shrunken away from the walls. The bobble-patterned window glass was painted black.

Despite the age, the room was spotlessly clean.

One feature was clearly new – a second shower curtain and pole had been added, dividing the room in two, isolating the toilet from the sink and bath tub; a dirty area and a clean. Surprisingly, there was no mirror, although, touching his bandages for a second time, Jason thought it was perhaps for the best, feeling sickened at the thought of having to face his disfigurement; concerned more how his wife would react. Heather might say all the right things, but how could she not be repulsed but it; by him.

Shortly after returning to the recovery room, Jason welcomed the arrival of a tray bearing a drink and something to eat – a flour-topped bread roll, filled with mature cheese. It was the sort he would have chosen himself. In fact, the products seemed identical to those he sold in store. The drink – a fruit smoothie – was not something he normally drank himself, but it was certainly something his wife always kept in the house. Was the surgeon's choice coincidence, or a subtle way of letting his captive know he knew things about him?

As far as Jason could tell, the surgeon remained at the other end of the property for the rest of the day, save for providing an evening meal and a late evening cup of tea.

A period of fitful sleep was followed by breakfast, lunch and an examination of the wound. The surgeon was clearly pleased with his work: very neat; healing nicely; no signs of infection.

Jason took the opportunity to ask a question that had been on his mind since he had been introduced to his missing ear.

'Those jars, are they all for me?'

The surgeon made no response until it was convenient for him to do so, his hands being unable to simultaneously apply new dressings and construct a new message. The delay was sufficiently long, that under different circumstances, the poser of the question might easily have forgotten he had asked it. As it was, Jason recognised his mistake and waited patiently for an answer.

Eventually, his stoicism was rewarded.

'Did you see your name on them?' The lady's voice asked, pleasantly.

'No.'

Jason expected his captor to elaborate. The fact he did not suggested there was no need for further explanation because the vessels had not been procured for the exclusive purpose of preserving Jason's body parts. There was probably someone else out there, minding their own business, who was destined to suffer the same fate. All things considered, he had not faired too badly; one of the jars had the capacity to hold a hand, or a foot.

'What is this place?'

Having completed his checks, the surgeon seemed more open to interrogation.

'A place of learning. Now you have learned something, I shall return you to your family.'

The words came as a relief, but brought further confusion.

'Have I learned anything?'

'If you have not, you must stay.'

Jason could have kicked himself, acting quickly to cover his error.

'I *have* learned something. I definitely have.'

The surgeon stared at his captive, challenging him to say precisely what he had learned.

'Sometimes...sometimes people do things wrong, and sometimes someone needs to be punished for them.'

With a swirl of his finger, the surgeon indicated Jason should continue.

'Sometimes the person who must be punished is not the person who has done wrong.'

The surgeon was evidently still not satisfied. His finger swirled a second time, his head nodding, encouraging Jason to say more. The captive felt he was nearly there, if only he could fabricate a greater understanding.

'Sometimes...to teach a person a lesson, you have to demonstrate the consequences of their actions to others.'

His eyes looked to his captor, pleading silently for the surgeon to accept his clumsy explanation. The wigged giant remained emotionless; unmoving. The pause lasted too long; so long, Jason wanted to scream at the man - the woman - however he identified himself.

Finally the iPad and stylus were raised.

'This evening you will be prepared for your return.'

The audience at an end. Having gathered his things, the surgeon left the room.

The first indication something was about to happen was the sound of an unknown number of heavy-footed people entering the property – in all likelihood, the return of the men in black. The second was the surgeon entering the recovery room, alone.

Avoiding the need for speech, the surgeon had brought with him a clipboard, the metal bar holding a single sheet of A4 paper, upon which was printed a checklist. Nothing was to be left to chance. In his other hand was gripped a hood, heavily impregnated with aromatic fabric softener, now familiar to the prisoner.

The hood was tossed onto Jason's bed. A visual instruction was issued. In total compliance, the captive picked it up and pulled it down over his head. The surgeon stepped forward to pull the draw-string tight. Having done so, he took a pen and ticked the first box with a flourish. Step two involved the men in black, stripping the patient bare. Fingernails were scrubbed; pungent disinfectant was rubbed across every surface of Jason's body; a gloved finger swept the inside of his mouth; his foreskin was retracted; his penis was placed inside a new plastic receptacle and taped in position; a liquid was injected through the cannula which was then removed carefully, the wound being bandaged with a forensically clean dressing.

Jason succumbed without resistance, not only because he was powerless to do anything else, but because this, he hoped, was the price he had to pay for his return to normality; to his wife; his children; his job.

6

Neville Eade – Nev - had been pleased to see his friend, Joe, at Joe's bachelor pad; he had been content to stay for a takeaway; he had been easily persuaded to consume six pints of lager over the course of the visit - slow and steady. It was only when he came to get behind the steering wheel, he was reminded that actions have consequences. By the time the ignition turned, it was already one o'clock in the morning and he was still far from home. To make matters worse, it being the early hours of Monday morning, he had precious little time ahead before he would need to be up and dressed for work.

Initially, to keep him awake, it was only necessary to play the radio and adjust the fan to cold and full, but within a quarter of an hour, his stay-conscious plan had evolved to include regular bursts, pounding the steering wheel with a clenched fist.

Neville glanced at the clock. It was one-thirty precisely. Asking himself the time made him think; thinking kept him focussed; focussing kept him from falling asleep at the wheel – at least he hoped it would. However, the potency of this technique soon diminished, and the satnav estimated he was still another twenty-three minutes from home. In the meantime, a battle raged between his eyebrows, lifting frantically, and weighty eyelids, determined to close.

Perhaps fortuitously, the front nearside tyre scuffed a kerb. The jolt, felt through the steering wheel, induced a brief sense of panic, triggering the production of sufficient adrenalin to restore alertness, albeit briefly. Desperate for new stimuli, Neville's eyes darted away from the road, to the fan control, hoping to boost the stream of cold air, already directed at his face. The distraction lasted no more than three seconds, but it was long enough for the surprise to have maximum impact, his attention returning to the road just as a naked man lumbered onto the opposite carriageway. If he had carried on driving, straight and narrow, his vehicle would have stood little chance of running the man down, but he did not. Startled, Neville instinctively took evasive action, directing the car away from one potential source of danger, only to point it at another - the base of a large oak tree that barely noticed the impact.

Craig Diggon, a newly qualified driver, had been following Neville's car for the past ten minutes, maintaining a safe distance behind. He had never before driven alone at this time of night. Consequently, he was nervous, especially as the driver ahead of him had been behaving erratically. He too witnessed a naked man stumble into the road. He too became startled, but instead of veering violently to the left, he brought his vehicle to a controlled stop, in such a manner his old driving instructor would have been proud of him.

Having bailed from his car, Craig checked first to see the condition of the naked man, who was already trying to get to his feet, and then of the blooded second driver, left hugging a deployed airbag. His next course of action was to call the emergency services – all of them.

PC Steve Billinge and his understudy, PC Dave Semmens, approached the scene. Someone had had the sense to deploy a warning triangle, at a safe distance from a lone, stationary car, parked on the clearway; its headlights and blinking flashers being the only source of illumination, the area being entirely devoid of street lights. As the patrol car slowed to stop, it became apparent a second vehicle was present, its front end wrapped round the base of a substantial tree. With no similar hazards to be found for hundreds of yards in either direction, the driver had exhibited the utmost misfortune in choosing to steer his vehicle in such a direction, at such a spot.

All lights blazing, Steve Billinge brought his car to a halt. A young man came out of the shadows to meet it, frantic but relieved he could hand over the mess to the professionals.

As the officers stepped foot outside their vehicle, two ambulances arrived in quick succession, followed soon after by a fire engine.

The young man did not know where to start. He pointed to the wreckage and described a man, trapped behind the wheel, groaning, but he was equally keen to speak of the naked man who was by now sheltering in the passenger seat of his car. He then described, in the fewest of words, what had happened.

Having quickly absorbed the scene, PC Billinge took charge.

'Right, let the fire and ambulance guys take care of the fella in the wreckage. Dave, you take some details from this fella...sorry, what's your name?'

'Craig Diggon'

'Okay,' the older officer continued, his hand indicating he was speaking to his colleague. 'You take some details from Craig while I have a word with this mysterious naked guy.'

'His name's Jason,' Craig interceded, helpfully. 'I had a quick chat with him to make sure he's all right. He fell into the road and was shivering, so I gave him my jacket and sat him in my car. He seems pissed or something.'

Dave Semmens had already made up his mind about Craig. Here was a young man with sculpted hair, driving an old car with a value many times less than the cost of the insurance - if indeed he had any.

'Come and sit in my car,' he said, pulling his note book from his pocket.

PC Billinge opened the passenger door of the youth's car, to be confronted by a man in his mid-thirties, wearing nothing more than a leather jacket, several sizes too small for him, and a crepe bandage, wrapped around his head.

He leaned in.

'You all right mate? Talk to me. My name is PC Steven Billinge; what's yours?'

The semi-naked man seemed confused, but had enough wits about him to respond.

'Jason...Jason Ressler.'

Steven Billinge cocked his head, the name being familiar to him.

'I know you, or at least I know your name. Is your wife Heather?'

Jason's neck disappeared as he shrugged against the cold, his hands gripping their opposite arm. He nodded.

'I was speaking to your wife a few days ago. Tell me, who is Anna?'

'What? Why? What do you mean?' Jason responded, his unfocussed eyes sagging downwards to stare blankly at his knees.

'Jason, we found your car abandoned. There was a note in it, from Anna.'

The officer appeared to have struck a nerve, the interviewee's head rising to loll on his shoulders, his eyes trying hard to fix on Billinge's face.

His response was delivered slowly, his words slurred.

'Why the fuck are you asking me about Anna? You should be asking me where I've been; about the fact I've been kidnapped by some cross-dressing maniac who cut off my fucking ear!'

Steve Billinge was temporarily lost for words.

Craig Diggon had not received any injuries, but was shaking, despite a paramedic having placed a blanket about his shoulders. There was little difference in ages between the witness and the officer, but Craig afforded him the respect the uniform deserved; more so than Dave Semmens had experienced during his short career to date. Far from dispelling the officer's initial suspicions, it had the opposite effect, convincing him this 'innocent' young bystander had something to hide.

'So, Craig, tell me what happened.'

'I've been at a mate's house all evening and was driving home.'

'Have you been drinking?'

'Diet Coke...I'm diabetic, so I have to watch the sugar, and no alcohol because I'm driving.'

'Any drugs?'

'I've never touched them...don't even smoke.'

'Okay, before we're finished I'll have to ask you to provide a breath test, but in the meantime I need as much information as you can give regarding what happened.'

'Okay, no problem. As I was saying, I was driving home and got stuck behind this fella.'

His finger pointed directly towards the wreckage of a previously pristine car, its sleek lines mangled by the collision.

'The guy was all over the place...You know, crossing the white line; speeding up and slowing down for no reason...If you don't believe me, check the video.'

'Video?'

'Yes, I only passed my test two months ago. To keep the insurance down, I agreed to install a dashcam. You've got to believe me, none of this is my fault. It's either the drunk guy in the car, or the naked guy who walked into the road.'

There were few things in the world capable of making PC Semmens doubt himself, but if the video corroborated the young driver's version of events, this had the potential to be one of them. Consequently, no sooner had the young man provided a specimen of alcohol-free breath, the officer hurried to his suspect's car to recover the device's memory card.

***

Neville Eade had been identified through his vehicle's index number and from a photo driving licence, found in his wallet, although the photo itself no longer bore any resemblance to the driver's face. A third officer had responded to the call and she had agreed to inform Mr Eade's next of kin, leaving Billinge and company to concentrate on the Resslers; a logical division of labour, given Billinge and Semmen's previous contact with the family.

Dressed in a hospital gown, lying on a bed behind a curtain in the Accident and Emergency department, Jason continued his recovery, his drunken appearance subsiding more rapidly than the officers would have expected.

The patient's voice did not portray any sense of emotional distress. Nevertheless, rivulets of water trickled continuously from his eyes, as though there was something wrong with the function of his tear ducts. Every few seconds he casually dabbed both cheeks in an attempt to stem the flow, doing so without making a sound; a sniffle; a whimper.

Billinge and his novice shared the space within the curtains. So swift was Jason's recovery, and despite the tears, the older officer had no qualms in asking questions.

'Jason, at the scene, you stated you had been kidnapped and that someone had cut off your ear. Is that true?'

The patient responded with an unflinching 'Yes', temporarily removing the tissue from his face, so to be clear.

'Jason, when you walked into the road, a car was forced to swerve to avoid you. That car hit a tree and the driver was seriously injured. We need you to tell us what really happened.'

The news caused a furrow to appear between the patient's eyebrows.

'Oh God, are they going to be all right?'

'I don't know the answer to that, Jason. He had to be cut from his car. His injuries are likely to be life changing. Do you understand? The surgeons are doing their best as we speak, but who knows what the outcome will be. I'm guessing probably not that good. Jason, you say you were kidnapped. We believe you went somewhere with a woman called Anna. Did her husband find you and cut your ear off? Have you been taking drugs?'

Jason's anger returned; an indignant, defiant anger.

'No! I was kidnapped by a surgeon who wore women's clothing. The crazy fuck cut off my ear while I was asleep. He drugged me. They threw me out of a van. I didn't know where I was. I...I must have wandered into the road.'

Despite the stutter, the speed with which he delivered his words suggested he was telling the truth...or that he had rehearsed his story well. Whatever the case, at that moment his own injuries were not his greatest concern.

'Oh God, have I killed someone?'

At last, a sound accompanied his tears, appropriate to the situation. Steven Billinge passed him the box of hospital tissues.

'Now Jason, I'm going to leave you for a short time. I'm going to see your wife, Heather. I'm going to tell her what's happened to you; that you're safe. You do want her to know you're back, don't you?'

Jason's expression was already formed of many facets - fear; anger; pain – and to these one more was added; anxiety, triggered by the mention of his wife.

'Of course I do. Why wouldn't I?'

'Then why the look?'

The patient dabbed his cheeks, then briefly shook his head slowly from side to side.

'Of course I want her to know I'm back. Of course I want to see her, but how's she going to react to this,'

The victim tapped his dressing gently.

The constable offered no advice. Instead he assured the patient he would not be left alone.

'PC Semmens will remain by your bed, so if you remember anything else you want to say, he'll be right here. In the meantime, I'll go and see your wife.'

'What about the kids?'

'I'm sure they're fine. I'll check on them when I speak with Heather.'

PC Billinge got up to leave. As he did so, his understudy excused himself for a minute, having something he urgently needed to discuss with his colleague. Once out of earshot, the young officer asked a question he could not keep to himself a moment longer.

'So, what do you think?'

'I think he's off his tits on drugs. He's been banging this Anna bird. Her husband's turned up and lopped off his ear. He can't tell the truth because he doesn't want his wife to know, so he's made up this crock of shit – although, that's just my opinion.'

***

PC Billinge pressed the doorbell at number 54, the chime audible from where he stood, inspiring confidence the occupier had been made aware of his arrival. Regardless of his initial optimism, Heather then appeared to be taking longer to respond than might be expected, suggesting she was away from the property entirely, in the back garden, or else she was in the shower. Such was the delay, the constable felt the need to apply the tip of his finger for a second time, to use the chromed knocker to produce a loud rat-tat-tat, and then take a step back, affording himself a clear view of the front windows, upstairs and down. There being no sign of life, even with his nose pressed against the glass, his flattened hand held across his brow in an attempt to reduce reflections, the officer released a frustrated huff and turned to leave. However, the sound of the door opening extended the manoeuvre from one-hundred-and-eighty degree to a full a three-sixty.

Heather's dishevelled appearance made it instantly clear the officer had been wrong to think she had been washing her hair; more likely, her legs had found difficulty carrying her the length of the hall.

She looked awful; as though she had not slept or showered for more than a week, despite it being little more than two days since her husband had gone missing.

Experience had taught the officer not to ask Heather to sit down to receive his news; not in these circumstances. To ask someone to sit was to assume they would collapse when hearing the worst. Although the return of her husband from another woman's arms was not good news, especially as he had been mutilated, at least the officer was not asking her to identify a body.

The constable adopted a neutral expression; one that Heather tried without success to gauge.

'Heather, do you remember me? PC Steven Billinge. I responded to your call at the lay-by.'

Heather, holding a dampened ball of tissues to her nose, nodded her head; more accurately described as a nervous vibration.

'It's good news. Jason's been found. He's safe, but he's in hospital. It's nothing life threatening, but he's been seriously assaulted...Don't worry, I can take you there.'

Heather's mind was once more thrown into turmoil, not aided by the officer adding a simple question which, although short, conjured a million scenarios.

'Heather, has Jason ever used drugs?'

She replied, to her knowledge, he had not. She wanted to know why the officer thought such a question was pertinent; she wanted to hear from her husband exactly what had happened; she wanted to know what Anna Richardson was to him; and she wanted to know how badly he had been injured.

'Are you all right, Heather?' the officer asked, placing gentle fingers on her upper arm, his eyes meeting hers.

'I'm sorry, I must have zoned out for a minute. It's just that I have thought about nothing else than this bloody Anna Richardson since your colleague found that love note on Friday.'

'Richardson? You know her surname?'

'I mentioned the name when I spoke to Jason's manager. Turns out the slut works under my husband – now there's a play on words.'

'How about we play it cool? I suggest you listen to what your husband has to say first before you jump to any conclusions.'

***

The journey to the hospital afforded the victim's troubled wife ample opportunity to interrogate her chauffeur, turning their normal roles on their heads. He judged it would be best to pre-warn his passenger with regard to the exact nature of her husband's injuries. He *had* decided it better to leave it to Jason to explain, in his own words, the events he claimed had taken place over the previous two days, but the revelation Jason had lost his ear caused Heather to badger the officer in to telling her everything he knew. In doing so, Billinge remained resolutely suspicious, while Heather's certainty began to wane. What if she had wrongly convicted him? What if she had avenged herself by hurting an innocent man? That thought being too horrible to contemplate, she chose to remain unconvinced.

By the time constable Billinge and Heather reached the hospital, Jason had already been examined by the duty doctor. Soon after, Heather was reunited with her husband, in the company of Billinge and Semmens, but before she was able to articulate a single word, a man in a surgical gown swept the curtain aside and stepped up to Jason's bed. Without a word of explanation, he removed the dressing from his patient's head, examined the wound in microscopic detail, replaced the bandage, and stood up.

'Mr Ressler, what do you remember of your ordeal?' he asked with the confidence of someone of high standing.

It was no hardship for the patient to retell his story, wanting the world to know what he had suffered, but before he could start, the consultant turned to face PC Billinge, a man who had to know the truth.

'Officer, this man has not been assaulted; he's been operated on.'

'What do you mean?'

'I mean, this man's ear has been surgically removed. I couldn't have done a better job myself. And he's been medicated via a cannula, here in his arm.'

The colour drained from Heather's face.

***

Billinge left the building in search of privacy. In sight of, but away from the smokers, he placed a call to the Force Control Room.

'I need to speak with the duty DI.'

'Can you give me any info?'

'Not really. I've been in this job twenty-four years now, and this is the first time I've felt so out of my depth.'

After only a short delay, Detective Inspector Robert Bickley returned the call.

'Steve, what's happened?'

'Boss, don't hang up. Honestly, this is what's happened. Young Dave Semmens and I answered a callout a few days ago. A man called Jason Ressler had gone missing on his way home from work. Although the circumstances were strange, the discovery of a love note pointed to him having run off with another woman. Well, tonight he's turned up again, missing his ear, and acting as though he's under the influence of drink or drugs. He claimed to have been abducted and operated upon by a transgender surgeon, before being dumped, naked, just outside town. I assumed he'd run away with the woman who'd written the note, been caught out by her husband, and he'd then sliced off Ressler's ear to teach him a lesson, leaving the victim to make up some cock and bull story so his missus would have him back.'

'But...?'

'But then a surgeon at the hospital comes in and informs me Jason's ear has been surgically removed.'

There followed a pause while the DI searched his brain for a set procedure that might cover such an eventuality. Clearly there was nothing specific, leaving him to think in general principals.

'Okay, I'll call in CSI and I'll send a couple of DCs to interview him when he's ready – probably tomorrow. In the meantime, have another chat with this Jason Ressler and make a note of everything he says.'

Having ended the call, Robert Bickley replaced the handset and beckoned to his office manager, Detective Sergeant Alan Honeyman, to come to his office.

'I've known Steve Billinge for a lot of years now and I trust him, and in all our years, neither of us have come across anything like this.'

7

Police Headquarters, Briefing Room, 09:00 hours, Monday, 26 September:

The windowless briefing room was modern, well-lit and had seating for fifty, most of which were occupied. A suited man stood at the front, to one side of a large smartboard, capable of displaying anything loaded onto the computer with a link to it.

'Good morning everybody.'

The room cut short a multitude of conversations; some relevant; some business-like; many about the weekend's football results. The man who spoke waited for his audience's undivided attention, and did not have to wait long.

'For anyone who does not know me, my Name is DI Robert Bickley. I am the SIO. Right, ladies and gentlemen, morning. We're here to investigate the serious assault of this man, Jason Ressler, a 36 year old husband and father of two. A seemingly innocent man.'

As if his words alone controlled the computer, two images appeared on the screen; a before and after. The one on the left depicted a smiling husband, credited as imaged from Facebook; the other a traumatised man, his hair cropped at one side of his head, his outer right ear missing. Further images appeared, homing in on the wound; neat and healing well.

'I'm going to build a picture of the events so far. Firstly, this call was made at 23:15 hours on Friday, the 23rd, to the non-emergency line, by Heather Ressler, Jason's wife.'

The computer operator seemed to read his mind, starting the first recording with impeccable timing. The short conversation required no explanation.

'Then, at 7 minutes past midnight, on Saturday morning, a 999 call was made by Heather's neighbour, Irene Spillman.'

The voice of an older lady played out over the speakers.

'PCs Steve Billinge and Dave Semmens responded to the call. Steve is with us to relate what they saw.'

The constable replaced his old boss at the front of the room. He spoke confidently, referring to his pocket book every now and then, ensuring his briefing was concise and accurate. Not only did he cover the night of the twenty-third, when he first discovered Jason Ressler missing, but also his part in the victim's return, informing Heather Ressler, and her discovery as to the full name of the Anna, thought to be Jason's lover. Once finished, a friendly hand, placed on his upper arm, guided him from the spotlight.

'Thanks Steve.'

The DI returned his attention to the room.

'DCs Chambley and Humfress, I want you to take the role of FLOs. Pay a visit to the hospital and conduct a video interview with Jason Ressler. They've moved him to a side room, so that shouldn't cause any problems. I'd like you then to speak with the Ressler's neighbours, Irene and Robert Spillman. How did Heather Ressler seem when she asked them for a lift? What did they talk about in the car? How did she act when they arrived at the lay-by?'

DCs Fallas and Pace, I want you both to go to Jason's place of work. Speak with his manager and find out everything you can about this woman - Anna Richardson. Speak to her colleagues. Did they notice anything about her relationship with Jason Ressler that led them to believe it had become more intimate? Also, see what CCTV we can lay our hands on.'

His focus moved from the individuals he had instructed, to the general gathering.

'At the moment we have no motive. This could be a case of mistaken identity. It's usually about drugs, love or money. Let's find out which one it is. Research Social Media and find out everything about them.

Thank you ladies and gentlemen. Let's get this thing solved.'

***

Drake Fallas steered his unmarked police car into the pick-up bay and stopped, despite there being plenty of empty spaces within ten metres of the supermarket's front entrance.

'Do you intend to leave it here?'

'Yep, why not? It's as good a place as any.'

'What's wrong with those?' Angela asked, pointing through her colleague's side window.

'Nah, too far. Besides, this could be a crime scene. We need to be close to the action. If we need to deploy some crime scene tape, you wouldn't want me to have to lug a roll of it half way across the car park, would you?'

'You're an arse. You're supposed to be fit.'

Drake produced a playful grin.

'I am fit and you know it. I've seen the way you look at me.'

'Tosser. In your dreams.'

'Always. I have to say, you scrub up well in my dreams.'

'As I say, you're an arse.'

The grin widened.

'A lovely Spanish arse.'

'You're not Spanish, not with an accent like that.'

'My parents are. Hence the even tan...all...over...my...body.'

Angela shook her head, her mouth turned down.

'I pity you.'

In Drake's mind, rejection and playing hard to get were merely two sides of the same coin. She would succumb...in time.

'Anyway, are we going to discuss my nice tight buttocks all day, or are we going to see if we can get an offer on a couple of meal deals, us being fine upstanding representatives of the law and all.'

'We're supposed to be investigating a kidnapping, not feeding your belly. Besides, if you want to keep your buns looking pert, I think maybe you should lay off the snacks a bit.'

'I knew you'd looked. Just say the word and I'll share them with you – my treat.'

Angela smiled, tempted by the offer.

'Time to go to work. We can discuss your buttocks later.'

Both detectives stepped up to the customer service desk, introduced themselves politely to the equally well-mannered lady holding the station, and produced their warrant cards to demonstrate to her they were the real deal.

An internal phone call was made, after which Jason's manager, Martin Feller, came to greet his visitors. Having shaken their hands, he walked them through to an office, away from the hubbub of staff and shoppers who infested every square inch of the premises. Children screamed; shelf-stackers faced-up the products, oblivious to their cages of goods causing bottlenecks in the aisles; old people supped their tea in the restaurant, discussing the state of their hips.

The door was well soundproofed and provided an appropriate venue for an informal interview.

Drake was first to speak.

'I understand Mrs Heather Ressler rang you on Saturday morning to inform you her husband, Jason Ressler, was missing.'

'That's correct.'

Martin had guessed the officers wanted to speak with him about Jason, but had no clue as to whether this was a missing persons enquiry, or whether they were hunting a murderer.

'Have you found him? Is he all right?'

'I'm pleased to say he has returned, but he has been seriously assaulted. Jason has made some claims and we are trying to establish the facts.'

Martin nodded, demonstrating his willingness to comply in any way he could.

'Okay, how can I help?'

'I understand you have an employee by the name of Anna Richardson. Is that right?'

'Yes,' Martin replied, his mind straining to see the relevance. 'She's on Jason's team.'

'Can we speak with her?'

'I'm afraid not. Anna is on a fortnight's annual leave. She left on Friday night.'

'The twenty-third? The night Jason Ressler went missing?'

'That's right.'

Drake paused while formulating his next question.

'What kind of person is Anna Richardson?'

'Well, she's a good employee; always on time; works hard; doesn't need anyone standing over her – one of the best. I guess it's down to her age. The youngsters don't seem to have the same work ethic these days.'

'Her age? How old is this lady?'

'Oh, I'd say she's in her early sixties. Her husband recently retired and got a lump sum. They've spent most of it taking their children and grandchildren to Florida for two weeks. I'm afraid, if you want to speak with her, you're going to have to wait a while, or book a flight to Disney.'

Martin saw his interrogator's reaction and mistook its meaning.

'I'm sorry, I didn't mean to be flippant.'

Angela responded on behalf of her partner whose train of thought had been derailed.'

'No need. You've been very helpful. We're going to need CCTV footage, inside and out, stretching back a month, if that's possible.'

'Of course, anything.'

'I understand Jason is a departmental manager.'

'Yes.'

How many staff does he have working under him?'

'Six.'

'Great. We'll need a list and we're going to need to speak with each of them.'

'No problem. Not all of them will be on shift, but I can give you their home addresses and contact numbers.'

'That would be splendid.'

Angela had given her colleague time to think of his next line of questioning.

'Tell me, what do you think of Mr Ressler?'

'He's a very good employee, and a very good manager – his staff love him. I think he's destined to go far in the company.'

The same question was asked of those on the list, Martin going the extra mile by summoning any of them who were on shift to his office, one by one, and allowing the detectives to call the remainder from his phone, all bar Anna Richardson who was non-contactable. All concurred with Martin Feller. Their boss was good-humoured and mucked in with the rest of them, leading by example. None had seen him since the night of the disappearance. However, they all recalled there was nothing out of the ordinary about him that night. None reported a special relationship with Anna Richardson, other than she acted like a mother to him, as she did to all of them.

Having achieved what they had set out to do, the detectives returned to their vehicle, Angela Pace holding a batch of DVDs, her partner clutching a sandwich, a packet of crisps and a can of diet coke.

'Anna in her sixties? Well, I didn't see that coming.'

Angela had to concur.

Back at base their findings were relayed to the office manager, DS Honeyman, the disks being handed to him, along with a small portrait photograph, obtained from the store's personnel department, an added touch Martin Feller thought the detectives might find useful.

***

DCs Nigel Chambley and Jane Humfress attended the hospital where they introduced themselves to Jason and Heather Ressler, as their Family Liaison Officers. Jane took the lead, her bedside manner being far superior to her colleague's.

'We'll pop round daily for a week or two, to keep you informed and to give you the opportunity to ask questions. Not now, but tomorrow – to give you time to rest and get the drugs out of your system - we're going to conduct a video interview, so we can record every detail while it's still fresh in your memory.'

The Detectives did not stay long, but left their cards in case either husband or wife needed to ask them something, or had recalled something important.

They left the hospital via the main concourse which, with its High Street outlets, was more like a shopping centre. Had it boasted a cinema or bowling alley, it would have made a good destination for a date. Despite the inflated prices, both officers grabbed a coffee and a Danish, before setting off to speak with the Ressler's next-door-neighbours, Bob and Irene Spillman, both of whom were at home, working on a jig-saw together.

The Detective Constables perched on the edge of a comfortable settee, so as not to spill their tea into their saucers.

'Irene, you took Heather to the lay-by. Is that right?'

'Yes, dear.'

She smiled at the young man who was asking her questions. He was in his mid-thirties, but still a young man in her eyes.

'Do the Resslers only have one car?'

'Yes, dear. Would you like a biscuit? I think we have some chocolate digestives.'

'Thank you, no.'

'Bob, bring in the biscuits. These two look as though they need a treat.'

Bob rose from his armchair to do his wife's bidding. He returned to the sitting room a few minutes later, refusing to remove the plate from under the officers' noses until they had each taken two biscuits.

Jane thanked the couple for their hospitality, but was keen to get the interview back on track.

'So, the Resslers have only the one car.'

She made a note in her pocket book.

'Of course, they used to have two...until Heather suffered an epileptic fit – poor dear – and hasn't been allowed to drive since.'

That too went in the pocket book.

***

Police Headquarters, Briefing Room, Tuesday, 27 September:
DI Bickley stood at the front of the packed room to receive feedback on the state of the investigation. There was nothing on Social Media. The Police National Computer held no details of Jason Ressler. However, Heather had a conviction for driving while unfit through drink and was currently on a ban.

That piece of information triggered DC Humfress to interject. She had her pocket book open, but did not need to refer to its pages. She knew what she had written.

'Yes, Jane?'

'Sir, DC Chambley and I spoke with Irene Spillman yesterday afternoon – the Ressler's neighbour. She was under the impression Heather Ressler had suffered an epileptic fit, giving that as the reason she doesn't drive. She clearly doesn't know about the drink driving conviction.'

Robert Bickley lifted a finger as if to highlight the significance of the evidence. It waggled as he spoke.

'Okay, Mrs Ressler may have wished to avoid embarrassment – that's understandable - but it does indicate she's not so squeaky clean after all. She has a driving ban *and* she's a liar. Anything else from the FLOs?'

Jane had started and so continued, answering for both of them.

'Nothing else from the Spillmans. We've introduced ourselves to the Resslers, but we're not conducting the video interview until later this morning. I believe Jason will be discharged this afternoon.'

Forensics were next up. The Crime Scene Investigation manager had not had personal contact with anyone in the case, to avoid genetic and fibre cross-contamination, but had received reports from his operatives who had attended the hospital. Given the victim had been dumped, naked, there had been little physical evidence to gather, other than two bandages: the dressing from around the victim's head; a smaller dressing, placed over the site of a cannula wound. Nevertheless, photographs had been captured, swabs taken, scrapes obtained from under Jason Ressler's nails – fingers and toes.

As previously diagnosed by the surgeon at the hospital, evidence indicated the victim's outer ear had been surgically removed. The incision; the stitching; and the dressing – all suggested the operation had been performed by someone with surgical experience, whether that was a hospital surgeon, or a vet. This was consistent with the statements the victim had made to PCs Billinge and Semmens at the hospital; that the work had been carried out by a man in a surgeon's gown, whose bedside manner and advice with regard to caring for the wound were textbook medical school.

Samples of Jason Ressler's blood had been taken. Analyses revealed the presence of two medications - Fentanyl and Midazolam. It was explained that Fentanyl was a potent, synthetic opioid analgesic with a rapid onset and short duration of action. It was doctor-speak, but nevertheless plain enough. Historically, the drug had been used to treat breakthrough pain and was currently commonly used in pre-procedures as a pain reliever, as well as an anesthetic, in combination with a benzodiazepine, for example Midazolam. Fentanyl was approximately eighty to one-hundred times more potent than morphine, and roughly forty to fifty times more potent than pharmaceutical grade heroin. The other drug – Midazolam – was a medication used for anesthesia; for procedural sedation; and to combat troubled sleeping and severe agitation. It made the patient sleepy, decreasing their anxiety, and causing a loss of ability to create new memories. It could be given by mouth, intravenously, by injection into a muscle, sprayed into the nose, or in the cheek. Jason Ressler's testimony was consistent with the wound in his arm, so it could reasonably be assumed the medications were administered intravenously and would typically begin working within five minutes. The effects lasted for between one and six hours. Importantly, these were both medications readily available to surgeons within the hospital setting.

A second CSI team had secured the holiday brochure and sticky note attached to it, originally supposed to have been written by the hand of Jason's lover. It had been handled, moved and thrown from a car window. DNA samples had been collected from all those who were known to have had contact with the items; their fingerprints taken. Every effort would be made to identify other genetic markers that could not be eliminated in this way.

Having thanked the CSI manager, DI Bickley turned his attention to DC Pace.

'Angela, DS Honeyman tells me you have an update on Anna Richardson?'

'Yes, Guv. Drake Fallas and I spoke with Jason Ressler's manager, Martin Feller. It seems we've either been sent on a wild goose chase, or there's another Anna out there we don't know of. Jason is responsible for six members of staff, one of whom is our Anna Richardson. However, it's unlikely she and Jason Ressler have been having an affair as she's in her early sixties. Her husband recently retired with a hefty golden handshake. They've used a large part of it taking their children and grandchildren to Florida for a fortnight. They left the night Jason went missing. We'll speak with her on her return, but as I say, she's unlikely to be involved; certainly her colleagues don't think there's anything going on between them.'

'Okay, thank you Angela.'

DI Bickley then summarised what they knew, drawing together information shared at both briefings.

'So we have a detached bungalow, probably in the middle of nowhere, with a gravel drive. Oh, and it may be a long way away...or close by. There are at least three heavies; a cross-dressing psychopath, trained as a surgeon, or a vet; and a crippled white Caucasian in Muslim attire. We're not even sure of their gender, but we do know the latter two have blue eyes. Brilliant! No sounds, smells or forensics, and no bloody motive!

'People, we have to do better than this. Any suggestions?'

A voice called out from the crowd.

'A shop keeper might remember selling a burka to a white man, but where would we start to find that particular shop. Clearly there are towns with strong Muslim communities, but they're all over the place.'

DI Bickley was hoping for more.

'It's a thought, but realistically we would have to appeal to the public via the media, and I don't think we're at that stage just yet. Right, suggestions of my own. I want background checks on the Ressler's finances. Both appear so innocent, one or both of them must be involved in something big. And I think it's time we made a call to the National Crime Agency. I want to know if there are any links between the Resslers and major crime. Best start with their phone numbers. I want to know why Jason Ressler was picked as a victim. What's the connection? What has he done?

'Meeting dismissed. Let's do this people.'

DI Bickley caught up with the FLOs who had plans to go straight from the briefing to the hospital.

'Hope you don't mind. I know I don't normally stray far from the office, but I need to look Jason Ressler and his wife in the eye.'

***

'Mr Ressler. Hello, I am Detective Inspector Robert Bickley, the Senior Investigation Officer in your case. I thought it only right to come and see you in person to find out how you're coping.'

Jason offered his hand and asked the DI to dispense with the formality of calling him Mr. He was Jason.

'The doctors are pleased with my progress and have promised to let me go once they've completed another set of observations.'

'That's great news. Now, Jason, you seem to already know my officers.'

'Yes, they introduced themselves yesterday and gave me their cards.'

'Good. Well, while you wait to go home, they're going to conduct a videoed interview with you. I believe they already explained the reason for it.'

Both Jason and his wife nodded.

'Good. I have spoken with the police constables who were at the crash site and with you here yesterday, and I've listened with interest to what they told me. It concerns me that the man who assaulted you intimated he will take you again, but we really have nothing to go on – that is, unless of course, you are holding something back from us that might help catch this person. Be honest, do either of you have any enemies?'

The couple looked to each other. Jason could not think of any occasion when he had upset anyone. His wife concurred.

'You're not very nice about Audi drivers, are you – all those things you say about them on Facebook. Steven Billinge tells me most of your posts appear to blame them for the problems of the world.'

'That's just a bit of fun. That's no reason to kidnap me and cut my bloody ear off, is it?'

The patient touched his fingertips tentatively against a fresh dressing, pressed against the side of his head.

'It may sound trivial to you, but do you really know who reads this stuff? Either way, we'll add that to the list of possible motives.'

'You have a list?'

'I'd love to say I have. The truth is, we have very little to go on at the moment, although we are following leads. It's not all bad. In our favour, there is no indication this surgeon knows where you live...'

'Maybe not, but they had no trouble finding me, did they? And they know my wife delivers CBT!'

'CBT?'

'Sorry, Cognitive Behavioural Therapy! She's a nurse.'

'I see. As I say, there is no indication this surgeon knows where you live. Maybe that's why he picked you up on your way home from work and dumped out of town.'

'Or maybe he knew there wouldn't be any cameras.'

'That is a possibility. For now, we'll give you a panic alarm. Press it and a car will be with you in minutes.'

'What about surveillance?'

'I'd love to say we'd arrange for a car to watch you around the clock, but the truth is, we don't have those kind of resources. We don't know when he might strike next. It may be tonight; it may be next year; it may be never - you said yourself he has other jars, but they haven't got your name on. On the other hand, he may be watching you and wait until we pull out and then attack. We just don't know. My officers can advise you about increasing your security. I'm sorry, but there's nothing more we can do for you. Of course we'll try our hardest to find him, but as I say, we have very little to go on.'

'You have nothing? You have me and you have a hole where my sodding ear used to be!'

The Detective Inspector remained calm.

'Mr Ressler...Jason...so far we have no clue as to the whereabouts of the place to which you were taken. We have your car, and Crime Scene Investigators will check it over, but bearing in mind your version of events, they're unlikely to find anything. It seems your kidnappers were not the least bit interested in your vehicle. We know you were transported in a white van. However, you cannot give us the licence number, not even the make of vehicle. We know you were taken to a residential property, but that could be anywhere in the country. You can provide no descriptions of the men who took you, other than they wore all black. No one spoke. You cannot relate sights, sounds or smells. You can describe a woman slumped in a wheelchair, wearing a burka, but given her eyes were blue, there's every possibility she wasn't a Muslim, but wearing said item of clothing to disguise her looks – and it seems to have been most effective. You cannot describe the perpetrator. You think he's probably a man, dressed as a woman. You don't know how tall he was because he was wearing heels. You have no idea what his real voice sounds like. You have no idea as to his build as he was wearing padding. All we do know is that he appears to be a trained surgeon, or a vet. Have you any idea how many surgeons there are, past and present? How do you propose I find the one nutter out of all of them?'

Jason could respond, but there was little fire left in his soul.

'I thought it would be like CSI on the TV.'

'Sadly not. We are working on the assumption your abduction needed a lot of pre-planning, so that is where we are concentrating our effort. Hopefully we'll find something on the CCTV taken from your place of work. That could take some time and we have to be lucky, but we must stay positive. 'Any questions?'

Jason had one.

'The man in the accident – the one who hit the tree – is he okay?'

The inspector looked to his constables. Jane Humfress provided an answer.

'He'll live. I don't think you have to worry about him, though. He was way over the limit and we have video from the car travelling behind him. Although you stumbled into the road, if he hadn't been under the influence, there was no need for him to swerve the way he did.'

Shortly afterwards, DI Bickley left the Family Liaison Officers to record their interview.

***

Later that evening, the Spillmans were kind enough to drive to the hospital and transport their neighbours home. They stayed a while, making conversation, before getting back to their jig-saw, which had less than one-hundred pieces still to do. Jason made her husband comfortable on the sofa and left the room.

'Don't go. I know I'm being a wimp, but I don't want to be on my own.'

Heather smiled and placed a comforting hand on his shoulder.

'I've just got to go to the car. I think I left my spare pair of glasses in the glovebox. I won't be a minute. Then we can watch TV together.'

Jason wondered why his wife felt the need to close the front door behind her, and why it took so long to search the glovebox, it having much the same capacity as an overnight wash bag. The truth was, he would never know what took her so long, even if he asked her outright. Her answer would be a lie.

Settled in the passenger seat, door closed, Heather was sure she was sufficiently isolated for her husband not to overhear her phone conversation.

'Hello, John? It's Heather.'

'I know, it comes up on my screen. How are you?'

'Not good. Listen, I have to be quick. Jason mustn't hear me talking to you.'

'Jason, but...'

'But nothing. He's back. I was tricked. He didn't run off with anyone. He was kidnapped and had his fucking ear cut off!'

'Wha...?'

'Precisely. Now, this is important. You and me? It never happened. Do you hear me?'

'Er...er...of course. Why would I tell anyone?'

'John, you have to delete the video. No one must ever know. Can you do that for me?'

'Er...er...I suppose. Yeah, sure. Hang on...There, I've done it.'

'Thanks John. Speak to you soon.'

'Fuck, Heather...'

'I know. Thanks for everything. Bye.'

'Bye.'

The call having ended, John Ainsley tapped the screen of his smart phone. A short video played.

'For the record, this isn't rape, it's revenge.'

John felt guilty for being unfaithful to his good friend, Jason. He felt guilty, too, for having lied to Heather, but he knew how delicate their relationship was now and how that could lead to accusations and counter accusations. Who knew, Heather might tell her husband she'd been raped in her darkest hour. He was not going to lay himself open to charges like that. Consequently, he had no choice but to keep the recording as insurance.

Heather returned to the living room, without her spare glasses.

'Never mind, I've found my regular pair,' she said, picking them up from the remote control basket on the coffee table.

***

In his office, DI Bickley took a call. DS Honeyman waited patiently at the door. As the Inspector replaced the handset, he beckoned his office manager forward. Alan Honeyman felt comfortable enough to take a seat without being asked.

'Well, boss, what's the next step?'

'We scale back. That was the Super. We've just been landed a murder on our patch.'

8

Two years ago

No one said it, but Charlotte Gosling had chosen an inconvenient time to take her own life. Being the opening days of a New Year, a back log formed, the consequence being that it was not until the first week of February before Kenneth and Jennifer got to lay their only child to rest – four weeks suffering an open wound; the remainder of their lives coping with the deep scars their loss had bequeathed them. Kenneth Gosling buried his head in his work; his wife remained absent from hers, sure she could never work again. It was only with the passing of their daughter she realised the truth – her family, not her career, was her purpose.

The moment had come. Charlotte's bedroom door had remained closed since she had taken herself from those who loved her. For weeks, the pain caused by the prospect of seeing the evidence of that night had been too great for her mother, but the day had finally come. Jennifer stood outside on the landing, a roll of black refuse sacks in hand, a bucket filled with cleaning sprays and cloths hanging over her arm. Her hand paused on the door knob. Jennifer steeled herself with a deep breath, and entered. The sight brought her close to fainting; to fall to the floor and pound the carpet; to howl - but she did none of these things. Instead, she stood quite still, her head panning slowly, left to right; her eyes scanning the enormity of the task. Her husband had suggested getting in the professionals; people used to cleaning up murder scenes and the apartments of lonely people who had died and lain unnoticed for weeks, or months, until the smell began to offend the noses of their neighbours. Jennifer was not in favour, believing this was the best she could do for her daughter; that and choose a luxurious coffin, and a restful place to have her earthly remains interred.

Charlotte's room was to become her shrine, but that did not mean leaving it as it was. There were signs that paramedics had been there; police too; and also the flotsam and jetsam, normally associated with a teenager's room. Bowls and drinking glasses were gathered on the side; discarded clothing lay on the floor. The bedding would need changing for the spare duvet cover and pillowcase set. The carpet would need special treatment to remove the spillage – brown stains that gave no hint of the life they once supported.

A dozen tea light candles, dead and empty, sat on convenient surfaces about the room. They could remain and perhaps be replaced from time to time, when Jennifer felt the need to lie upon her daughter's bed and feel they were together once again.

The process took from early morning until late evening, the only thoughts filling her head being those of her last hours together with her daughter. Charlotte had eaten her evening meal in the company of her parents, sitting at the dining table. For Jennifer and Kenneth, it had made a pleasant change to find their daughter happy; relaxed; conversational. Unusually, despite being the first to lay her knife and fork down, Charlotte had made no move to leave the table, excused or otherwise. Instead, she waited patiently until her parents had finished eating and had drained their accompanying glasses of red wine, before helping her mother stack the used plates, cutlery and glasses into the dishwasher. Even then, she had ignored the lure of her bedroom, choosing instead to settle down with her parents to watch TV – a recorded art history programme in which she clearly had no interest.

As the presenter paved the way for the next week's episode, tantalising his audience with clips of great art works to come, Charlotte had issued a convincing yawn and rose from the settee with the apathy of someone so desperate for bed, it was touch and go whether she would make the stairs. Perhaps to avoid appearing rude, before heading up, she first excused herself, explaining she was tired; reminding her parents she had school in the morning. She had given each a hug – something neither parent had experienced in a very long time. At the living room door, she had paused and turned to apologise for having been grumpy of late. Jennifer and Kenneth had responded, telling Charlotte how only earlier in the day they had spoken of how she seemed to have perked up recently and how nice that was.

Charlotte had smiled at them before leaving her parents to catch up on the day's news. At the lounge door, she had paused and turned back into the room.

'Love you.'

Those were her last words.

Jennifer remembered every nuance of that evening; she could not forget; she could not help but analyse each and every moment, searching for its true meaning.

Jennifer had chosen a day when her husband would be out of the house. That was easy these days as he seldom came home, preferring to bury his thoughts in his work at the hospital, returning late to avoid conversation with his wife. When he did speak, interaction was nothing more than him asking where the corkscrew had gone. Jennifer felt he should know, Kenneth being the only person in the house to use it. It was a wonder to her he could operate on anyone at all.

By the end of the day, the blood-stained mattress had been turned, the bedding had been changed, the carpet looked presentable, Charlotte's clothes had been binned or laundered, and a fresh glass of water had been placed on the bedside table.   It would need changing daily.

In the course of her work, Jennifer had found her daughter's private journal, hidden well. A five-year diary, it was fat and up to date. It promised answers that her daughter's suicide note had only touched upon, but it was private. Jennifer was torn between her desire to know the truth, and her respect for the dead – her daughter. After much internal discussion she found a compromise, deciding to begin at the end and read backwards until she had discovered all she needed to know, but no more. Charlotte would have her secrets.

The last entry set out her plans, and recorded how, as a result, she suddenly felt at peace, having found a solution to her problems, but it did not reveal what those problems were. Previous entries revealed she had discovered a website, dedicated to the subject of self-harm and suicide – not encouraging it, but talking openly about feelings, reading the signs and supporting those in crisis. Charlotte particularly liked that it was a resource aimed at people of her own age.

Going further back, Jennifer began to build a picture of a life she knew nothing about: her daughter being bullied at school; being abandoned by those she had called her friends; being unable to understand what was happening to her; her parents remaining oblivious to her problems.

Reluctantly, Jennifer trawled back even further, through pages crinkled by the pressure of a firmly held pen, to 7 November, the handwritten words marking the passing of Kenneth's mother; Charlotte's grandmother – Nan. Charlotte had received the news badly, as any teenager might react to the loss of someone who had been part of their life since birth, but her entry portrayed a much deeper loss.

Unsettled, Jennifer continued to turn back the pages, and there it was; evidence of a troubled young woman confiding in Nan, choosing to skip a generation in search of the support she craved. Why had Charlotte not confided in her parents? Why had Kenneth's own mother not told him that his daughter was in crisis? Had Charlotte and her grandmother had such little regard for Jennifer and Kenneth's ability to listen and to act?

Jennifer's feelings of guilt strengthened; a guilt that had swamped her the moment her husband had cried out in despair, when he discovered he was too late; a guilt that had continued to fill every moment of her waking day, and much of her sleep; a guilt now justified by the words of her daughter, lost to her before her precious Charlotte had ever tasted independence.

Sitting on her daughter's bed, Jennifer read forward through the pages again, trying to make sense of it all. Having absorbed the last entry, she allowed the journal to drop to her lap, and her body to collapse to one side, adopting the foetal position, her head resting on the pillow. She instantly regretted having laundered the original slip, the washed and ironed pillowcase retaining none of the essences that might otherwise have triggered memories of her daughter. Nevertheless, it allowed her think and in doing so she formed a plan.

When Kenneth finally returned home, unusually his wife was there to receive him. He was not in the mood for talking, deep and meaningful conversation or otherwise, but Jennifer had already determined he would. She let him pour a large glass of red wine, gulp half its contents, and top it up again before he sat down. As if playing a decisive poker hand, she then placed their daughter's diary on the coffee table between them. Kenneth left it where it lay.

'I finally got round to tackling Charlotte's room today. It looks much better now.'

The words drew no reaction from her husband who seemed interested in his socked feet; the way the shape of his large toes nail was visible through the material.

'While I was tidying up, I found this,' she said, placing a hand on the cover. 'It's her diary.'

Still there was no visible reaction.

'I read some of it – I wanted to know why she…'

Jennifer could not bring herself to finish the sentence. There was no need.

'Did you know Charlotte confided in your mum? Told her everything?'

Kenneth remained silent, but his head lifted to face his wife, his expression one of curiosity.

'You should read it too. Then you'll know how we let her down.'

Kenneth took a calculated sip of wine and stared at the journal. Without another word, his wife rose to her feet and left the room, calling back to him from the door.

'I'll leave you to it.'

Jennifer retired to the spare room, settling down for another sleepless night, despite her physical exhaustion. She soon began to think of Charlotte's friends, of whom she had met several in the past. Over the years, old had been replaced with new as friends fell out of favour and new ones took their place. Allegiances had been forged and broken, but there had always been someone paying a visit, meeting Charlotte's mother for the first time, introducing themselves with a, 'Hello Mrs Gosling', to which she would answer, 'Call me Jennifer.'

Over the years, many of them had stayed for sleepovers; they had paired up with Charlotte as buddies on school trips; they had accompanied the Goslings on family minibreaks, providing Charlotte a lifeline during those times when her parents became too dull for company. In recalling the past, Jennifer realised that in recent months, those occasions had tailed off. She wondered why she had not noticed before. Further, she realised Charlotte had not mentioned any of her friends of late, had seen precious little of them outside school and there was no mention of them in the diary. Why?

The next day, Jennifer was already standing at the entrance to 'The Grange' when the bell announced the end of the school day. She had chosen to stand next to an outward-facing sign, painted in gold lettering on a background of royal blue, designed to promote an image of superiority over the two comprehensives at the other end of town – 'The Grange' was a seat of learning for the middle classes.

A short delay was followed by the emergence of a herd of well-groomed pupils, babbling among themselves; the boys wearing traditional blazers; the girls wearing smart dresses. Everyone appeared excited: full of life; glad to be free. Andrea was among their number. She knew Jennifer well, but failed to see her at first, Andrea being engaged in conversation about shoes, and Jennifer being partially obscured by the school sign. They were still fifty paces apart when their eyes met, at which point Andrea immediately lost forward momentum, bade her friends to continue on without her, dropped her head to her chest and sloped to the spot where Jennifer waited, smiling benevolently.

Keen to demonstrate she meant no harm, Jennifer put a friendly hand against Andrea's elbow.

'How are you? Are you okay to talk?' she asked in gentle tones.

Andrea lifted her head. She was crying.

'Oh, you poor thing. Here, have a tissue. It's clean.'

The pair took advantage of a convenient bench, positioned away from the lanes of human traffic.

'I'm sorry,' Andrea said, sobbing quietly.

'What for?'

'I should have told someone. I should have helped Charlotte.'

The conversation that followed revealed information that was as difficult for the young woman to deliver as it was for Jennifer to receive. If Andrea was to be believed, in recent months her daughter had led a life about which she knew nothing. Charlotte had begun to question her own sexuality, confided in the wrong people and become the target for bullies who used psychological warfare to reduce her to a point where she doubted her validity. Friends began to abandon her, one by one, not wishing to become targets themselves. Andrea was one of them, leaving her guilt-ridden ever since. Charlotte's grades began to suffer. Teachers missed the signs, only seeing a prize pupil who had turned her back on her studies; probably because she had discovered boys. Nothing could have been further from the truth. The teachers' solution had been to threaten detention and to inform her parents. It was as though they had become bullies too. All Charlotte had needed was someone to stop the bullying and help her find herself. She felt so alone. All she had was her Nan.

'She didn't feel she could come to us?' Jennifer asked wistfully.

'I'm sorry Mrs Gosling, but no.'

Jennifer knew it was common for the parents of a child who had taken their own life to feel they were at least partially to blame; that they could have done something differently. The diary had played its part in Jennifer believing these feelings were not without grounds. Andrea's revelations had confirmed them to be true.

If asked, Jennifer would not have been able to describe how she had made her way home, nor how she had found her key to operate the front door, nor how she found herself sitting on the settee, still wearing her coat and outdoor shoes.

The diary remained on the coffee table, in exactly the same position she had left it the night before. Her investigation was complete; her knowledge of the circumstances surrounding the death of her beloved only child being as complete as it needed to be. Charlotte had been tortured and no one had done anything to rescue her. It was one thing for her tutors to have missed the signs; another for her friends to have distanced themselves for fear of reprisal. However, it was unforgiveable that her parents had not noticed the changes; worse they had raised such barriers their own child would rather confide in her grandmother and an internet website. Jennifer knew what she had to do and how to make her husband accept the truth.

Turning to the current date in Charlotte's journal, she made a fresh entry.

I cannot live knowing I have played my part in the death of our wonderful daughter, Charlotte. If there is a heaven, I want to say sorry to her for letting her down. If there is no heaven, at least I will have paid my penance...

There followed a précis of her investigation and conclusion.

Soon afterwards, the diary was placed on Charlotte's bedside table, the pages weighted open. Jennifer stood upon her daughter's dressing table stool, a cord tied round her neck, the other end secured to the curtain pole bracket. She tested it for strength and found it suitable. Without further delay or thought, she upset the stool, causing her body to drop with a jerk, and the cord to tighten.

Jennifer's legs convulsed several times, kicking an adjacent piece of furniture with such ferocity a heavy glass candle holder was knocked onto its side.

Kenneth attended work as usual, the already heavy cloud that had descended upon his shoulders the day after his daughter had been taken from him, and which had never lifted since, being added to by the events of the previous evening. Some of what his wife said had pierced his armour. Consequently, he left for home early, claiming to be unwell. Nobody questioned a man possessing such an impeccable work ethic; a man who had suffered such a loss. The sound of his key turning in the door disguised the fall of the stool in the bedroom above his head. He called out, keen to wrap his arms round his wife and issue an apology. His voice received no response.

In Charlotte's bedroom, the candle holder rolled slowly to the edge of the cabinet and dropped to the floor, its heavy weight causing almost as much of a thump as had the stool. In an otherwise silent house, the sound could be heard downstairs, drawing Kenneth to it. He climbed the stairs slowly, affording himself time to consider what he might say by way of an apology. Reaching the top of the stairs he called out a second time, looking about the landing, expecting a response from the master bedroom, or the family bathroom. Still there was nothing, but it was odd Charlotte's door should be open. It was never left open. No sounds came from within. If Jennifer was in there, Kenneth expected to find her sitting, or lying on their daughter's bed, lost in thought.

His hand swept the door gently to one side, revealing a scene so unexpected, so shocking, it defied time, causing his world to shift in to slow motion.

Jennifer's face was grotesque; her skin purple; her eyes bulging; her tongue protruding from her mouth. Her body convulsed at one end of a dark cord, the other end of which was knotted about a curtain pole bracket that was pulling away from the wall, already exposing one of two anchor fixings.

The sudden presence of adrenalin coursing through Kenneth's veins presented him with choices – to fight or to take flight. Instinctively, he chose to face his fear; to stride the short distance across the room; to grasp his wife about her hips; to lift her up and so relieve the pressure on her neck. However, before he had taken his first step, the bracket gave way completely, dropping his wife to the floor, the pole and curtains tumbling on top of her. Although Jennifer landed hard, at least her chances of survival had improved. However, while the knot could not tighten further, neither could it loosen; not on its own; not even with the aid of finger nails tearing and picking at the binding.

Kenneth called for help, bellowing as he had never done before, his voice exploding from the pit of his stomach, but his effort was to no avail. The windows being closed, the detached house surrounded on all sides by garden, trees and bushes, no one heard his calls.

Valuable seconds were wasted as Kenneth wracked his brain for the location of anything that might sever the noose. The bathroom came to mind, the mirrored cabinet providing a pair of nail scissors. Reluctantly, he left his wife's side, dashed across the landing, in doing so, stumbled into one doorframe, then another, his normally well-honed motor skills impaired by his body's own high octane boost.

Scissors in hand, Kenneth dashed back to his daughter's bedroom, leaned his wife's motionless body against his chest, and set the blades to work, the sharp tips of the instrument tearing into Jennifer's skin.

In time the noose gave. Jennifer had a pulse, but it was weak, if there at all.

A phone call brought the paramedics. In the meantime, Kenneth became her heart and lungs, the heel of his hand pumping her chest rhythmically until sweat dripped from his brow, the only respite being to deliver second-hand breath. An ambulance with blue flashing lights and deafening sirens took Jennifer to the Accident and Emergency department; to the same hospital in which Mr Gosling, consultant, operated daily. People he knew delivered the prognosis; people who knew his level of knowledge; people who knew there was little point in trying to soften the blow.

'Kenneth, Jennifer will probably live, but we fear her brain was starved of oxygen for a prolonged period and is likely to have suffered irreparable damaged as a consequence.'

Kenneth took the news impassively.

The consultant who delivered the news had not finished.

'There's more. We believe Jennifer has also sustained a spinal injury – a result of her sudden drop to the floor. It's too early to say for certain, but we fear she will never walk again.'

9

Heather guarded a small table in the window of a busy coffee shop. It was no place for people to drink alone. A minimum of two patrons were required; one to stake a spot; one to join the endlessly replenishing queue. As she waited, she wondered when Britain – a nation of tea lovers – had transformed into a nation of coffee drinkers. Within 0.73 seconds, Google provided myriad answers, sufficient to keep her occupied for the rest of her life, but before she had accessed the first article, her friend, Natasha, stepped up to the table, holding a tray.

Heather unloaded an oversized cup and saucer, a teapot and a milk jug onto the table; Natasha laid claim to a bucket of frothy coffee and shared the array of chocolate cakes between them.

There was a conversation to be had, but neither knew where to start.

Heather was the first to break the silence.

'It's funny, we talk about stress, anxiety, depression and all manner of problems on a daily basis. We always have the answers. It's easy. But when it happens to you...I mean, who would have thought I would need counselling?'

'Heather, you're not seeing a counsellor; you're having coffee with a friend who just happens to be a colleague.'

'But I should be able to deal with this on my own. I know the techniques.'

'Is that what you'd say to your clients?'

Heather had to admit she would not.

'How is Jason?'

'If you were to see him, you'd probably think he's doing okay. I mean, he's ignored all the advice to rest and instead has been working his way through all the things I've been asking him to do for years – stopping the tap dripping, that sort of thing. He's found a real appetite for it.'

Heather abandoned a half-formed smile and fell silent, her answer not fully given.

'But?'

Heather accepted the prompt.

'But scratch beneath the surface and he's really not good at all. I've had to ask Irene round to babysit. He panics if he's left alone, but I have to get out, or I'd go mad.'

At that moment, her phone chimed. She glanced at the screen and saw the face of a clown.

'It's him.'

Over the years they had known each other, Natasha and Heather established an unbreakable rule – no phones in cafes or restaurants. However, given the circumstances, Natasha was prepared to make allowances, waiting for her friend to respond, without making judgement.

'Is he okay?'

'He's fine. He just wanted to let me know Irene has got him started on a 5000 piece jigsaw. Bless her.'

Natasha issued an appropriate smile.

'And in general?'

'As I say, not good. He's got this thing about his missing ear. He's removed or covered all the mirrors in the house – you can imagine how difficult that makes it doing my hair. I can't dry it while he's in the room and he won't let me out of his sight for more than ten minutes at a time. I have to be quick.'

Natasha's expression looked almost horrified. Her friend had further ammunition to ensure it did.

'It gets worse. I understand he's not ready to return to work at the moment, but he won't even drive along the road to get there. He'll only travel during daylight and he's talking of turning the box room into a panic room. He carries a spray and a personal alarm wherever he goes and I'm pretty sure he has a knife.'

There it was – horrified.

'God, that's awful.'

Heather lowered her tone so as not to be heard by those around her. Clearly, her next revelation needed a degree of confidentiality.

'And there's more. He wet himself the other night. I'd changed the bedding and apparently the softener I used had the same smell as the pillowcase placed over his head by the kidnappers.'

Natasha imagined the scene was not as passive as described, Jason laying his head gently on his pillow, a small trickle of urine dampening the front of his pyjamas. Only Jason and Heather could know the trauma he had suffered.

'And he talks to himself when he's driving, assessing potential dangers; cars that have followed him for more than a mile; lay-bys; police in hi-vis jackets who might be kidnappers in disguise; anyone wearing black – white vans are a particular problem and there are so many of them.

'I just want my Jason back. Do you know the thing I miss the most? It's his stupid sense of humour. He was always doing silly things to make me smile. I'm sure he takes his job seriously, but as soon as he sets foot outside that supermarket, it's like he never grew up.'

With Heather having emptied her buffer, the conversation stalled, at which point Natasha leant forward, cut her friend's chocolate chip muffin in two and pushed the plate towards her.

'Eat this. It's gorgeous and then I'm going to tell you what to do.'

Natasha's plan was to take it easy, but to break the cycle. Heather was advised to make her husband visit his place of work, if needs be threatening she would otherwise leave him alone in the house with his jigsaw. To avoid the road that caused him so much anxiety, they would travel by bus; not the direct route; the number 36 which went all round the houses. He could wear a hoody and trendy new headphones, the sort that would once have been the preserve of recording studios, large enough to make it impossible to tell who had and had not got ears. No one would know he had only one. Heather was to pre-warn his manager of Jason's arrival, ensuring they could meet discretely; without bumping into his colleagues. Most of all, Heather was to keep in touch with her friends and colleagues for coffee and cake. Heather preferred tea.

The advice was not perfect, but well worth a try. For a short while Heather felt relaxed; perhaps it was the cake; perhaps it was the everyday conversation that followed. Nevertheless, when it was time for Natasha to drop her friend home, the butterflies once again took flight.

Heather provided her husband with a fresh mug of English breakfast tea and a brace of dunking biscuits, joining him at the dining table. Oblivious to his chosen plan of attack, she put into action one of her own, picking carefully through a spread of nobbly cardboard pieces, searching for anything bearing a certain shade of red. For a while, the only sounds to be heard were those of shuffling fingertips, the slurp of lips drawing in hot tea, and the occasional, 'Got it,' synchronous with a gentle snap and a double tap. By the time both mugs were drained, Heather had formed a Victorian post box, while her husband, to his great satisfaction, had discovered he could join several islands together, transforming a hole with pictures in it, to a picture with holes in it.

Lost in their respective tasks, any subject then broached would appear secondary; an incidental thought, or so Heather hoped.

'I spoke with my colleague when I went out this morning.'

Heather deliberately chose 'colleague', not 'friend', believing the more she disassociated herself, the more likely Jason was to accept Natasha's plan.

'Oh yes?'

'I'd like you to see her. Her name's Natasha. I've probably mentioned her before. She's very good.'

'Got it!'

Jason plugged one of the remaining holes.

There was little to gain in Heather becoming riled by her husband's lack of focus. Instead, she paused, re-establishing her pretence at nonchalance.

'Well? Will you see her? I think you should.'

Before responding, Jason tried and failed to fit another piece.

'It's funny,' he said in a matter of fact way, 'the surgeon knew what you do for a living, but advised me to get counselling from someone not so emotionally attached. The man cut my ear off, but then wanted what was best for me – funny.'

Evidently he had been paying more attention than Heather thought.

'So, will you see her?'

Jason concentrated on a patch of foliage, determining the subtle differences between one frond and another, so he might piece together the bottom left corner of the puzzle. His decision could not be rushed.

'I do need to sort myself out. I want to be well enough for the children to come home. I know my behaviour's been a bit strange since my return, but I really am trying.'

He could say no more. Having dropped a distinctive light green leaf back into the box, his head fell into his empty palms, a sniffle and reddening forehead indicating he was crying.

Heather left her seat, moved round the table and engulfed him in her arms from behind.

'There's no hurry. When you're ready.'

The crying stopped abruptly, Jason having quickly regained control of his wayward emotions.

'Better sooner rather than later, don't you think?'

Natasha was available the next day; a one-to-one session, squeezed between the morning clients and an afternoon group therapy. Jason was not bothered that she ate her sandwiches as they spoke. He was simply grateful she was prepared to give up her free time to help.

Over the course of an hour, the counsellor listened to her patient's anxieties and steered conversation towards her ultimate goal – to explain her grand plan; more importantly to get Jason to buy into it.

'So, how did it go?'

'She's good. I mean you're good too, but…'

'I understand. No offence taken. So, are we getting the bus?'

'No, I'm going to try driving the route again, or at least a route. Forget the bus. There are loads of different ways I can go. Of course, it'll take longer getting there, but you gotta keep them guessing, haven't you?'

Martin Feller was genuinely pleased to see Jason able to step foot over the threshold once more. He did not want one of the company's star pupils feeling pressured to return to work before he was ready, but he was of the firm opinion it was necessary to get back on the horse as soon as possible, or face never being able to ride again. He was also a great believer in idioms, using them as regular as clockwork.

'It made the papers,' Martin said, excitedly.

'It did,' Jason replied, less enthusiastically.

'Oh, don't be like that. We can put this to our advantage. Get you fixed up double quick.'

Jason and his wife were hooked.

'How?'

'You gotta love the NHS, but they can be a bit slow, can't they. In your case, private's the way to go.'

Jason's eyes narrowed; his wife rocked forward in her chair.

'When you rang to say you were coming in, I spoke with the boss and squared it away, and he phoned head office, and they're right behind the idea.'

'What idea?'

Martin spoke as though trying to present a sales drive to his managers; to get them as fired up as he was.

'You know we're always running campaigns for charity. Well, I thought that charity could be you.'

Jason was not sure he liked the idea of being a charity.

'A good cause then. Anyway, my idea is to run a promotion at the tills – make a connection between the newspaper article, a local man, and the store. It's bound to be a success. We'll pledge to match donations and you'll be in a private surgery in two shakes of a lamb's tail, and then you can do away with the hoody.'

Jason was suddenly aware how out of place he looked, sitting in an office, a teenage thug's outer garment substituting his smart blazer.

Heather could tell her husband was troubled. Perhaps it was all too much for him to consider.

'And what if the customers are not as generous as you think?' she asked, concerned Jason's hopes were being raised too high.

'We run these things all the time. Jason knows. If we can raise enough money to put a new roof on the Scout hut, I'm sure we can do the same for your husband. Besides, the local rag wants to do a piece on it. That means advertising. That means Head Office will want this to be a success. One way or the other, we *will* get the funds.'

Her concerns mollified, Heather gave her husband's hand a reassuring squeeze, her eyes trying to connect with his, beneath his downturned head.

Martin had gone out on a limb, but it was not plain to understand his motive: to help heal the physical and mental scars endured by a loyal and worthy employee; or to benefit the company, depicting it as the caring uncle of the community. Of course, it might have been both, but it came across more as a sales pitch than a support mechanism.

'Look, Jason, the sooner you feel normal again, the sooner you can return to work and get back to that career we both know you have ahead of you.'

The thirty-something teenager thought for a moment, his wife still holding his hand, willing him to make the right choice. He raised his head, making visual contact with his boss. Whatever Martin Feller's motive, or that of his employer, it meant a boost to his recovery and a leap closer to normality. Weekly sessions with the lovely Natasha would do the rest.

'Go for it.'

Jason had visited a number of hospital departments in his time and knew the routine. Hence, when he reached the waiting area, he settled down with a magazine, expecting to read it from cover to cover, giving time to articles and items he would normally skim across. He had not been to a private hospital before, so was in for a pleasant surprise. Barely had he got past the contents page before he and his wife were being called through to see the consultant.

Overnight, Jason had developed a phobia. It was only now he realised it was not hospitals he feared, but medical men dressed as surgeons. Thankfully, Mr Farnorth was a short, balding man, wearing an expensive suit, his overall appearance bearing no resemblance to the man responsible for his missing ear. Nor did this surgeon feel the need to disguise his voice; well spoken; confident; relaxed; the voice of a man, not a machine. So far, Jason's pulse rate barely rose above normal.

'Right, Mr Ressler, with regard to auricular reconstruction, we can offer you three alternatives. Firstly, we can take a graft, using rib cage cartilage, to form you a new ear.'

Mr Farnorth tapped his patient's side.

'One major advantage is that we use your own tissue, avoiding complications. However, this would require up to four procedures.'

As keen as Jason was to be restored to his original specifications – two eyes, one nose, one mouth, and two ears - he did not like the idea of multiple operations, or having a second area of his body disfigured by the surgeon's knife. His face remained unimpressed.

'If I can't excite you with that, secondly, we can reconstruct your ear using a plastic implant. This normally requires only one or two procedures as an outpatient.'

Jason picked up that this surgeon used contractions; another indication he was not the transgender monster who had stolen his ear.

Mr Farnorth detected his patient's difficulty maintaining attention and paused until Jason's eyes flickered, indicating his mind was back in the room. The consultant must have had some understanding as to what his patient had been through, as he appeared not the least bit irritated.

'The implant is actually a porous framework that allows your tissue to grow into the material. We cover this with a flap of your own tissue – your skin - to form a new ear, in a single procedure, with a small secondary surgery three to six months later to make adjustments.'

Mr Farnorth paused again to assess whether the information was still being absorbed. Satisfied it was, he continued.

'The third technique involves providing you with an auricular prosthesis, custom made to mirror your surviving ear. They can appear very realistic, but require a few minutes of care each day. That shouldn't be any more burdensome that caring for false teeth or contact lenses.'

'Are you suggesting I put my ear in a glass on the bedside cabinet at night time?' Jason snapped sarcastically.

'Jason!'

Heather turned first to her husband and then quickly to the surgeon, her face a picture of shock and embarrassment.

'I'm sorry, you'll have to forgive him. He's been through a lot lately.'

Jason knew he had been flippant; knew he was not in the best of moods, but found his emotions sometimes got the better of him.

'There's no need to apologise on my account. I'm capable of doing that myself. Sorry, it's not aimed at you.'

'No offence taken. Shall we continue?'

Both Jason and his wife nodded silently.

'Okay, they're made of silicone, coloured to match the surrounding skin. They can be attached with adhesive, but I prefer using titanium screws, inserted into the skull, to which the prosthetic is attached. The biggest advantage of this option, over surgery, is that the prosthetic best restores the appearance of the missing natural ear. The biggest disadvantage, other than the daily care required, is you'll know it's not real.'

None of the options appeared without disadvantage.

'What would you recommend?'

'If your ultimate goal is for your appearance to look as natural as possible, I would recommend the third option.'

A date was fixed for two weeks hence.

In quick succession, Jason had begun his counselling, overcome his fear of driving to work, and received the news his physical appearance was to be restored to normal - three actions that promoted a sudden recovery; so effective and so rapid, all parties deemed it right and safe for Charlie and Lily to cut short their unscheduled holiday with their grandparents, and return home. The restoration of the family unit acted to consolidate Jason's progress.

Days returned to normal. The children returned to school. Jason was not yet emotionally strong enough to be there for them, outside the school gates, but he welcomed the idea of doing so the moment his new silicone ear had cured. Not since he was a child, counting the days to Christmas, had he felt such impatient excitement, and just as he had been at the age of five, he found it almost impossible to sleep on the eve of the operation. Finally, Jason padded wearily upstairs to bed. Having donned his pyjamas, he padded, barefoot, across the landing to the bathroom. Having brushed his teeth, he pulled down the towel from the medicine cabinet door to brave a defiant look in the mirror at his a-symmetrical face.

The house remained quiet, even as the masked men entered the master bedroom. Gloved hands were placed over the sleeping couple's mouths, only long enough for them to wake, come to their senses and see the gun. The gloves absorbed the initial yelps; the automatic pistol ensured continued silence. The panic button was so close, but utterly impotent. For the first time, Heather knew first-hand the terror of being at the mercy of silent figures with no identity; of men who communicated only through sign language, making themselves understood with a nod of the head, or a flick of the barrel. For the first time, Heather knew first-hand the terror of being injected; being powerless to prevent it.
In a strange way, Jason was relieved his wife's suffering was short-lived. He took comfort in the belief she would wake unharmed and that his children would be spared.
The kidnappers both wore black, although their choice of attire differed. One preferred a ribbed pullover; the other a black bomber jacket, his chest bulging unnaturally.
The man with the jumper held the gun, allowing his associate to work freely with both hands. The man wearing the jacket patted his empty pockets, failing to find was he was feeling for. He pulled the zip down to his stomach, reached into his clothing and withdrew a now familiar-looking, drawstring hood. Slinging it across his shoulder, he frisked himself, patting and rubbing flattened palms around his midriff. Clearly, whatever he was looking for was not there. Nor was it on the floor in the immediate vicinity. The man in the jumper made a gesture, querying what the problem was. His associate mimed a roll of tape which he had forgotten to bring, or had misplaced as they crept through the house. The eyes alone of one asked how the other could have been so stupid. Shrugging his shoulders, the man in the jacket turned to their captive, raised a finger to him, and issued a 'Shhh!' In the circumstances, fear of reprisal would have to substitute for a length of sticky tape.

The hood was pulled down over Jason's head, the familiar fragrance of raw fabric softener overpowering his senses, causing his bladder to loosen, as it did whenever his mind made the connection between that particular scent and the trauma he had previously suffered.

He made no attempt to prevent himself being thrown over one of the masked men's shoulders, to be transported downstairs, maintaining silence so that Charlie and Lily would not wake and become a problem. Supported at either side, his bare feet kept pace with his captors, trotting the length of the back garden, the occasional pebble under foot and scuffing of skin on concrete causing him to wince; a broken snail oozing between his toes causing him to cringe. A rusty latch scratched his side through his pyjamas as he was rotated through ninety degrees to facilitate three men passing through a gateway designed for one. The van was close by; ready to receive.

10

Kenneth Gosling applied pressure to the plunger, delivering a liquefied meal directly to his wife's stomach, via a nasal tube. She was neither grateful nor ungrateful. She had no opinion, or if she did, she could not express it. Her only reaction was to dribble; something she did a lot, requiring the application of a barrier cream to combat sores. Kenneth mopped the saliva from her chin, using a cloth that had been laid purposely to hand by Jennifer's paid carer, but for all the care and kindness he lavished upon her, her pale blue eyes rarely diverted from their daughter's childhood doll, which lay on her lap.

Trapped in a damaged mind, what remained of Kenneth's invalid wife still blamed him; punished him. Nevertheless, he planted a gentle kiss on her forehead and wished her 'Goodnight', cradling her arm around the doll for comfort; tucking a towel beneath her chin to keep her nightdress dry. So incapable of acting alone, a light stroke of her husband's palm was required to close her eyelids.

It was still early.

The forensic explanation for this formally bright and intelligent middle-aged woman being reduced to a near-vegetative state was the prolonged lack of oxygen to her brain, caused by self-strangulation. The generally accepted view was that Jennifer believed she had failed to notice the distress suffered by her only child, had felt responsible for Charlotte taking her own life, and had therefore sought to make amends by intending to take her own. This conclusion was backed with hard evidence – the lengthy, self-damning suicide entry she had added to her daughter's journal. To most, nothing could be clearer, but not to Jennifer's husband, who preferred to consider the bigger picture. Something or someone must have triggered Charlotte to destroy her own existence and of those closest to her.

Thinking back to his daughter's final hours, Kenneth did not recall a teenager who was out to teach her parents a lesson. Far from it. To Kenneth's mind, it was evident she had gone to great pains to ensure their enduring memory of her would be of the sweet, beautiful, caring person she had been. Others might have construed her actions as those of a lost young woman saying goodbye, relieved she had found a solution to end her pain. Alternatively, she might have intended giving her parents one last chance at redemption; to notice her struggle and save her. Kenneth would never join either camp, preferring to believe his daughter had been saying sorry for taking action that had been forced upon her by someone or something unknown. It was the mechanism by which she had reached her decision that her father now wanted so desperately to understand.

The police had been interested in Charlotte's diary, but no longer. To them it had been a piece of evidence that might have convicted a murderer, if it had not been concluded there were none. It had been returned, sealed in a clear plastic evidence bag and had sat on the coffee table ever since, in almost the same position Jennifer had left it in the hope her husband would take it in his hands and read the pages within.

Kenneth's bloodstream having absorbed more alcohol than he was used to – even by recent standards – he leaned forward, picked up the package and sat back again, sinking into an untidy heap of cushions. The interior décor had suffered since Jennifer had effectively left him and there seemed little point hiring a cleaner to restore its former glory as he no longer entertained visitors who might be impressed by it.

His subconscious was more courageous than his thinking mind, his hands and fingers working autonomously in opposition to rip the bag apart. This had not been a spur of the moment decision. Steps had been taken throughout the day, easing incrementally closer to the moment. A note pad, a pencil and a dispenser of sticky page markers lay beside him in readiness for the examination.

The discarded evidence bag fell to the floor.

The journal rested in Kenneth's hands. He took a moment to feel its weight, its texture. Then he took a deep breath and opened the pages, quickly flicking to the last of Charlotte's entries, disregarding his wife's later addition.

Kenneth read the same words as his wife, but saw different meanings – evidence that neither he nor Jennifer might be to blame after all. He had seen the final entry in the book, written moments before his wife had exchanged unhappiness and guilt for an unthinking existence, one that lacked blame, but also purpose, understanding, life. He knew its content; a summary of the investigation she had carried out; the school children she had interrogated; the conclusions she had drawn. Now he suspected she had been wrong.

In her darkest hour, having lost her grandmother, and feeling her secrets could not be shared with her parents, Charlotte had turned to the internet; specifically one particular site, the name of which cropped up more than once – 'Heather Cares'.

A few taps on the screen of his iPad brought Kenneth straight there; to a site dedicated to the suicidal young. Hypertext linked to subject matter: warning signs; getting help; causes; self-harm; a forum. Each linked to more information; each piece of information – seemingly each paragraph – riddled with the word 'suicide'.

Kenneth imagined if he was feeling low, how the mere sight of that word, repeated over and over, would plant a seed he would find impossible to resist. Given the site was aimed at young people, with impressionable minds, it was inevitable that some would be pushed over the edge. Here was the cause of his beloved daughter's early death. Whoever was responsible for creating and administering the site was also responsible for murdering his child.

Without any idea to whom he directed his anger, Kenneth vented a statement aloud.

'I am going to make you pay for this.'

The words were delivered slowly; deliberately.

Despite the muscle-relaxing qualities of the wine in his belly, Kenneth's face became rigid, his eyes narrowed, his lips puckered and white.

'Damn, I am going to make you pay.'

Striking while the iron was still hot, he moved the cursor over the 'contact us' button and clicked, opening a box within which he could write a message.

It was here he paused, considering how to write to someone he wished to exact revenge upon.

Despite the effects of alcohol, Kenneth still had a fine mind, so it required less than a minute before he had a plan and had formulated the words with which to start the ball rolling.

> *Hello, I am a great admirer of your website. You appear to be offering a very valuable service and because of this, I would like to meet with you to discuss the possibility of me making a substantial contribution to your cause. Kind regards, Kenneth Gosling.*

Only once the message had been sent did Kenneth consider it might have been wiser to use a nom de plume.

The reply came swiftly, thanking Kenneth for his kindness and suggesting ways he could donate without meeting. It was signed Heather. A second exchange was needed, during which the benefactor spoke of wishing to ensure he was making the right investment, given the sum of money he was prepared to offer - £10,000. Heather agreed. Another exchange determined the area of the country in which she was based, several hundred miles away, but her exact location was disguised by her suggestion they meet at a tea room as she did not operate out of business premises. Kenneth did not push further, but merely arranged a time and date, omitting to inform her he would have to drive for several hours if he were to make the rendezvous at the appointed time, thus disguising his own place of residence.

Kenneth arrived early, taking the opportunity to walk the route to the tea shop, before parking some distance away so his mark would not discover the make or registration number of his vehicle. There was still time to doze for half an hour, but at eleven minutes to nine, the car's security system bleeped, signifying the start of a brisk walk that carried a vengeful mind to its destination, arriving just as the big hand of the church clock reached the top of its arc.

All was set.

The door to 'The Cup and Saucer' was fitted with an old fashioned bell that tinkled every time a customer arrived or left. The interior was old fashioned too: mismatched furniture, covered with doilies; chipped bygone teapots lining the shelves of several Welsh dressers; homemade bakery, protected from the flies beneath glass-domed, flower-patterned cake stands.

Neither Heather nor Kenneth had thought to exchange a method of identification, but thankfully this proved unnecessary – a woman sitting alone; a lone gentleman entering the premises at the appointed time.

Heather rose from her seat.

'Kenneth?'

'Heather. Nice to meet you.'

Kenneth accepted her outstretched hand and shook it firmly, but without an air of dominance. None of his hatred for her showed.

The waitress brought menus. Kenneth cast his eyes over a long list of hot beverages, sandwiches and light bites. Reluctantly he accepted it was too early for wine. Besides, the premises appeared not to have a licence to sell alcohol. Just as well, he thought. If they had met later in the day, he might have suggested a pub, in which case he would have consumed too much alcohol, and he needed to keep a clear head for what he was about to do.

'What do you fancy? I shall put it down to expenses.'

As Heather accepted Kenneth's kind offer, she considered the man before her. He spoke with a well-educated voice, with a neutral accent, hard to place, just as she had imagined a generous benefactor to be. He had a calmness about him; self-assured, but he looked drawn, as though he had missed too many hours sleep.

Kenneth had no appetite. Nothing on the menu took his fancy, so he simply ordered two of the same.

As they awaited the arrival of a pot of tea for two, he broke the ice.

'Tell me about yourself.'

Heather looked surprised.

'Me?'

Kenneth reminded himself why he was there. This was not a date; it was a business meeting. The circumstances were bound to have unsettled his mark, without him compounding the problem by asking about her personal life. That could wait.

'You can if you want, but I was thinking more about your website; the charity.'

A faint hint of embarrassment flashed across Heather's face, indicating Kenneth had recovered well.

'Well, I've been a Cognitive Behavioural Therapist for many years now.'

Her audience of one claimed ignorance of the subject, challenging Heather to explain it in layman's terms.

'Well, CBT aims to stop negative cycles, and we do that by breaking down things that make you feel bad, anxious or scared. We aim to make your problems more manageable, and help you change your negative thought patterns to improve the way you feel.'

It sounded simple enough, but Kenneth's body language indicated he wanted more.

'Okay, so stress can affect the way you feel, think, behave, and even how your body functions. It can cause symptoms such as sleeping problems, sweating, loss of appetite and lack of concentration. You might feel anxious, irritable, or suffer low self-esteem. You might find that you are having racing thoughts, or that you are worrying all the time. You might lose your temper more easily, begin drinking more, or start acting unreasonably.'

Kenneth recognised much of what she was listing in himself.

'And you help combat this?'

'Yes. In principal, it's simple. As I say, it's a cycle. In essence, what I try to do is help you break that cycle.'

'And does it work?'

'Not for everybody, but in my time I've helped many people cope with depression, anxiety and stress. Many of them have been young and many of those young people had considered suicide before they came to me. When you get to that stage, you often don't know you have a problem and it takes others to notice. People don't know what the signs mean, or what to do if they recognise them. I wanted to make information available, giving sound advice they might not otherwise get because the sufferer did not want to come forward, or because those who care for them don't know what to do.

'I'm really pleased I did it, but to be honest, it's all getting too much. I'm a one-woman band and it's a lot for one person to administer a site like mine. I'd pack it up if it wasn't for the feedback.'

'And that is good?'

'Very good. I like to think my site's saved a lot of people.'

Kenneth resisted the temptation to issue a dismissive, 'Hmmm.'

'So, you're solely responsible for the whole thing?'

Heather suddenly became worried her potential investor might withdraw his offer if he saw her charity as too small to invest in.

'I am, but with a little funding, I'm sure I could spread the word even further; perhaps get some help – someone to design the site; add facilities.'

Kenneth sensed her concern.

'Do not worry, my offer still stands, but are you not concerned you might be putting ideas in young people's heads?'

'Ah, that's a common misconception. The less well informed believe if you mention the word suicide, it raises the chance of it happening. It's simply not the case. The best way is to be honest and open. I take it you agree. You've seen the site and you're here now.'

Kenneth gave a reassuring nod.

'Exactly.'

The conversation had been so intense, the arrival of the tea pot and its accoutrements had not registered with either party.

Heather was first to notice.

'Shall I pour?'

As she did so, Kenneth wrote a cheque for £10,000.

'To whom should I make this out?'

'Heather Ressler, please.'

Kenneth signed with a flourish, pleased to have learned his mark's surname. However, his clever manipulation was unnecessary. Having buttered her toasted tea cake, Heather paused to give her benefactor a leaflet.

'I brought this with me. I thought it might interest you.'

She placed a bi-fold sheet of paper in front of him – home grown on a domestic printer - aimed at drawing those in need of advice and guidance to the Heather Cares website, explaining its purpose and providing the full name and a picture of the charity's founder.

'Thank you. This is very helpful. Perhaps you can use some of the money to print more like this.'

Kenneth was genuinely grateful. Having a picture of his mark meant he did not have to obtain one surreptitiously, pointing his phone in her direction while he pretended to text.

Kenneth paid the bill, after which he and Heather stepped outside, causing the bell to wish them goodbye. It was raining.

'Where are you parked?'

'I have to confess, I did not know where the tea room was in relation to the cark park, so I left it in the long-stay at the other end of the High Street.'

'That's a long way. You'll get soaked. Let me give you a lift. I'm parked right here.'

Kenneth accepted her kind offer, determined he would only allow her to drop him at the car park, not in it. In this way he would at least keep the identity of his vehicle a secret and hoped then to pick up her trail, following her home without being spotted.

The plan was one devised by an amateur; bound to fail. In all likelihood, she would inadvertently give him the slip as soon as they bade each other farewell. At least this was an improvement on his position. Had she not offered him a lift, she would have been out of sight before he had covered a dozen steps.

Thankfully, luck was on Kenneth's side, there being a small batch of unopened letters stuffed in the passenger door pocket, handed to Heather by the postman who caught her as she left from home that morning. Glancing down, the passenger could see his mark's name, confirming the envelopes were inbound, destined for the Ressler household. Only a slight distraction was needed for Kenneth to be able to access the full address, but the potential for failure rendered the risk too great to contemplate. Frustration might have got the better of him were it not for his luck holding.

Although, by car, the route was short, Heather asked if her passenger minded that she pull over briefly, to deliver a bag of unwanted clothes to a charity shop. He most certainly did not.

Threatened frustration quickly gave way to anticipation as Heather stepped from the car, collected her bags from the boot, navigated her way to and through the entrance of the local animal protection store, and disappeared from view. Although Kenneth hoped for minutes, he worked to a time frame of mere seconds. Grabbing the small wad of mail in his left hand, he held it close to his lap to avoid discovery, working on the assumption his mark might return at any moment. Not only did the items provide an address – 54 Russell Way, Deepwell – but revealed Heather was married, her husband's forename beginning with a J.

The precise way in which the post had been stored within the door pocket was not something Heather was likely to have paid attention to when depositing it there. Nevertheless, to avoid any possibility of suspicion, Kenneth returned the bundle as best he could to its unique position.

Within less than one minute of her entering the charity shop, unaware she had lost her anonymity, Heather returned to her vehicle, drove her passenger to the long stay car park, thanked her benefactor for his generous donation and waved him goodbye.

***

The following morning, Kenneth rang the council to whom Heather paid her local taxes. On the pretext he was someone who had just moved to the area, he asked on what day of the week the bins were collected. The answer was not so simple as the question, the advisor insisting on listing a whole list of dos, don'ts and provisos, not forgetting to point out that the glass was collected every second week.

The ruse was effective.

Kenneth arrived at Russell Way in the early hours of Tuesday morning. As hoped, many of the local residents had already put out their rubbish the previous evening, clusters of bins, bags and boxes temporarily spoiling the look of a normally well-kept road. Outside number 54, waste had been separated into green, recyclables and other, but it was only the sacks containing the recyclables that excited Kenneth, they containing paper; hopefully the identifiable fragments of the Ressler's lives.

Kenneth feared that if he simply took the pink sacks, either Heather or her husband might think it strange. To avoid suspicion, having carried his quarry from the scene to his car, parked round the corner, he returned to the footpath outside the Ressler residence to disguise the theft, replacing each of the missing sacks with one taken from each of three of their neighbours.

It was worth the effort; the early mornings; the expense; the jiggling of his list of surgical operations.

Over the course of several weeks, Kenneth's lever arch file became swollen with retrieved pieces of evidence, each protected within its own plastic pouch. The visible clue of booster seats in the rear of the Ressler family car revealed the number of their children; letters from the school revealed their names and ages.

As Kenneth prepared his wife's supper, drawing it into a large syringe, he spoke to her, reporting his progress, buoyed by his success.

'Do you remember I told you I found the website Charlotte visited, and how I believe it was the so called advice pedalled there that led to our dear daughter taking her life?'

Jennifer showed no recollection, or any reaction at all.

'And you will remember how I met with the administrator. Well, I have formed the opinion she must be stopped, before she causes the death of anyone else. I am also of the opinion, and always have been, that she must pay for her actions. Over these past weeks, I have come to know the Resslers quite well and I have developed a plan in my head, designed to deliver a fitting punishment. My only trouble is, my dear, that although I want her family to suffer just as we have done, I am no master criminal and have no current means of putting it into action. Lord knows, I have made some mistakes already, but rest assured, I *am* getting better and I am of the firm belief the time will come when you and I shall have justice.'

11

Unseen by Jason, the man in the black ribbed pullover took control of his captive's arms, holding his biceps in a vice-like grip, while the man wearing the bomber jacket flung open the rear doors of the waiting van and leapt inside, demonstrating athletic prowess. The man in the pullover then passed the victim to his associate who pulled him inside and dumped him on the floor. Jason's palms fell against a corrugated surface - scarred and rough through years of heavy use - an indication this was not the same vehicle as before.

A strong hand took hold of Jason's pyjama top. Moments later, a distinct sound could be heard; that of something sharp piercing and cutting the cotton material, the tattered cloth falling away, causing an immediate drop in skin temperature. With no consideration given to his comfort, the victim was rolled to one side, allowing the rags to be pulled from beneath him. Then came his pyjama bottoms, a large patch of which were soaked in urine. The cargo handler's throat generated an incoherent noise - as though stifling a guttural cuss - the grunt conveying disgust, contempt and anger.

The man in the bomber jacket loosened the drawstring he had tightened in the Ressler's bedroom, removed the hood and shone a torch into his captive's eyes, simultaneously wiping the sodden bottoms across an exposed mouth and nose. Jason's lids closed tight, protecting his eyes from the intensity of the beam, and in doing so squeezed a teardrop onto his cheek. His lips rolled inwards between his teeth, sealing his mouth against the taste of his own bodily waste.

The onslaught was short-lived; the torch being directed elsewhere; the soaked rag dragged from his face.

Jason's eyes relaxed, allowing them to open; to see the glint of the blade that had shredded his clothing. He could feel the dampness across his face, evaporating and cooling his skin. He wanted desperately to wipe his hand across his mouth, but fear of reprisals prevented him.

Powerless to stop himself, Jason spoke aloud, but without force behind his words.

'Kill me. I can't do this again. Please, just kill me.'

The loadmaster's head whipped round; the aggression expressed in his body language so effective it would be to the delight of any mime artist seeing it, appreciating the art of speaking without words.

Jason's body tensed as it shook, his body's semi-autonomic response closing his eyes once more, pitting the thinnest of skin membranes against the might of a muscular man with anger coursing through his veins. His captor preferred them open, patting Jason's cheek until he complied. He then showed his captive the urine bag he had planned to tape to his groin, slapping it several times across his victim's face, before discarding the item to one side; a contemptuous demonstration it was no longer needed.

The mild impacts did not bring pain but served to increase the fear of pain. Nevertheless, despite the best advice of his inner voice, Jason spoke again.

'Please don't hurt me.'

The kidnapper's response was immediate.

'Linişte!'

This single, unfathomable word was delivered with passion, leaving Jason instantly to regret having issued his simple plea for mercy.

A foreign reprimand was not enough to satiate the kidnapper's desire to punish disobedience, even if the subject of his lesson had no idea what instruction he had disobeyed. The loadmaster picked up the remnants of sodden pyjama bottoms and stuffed the dampest portion into his victim's mouth. Jason's facial muscles reacted, forming an expression of disgust, and then one of terror as the man's knife was held close to his mouth, the edge threatening to widen his smile.

'Linişte!'

The word was spoken again, this time growled through closed teeth.

The man in the pullover had stepped to the passenger door to retrieve something, not far enough to prevent him hearing the instructions he had given at the pre-operation briefing being ignored. Following a quick rummage in the darkened footwell, he returned to the cargo bay in time to witness his associate speak for the second time, fully aware of the lengths to which the gang's leader had gone in denying his captive audible clues.

To Jason's terrified eyes, it was clear the henchman in the jacket had acted without authority and might have just lost himself his place on the team. In this, Jason judged correctly. The man in the pullover had already decided to make the cut, but the more important decision - how the hired hand might *retire* – would be reserved for a later date.

Stepping up to the rear of the van, the man in the pullover thrust a roll of tape hard against his associate's shoulder. His associate reacted badly, exacerbating his position.

'Rahat!'

The single word was spoken loudly and with clarity, as though he wanted the victim to learn the rudiments of his language.

The leader's stare intensified, making his displeasure clear. His extended index finger raised to press against his lips, then pointed at Jason's clothing, motioning a reminder to his colleague what had previously been agreed – to discard them on the road.

As would a sulking child, the man wearing the jacket gave his captive one last slap about the head, pulled the pyjama bottoms from Jason's mouth, gathered them together with the torn top, and discarded both remnants through the rear doors, happy to see them hit his associate squarely in the chest. A strip of gaffer tape was then torn from the roll and applied to Jason's mouth before the hood was replaced, the drawstrings pulled tight.

The man standing outside the vehicle, angered by the actions of his associate, but possessing greater self-control, climbed into the rear of the van, intent on speeding up the process. Even Jason, paralysed with fear, noted the team were taking too long. It was almost a relief when his wrists and ankles were bound so they might get under way without anyone feeling the need to inflict further ill treatment. As the van finally moved off, the random soundtrack returned to fill the interior.

Jason feared he would spend the long journey naked, cold and exposed. Thankfully, he was proved wrong. In what he considered a small act of kindness and humility, a blanket was thrown across him, covering his shoulders to his ankles. It did not seem like the action of the man who had forced Jason to taste his own urine, so it had to be assumed he had been banished to the passenger seat – a welcome thought. By rolling first to one side, then the other, Jason managed to encourage a portion of the blanket to settle between his hip, shoulder and elbow, and the corrugated metal floor, reducing his discomfort to a level at which meditation became possible. Of this, Jason had no previous experience, but instinct and the lesson of the first journey taught him to lay still and shut his ears to the endless audible camouflage. This allowed him to draw sufficient breath into his lungs, despite the restriction to his airways caused by the tethered hood and the tape that sealed his lips. It also permitted him to replace fear with other thoughts. It was only then he realised not only had he heard his abductor speak for the first time, his subconscious had continued to repeat the two words over and over, their pronunciation bouncing around inside his head.

'Liniște, liniște, rahat, liniște, rahat.'

Their origin was clearly foreign, the significance of which could not be more apparent. If Jason could recall them when next he spoke with the police – assuming he was given that opportunity - these two words might be translated, providing a key piece of evidence, leading to arrests and an end to this nightmare. *If* was the appropriate word. *If* the second abduction followed the path of the first, these unfamiliar words would have to stay with him through trauma, several days in captivity, and a fair amount of drug-induced unconsciousness. The only hope of this happening was to use a technique he had once heard described by a memory champion on the TV, ahead of a world tournament. Thanks to him, Jason still recalled a small shopping list from a decade ago.

The first task broke the words into syllables – lin–ish–tay and ra-hat. The second assigned an image to each. The third brought the images together to form an unforgettable event; the more bizarre, the better.

With regard to '*lin*', there was only one choice – Lynn being his mother-in-law's first name. I*sh* was a headless fish, having lost its *F*. *Tay* was trickier, the only thing springing to mind being the vague recollection of a Scottish poem about the Tay bridge disaster. Jason remembered nothing of the verse and knew nothing of what the bridge had looked like before it fell beneath the *silv'ry waters*, but the association was memorable – his mother-in-law releasing a headless fish to swim beneath a large iron span. Jason repeated the pronunciation over and over; repeated the connection over and over, until indestructible neural pathways had been formed. Only once he was confident that no matter what drugs were pumped into his system, or how often they were administered, he would still recall those same three syllables, did his attention turn to the second word: rahat – ra-hat. Jason could not recall which one, but did remember an ancient Egyptian god called Ra. He imagined one of those familiar figures, painted on the walls of tombs, of pharaohs wearing bottle-shaped crowns, his mind exchanging the original for a wide-brimmed floral hat. Again he recited the connection over and over, encoding new and permanent memories, tested many times throughout the course of the journey to ensure they remain firm.

By the time the van arrived at its destination, the ribbed pressed-steel floor had tenderised Jason's muscles, pressing and grinding them against his bones, and although the blanket had prevented heat being lost upwards, contact with the metal has chilled him to the core. The van stopped, so too did the endless recording of animal noises and other miscellaneous sound effects, re-stoking apprehension for what lay ahead. Jason could cope with being there. He had become accustomed to the sight of the surgeon in his strange disguise. He could accept being drugged and tethered. He could endure all this, believing he would then be taken home, but none of it could detract from the fact that in a few hours he would be missing another part of his body; which part, only the surgeon knew. Accepting he could do nothing to change this, he concentrated on the hope that in the short term he would at least be made more comfortable and that he would soon be able to breathe.

The doors opened; the blanket was thrown to one side; his personal guard jumped onto the gravel drive. Such was the degradation Jason had already experienced at the hands of his captors - this and the last time - the act of being naked and manhandled by strangers no longer felt humiliating, even though he was fully aware those parts of his body that made him a man were exposed to anyone who cared to look, flopping about in full view. It mattered not whether they judged him. The key consideration was his ability to breathe; his sole aim being to remain calm and co-operate as much as he was able, to bring about the transfer from van to bed in as short a time as possible, where he hoped the hood and gag would be removed.

The roughened metal floor of the vehicle scuffed Jason's skin as his body was dragged across it, into the arms of his captors, causing a momentary loss of focus. However, once suspended by four strong arms his ability to think returned, leaving him to wonder why they carried him so openly - naked and hooded - from the van to the entrance of the 'hospital'. Surely it raised the risk of being discovered. It had to say something of the area – that it was not overlooked, perhaps isolated.

Jason's eyes were shut beneath the hood, helping him predict and follow his arrival, the familiarity of the short journey continuing to dampen his fear of the unknown. His ears detected the sound of gravel beneath laden feet, replaced by the crumpling of heavy gauge plastic and the exact same soundtrack, playing perpetually from numerous sources, each out of synch with the other.

Anticipation grew, Jason knowing he would soon be able to breathe freely. At last he felt the padded surface of the hospital bed beneath him, and the straps being applied to hold him still.

The hood was raised partially as before, permitting him to experience the first whiff of clean, unscented air in hours. Fingers touched the side of his mouth. He braced for the brief sting of adhesive tearing from his lips. The pain was short lived; the reward was immense, Jason being able to take a deep breath, filling his lungs to capacity.

A hand gripped the top of the hood and pulled it clear, revealing the same post-op room as before. Being naked and unable to move much more than a wriggle, Jason felt vulnerable. His eyes looked down the length of his body, to his unprotected genitalia trapped between his thighs. They were in need of readjustment; a quick flick of his fingers to make everything right, but his hands were immobile. Frustration at not being able to do anything about it threatened to rule his thoughts, as might an itch in a space helmet. Needing distraction, he turned his thoughts to something else on which he could focus, bringing to mind a headless fish swimming beneath a great iron girder bridge, his mother-in-law cheering it on, and then to an Egyptian god wearing a broad-rimmed floral hat.

Satisfied the words were still within him, his thoughts returned to the room; to his naked body, strapped helpless to a makeshift gurney.

So far, other than the place of abduction and the incompetence of his handler, the modus operandi had followed much the same path as before, the most noticeable difference being that his clothes had been cut from his body and discarded. He could not help but wonder whether there was something malevolent in this. Was this preparation for the next procedure? Was he about to lose the thing that brought him most pleasure in life?

With this thought trumping all others, Jason's breathing suddenly became more apparent, his chest rising and falling more prominently; his arms and ankles straining against their bindings. He was confident he was not about to be tortured, murdered or flayed, and he expected the surgeon would treat him well with regard to infection control, aftercare, and catering. However, none of that made a jot of difference if he was about to lose his dick. An ear could be replaced, but not that.

The temptation was to break down, as he had done on many occasions of late, but with the aid of his counsellor, he had learned to cling to every positive, however small; not dwell on the negatives. Jason was the first to recognise this philosophy was easier to achieve during his weekly session, and in the company of his wife and friends, than it was when strapped, naked, to an operating table, anticipating the arrival of a cross-dressing psychopath. Nevertheless, he clung to the notion his ordeal would be relatively short-lived, and that when he returned home, he would possess a raft of tangible clues to pass to the authorities. In the meantime, there was little more he could do other than endure, survive and gather further evidence.

He had often heard advice, given to prospective employees, to imagine the interviewers naked, to put the interviewee at ease in an otherwise uneasy environment. Whether or not this worked, Jason felt he could face the surgeon with a similar frame of mind. Having memorised two foreign words, he had created a chink in his adversary's seemingly impenetrable armour. His captor would enter the room, smug in the knowledge his victim knew nothing about him, but he would be wrong. As someone once said, 'knowledge is power.' Accepting this as truth, Jason believed the table had turned slightly in his favour.

The wait was not long. The surgeon made his grand entrance almost on cue, presenting himself wearing the same style of clothing as before. Jason said nothing to him, but instead stared defiantly into the man's eyes, taunting his captor with an inner voice.

'Okay Mr or Mrs Psycho - whatever you are - let's get this out of the way. I've got you, you freak, and when I get home, I'm going to make sure you burn in hell, you bastard.'

Such was the ferocity of this silent onslaught, the muscles of his lips formed ghosts of the words. Thankfully, the surgeon was pre-occupied and noted none of it

Given the man had proven himself to be a sadistic torturer, his reaction at seeing his patient bound and naked came as something of a surprise, the surgeon shaking his head in disheartened disbelief, immediately covering his captive with a fresh blanket, restoring his modesty and improving his comfort. Only then did he take up his iPad and stylus in gloved hands, tapping the screen, activating a pre-prepared message.

'I am sorry you had to travel naked. My associates were concerned the police might have used a wire or some such tracking device. I have placed alternative clothing here in the recovery room. I believe they will fit, but you will not need them until tomorrow afternoon.'

The words reminded Jason of the reality of his circumstances; the fact he was to be operated on first thing in the morning. Defiance melted away, and yet there was still more to come, typed ad hoc.

'My colleagues inform me you begged to be killed. Is this true?'

Jason's head managed a barely perceptible nod.

There followed a pause while the mute surgeon selected an audio file.

Attempting to regain his former confidence, Jason made further remarks that only he could hear.

'Yeah, and I bet they didn't tell you they'd spoken to me, did they?'

Even inside his head this defiant comeback was delivered in nothing more than a whisper.

The surgeon 'spoke' again.

'You must be strong. If you do not continue to attend your appointments, I may be forced to turn my attention to your children.'

That which remained of Jason's hidden smile melted.

'The truth is, Mr Ressler, I am going to test your mettle. You might consider trying to hide. You might even consider taking your own life to avoid what is in store. However, you must know this; my associates have a particular skill in finding those who do not wish to be found. You might say, they have many fingers in many pies. More accurately, you might say they have many connections in many organisations. Try to hide, or try to take your own life, and I shall merely turn my attention to the next member of your family...how are Charlie and Lily enjoying school? They are getting big now. You must be very pleased with their progress. The teachers certainly are.'

The words seemed even more evil, the written text being interpreted by a lady with a soft voice of calm and serenity.

Jason froze.

'Less of this unpleasantness. Please forgive me that I could not fit you in sooner. My clients needed my assistance. I would have saved you the trauma of such a long and uncomfortable journey, but I would not trust those oafs to inject you. This will be the routine. I can continue to sedate you for the journey home, but not for the journey here.'

Jason could not contain himself.

'Well they bloody well injected my wife.'

Even behind the disguise, it was clear the surgeon was taken aback, the stylus immediately being put to work, tapping a hastily constructed response.

'I am sorry. I gave them instructions not to. I shall speak with them.'

The device was set down; the time for conversation seemingly having past.

A white, enamelled baking dish was placed between Jason's ankles, most likely the same as before. Given the surgeon was a sadistic madman, his bedside manner could not be faulted.

The stylus was put to use once again.

'Shall I put it in the other hand this time?' he asked, taking a cannula from the dish, pausing to activate another pre-recorded message.

Jason nodded, his mind, body and spirit numbed by a combination of confusion and fear.

He braced for the 'small scratch' of which administering doctors and nurses always spoke; he listened to the preparation of the syringe; he accepted unconsciousness as a better alternative than being awake; as a step closer to being home.

Jason woke the following morning, back in the makeshift operating theatre, to discover the blanket had been replaced with a clean white sheet, covering him from ankles to beneath his chin. He could feel the catheter had returned, mitigating any previous notion he had he was about to lose his penis, recognising the tube would doubtless interfere with the operation, had that been the surgeon's intention.

He checked his surroundings, moving his foot to one side to reveal what appeared to be the same cloaked figure as had witnessed the first procedure. As before, motionless eyes were windows to a seemingly absent mind.

The sound of a key turning in the door lock, and the re-appearance of the cross-dressing surgeon, re-focussed Jason's thoughts, from the wheelchair on the far side of the room to the man intent on mutilating him further.

As the surgeon went about his business in silence, his captive repeated the only clue he clung to; the only piece of evidence that gave the ordeal meaning.

'Lin-ish-tay. Lin-ish-tay,' Lynn casting a headless fish into the water, downriver from a girder bridge.

'Ra-hat. Ra-hat,' a long-dead Egyptian king wearing a floral bonnet.

This distraction had limited effect, holding his thoughts and his silence only briefly.

'Why me? Why are you doing this to me?'

Surprisingly, the surgeon was not angered by his patient's outburst. By his actions it appeared he had foreseen the question and pre-prepared an answer. Placing down his surgical instruments, he picked up his stylus and activated the electronic tablet where it lay.

'Buddhists believe we are reincarnated to learn lessons, rise through levels and reach Nirvana. I want you to learn lessons. I want you to reach Nirvana.'

The surgeon waited until the posh lady had finished speaking before administering a measured quantity of something to the cannula, still embedded in Jason's vein.

The stylus jabbed the screen once more.

'Now, get some rest. We both have a busy day ahead of us.'

12

Heather woke from a dreamless sleep to the unpleasant sensation of her face moistened by a pool of her own drool, and to the rolling of the mattress upon which she lay; a motion caused by her daughter, Lily, bouncing up and down on the bed. Aged eight, Charlie, being two years older than his sister, took a different approach in trying to wake their mother. He stood next to her, his hands placed on her shoulder, shaking her to consciousness. She looked at him through drowsy eyelids, at first not recognising him or realising what was happening.

'Has Daddy gone away again?'

Charlie's question set his mother's train of thought on a journey. It took a while to get up to speed, but then memories of masked men, guns and needles came flooding back, powering her arms to push her upright. The motion was too fast, confusing her inner ear, telling her the room was moving. She collapsed back and stared towards the ceiling, bewildered.

'Mummy, are you all right?'

Heather tried to answer her daughter but instantly discovered her throat was parched and incapable. She sat up again, but this time more slowly, then reached her arm out towards a glass of water that sat on her husband's bedside cabinet. Charlie took it and passed it to his mother who drank greedily until the vessel was dry.

'Thanks Charlie,' she said, hoarsely. 'Don't worry, everything's going to be just fine.'

Only a mother could tell such an uncertain truth with so much conviction.

Somewhat restored, Heather reached to her side of the bed, ripped the charger from her phone, made several swipes and taps, and finally jabbed the same digit, three times. The response was far removed from the doubting politeness of her first call to the police, on the night of her husband's first disappearance. Her address having been flagged on the control room's screen, uniformed officers were despatched immediately with instructions to check Heather and her children were unharmed - but they were not to enter the house.

Two officers knocked on the Ressler's front door and when Heather responded, she and her children were requested politely to come as they were - the children being still in their pyjamas - to take refuge in the patrol car. Heather had used the response time to dress, hastily throwing on casualwear, the kind of which she normally reserved for lounging about the house on lazy Sunday afternoons. Given the events she had endured, making herself presentable might not have been on everyone's list of priorities, but Heather saw it as a matter of avoiding further trauma, not wishing to be seen and interrogated in her nightwear.

Having established there was nobody else in the house, the same officers then set about cordoning off the property, assisted by colleagues whose vehicles pulled up shortly afterwards. By the time Superintendent Ormsby, DI Bickley and both Family Liaison Officers - Nigel Chambley and Jane Humfress - arrived, the property had been ringed with blue and white plastic 'police' tape, denying members of the public access across the front and rear boundaries, incorporating the paths and a portion of road leading to the rear garden gate.

Superintendent Ormsby introduced himself to an officer, one of several who maintained the border. Even as the tape was lifting to allow the four detectives passage, the Superintendent was spotted by one of the Crime Scene Investigators, the leader of a herd of men, dressed in white suits with blue backs, blue latex gloves and white face masks, who continued to scour the area for evidence.

The man lowered his paper mask to speak, before delivering a concise report with calm professionalism.

'Police Officers have secured the scene to the rear of the property; we have picked up a number of footprints in the lawn and indications of a third party being dragged in the upright position. There are no tyre tracks, but we believe the victim was removed to a vehicle waiting in the cul-de-sac, accessible via a gate at the bottom of the back garden. That's all been photographed and taken care of. A set of pyjama top and bottoms have been found, which appear to have been cut from the victim. Mrs Heather Ressler, the occupant of the house, and wife of the missing man, confirms they belong to her husband. We've also seized the nightdress she was wearing, and the duvet from the master bedroom, both for further examination. We've also dusted for prints.'

'Excellent. Can we have a look around?'

The police officers donned the same paper over-garments as modelled by the CSI team, before being given a tour of the cordoned area, inside and out. The party proceeded in-line, keeping to a minimum the area trodden down by their footfall, making the subconscious decision to follow each other in order of rank. Their guide pointed to areas of interest, while answering, as best he could, the many questions put to him by his police colleagues. Fingerprint dust covered many surfaces. Small, yellow, numbered, cones marked multiple areas of interest, each of which had been captured as a series of digital images.

The party came to a halt at the spot on which it was believed a getaway vehicle had been parked. Here, the tour guide made his closing remarks.

'My manager will send our report in due course, but in the meantime, you might be interested to know, we scanned the master bedroom with UV light and found semen on the back wall, the bedside cabinet and headboard. The patterns suggest one event. Someone's been having a good time. Really messy. There's nothing on the bedding though, so it must have been washed since. Samples have been taken, but DNA analysis will take time.'

Jane Humfress' ears pricked, but not because the man from CSI had dropped his air of professionalism.

'Strange, DC Chambley and I have come to know the family pretty well since Jason was taken the first time. When we last saw them and asked how they were coping, Heather confided in me that their sex life had become non-existent.'

***

Heather, Charlie and Lily had been rescued from the patrol car by their neighbours, Irene Spillman having sent her husband out in his dressing gown to make enquiries. With the blessing of the police officer, whose patrol car it was, Heather and the children had been invited inside number 52, accepting Bob's offer with gratitude. It was fortunate the Resslers had such kind hearted friends as it was some time before the Family Liaison Officers arrived to speak with Heather, who was to be found in the kitchen being comforted and cared for by her host. The children were sat at the dining table with 'uncle' Bob, colouring in pictures, torn from a book, purchased to keep their own grandchildren occupied on babysitting days, of which there were many. For the same reason, Irene and Bob also had a stock of unhealthy foodstuffs into which Charlie and Lily had made inroads.

The officers, each having accepted a cup of tea and a plate of biscuits, Nigel taking two to his colleague's one, made small talk until they felt Heather was sufficiently prepared to answer a few questions. Bearing in mind the sensitive nature of the matters Jane Humfress wished to discuss, Nigel was silently given the task of removing Irene from the room.

'I'm sorry this will sound very personal, but it may be important. Have you and Jason had sex since he was taken the first time?'

Heather was slow to answer, her eyes looking first outraged and then sad.

'No.'

'It's just that forensics have found semen and have taken samples for testing.'

Heather looked shocked.

'Is it Jason's?' the detective asked, gently.

Again there was a pause.

'I don't know.'

Heather's answer was delivered in a whisper, her eyes directed to the cup she held in her hands.

'Then there's a possibility it could be someone else's?'

The interviewee's eyes did not lift.

'Yes,' she answered, quietly.

'Who?'

Heather sighed and raised her head, trying not to cry.

'John Ainsley. He's a mutual friend.'

'Has this been going on long?'

'No, Heather replied indignantly, before quickly realising she had no right to be.

Jane waited for her to settle; to answer in her own time. She did not have to wait long.

'Only the once. I thought Jason had run off with another woman. I was upset. John came round to see if there was anything he could do. It turned out I thought he could. I almost forced him to have sex...as a way of getting revenge. I was going to humiliate Jason when I saw him...tell him John was so much bigger and better than him, but then...'

'But then?'

'Then Jason came back the next day. You can't imagine how that makes me feel. All the time I was shagging his best friend, he was being tortured, thinking he was going to die.'

The detective pushed a box of tissues across the table so Heather might catch the tears and mucus that threatened to fall from her face.

'I see. Heather, we're going to have to speak with John Ainsley. You do understand, this makes him a suspect?'

The detective's words had the potential to intensify her interviewee's tears, but instead it put her emotions in check.

'Oh God, don't tell Jason. He's been through enough as it is. And don't be too hard on John, he's done nothing wrong.'

Jane could not give her word, but instead shifted the questioning to aspects of the kidnapping itself. When she was finally done, Jane collected her colleague from the kitchen, where she discovered Nigel had embraced the baby sitting duties his colleague had forced upon him. Nigel seemed to relish the opportunity to entertain the Ressler children - only a few years older than his own. He too had acquired a page, torn from the Spillman's Bumper Colouring Book, and could be seen applying a felt-tipped pen to it, at great pains to keep it within the lines. In his free hand he held an opened mini Swiss roll which he finished off with a single careless bite and the push of a finger, tucking the stub into his mouth. He then dropped the wrapper among the packaging of several other food items that he, Charlie and Lily had apparently gorged themselves on.

Jane's eyes looked first to her colleague and then to the pile of rubbish he had helped create.

'Really?'

Bob smiled.

'Oh that's all right. They've all been very good together.'

It was Jane's turn to smile.

'Come on you, let's get you home.'

***

Superintendent Brian Ormsby had invited DI Bickley into his office to review the Ressler file. The former was a hard man to warm to and even though the two had known each other as colleagues for many years, the barrier of rank nevertheless held firm.

'Well, Robert, I fear this mess is going to reflect poorly on the Service. We need it solved.'

The inspector read into this statement what he was supposed to – to mobilise the resources at his disposal; a team of approximately fifty men and women; operational and non-operational staff; all highly competent within their field. Superintendent Ormsby had provided the ball and it was now DI Bickley's job to get it rolling, and for that he turned to his office manager, a man in whom he had the utmost faith, Detective Sergeant Alan Honeyman.

The sergeant rose to the challenge as he would any other case, preparing for a briefing the following morning.

Police Headquarters, Briefing Room, 09:00 hours, Sunday, 23 October:
DI Bickley was first to take up position at the front of the room, standing to one side of the large smart board.

'Good morning everybody. For those of you who are not already aware, Jason Ressler has been abducted for a second time, we believe by a man skilled in surgical procedures who, in all likelihood, intends to remove another piece of Mr Ressler's body.'

Although widely experienced, some members of the gathering winced.

'Now, I know we've been caught up with this murder, and we're most certainly not taking our foot off the pedal on that one, but this second abduction puts us in a poor light, so we must resolve it and do so quickly. Initially we dismissed this as a routine missing person. However, the victim has since been returned, missing an ear. There being very little to go on, we conducted a routine follow up, installed a panic button and effectively left the Ressler family to get on with it. In hindsight, the Superintendent doesn't think we did enough to satisfy public expectation.

'Of greatest concern to Superintendent Ormsby is that the debrief following the first abduction suggested a strong likelihood Jason Ressler would be taken again…and again, the intention of the perpetrator being to remove another piece of the victim each time.'

As the inspector spoke, his hand drew the room's attention to images displayed on the screen, reminding his staff they were not dealing with a faceless statistic, but a human being in desperate circumstances. The image on the right showed the bright face of a man with both ears. Next to it, a second image showed the same man with just one ear and a tortured expression.

'As strange as this may seem, with limited resources, the murder is going to have to play second fiddle to the abduction. Of course, it goes without saying, the murderer must be caught as quickly as possible, but then again we are working on the basis he reacted to a specific set of circumstances which are unlikely to be repeated, and in that respect time is on our side. On the other hand, in Jason Ressler's case, we are dealing with something tantamount to a serial killer, who threatens to strike again and again, until we are left with nothing more than a bunch of spare parts.'

There followed a résumé of the first incident and of the investigations resulting.

'Right, did we ever get final confirmation Anna Richardson is a false lead?'

DI Bickley looked to DC Drake Fallas who responded with confidence.

'She checks out, Guv. DC Pace and I spoke with Mrs Richardson and her husband the day after they returned from Florida. They looked tanned and exhausted and were keen to show us photos of their grandchildren cuddling Disney characters. There were loads of pictures with her in them and the date stamp indicates they were in an airport hotel on the night of the kidnapping. There's either another Anna or Mrs Richardson has been used to throw us off the scent.'

'Thanks Drake. Right, in order to kidnap Jason Ressler at the lay-by, the perpetrators would have to have a detailed plan; to know his movements. They may have been staking out the supermarket for weeks prior to the incident. So, anything from the CCTV?'

The answer was provided by Drake's partner, DC Angela Pace.

'I'm sorry, Guv. That was put on the back burner when the murder came in.'

DI Bickley accepted her excuse, knowing full well the team was currently stretched, but had hoped someone in the back room would have looked at the footage by now.

'Okay, thank you Angela. We need to make that a priority.'

DI Bickley looked to a notebook in which he had written several bullet points.

'The victim himself; anything from an intel point of view?'

A voice responded from the audience.

'There's absolutely no intelligence that's come in.'

'Nothing. Hmm. Okay, shall we move on to the current situation?'

Having delivered a précis, speaking with the knowledge of a man who had visited the scene of the crime, DI Bickley then invited the Family Liaison Officers to provide their input.

The first to respond was Detective Constable Chambley, who spoke with professional melancholy.

'We interviewed Heather Ressler who was being looked after by her neighbours. Heather gave a good description of the muzzle of an automatic pistol, but she couldn't say anything about the perpetrators, other than they were wearing black and that they said nothing. Instead they used hand gestures and waved the gun about.'

'Have we got anything on the gun?'

'Sorry, Guv. All we can say is that it was an automatic and it was pressed to Heather Ressler's head, but not enough to leave forensic traces.'

'How is Mrs Ressler?'

'Shaken. She wet the bed.'

'I understand she was drugged. Is this the same drug used on her husband?'

The question was fielded by a man in possession of a preliminary forensics report.

'Too soon to say, I'm afraid. She was injected. We took bloods and we're now waiting analysis. In the meantime, I can say that the man who administered the injection was no professional, given the bruising he caused her.'

'Okay, thank you. I look forward to receiving your full report.'

Having finished with the individual, the inspector widened his focus in order to address the team as a whole.

'So, we have a skilled surgeon on the loose who operates in full view of a woman in a wheelchair, and a group of at least three co-conspirators who it seems are tasked only with the capture and transportation of the victim. Any questions so far?'

DC Peter Graham was new to the team and keen to prove his worth, believing it was better to be heard and shot down, than to be mistaken for wallpaper. As a consequence, he raised his fingers to shoulder height and spoke.

'Guv, the woman in the wheelchair…'

DI Bickley wrongly took this as a request for more information.

'Yes, the mysterious figure in the operating theatre. Well, other than she has blue eyes, we know next to nothing about her. Thanks to the heavy disguise, we're not even sure she is a woman. Indications suggest she is disabled. I say that not only because of the wheelchair, but because her eyes are reported as being distant. It's my hunch she is related to the surgeon and perhaps is placed there to witness Mr Ressler paying for whatever he has done to her. Although I have no idea what that might be.'

Although accepting his boss' theory, it was evident from his body language that DC Graham had an alternative proposal.

A nod from the inspector invited him to share it.

'I was thinking, maybe she's drugged too. Maybe her punishment is being made to watch Jason Ressler being carved up while not being able to do anything about it.'

Robert Bickley had to concede this was a possibility, in which case he was forced to concede also that he understood even less about the case than he had done before. It was clear that discovering the identity of the person in the wheelchair would explain a lot, but that line of enquiry was yet to deliver a single lead.

'Okay, Jane, Nigel, anything more from Heather Ressler?'

DC Humfress liked her colleague – she liked him very much, both as a colleague and a friend. Nevertheless, she was keen for the room to receive her input before he had the opportunity to step in and steal her glory, as was often the case.

'Yes, Guv. As you know, CSI found traces of semen in the Ressler's master bedroom – the scene of the abduction. That wouldn't seem odd but Heather had previously confided in me she and her husband have not had sex since his return. Apparently, he has become too self-conscious of his missing ear to perform. I know it could have pre-dated the first abduction, but something didn't seem right. Anyway, I put it to her and she spilled the beans. The day after her husband was taken, she threw herself at one John Ainsley, a mutual friend of Heather and her husband. She excuses her actions, saying she thought Jason had run off with another woman – Anna – and wanted to get revenge. She claims it was a one-off and that she has never been unfaithful before.'

'Interesting. Okay, at last we might be getting somewhere. This may be our motive. I want you to speak with Mr Ainsley as soon as possible.'

Jane Humfress nodded, her external appearance remaining professional; her internal expression gloating.

With nothing more to discuss, the inspector made his closing remarks.

'Right, this is what I want. We need to establish a time-line for the evening of the 23rd September to the 24th and for 21st to 22nd October. I want the supermarket CCTV gone through with a fine toothed comb, and while you're at it, take a look at the neighbour's CCTV too. I know it only covers the front but it might show something. I want ANPR checks. I want the lay-by searched again and I want it done thoroughly – CSI can do that. If you have a CHIS, get onto them. There's no point having informants if they don't give us any information. And find me something on Heather Ressler. I like her less and less every time I hear her name. First she gets a driving ban, then she lies to her neighbour about it, and now she's sleeping with her husband's best friend as soon as his back is turned. DS Honeyman will assign the work to you. As usual, feed your results back through him.'

***

Heather invited the two, now familiar, Family Liaison Officers into her home. Her eyes were red, a sure indication she had been crying. Responding to one of Jane's knuckles pressing into his thigh, and a nod, Nigel Chambley disappeared to the kitchen to make teas and coffees, allowing Heather to return to the sofa, where she had remained all afternoon. There she took up a crumpled pair of men's jeans and squeezed them tightly in clenched hands and arms, as a small child would hug their favourite comfort blanket. An expression sculpted DC Humfress' face, her body language posing a question as clearly as if she had articulated it in words; so clearly, in fact, Heather responded as though she had heard it spoken aloud.

'I know it sounds weird, but I feel I'm with Jason when I hold them.'

Her voice was feeble. Her head dropped, directing a pitiful gaze towards the denim, as though it was necessary to clarify to what she referred.

'When they let me back in the house, there were smudges of fingerprint dust everywhere. The place felt dirty, so I started cleaning as though my life depended on it. Clearly, I needed something to keep my mind occupied because I carried on until I was utterly exhausted, but even then the thoughts were still there. I can't stop wondering how he feels; what he must be going through; what that monster is doing to him, and I keep asking myself if I could have done something else…if I could have pressed the damned panic button? Anyway, I started feeling guilty that I'd washed away all traces of him. I had to have something to connect us; something with his smell on it.'

Heather wafted away the air of melancholy surrounding her, smiling while describing how she had run round the house like a mad woman, searching everywhere for an unwashed tee-shirt, or a pair of his pants to wear. Jane mirrored the smile, confirming she was listening.

'Thankfully I found his trousers under the bed. That's typical Jason; he never has known where the laundry bin is. At least once I'd found them I could relax, but now I keep asking myself the same question, over and over. Why? Why would someone want to hurt my Jason? He's so harmless. He doesn't deserve any of this.'

Aware of the suspicion DI Bickley harboured for the victim's wife, Jane could not help but listen with a clear head and a cold heart, wondering whether this had been rehearsed in front of the bathroom mirror; whether the tears that ran in rivulets down Heather's cheeks were genuine, or the skill of an actor.

Heather sensed she was being judged by the detective, a woman who knew of her infidelity.

'I really don't know if I'm going to get through this,' she added, her voice quavering.

'Try not to worry,' the detective responded, feeling it was the professional thing to say, despite her reservations. 'If things go the same way as before, Jason will be returned any time soon With any luck he'll have that vital piece of evidence we need to catch this gang.'

The conversation stalled. Jane found silence a powerful tool and was happy to bathe in it, hoping her interviewee would feel the need to fill it with a confession, or at least something she wished to keep secret. Conversely, Heather was left feeling intimidated; longing for it to be broken by the timely arrival of the second detective, carrying hot drinks to the table. However, her wish would not be granted; Nigel would never be given employment in a coffee house, given the time it took him to fulfil the order.

Heather could stand the silence no more.

'Have you seen John yet?'

Jane smiled inwardly, having discovered what was truly on Heather's mind. All that tosh about her husband while, in reality, she was thinking only about herself; how her infidelity might play out.

'No, not yet. We were thinking of popping along to see him this afternoon.'

The drinks arrived, too late to save Heather from her own conscience.

Silence returned, broken only by the occasional sip and the snap of a biscuit which Nigel had thought to provide from the Ressler's barrel. Heather gripped her husband's jeans tighter and concentrated on her tea, avoiding the compulsion to speak again. Jane could only imagine she was contemplating the result of the conversation that was to be had with Heather's lover.

DC Humfress watched her colleague tuck into a second biscuit before choosing her moment to further their investigation.

'Heather, it would help if we could look through your husband's things. It might give us a clue as to why he has been targeted.'

'Of course. Anything.'

If Heather was intent on hiding her involvement in a conspiracy to kidnap, maim and torture her own husband, she was either confident she had covered her tracks thoroughly, or she was not very good at the game. The alternative scenario, which Jane felt obliged to consider, was that Heather was entirely innocent, despite evidence to the contrary. As a detective, Jane had been conditioned to suspect guilt in everyone; to expect the spoken words of witnesses to be, at best, a distorted truth; at worst, practised lies.

Disguising their impatience to get started, the detectives drained their coffee cups, before commencing their search.

'You'll probably want to start in his workshop,' Heather suggested, helpfully.

Nigel took Heather's empty mug and placed it on a coaster, freeing their host's hands to push herself up from the sofa. It took more effort than it ought to have for someone so young. Nevertheless, she declined the offer of a strong arm for support.

Nigel and his colleague were shown through a door, off the hallway, to the vestiges of an integral garage. The installation of a downstairs toilet and shower room had rendered the space too small to shelter a car ever again, and so it had been re-imagined as a hobby/utility room. The majority of the remaining space was taken up by workbenches; delicate tools; materials of many different kinds; a host of dolls' houses in various stages of completion; miniature furniture; and groups of little people, some clothed, others naked. One such group represented the Ressler family, the clothing and facial features accurately copied from a family photograph in which everyone looked happy to be together; happy to be alive.

Although interested in its contents, the detectives did not restrict their search to a single room, taking time to check the contents of cupboards and drawers throughout the property. By the time they had finished, Heather was to be found back on the settee, clutching her husband's trousers once more.

Jane took a seat close by and produced a sheet of paper; a document, folded into thirds.

'Heather, I have to ask, you recently increased your life insurance. You stand to gain quite a lot of money should Jason die. Can you help me with that?'

Heather's reaction was to express indignation and hurt. Here was a so-called Family Liaison Officer, tasked with looking after the family of the victim, insinuating she had arranged the double abduction of her husband to raise twenty grand on an insurance scam.

'We took out another mortgage against the house to convert the garage. Any loan like that needs additional life insurance.'

Gone was the frailty of voice; her words delivered slowly, purposefully.

'Sorry Heather, I wasn't accusing you, just clearing up loose ends. I hope you understand.'

The detectives left soon afterwards, Nigel thinking about lunch and what he might like to ask John Ainsley later in the day; Jane worried she had handled the victim's wife poorly and that their relationship had been damaged as a result.

***

DS Honeyman knocked on DI Bickley's office door and entered before being invited.

'Hello, Alan. Got anything for me?'

'Sadly not.'

Robert Bickley opened his desk draw, pulled out an opened packet of Jaffa cakes, offered it forward and then selected two for himself.

Alan Honeyman smiled as he broke off an edge, the first step in the process of deconstructing the offering as he always did.

'Funny, if this was the 1970s, you'd have pulled a bottle of whisky and a couple of glasses from that draw – how times have changed.'

His boss managed an approving chuckle.

'Given that this is not the 1970s, it is my opinion that the humble Jaffa cake makes a very good substitute.'

Sponge and chocolate coating removed, Alan placed the filleted slice of orange jelly onto his tongue.

'Agreed.'

The moment of light relief having come and gone, DI Bickley confirmed what the office manager had imagined, that he had spent much of the afternoon and evening reviewing the evidence in the Ressler case; staring at his computer screen which displayed an electronic incident board, a modern version of the old displays of hard copied photographs, annotated and connected with marker pens.

'What's going through this surgeon's mind?'

The Inspector did not expect his colleague to have an answer but was always grateful to have someone off which he could bounce ideas. Although now primarily an office manager, Alan Honeyman had a wealth of investigative experience behind him and was more than happy to step through the door when he could see his boss had hit a wall.

Together they agreed the perpetrator was probably not local, given the length of the drive following kidnap. That made establishing a connection between the victim and surgeon considerably more difficult. They also gave thought to who this cross-dressing man was; whether his attire was a statement of his sexuality, or simply a disguise. The man had skills as a surgeon, but how would he have become so proficient at kidnapping? Perhaps he had military experience. Perhaps he used hired hands. If so, how would a skilled surgeon meet the men he needed when they lived such disparate lives?

Next up were potential suspects, of which the DI had only one, and was keen to see if his colleague shared the same view.

'What about this Heather Ressler? She smells wrong.'

'I agree. She's a counsellor isn't she? Doesn't she work for the NHS? Perhaps that's her connection to the surgeon.'

'Hmm, DS Honeyman, you might be on to something there. Let's get someone on it first thing in the morning.'

The DI clipped his pen inside his suit jacket, pushed his chair away from his desk and stood up.

'Fancy a drink? I believe there's a couple of pints waiting for us at The Saracen's Head.'

DS Honeyman nodded.

'Why not? Maybe we'll think better with an unclear head.'

***

Robert Bickley and his office manager were quick to succumb to sleep, almost as soon as their heads touched their respective pillows. They had already forgotten the name Jason Ressler; a deliberate ploy on the part of the inspector who recognised he was suffering with what he termed 'detective's block'. Even though alcohol consumption was sure to impact adversely his REM sleep, he remained confident a flash of inspiration would come to him when he awoke, and the block would be gone. The unconscious labours of the inspector's mind, joining together snippets of knowledge throughout the course of the night, would often reveal themselves to him as he stood beneath the showerhead, first thing in the morning. There was no reason to believe this occasion would be any different, but he was wrong. On this occasion, he was denied the opportunity for a shower, his mobile phone waking him from a restless slumber in the early hours.

'DI Bickley.'

'Guv, he's back.'

13

Six months ago

Kenneth Gosling walked towards his vehicle, parked in the staff car park, vaguely aware the area was less illuminated than usual. He noted some of the security lights were out and muttered beneath his breath, words that if heard would not have been received well by the maintenance department. To let one bulb blow was acceptable – it might have only just gone. To let two or three go at the same time was nothing short of negligence.

Kenneth might have been in a more forgiving mood had he not just experienced standing at the operating table for a full nine hours. While focussed on the anatomy and inner workings of the human body, he thought nothing of the discomfort he endured, but without that distraction it was impossible to disregard his throbbing feet and the tightening of his empty stomach which now threatened to turn in upon itself.

Despite the late hour, Kenneth yearned to flop down onto the settee with a generous portion of microwaved linguine; more importantly, to wash it down with a large glass or two of refrigerated Chardonnay. Crawling beneath clean linen on a full stomach - his blood substantially diluted with alcohol - his sleep would doubtless be restless, but in truth, it was unlikely to make matters any worse than he had grown accustomed to. Since the loss of his beloved Charlotte, and the subsequent tragedy that had befallen Jennifer, Kenneth had not enjoyed a single unbroken night's sleep. Whenever he tried to relax, images of his daughter's lifeless body sprang cruelly from nowhere to torment his mind, but when he busied himself, caring for his wife, he was constantly reminded how she had become merely a breathing, dribbling carcass. Although Kenneth still loved her - every bit as much as the day he had plucked up the courage to ask for her hand in marriage – the reality was that his soul mate had been lost to him, at the end of a knotted cord.

Kenneth continued the walk towards his car. An old van stood in his path; the overall condition and a missing a rear number plate telling him all he needed to know about its owner. Although they had never met, the surgeon held the man in contempt - there being no doubt in his mind, the driver was a indeed a man. What galled him the most was that such an eyesore had been parked among the better cars: the Jaguars; the Mercedes; the BMWs.

With a disapproving shake of his head, Kenneth turned his attention to his phone, his intention being to inform his wife's carer of his imminent departure. Madeline was a God send. Knowing and accepting the unpredictability of her employer's working hours, she was prepared to stay all night, at short notice, never once complaining. It helped she was paid handsomely, but if she could have afforded to, the surgeon suspected she would have offered her services for free, such was her dedication.

As his thumb pressed down upon the screen, the phone was snatched from his hand. A moment later his mouth was taped shut; a hood was pulled down over his head; his wrists were thrust behind his back and bound.

The men who grabbed him - who cast him into the cargo bay – were practised. Helpless to resist, all Kenneth could do was hum a muted protest, as audible as the gag would permit. In response, the hood was lifted briefly, long enough for him to see a man in black crouched over him; long enough to see the rifled barrel tip of an automatic weapon. The message was effective.

The journey was uncomfortable, but not long. It ended at an abandoned industrial unit, the captor being dragged through to offices associated with a long-forgotten warehouse. Only when he had been forcibly seated was the hood removed; only once he had been reminded at gunpoint he had no hand to play was his gag ripped from his skin; only then were his hands freed. His position having been explained in near silence, two masked men raised Kenneth to his feet and guided him through to a second room, following the man with the gun, who appeared to be their leader. As soon as he stepped across the threshold, the reason for his abduction was clear. A fourth man lay on an improvised operating table, blood – an awful lot of blood - discolouring the skin and the bandages that had been applied to an abdominal wound. Without them, the man would have died, but without treatment he would still do so just as certainly as if the first aider had not bothered.

In that moment, Kenneth did not consider who this man was, or what he had done to receive such a wound. All he wished for was to be left alone to get on with his job, and to have the tools with which to do it. There was little point in speaking those clichéd theatrical words, 'This man needs a hospital'. Clearly, if his captors had considered that a possibility, they would have brought the horse to the cart, not the other way round.

The leader waved his pistol, attracting the surgeon's attention. Having got it, he held up pictures in his free hand, picking them up, one by one from a shelf, each an image of his car, his house, taken at a distance and up close. The threat was crude but clear.

'Fix him.'

To hammer his position home, the chief abductor had saved one photograph until last. Poor Madeline had been mistaken for Kenneth's wife.

Kenneth showed no reaction to the images, seeing them merely as an unnecessary and unwelcome delay. Time was of the essence.

'I will need to scrub up and I will need drugs and instruments.'

The leader pulled aside a small, clean sheet – possibly a table napkin – revealing an ice bucket beneath, filled with steaming water and a host of stainless steel tools, something akin to a kitchen utensils pot. The removal of a second napkin revealed packets, well known to the surgeon: sutures; bandages; pain relief; syringes. Kenneth nodded his approval.

The adjacent room was a kitchenette. On the draining board was an anti-bacterial liquid soap dispenser, a box of large latex gloves and a pack of paper towels. On the counter was a neat pile of clothing: a surgeon's working clothes, including hat, mask and plastic slip-on sandals. So familiar were they, Kenneth suspected they had been stolen from the hospital, if not the very department in which he normally worked.

Kitted and clean, the surgeon assessed his patient, inserted a cannula, through which he introduced saline to replace lost fluid, removed the dressing and set about staunching the flow of blood. He was in his element; relaxed, capable and confident - enough to ask for music to be played, one of the missing ingredients of a successful operation. With some reluctance, a radio was tuned to several stations, until one was reached that filled the room with Mozart – his concerto for violin and orchestra number three, in G major. Kenneth knew it well. Another missing ingredient was conversation. Although it seemed inappropriate to discuss his plans for the weekend, nevertheless he liked to while away the hours, conversing with his colleagues.

'On the whole, you have impressed me,' Kenneth said, without warning.

Only one of three kidnappers reacted to this unexpected statement, leaving Kenneth to suspect only one of his abductors spoke English. Maybe the one who lay beneath his fingers had no grasp of the English language either, but that hypothesis would remain untested until the operation was complete, and only then if it was successful.

'What is this?'

The more words the gang's leader spoke, the more it was evident he was not from these parts – probably Eastern European. The Balkans maybe.

'Well, my good man, I have been impressed by the way you took me – very efficient. I have no idea where we are and I have no idea who you are. I am also impressed by your preparations. I could probably have made do with a kitchen knife and a sewing kit, but I very much appreciate the equipment you have provided. It makes the outcome so much more predictable.'

'Be quiet,' the leader said, aggressively, holding his gun to Kenneth's temple, 'I warn you, our last doctor died.'

The surgeon ignored the words as an empty threat. Despite the pistol being waved in his general direction, Kenneth judged he now had the upper hand – at least for the moment. What he had to speak of would hopefully prolong his own life and allow him to activate the plan that had been brewing in his mind for far too long.

'As I said, you have impressed me…for the most part.'

The leader said nothing, but the angle of his masked head and his narrowed eyes indicated he was keen to hear an explanation.

'Firstly, if you are going to threaten me by demonstrating the vulnerability of my family, please get your facts right. I refer to the photograph you showed me of the woman entering my house. She is not my wife, she is my wife's nurse. Secondly, I have an Achilles heel, as does every man. I assume you believe you have found mine, but let me assure you, you have not. You see, my only daughter is dead and my wife is as good as dead, and would probably relish being freed from her body.'

The man with the gun considered the surgeon's statement, before asking a question.

'If I have nothing over you, why do you fix my friend?'

'Look Mr…'

The leader did not look as though he was about to disclose his name.

'Look, I shall fix your friend because that is what I do. I shall make him as good as new. Rest assured, I have no intention of reporting you to the authorities; rather, I believe we might forge a relationship of mutual benefit.'

Again, the leader's body language urged his captive to provide an explanation, but before Kenneth could continue, the two men were interrupted by another of the kidnappers.

'Ce Zice?'

Annoyed, the leader snapped a reply.

'Shh, lăsați acest lucru pentru mine.'

The leader returned his focus to the surgeon and indicated with his free hand to continue. Kenneth was happy to oblige.

'You see, Mr Kidnapper, you meet my needs perfectly.'

A wave of the pistol demonstrated the leader was an impatient man who was sensing loss of control.

'Please, put your gun down. I have no desire to die this evening, not because I value my life, but because I wish to enact a plan I have developed over time, to avenge my family. Not only have I got every intention of saving your associate, I am prepared to act as your go-to surgeon if ever you have need in future; all beneath the radar, of course, and at no cost. All I ask in return is that you bring a particular person to me once in a while so I can deconstruct him, piece by piece.'

The English speaking abductor's eyes narrowed. The surgeon was serious.

Kenneth had one more thing he wished to say, appropriate to the moment.

'For many years I have considered myself a devout atheist, but events such as these would test the most ardent disbeliever. I mean to say, where would a professional such as myself hope to find someone capable of abducting a man and putting into operation a plan I have given constant consideration to, but have always doubted could ever happen.'

'You were not a religious man?'

The kidnapper seemed surprised, as though he himself was, and assumed everyone else was too.

'No, my friend, not then and not even now. Too much harm has been done to my family to be undone by a simple coincidence.'

Despite their theological differences, and even though Kenneth did not know it, the deal was almost done.

Having made his position clear, the surgeon quickly changed the subject.

'Now, if you wish to avoid my wife's carer calling the police, I suggest you permit me to ring her.'

The fact the chief abductor dialled the number and held the surgeon's phone to his ear, suggested he was at least interested in the proposal.

The clincher was the survival of his patient who, by the following morning, was conscious and recovering. Only then was the leader prepared to discuss details. For this, he and his associates had removed their disguise. If all went well, they would be working together and anonymity would no longer matter; if badly, Kenneth suspected he would not be given the chance to describe a photofit of his abductors to the authorities.

'Tell me, why did you choose me?'

The response was not as flattering as the surgeon had hoped.

'I plan for problems. I have spent many time identifying surgeons…in case we need one. I saw your face in local paper. It said you had done something good, but I no care. It said you were surgeon and where you work, and I have your photo. We follow you and find where you live. There are others. At other hospitals.'

'And what would your plans normally be…for those surgeons you have used?'

'It depends. Kill them I think…if they talk.'

As stark as this answer was, Kenneth saw it as a bargaining tool.

'Okay, think of the benefits: no more finding surgeons; no more worrying whether they are going to inform the police; no dead surgeons leading a trail to your door; and I have a proven record. Also, I have some ideas how you can improve your operation.'

A handshake sealed the deal.

If the kidnappers had doubted Kenneth's intentions, their concerns were put to rest soon after they returned him to the hospital to collect his car, and had then followed him home. Kenneth went indoors, made his apologies to Madeline, dismissed her for the rest of the day, spent five minutes with his wife, and then invited his erstwhile abductors into the living room for a cup of thick, black, sweet coffee, just as he imagined they liked it. Once settled, he produced a plastic storage box and took from it his daughter's diary and a folder full of clear plastic pouches, each containing a snippet of evidence he had retrieved from the Ressler's waste. He also produced a notebook in which he had formulated his plan and brought together all the strands of information he had obtained. A genealogist would have been extremely pleased to have gathered so much information about just one person, but he had it on an entire family – photographs; places of work; achievements; movements; holidays - the detail meeting the standard of a professional private investigator.

'There is no timescale. I am a patient man. I have had to be. Take time to make your preparations and let me know when you are ready to strike so I can adjust my workload accordingly. I have in mind a place I can utilise as a temporary hospital. The situation is perfect, but it will need modification. I shall do the work myself. The less people involved the better. Please think about the improvements I suggested. Silence is golden. If I was minded to, I could have guessed your nationality, and I could hear rain outside and heavy traffic. The police could have ascertained where it had been raining at that time, and would have known the premises were in close proximity to a main road, one that stays busy late into the night. It does not sound much, but it is a risk you need not have taken.'

As grateful as the leader was to receive Kenneth's suggestions, he was the professional, with access to many phones, stolen vehicles and men, all with immense experience in the world of organised crime. Compared with sex trafficking and arms smuggling, the task given to them would be nothing more than a tradesperson taking on a private job at the weekend.

With almost immediate effect, Jason's workplace was placed under observation, inside and out. Shifts were established; opportunities noted. Despite the intensity of recognisance, none of the activity raised suspicion, the contractors rotating men, vehicle registration plates and phone SIM cards.

By the time the makeshift hospital was ready, the kidnappers were champing at the bit to finally get the job done, but first they wanted one more thing – an up-to-date photograph of the mark, to circulate to everyone involved, avoiding unnecessary mistakes.

An anonymous man, wearing forgettable clothes, pushed a trolley up and down the aisles, collecting random items that would suggest he lived in a household of cats and dogs; of young and old; and of meat-eating vegans. He wore gloves and a baseball cap, neither of which looked out of place among the other clientele, some of whom appeared to have come shopping in their night clothes.

The man spotted his mark, who was standing with a female colleague, discussing work matters. To get closer, the miscellaneous customer sidled up to the shoe polish, pretending to have some difficulty choosing just the right colour, brand, application and weight. Unsure, he held up a tin of tan wax to his phone, seemingly to photograph it as an aide memoir, or to message it to someone else for confirmation. The phone captured silently the tin and then Jason Ressler, who remained oblivious to the stolen image. All the time, the anonymous shopper's ears were open to anything useful. For this purpose, it was fortunate he was one of the few gang members to have attained a strong grasp of the English language.

As the lone kidnapper replaced the item on the shelf, Jason could be heard discussing holidays.

'Don't forget, my last shift is Friday night, the twenty-third. After that I'm away for two weeks in Florida.'

The woman - well beyond her prime – spoke to her boss as a mother might speak to her son, or an aunt to her nephew. Jason responded as though he accepted the role.

'Florida! I'm so jealous. I'd love to take the kids there.'

The kidnapper made a mental note, slipped away silently and abandoned his trolley for someone to find later and restack the contents.

14

Jason woke in the recovery room, jolted from his drug-induced slumber by the same blood pressure monitor as before. So deep had been his sleep, it took staring eyes a few moments to feed his brain with sufficient data to determine where he was, but when it had, it felt no different than waking after a night on the tiles, in the unfamiliar surroundings of a friend's spare bedroom, naked. The surgeon was present, as usual wearing women's apparel. The clothing neither suited nor fitted him well, suggesting it was worn as a disguise rather than a lifestyle choice. The fashion was that of an older person. Jason wondered whether he wore the items simply because they were the largest the local charity shop had in stock, or whether he had another source – perhaps the woman in the wheelchair, if indeed the silent witness was a woman. It was an attractive notion, but one quickly dismissed, the age of the unidentifiable person's eyes being too young to belong to the original owner of the surgeon's garb, it being more suited to a person who had long since retired; or died.

Jason felt something being introduced into his veins; presumably a pain killer, the psychotic offspring of Florence Nightingale being, at the same time, cruel yet caring.

In truth, the analgesic was unnecessary, the patient experiencing no pain. Although, in many ways a desirable position to be in, it had one drawback, there being no clue as to the piece of his body the surgeon had claimed. The captive patient would have examined himself had it not been for the straps and bindings that held him tight to the washable mattress. The alternative was to risk triggering the wrath of an unbalanced man by asking him directly; risky, but apparently his only option.

'Please, I have to know. What have you taken?'

The words were delivered in a voice that croaked, coming as a surprise to the patient who was unaware how parched his throat had become.

The surgeon's response was to drop the used syringe into a yellow sharps bin and leave the room in silence. He returned after a short absence with a plastic beaker, a straw protruding from a non-spill lid. The vessel contained only water but the reluctant patient sucked the contents from it as though he was bound by an addiction. The cup was soon empty, at which point the surgeon placed it down and took up the tablet.

It was not lost on Jason how remarkably quickly he had adapted, finding himself waiting calmly, patiently, for answers to be typed.

'I have conducted an orchidectomy.'

Only four words had any meaning, the fifth, and most important, causing Jason's face to adopt a look of confusion. The surgeon had rightly predicted his patient would not be familiar with the term and had prepared an explanation.

'I have removed one of your testes. Do not worry, it required only a small incision, so the chances of infection or complication are minimal, and it will not have affected the potency of the remaining gland which I currently have no intention of taking.'

As the voice spoke, the surgeon's hand swept across his body, inviting Jason's eyes to look to one side. Obediently, the patient craned his neck, his eyes reaching the extreme end of their travel. There they made a discovery - a second jar had been filled with formaldehyde, preserving a single testicle – not that he had seen such an organ out of its protective sack before, or that it had any distinguishing features signifying it was his own, but there being no evidence to the contrary, he accepted it was his.

The briefest glance provided all the information his mind needed, or could cope with, after which he turned his stare to the ceiling as his stomach began to retch, over and over. Rapid, shallow breathing through pursed lips brought the convulsions under control, preventing the contents of his stomach being ejected from his body, but his limbs were left trembling; his heart sinking more than he could have imagined. His mind would have benefitted if only he could change his train of thought, but he could not.

Despite the shock, he wondered how he might have felt different if the piece of him removed had been something else. Losing a finger, a toe, or even his nose would have been equally traumatic, but somehow this was almost the worst of a bad situation. At least his penis had been left for another day. Nevertheless, of everything else he might have lost, this made him feel less whole; less of a man; less the person he had been, and for what purpose? It was not a necessary evil; suffering amputation to save a life. Nor had he suffered an accident. This was simply revenge for something he had no knowledge of, carried out by a perpetrator about whom he knew nothing. As anger welled within him, so despair smothered his rage, leaving him sad and impotent.

The jar containing the lone testicle rested on the same chromed trolley as before, next to the jar that contained his severed ear, which the passage of time had not altered in any way. As life changing as the loss of two individual pieces of his body had been, and continued to be, it was not so much the nature of the pieces removed that was of greatest concern; it was the number. One was an individual statement; two had the makings of a collection; not forgetting the trolley supported at least a dozen empty jars - like having an album into which a collector could slot coins, cigarette cards or stamps, leaving spare pouches which he hoped eventually to fill with future acquisitions. If there were a dozen jars, the surgeon clearly desired to harvest at least a dozen body parts. The question arose, was this cross-dressing madman interested in British coins alone, or did his interest look to the wider world. In other words, if the surgeon had a particular penchant for all things Jason, this two-times victim was in a lot of trouble, but if the jars were eventually to contain donations from several people, that was another matter. Given the evidence before him, the situation looked grim. So far, the collection amounted to two pieces, both from the same man. If there were other intended contributors, surely the surgeon would have rotated his victims – unless his intention was to cannibalise his chosen donor of all his best bits and then dump the body, before finding a new victim.

The surgeon observed his patient's reaction and permitted him a moment of reflection and adjustment, using the time to construct another, short, message.

'I advise you to continue seeing a counsellor. You have chosen well with Natasha.'

Jason wanted to scream. Was there anything this psycho did not know about him?

The captive had only a moment to consider the answer before the plummy English lady spoke again, inviting new thoughts.

'You will probably experience some discomfort. While you remain here, I will administer painkillers as necessary. If you continue to experience discomfort once you are home, I recommend Paracetamol. Do not worry about brand names – you are only paying for the name. I am sure you can obtain some from your work place as necessary, but be careful not to exceed the recommended dose; it can do irreparable damage to your organs.

'The site should settle down after a few days, but if it does not, please contact your doctor. Make sure you keep your wound clean and dry. You will find it more comfortable to wear loose fitting underwear. A brief daily shower can help the healing process, but you should not soak for long periods or use soap directly on the wound. Dry yourself thoroughly by patting gently with a piece of gauze. Do not rub the area. A sensible alternative is to use Heather's hairdryer on a very low heat to dry the area.

'You may develop some bruising of the scrotum – this is quite normal. Please do not touch your wound with your hands unless you have washed them thoroughly – this will help to prevent infection.'

Jason listened passively, becoming ever more bewildered by his captor's bi-polar mind-set. If the man truly cared for his patient's welfare, why then did he go to such great effort to torture him first?

The recording ended, the speech being so protracted, Jason half expected it to close with, 'Any questions?' Given the awkward silence that followed - not silence in the true sense of the meaning, there never being any, day or night – the patient chose to believe the question had been asked, and would have raised his hand had his arms not been immobilised.

'Why are you doing this to me? I don't know what I've done. Whatever it is, I'm sorry. Please don't take me again; not just for my sake, but for my wife; my children.'

The surgeon issued no acknowledgement of his captive's plea, but Jason could see he had been heard - his question had not been ignored – the surgeon's stylus working against the iPad's screen.

The reply was a long time coming.

'As before, I have some business to attend to, so I must leave you alone. The catheter will remain in place until my return. I will then put you on the leash to give you access to the facilities next door.'

This told Jason nothing, leaving him feeling cheated, having waited patiently only to discover he had been ignored after all, but as he lay seething, the surgeon continued to type.

'While I am gone, think on this. Is the man who encourages another to murder as guilty as the man who wields the knife?'

Having issued such a provocative statement, the surgeon made to leave the room, pushing the chromed trolley before him, jars, empty and full, chinking against one another.

Jason panicked. The loss of a testicle had to attain a better price than a few foreign words and a cryptic sentence. He had to be able to give the police more than that. Throwing caution to the wind, an unstoppable question breached his sealed lips.

'Who is the person in the wheelchair?'

He tried to sound non-demanding; friendly.

It took a matter of a second to realise the question should have remained a thought inside his head, anger visibly taking hold of his captor who nonetheless managed to maintain his mute disguise. The stylus attacked the screen and within seconds the captive had his response.

'Do not mention her again.'

The voice being synthetic, the words portrayed no malice, but the expression on the face of their author most certainly did. Anticipating retribution, Jason at least had the satisfaction of having forced an error, the surgeon having inadvertently confirmed the person in the wheelchair was indeed a woman. The maniac's sensitivity to the question suggested that woman was close to him – a relative, perhaps; certainly not another victim.

For a moment it seemed venting his anger orally would be sufficient to calm the surgeon's wrath, but then, having turned towards the doorway, he stopped. Abandoning the electronic tablet on the trolley, a preparation was extracted from his pocket – another injection, forced under pressure through the cannula embedded in Jason's immobilised arm.

'No, please. I'm sorry.'

Jason's petition fell on deaf ears, but soon he did not care that he was ignored.

The patient woke to find the bindings that had held him fast had been removed, affording him the freedom promised him, to wander as far as the restricting leash would allow – most of the room in which he recovered; the corner of the L-shaped hall; and the whole of the modestly-sized bathroom.

The relaxant, administered by the surgeon, encouraged an unnatural sleep. Rousing from it was far from the experience of waking at home where his sleep would become shallower, until broken by the alarm. Current circumstances prevented him bounding from his bed. Instead, Jason swung his legs over the side and sat up, taking time to find his bearings; to let the fuzziness of thought clear.

Senses returned in stages.

First, Jason became aware he had been clothed in the same pyjama bottoms and adapted top as before.

Second, he noticed food had been provided as before. Without exception, every ingredient was familiar to the shelf-stackers whom he was normally employed to manage; items bought by his family on a weekly basis. As previously the case, the choice appeared to be beyond mere coincidence, leaving Jason convinced the maniac behind the menu knew exactly what the Ressler family kept in their cupboards.

Then came his sense of feeling, his bladder making patient suggestions, warning him of the need to use the toilet. It was then he realised the uncomfortable catheter had been removed. Until this most recent experience, the patient had never given thought to the process of using the toilet. Under normal circumstances, whether at the pub or at home, he stood; he urinated; he tucked everything away again; he often washed his hands, especially if others were present; then he was done. The operation had changed all that. The process was no longer an inconvenient departure from the bar; a paused TV. The act had suddenly become the conversation; had become the subject that held his attention.

To Jason's mind, this second disfigurement was not a reality until he saw it; felt it. Worse than denying himself these things was to imagine how he would look in the mirror; how he would be judged silently by his wife. What would Heather say; more importantly, think? Outwardly, she had accepted the loss of his ear; had made all the right noises about loving him just as much with or without it; had supported him on his road to recovery. Jason could only guess what was really in her mind; how he might think if the tables were turned. He concluded his feelings for his wife would not change, but he was no longer talking about an ear; this was different. With the lights out, Heather's passion would not be stifled by the absence of a lesser feature of his head, partially disguised by his hair line, but when they made love, it was inevitable she would see, or at least feel, a missing testicle. In that moment he knew he and his wife would never again become intimate. Left only to his imagination, the gulf between reality and perception grew quickly to staggering proportions, the site of the operation becoming grotesque; something worthy of a horror chamber; something that should never be seen by anyone; not a doctor, a collector of the macabre, and certainly not his wife. Yet still he had to answer the call of nature.

The steel leash slid along the fixed cable with ease. In the bathroom, Jason exposed himself with care, avoiding touching anything other than his penis; avoiding sight of his remaining genitalia. Having tucked himself back into his pyjama bottoms, the patient washed his hands more thoroughly than usual before returning to the recovery room. There he distracted his thoughts, devouring the waiting sandwich, one he had to concede was well constructed. As he ate, the surgeon entered the room, his body language indicating a man whose mood had improved considerably.

'I am sorry for my earlier actions. I should not have administered the drug without clinical need. If it caused you undue trauma, I apologise.'

For once the posh lady's voice matched the text it conveyed.

'By way of recompense, I invite you to pose one question. Of course, I may choose not to answer it.

I will make you a mint hot chocolate. I know you like it. I shall give you until it is made to consider what it is you wish to ask.'

The surgeon exited the room, leaving Jason, a victim, with a head full of confused internal dialogue. How could this maniac torture and then apologise? Why did he feel compelled to make amends for his lack of professionalism in administering drugs unnecessarily when it bothered him not that he had twice removed healthy tissue for no other purpose than seeking revenge? How did he know Jason's family bought a particular beverage? Why did he invite questions after he had gone to such efforts to give nothing away? None of it made sense.

At most, Jason knew he had minutes to consider the question he would put. Previous attempts at obtaining answers had fallen on deaf ears, or brought retaliation. He had to be careful.

The captor returned, placing a mug of mint hot chocolate down beside his patient. He had gone that extra mile, sprinkling mini marshmallows upon its frothy surface; just another bizarre inconsistency, once again proving the man was mad.

The cross-dressing maniac gestured for Jason to speak, who made sure to thank his captor for his kindness before making his permitted enquiry.

'Have I, or someone close to me, hurt you or someone close to you?'

The surgeon's face, over worked with makeup, remained expressionless. Reaction was slow, presumably while a response was considered. Finally, the words had been chosen, written and were published, spoken by the lady who knew no difference between threat and declaration of love.

'Enjoy your drink.'

As forewarned, the surgeon had chosen not to answer.

Far from being frustrated or disappointed, Jason could sense there was a greater meaning to the response, if only he could put it into words. A simple yes or no would have sufficed, yet the captor had felt unable to provide either – why? Placing himself in the surgeon's position, he thought about the implications had he committed to either monosyllabic response.

'Yes' would have vastly reduced the size of the haystack in which Jason and the police sought to find a needle. A 'yes' would imply someone in his small family must have done something with devastating consequences for someone close to the surgeon. In this regard, there were two pieces of evidence to consider: the surgeon's previous cryptic comments suggesting Jason himself was not the perpetrator; the presence of the woman in the wheelchair seeming to identify her as the person wronged. However, it was ludicrous to believe a member of Jason's closest family could cause another person to become disabled without him knowing. If this was the surgeon's contention, he had to be mistaken as to the identity of the person warranting his attention.

If the surgeon had chosen to say 'No', all sorts of possibilities would have to have been considered, making life much harder for the investigators. Nevertheless, the surgeon had felt he could not give it, suggesting he felt morally obliged to tell the truth. Realising a 'yes' would weaken his position, he had opted to change the subject. To Jason's mind, he had his answer after all.

The mint chocolate tasted good.

Jason knew when he woke that he was on the final stretch of his current journey, so long as the day followed the same or similar pattern as before. It did. Breakfast was followed by lunch and an examination of the wound, from which Jason averted his eyes. The surgeon was satisfied with his work and with the healing process. The captive remained silent throughout, not wishing to give his captor reason to test him for what he had learned from the experiences of the past few days. Having formed a theory, he did not want to share it, fearing that if it was too close to the truth, he might not be returned to his family after all.

Several hours after tea, Jason was pleased to finally detect the return of the surgeon's henchmen, hearing heavy-footed people gather in the hall.

The surgeon re-entered the recovery room.

The posh lady spoke.

'You will now be prepared for your return journey. I suggest that in future you get out more, and do so alone. It would be so much less traumatic for Heather and the children if next time we picked you up away from your home.'

So, there was to be a next time. Jason's heart sank at the thought.

No longer using a clipboard, the surgeon had created a check-list on his electronic tablet, the first order of the evening being to strip the patient naked. One of the foreign hired hands entered the room, holding a pair of ring spanners. These he used to free the tether's loop from the guide wire, anchored at one end to the stud wall in the recovery room; to the bathroom wall at the other. All the while, the surgeon held the captive at gunpoint. Jason was confused why this might be. Surely his captor could see he had no intention of escape. If truth be known, even if he were handed the pistol, he would not use it, in the knowledge his captor and one of the henchmen might be dead, but the rest of the organisation would then quickly seek revenge on his family.

With the cable no longer causing an obstruction, Jason was dressed in a paper suit, one arm remaining free. His bare feet were then covered with disposable overshoes before he was invited to sit. The cannula was used for its last time, before being removed, the wound dressed with a small piece of surgical tape, holding firm a wad of sterile cotton wool.

Each stage earned a single tap of the screen.

His arm, increasingly relaxed, was fed into the suit, the captive having no concerns about the hood being placed over his head, or about being carried to the van, waiting outside.

15

Police Constable Steven Billinge was asleep, gently breathing sounds of serenity. His eyes fluttered beneath closed lids; his brain busy fabricating a mixed world of familiar faces in unfamiliar situations. The scenario was a keeper – one to relate to his wife, Elaine, in the morning – or it would have been had his sleeping cycle not been devastated by the sound of a window breaking downstairs. Both Steve and his wife woke in an instant, although she, being in a different phase to her husband, would take several minutes to overcome the disorientation and confusion she experienced on opening her eyes in a room almost entirely devoid of light.

The off-duty officer's instinct caused him to make a mental note of the time - 03:37 hours. As keen as he was to investigate the source of the disturbance, being naked, he delayed his response long enough to grope for and then don his bathrobe.

The sudden illumination of the landing light forewarned anyone on the premises of the officer's rapid descent to the ground floor. At the bottom of the stairs, Steve was drawn towards the front room by a breeze that should not have been there. The main light revealed no sign of an intruder, but the curtains billowed, indicating the source of the noise was hidden behind the fall of cotton damask.

Very little time had elapsed between the shattering crash and his arrival at the scene. There was just a chance a quick-thinking person might catch the perpetrator, or at least, capture a description of a fleeing vandal. Steve was such a person, turning his attention away from the window, which could await forensic examination at a later time, towards the front door. Retrieving the key to release the dead bolts caused a frustrating delay; an unfortunate consequence of being ahead of the pack with regard to home security, accepting a smaller-framed burglar might gain entrance through the Billinge's oversized dog flap, but could not then leave conveniently with the goods via a window or door.

Swinging the front door wide, the off-duty officer was surprised to find he was not too late, the evidence being there in front of him – a naked man, writhing about on the block-paved drive. A torch, grabbed from a shelf situated above a well-stocked shoe rack, revealed the trespasser's identity.

'Jason? Jason Ressler?'

The man tried to sit up but failed, his only verbal response being an unintelligible groan.

'What are you doing here?'

The naked man's unfocussed eyes looked up to meet with those of the man in the bathrobe; a man who looked familiar; someone he had definitely met before.

'Here?'

'Jason, do you remember me? My name is PC Steven Billinge. This is my house. This is where I live.'

The naked man repeated his interrogator's name, slurring the pronunciation. There followed a degree of cerebral processing before he suddenly became alive; as though a coin had been dropped into a mechanical arcade machine.

'Don't you see? It all makes sense. They have a mole who's told them where you live and that you've been involved in the case. It's what I've been saying all along; my family isn't safe.'

The officer knelt down to help the stricken man sit up. He would have taken him indoors but rightly judged his legs too weak to support his own weight.

'What do you mean? Who has a mole?'

'The men who took me!'

'Don't be ridiculous. There are no moles in the police service. Especially round these parts.'

'Oh yeah! Well, they know everything about me; my family…my kid's names; how they are doing at school; the name of my counsellor. Christ, they even know what we eat.'

'Okay, okay. Jason, are you all right? Are you hurt?'

Aided by the light of his torch, a quick scan of those parts of Jason's body he could see revealed no obvious injury. The cannula wound was small and by now the dressing had been removed, along with the paper clothing he had been provided for the journey; one of the final operations carried out by Jason's guards before they lifted him silently from the van and delivered him to PC Billinge's doorstep. Their penultimate operation had been to free their captive's bindings; the final task having been to take a carefully selected brick from a sealable plastic bag and throw it through the front window, wearing latex gloves to avoid transference of DNA.

The returned victim began to cry, as if only just reminded of his ordeal.

'He's taken one of my bollocks! What's Heather going to say?'

A seasoned professional, the officer had no problem remaining calm.

'It's okay. We'll get you sorted out.'

'I have evidence…the person in the wheelchair, it's definitely a woman.'

'That's good.'

At that moment, the officer was relieved to see his wife appear at the door, smart phone in hand.

'There's more. They're foreign, or at least the men who took me are. One of them said a couple of words. I memorised them.'

'Okay, Jason, hold that thought for a moment. We need to get you some help.'

The officer took the phone from his wife and placed a couple of calls; one for an ambulance; one to the police station. During the conversations, Jason's tears dried, his mind unable to simultaneously generate symptoms of trauma, sadness and upset, while accessing memories he felt important to the case. His emotions once more his slave, not his master, Jason recalled two unforgettable scenarios; two ingrained words of unknown origin. He wondered how they might be translated. The police could not simply keep asking people of foreign descent, hoping to stumble upon someone who recognised the words.

Elaine placed a coat across Jason's bare shoulders, just as the second call ended. Seeing the phone hang down in the officer's hand, a possible solution was born.

'Give it to me,' Jason demanded, desperately.

'What?'

'Give me the phone.'

Rightly or wrongly and without question, Steve Billinge passed the device to the victim.

Struggling as would someone suffering drink-induced myopia, Jason nevertheless managed to connect to the internet, hunt for Google and activate the microphone.

The device bleeped twice; a single word appearing on the screen advising it was *listening*, prompting Jason to issue a simple, well-enunciated instruction.

'Translate lin-ish-tay.'

With hardly any hesitation, the phone replied in a pleasant, American, female voice, ending with a rising inflection, designed to demonstrate artificial intelligence no longer articulated in monotone, as did the imagined robots of the 1950s.

'Quiet.'

The translation appeared simultaneously on the screen as several lines of text.

'There, his cronies, they're Romanian.'

Buoyed by his apparent success, Jason spoke again.

'Translate ra-hat.'

This time the response was not so successful, triggering almost half a million results in as many fractions of a second, the top most suggesting it might be Arabic or Turkish for *comfort*. In this case, the translation made no sense, Jason recalling the original was spat in response to one kidnapper thrusting a roll of tape against the bicep of his colleague.

'It doesn't fit.'

'What do you mean?'

'One of the kidnappers said two words. I memorised them, but Google's getting confused. If someone punched you in the arm, you wouldn't say *comfort* would you?'

PC Billinge agreed he would not, and gave the matter quick thought. After a few seconds, his eyes revealed an idea. Taking back the device, the officer tried again.

'Romanian ra-hat.'

Another quarter-of a million results, the top answers revealing *rahat* was indeed a word in Romanian, but far removed from its Turkish equivalent.

'Shit. It's Romanian for *shit*.'

The officer's success marked the conclusion of Jason's primary mission, causing a look of relief to flash across his face. However, his expression was short-lived, it being wiped from his face as he collapsed into Elaine's arms.

16

Police Headquarters, Briefing Room, 09:00 hours, Tuesday, 25 October:
Whereas the morning briefing of the previous day had been routine, disappointingly delivering no new breakthroughs, that of the 25th had much to discuss.

DI Robert Bickley drew the attention of the room. His face looked stern; the same expression used when reprimanding a subordinate for breaching the code of conduct, or for simply having acted with stupidity. However, his opening words were not born of anger; rather frustration and disappointment, the lack of progress gnawing at his pride.

'Morning everyone. The good news is, Jason Ressler is back, but he's been drugged and he's missing a testicle.'

His open hand indicated an image of the victim, displayed on the smart board for all to see.

'Let's take a second here to remind ourselves we are dealing with a real person, not just a name on the cover of a file.'

'At 03:37 hours this morning, Jason Ressler was dumped, naked, on the driveway of PC Billinge's property. What intrigues me the most is how the perpetrator knew Steve was involved in the case; how they knew what he looks like; and how the hell they knew where he lives. We all know there are no moles in this organisation, but how are we going to convince the victim of that when he sees evidence to the contrary. Christ, they're probably just sifting through his bins. Anyway, I don't care how you find out, or who you ask, but I want those questions answered, preferably by tomorrow morning, and I won't be best pleased if I find it's down to careless talk from within these walls.'

No one person was chosen to fulfil this task, the boss' eyes scanning the room, issuing it as a challenge to whomever could produce the answer first.

'Right, Steve has some new information for us.'

PC Billinge moved to the front of the room and produced a pocket book; there should he need it.

'At 03:37 hours this morning, I was woken by a brick, thrown through my living room window. On investigation, I found the victim, Jason Ressler, lying naked on the drive outside my front door. At first he was confused and incoherent, but was soon able to give information with regard to his abduction. Firstly, he confirmed the person in the wheelchair, present during both operations, is indeed a woman, although how he is able to say this is not known as he fainted immediately after having provided his second piece of evidence, which is….'

At this, PC Billinge referred to his notes.

'...The victim overheard one of the kidnappers say two words in a foreign language that he did not recognise. *Linişte* and *rahat*. You'll have to forgive my pronunciation. Anyway, he memorised these and was able to translate them using my wife's phone. The best match for both these indicates the kidnapper was speaking Romanian.'

'He also stated one of his testicles had been removed by his abductors.'

The men in the room winced for a second time in as many minutes. Unaware, the constable continued.

'With regard to the brick, forensics have taken it and are looking for any fibres or fingerprints, or any distinguishing marks that might be unique to an area it was taken from or used.'

Having delivered his evidence concisely, the officer returned to his seat.

DI Bickley was keen to hear the reaction of his team.

'Well, I think we all agree this is a breakthrough and that can only be good. However, what is not so good is the fact that our only progress has come as a result of the efforts made by the victim, and he's had to pay a pretty high price to get it.

'Right, thoughts on what we've just heard.'

Voices from the floor suggested it might mean the involvement of the Romanian mafia; possibly drugs and sex trafficking. This begged the question, how had the Resslers – a seemingly average, working class family – become involved? Was there a connection between either the victim or his wife, and the Romanian underworld?

As far as those in the investigating team could tell, the surgeon was not foreign, based on the style of speech reported to them, rather than accent, which was that of a machine. They had concluded he was well educated, given he used no contractions. As he spoke only through a computer tablet he could of course be using it to translate, but in that case there would bound to have been some glaring errors. These assumptions presented another question. How might a well-educated, medically trained surgeon from the UK become involved with the Romanian mafia? Of course, everyone could see how a surgeon might be of use to an Eastern European gang, but in this case they seemed to be working for him, not vice versa.

The link with the Romanians would need further, urgent, investigation.

DI Bickley turned his attention to DCs Chambley and Humfress.

'Right, anything from the FLOs about this John Ainsley character?'

Although it was often Jane Humfress who did most of the talking when they interrogated witnesses and suspects together, it was more often the case that her colleague, Nigel Chambley, presented the results, especially when it was to a large briefing, hosted by the Detective Inspector. Nigel had a knack of getting the first word out at which point any interjection from Jane would seem unprofessional.

'Yes Guv, we spoke with John Ainsley, aged 32, at his home, yesterday afternoon. He lives in a flat on his own, has no current partner and has been a mutual friend of the Resslers for approximately ten years. Prior to that, he had been a friend of Heather Ressler alone. Jason was introduced to him at John Ainsley's wedding. However, that marriage ended four years ago. Now, I don't know whether he was tipped off by Mrs Ressler, but he was clearly expecting our arrival, stating, 'I wondered when you lot would show up.''

DC Chambley referred to his pocket book to ensure he repeated the phrase verbatim.

'He claims they were in a relationship before Jason Ressler came on the scene, and let himself be easily seduced by her during the evening of Saturday, 24 September, less than 24 hours after the disappearance of her husband. Although happy to take advantage of her vulnerability, he was worried it might lead to an accusation of rape at a later date. Apparently she sensed his reluctance and made a short video on his phone to put him at ease.'

A copy of the video had been submitted to the office manager, DS Honeyman, who fed it to the smart board and pressed play in response to a nod from the constable. Everyone in the room was instantly treated to footage of Heather Ressler, naked, holding her lover's groin, bulging through his jeans, while she spoke the words, 'For the record, this isn't rape; it's revenge.' She looked as though she had been crying and had drunk too much, but not to such a degree to suggest it was not her decision.

'Soon after Jason Ressler was returned, Heather Ressler contacted Mr Ainsley, asking him to delete the video. He told her he had, but kept it as he feared the incident would come out and she would cry rape to cover her infidelity. If you ask me, even if it was a genuine mistake on the part of Heather Ressler, it shows what kind of woman she really is.'

'Excellent, Nigel. Great work.'

DC Humfress raised a finger, not wishing to remain in her colleague's shadow a moment longer.

'Yes, Jane,' DI Bickley responded.

'Guv, there's something else. We spoke with Heather yesterday morning with a view to establishing the state of their family unit. Everything points to them being as close knit and loving as they would have us believe. They have photographs of the children, the family as a group, and of Jason and Heather together, all over the house. He's even made the kids a dolls' house and figures to put in it, made to look like each of them. However, we also discovered they have recently taken out another twenty-thousand pounds of life insurance. Heather said it's to cover the additional mortgage they recently secured to pay for a raft of home improvements. It's true, they have converted the garage to a downstairs bathroom, utility room and workshop, but I thought it best to mention.'

'Thank you Jane. That might be significant.'

Jane glowed inwardly, becoming a schoolgirl once more, praised for her work by her teacher - only a superstar sticker could have made the moment more fulfilling.

The next item on the DI's agenda was the CCTV footage retrieved from the superstore in which Jason normally worked. Mikala Braid, who always wore thick-rimmed glasses, had spent many hours getting to know every frame intimately. The temporary damage her eyesight had sustained during her toil had been worth it. Excerpts were sent to the smart board, Robert Bickley moving to one side to afford everyone in the room an unobstructed view.

A man could be seen entering the store, wearing a black bomber jacket, blue jeans, gloves and white trainers. His face was obscured from view by a logo-free, deep-brimmed baseball cap. The analyst confirmed he appeared many times throughout the recovered recordings, but his face was never fully visible in any of them; only sufficient to determine it was a white male. One week before the first abduction, he could then be seen approaching an area close to where Jason Ressler – suited – was engaged in conversation with a shelf-stacker; a woman of advancing years, recognised by DCs Drake Fallas and Angela Pace as being Mrs Anna Richardson, for a short time thought to be Jason Ressler's lover. Although the images were by no means close up, still the section manager's mouth could be seen moving with enough clarity, a lip reader had been able to decipher one or two words of the conversation, including 'Florida.'

DI Bickley raised a finger, interrupting his colleague's presentation.

'Sorry, Mikala, but I think this is important. Perhaps this was how the perpetrators happened upon Anna's name, deciding to use it to create a false trail. I bet you, if we could hear both sides of the conversation, Anna Richardson would have confirmed when she was going on holiday, where and for how long.'

His eyebrows raised, forcing his head down slightly and to one side, challenging his team to tell him he was wrong. No one did.

The analyst was allowed to continue.

'Given the height of the victim is known, we have estimated our man of interest to be approximately 1.70 metres in height. As you can see, he appears to be of athletic build.'

With Jason Ressler's attention engaged, the man with the cap appeared to be taking sideways glances at the victim's name badge, although his eyes were not visible. He then appeared to be using a mobile phone, covertly taking a photograph, while pretending to capture an image of a randomly selected item of produce.

Having identified this figure as a person of interest, the analyst had followed his movements, establishing that he made regular appearances at and around the store during previous and subsequent days. The man parked near the staff entrance. A vehicle - a black Vauxhall Vectra - seemingly identical in appearance on all occasions, could be seen to draw up at roughly the same position, at about the same time, throughout the week. However, the number plate was never the same. The conclusion was that false plates had been used and that the man in the baseball cap appeared to be establishing Jason's shift pattern with the emphasis on his finishing times.

'I've done what the man in black could not do,' Mikala said, smugly, 'and rung the victim's boss. Jason Ressler maintained a predictable pattern, working the late shift, five days in a row, including every weekend.

'His wife must love him.'

'I've also run the false index plates. They all originate from other black Vauxhall Vectra motor vehicles, although differing in exact model and year. Of interest, none of the owners of these vehicles have reported their index plates missing, implying the gang must be making their own.'

The presentation continued. Occasionally, the vehicle with the ever changing number plate was seen to leave the car park at the same time as Jason, probably checking the mark's route home and those points along the way when he was most vulnerable.

On the night the victim went missing, the Vectra could be seen again, leaving shortly after him. Although the analyst had not seen any visual evidence, it was likely the person of interest had phoned ahead, warning his associates to be ready, perhaps using the phone he was seen to have in possession in store.

The screen returned to a still image of Jason Ressler, and beside it, a still image, captured from the video, offering as clear a picture of the man of interest as could be found.

'Thank you Mikala,' DI Bickley said, smiling. 'Okay everyone, we have to focus on the details. Any little piece could be relevant. In the CCTV, the suspect appears to be using a mobile phone. As we've heard, it's also likely he used a phone on the night of the first abduction. If he's prepared to change a number plate every night, he may have done the same with his SIM card. Nevertheless, we need to identify his device and establish to whom he was speaking.

Right, anything from anyone else before we seize the day?'

DC Drake Fallas spoke up.

'I was thinking, Sir, maybe it's not about the money at all. Maybe Jason Ressler plays around - or at least Heather thinks he does - and she's had enough. We've already seen how quickly she's prepared to jump into bed to exact her revenge – less than 24 hours after her husband's been taken.'

The constable paused to determine whether his boss thought his theory had sufficient merit for him to continue.

'Interesting. Go on.'

'Well, Sir, maybe Heather Ressler happened to befriend a surgeon, and persuaded him to slice bits from her husband, either to teach him a lesson, or to make Jason less attractive to other women. I think the woman in the wheelchair is his wife. Clearly she's not seeing to his sexual needs – by all accounts she's hardly capable of lifting her own head. It's just possible that Heather Ressler provides him a sexual service in exchange for him carrying out a few operations. Of course she seems upset in the video and whenever anyone speaks to her – hardly surprising as her husband has been playing away and she blames him for making her take such drastic action.

'With regard to the surgeon's wife, I reckon she isn't there to witness the operation at all; it's probably just that she's so disabled she can't be left alone.'

Having finished his presentation, DC Fallas held his breath in anticipation while the DI mulled over the proposed theory. Although the Inspector had a tendency to react on gut instinct, speeding up the process, the pause was nonetheless sufficiently protracted for his constable to experience the onset of oxygen starvation. In the end, his approval came not only by way of accepting DC Fallas' notion, but also by embellishing it.

'And in the same way as Heather is offering a service to the surgeon, he might be offering a service to the Romanians, in exchange for them kidnapping the victim. Perhaps there is a mole after all – one within the family, and we all know who that might be – Heather Ressler.

'Okay, I like it. Let's dig around and find out whether Jason Ressler plays the field. Drake and Angela, I'll leave that one with you.

'Right, Jane and Nigel, you're the FLOs. I want you to interview Jason Ressler this morning, if you please…as soon as the doc says he's fit to talk. Mikala, I want your team to concentrate on the mobile phones. The rest of you, DS Honeyman will assign each of you tasks. Feed back to him anything you find. Good hunting ladies and gentlemen.'

***

Jason recognised instantly the Family Liaison Officers as they approached his hospital bed, situated in one of the ward's few side rooms. He greeted them before offering each a chair. DC Humfress asked the victim whether he would be more comfortable with the end of the bed raised, allowing him to sit up. Jason accepted her suggestion with gratitude and her colleague leapt from his hard plastic chair to perform the task, eager to demonstrate he was no less empathic than his partner, although he was, and always would be.

Jason appeared stoic, accepting his ordeal without complaint, for to do so would suggest *his* wellbeing was his foremost concern.

'Don't get me wrong, I don't want to be taken again, but if I stop them, they said they'd take my children instead. I don't know if either of you have kids, but what would you do? On the other hand, if you don't do something soon, there won't be anything left of me; at least nothing worth saving.'

Seeing his colleague struggling to find the right answer, it was left to Nigel Chambley to respond.

'As it happens, I do have kids – two young boys; five and three. In answer to your question, I don't know what I would do, but looking at your situation from the outside, with a clear head, I think you really have to consider going into hiding. Of course you're afraid of this madman. Who wouldn't be? But he's not this all-seeing omnipotent being you make him out to be. They won't take your kids because they won't be able to find any of you.'

Jason dismissed the suggestion out of hand.

'The surgeon was very clear. He said his associates have – and I quote - *many connections in many organisations.* To my mind, that means he has an inside man. It wouldn't matter where you sent us, he'd know.'

Wary that if not handled with sufficient care, Jason might cease to want anything to do with either of them, Jane stepped in, her tone oozing tact and diplomacy. Even her eyes played their part, looking to her folded hands until the question was put, avoiding the antagonistic stare of an interrogator.

'Can we explore that a little more? You told Steve Billinge the surgeon knows all about you and your family. Do you want to tell me what he knows?'

'Okay, for a start he knew where the officer lives, didn't he? He knows where to find me: where I work; where I live; my movements. He knows my kids' names and how they're doing at school. He knows I have been seeing a counsellor, and her name. He even knows what groceries we buy. Everything he's fed me could have been taken from our cupboards at home.'

'Okay, we can explore all that, but what interests me most is how your kidnappers came to know of PC Billinge. You'll be aware he is not part of the investigating team, his only involvement being that he happened, by chance, to respond to the call when you were first reported missing, and then when you were first returned. Jason, while you were away, did you mention anything about him to your captors? Might you have said something while you were under the influence of the drugs he's been pumping into you?'

'No, I'm hardly allowed to talk. He doesn't ask me anything. He already knows it and I think he gets some sort of kick in letting me know he knows it.'

'The idea has been put forward that the men responsible for all this may have simply been going through your rubbish.'

Jason could not instantly conceive a counter-argument.

'It's possible, I suppose.'

'Can you see, it's more likely that their source is a dustbin sack than a mole within the department, in which case, if we took you somewhere remote, they wouldn't find you.'

'Firstly, would you take that risk if it were your family? Secondly, if I'm out of the way, how do you propose to catch him? If you don't, I'm destined to spend the remainder of my life in hiding. We'd never be able to see the rest of our family and friends again and I can't accept that.'

'Okay, Jason, the other thing you said to PC Billinge was that you were pretty sure the person in the wheelchair is a woman...'

'Not just any woman. I think they're close...a wife, or sister, or something. He seems to think she was put in a wheelchair by someone close to me.'

'Is that possible?'

'We don't have a big family. What family I do have is pretty close, so I'd know if someone did anything like that.'

Nigel detected a pause and used the opportunity to slip in further questions from a list that had begun to stack at the forefront of his mind.

'The journey there and back; can you tell us anything about it?'

'Well, I can't say with any degree of accuracy, but the trip there seemed to take about as long as last time. Of course, I was out of it on the way back – drugged – so I have no idea about that. I do know one thing though, the van wasn't the same as before.'

'Interesting, why do you say that?'

'I was naked. I could feel every lump and bump in the floor. It's true, last time I was wearing clothes, but my hands were in contact with the floor and I could feel the general shape through my trousers.'

'Okay, assuming the kidnappers are not driving round in circles to disguise distance, have you any idea why they might have taken you so far?'

'My guess is the woman in the wheelchair lives nearby. On both occasions he's left me on my tod while he takes her home. He's not gone long.'

Both detectives nodded as they made notes.

Jane took back the reins.

'Do you know anyone who lives that sort distance from you, or have any of your family visited someone who lives that far away? I'm wondering if perhaps your wife did something and didn't realise it – caused an accident in her rear view mirror – that sort of thing.'

Jason looked somewhat taken aback.

'You'd have to ask her that one, but I don't recall either of us having driven any great distance in years. What family we have lives no more than an hour away, and we always holiday abroad. My shifts don't really allow many family weekends away in the UK. Anyway, why do you mention my wife as though she's to blame for all this? I'm telling you, if Heather had done something that resulted in a woman becoming disabled, I'd know.'

'Try not to get upset. We're not accusing anyone; we're simply exploring every avenue.'

Jane paused. Then, judging the victim had recovered sufficiently, she decided she could stretch the boundaries just a little bit more.

'...It's just that we know of Heather's conviction for driving while under the influence of alcohol. Might that not have led to something happening?'

'No, not at all! Heather was convicted for doing something stupid. She drank too much at the Christmas party, got in the car, realised it wasn't safe and fell asleep with the engine running, without ever having left the parking space. We both know she shouldn't have gone anywhere near her car in that state, but she was never in any danger of hurting anyone.'

Seeing their interviewee was getting more and more agitated by the minute, Nigel Chambley swiftly changed the subject.

'Okay Jason, let's not get hung up on your family. We're not here to blame them. We're here to find the people who have done these things to you.'

Jason's indignation melted somewhat, having said his piece and put things straight.

'Jason, I'm impressed. Steve Billinge told us you managed to work out that the men who took you were Romanian. Can you tell us anything more about them?'

The victim paused before answering, allowing his resentment to pass.

'The leader of the men who kidnapped me could have been the same man – very professional; very slick and kept his mouth shut. The guy who dragged me into the back of the van was an amateur. It seemed to be his fault we took forever to set off. He got angry and spoke two words. I memorised them. As soon as I could I used the officer's phone to translate them. Actually, I think it was his wife's phone, but I don't suppose that really matters. Turns out both words are Romanian, meaning *quiet* and *shit*. It makes sense. He said the first word when I spoke in the back of the van. And he said the other when the leader thrust a roll of tape into his arm. It must have hurt. Oh, and the new fella had a shiny knife and a torch.'

Hoping the victim had forgiven her for suggesting his wife was involved, DC Humfress spoke again.

'Excellent. And is there anything else you think might help?'

'Well, I reckon the *hospital* must be pretty isolated, otherwise they wouldn't have carried me naked so openly.'

'Good point.'

As she made a note, Jason thought to issue an addendum.

'He told me I'll be kidnapped again.'

Seeing his colleague's head directed towards her pocket book, DC Chambley picked up the lead.

'Did he actually say that?'

'Not exactly. I asked the surgeon why he was doing it. He told me he wants me to reach Nirvana – something to do with Buddhists. He wants me to learn lessons and rise through levels of some sort.'

Both detectives looked to the victim, their faces pictures of confusion.

With little else to be gained, the interview ended shortly afterwards with promises that both detectives would continue to support the Resslers in any way they could. Jason thanked them. He was glad to have been given the chance to relay the evidence he had paid so much to gather and could fight the need to sleep no more. He yearned for natural slumber, free from forced medication, but at the same time, feared the terrifying memories that might invade his dreams.

17

Police Headquarters, Briefing Room, 09:00 hours, Wednesday, 26 October:
DI Robert Bickley cleared his throat, achieving almost immediate silence.
'First, let's have feedback from the FLOs.'

Anticipating the prompt, Nigel Chambley was first to respond, leaving Jane annoyed for having missed an opportunity for her hard work – at least her part in the investigation - to be recognised.

Oblivious to his colleague's feelings, Nigel reported that Jason continued to refuse all offers of protection for him and his family, citing evidence leading him to believe his abductors had infiltrated the police.

The inspector reacted badly, taking a deep breath, just so he could exhale again, letting his upper body slump, his eyes to close briefly; visible signs of his frustration.

For once, Jane was glad her colleague had ridden roughshod over her. Claiming the update as his own meant he alone would forever be linked to such an unpalatable suggestion; one that insulted everything the inspector stood for. A slight on the integrity of the police was a personal attack on each and every person who worked within the organisation. 'Don't kill the harbinger' would not cut it with DI Bickley. Everyone knew that.

The Inspector's recovery was quick, but Jane suspected the moment had been stored; that Nigel would never make Sergeant – or was that simply wishful thinking.

'So, Mr Ressler thinks we have a mole, does he? *You* know the idea is ridiculous, *I* know the idea is ridiculous, but have we got anything to refute the accusation. DC Chambley, please tell me we do.'

There it was; the cordial use of the officer's first name had been dropped for something far more formal, and the change had not gone unnoticed, Nigel's response suddenly lacking the absolute confidence his voice normally carried.

'Nothing, Sir, other than Jason remains adamant he has not knowingly mentioned Steve Billinge's name, or his connection with the case.'

Luckily, DC Chambley was saved further interrogation by the timely interjection of another of the team. Mikala Braid had worked beyond her remit by checking media coverage. PC Billinge had appeared in the local newspaper, which had dedicated its entire centre spread to raising funds for Jason's operation to restore his missing ear. A photograph showed the staff at the supermarket, headed by Jason's boss, Martin Feller, standing by collection buckets, a thermometer-shaped totaliser and plenty of examples of the store's corporate logo. In the foreground, forming a semi-circle behind Mr Feller, stood Jason's team of six, including Anna Richardson, recently returned from her holiday of a lifetime in Florida. To the back of the shot, other contributors to the effort could be seen, one of whom wore the uniform of a police constable. Although not the clearest of images, making the officer recognisable only to those who already knew him, his name was disclosed in the accompanying text. Knowing his name, it was a simple task for the kidnappers to then reference a clearer picture, available to all on the force's community policing web pages. The kidnappers had then only to follow him home at the end of his shift.

Richard Bickley thanked the contributor.

'Thanks Mikala. There ladies and gentlemen, I think we have our answer. As I said, no mole. Nigel, make sure Jason and his wife know of this. It might just alter his mind about going into hiding.'

Not only had Mikala solved the conundrum, but in doing so she had returned Nigel's name to the inspector's lexicon and restored the constable's self-confidence.

'Will do, Guv, but I doubt it will change anything? We've already explained how much information the family have probably given the perps via their rubbish sacks.'

'And he continues to believe the existence of the mole?'

'Not necessarily, but he's not willing to take the risk. After all, *it is just a theory* – Jason's words, not mine.'

After a short pause, Nigel continued his report, referring to bullet points he had made in his pocket book, leaving no opportunity for Jane to show she was more than the silent partner.

'Jason believes that the woman in the wheelchair is closely related to the surgeon. On both occasions the surgeon has left the hospital, presumably to return her home, but has not been gone long. That means she must live locally.

'He also believes the surgeon blames Jason in some way for the woman's disability, although Jason was adamant nobody in his family has ever caused an accident.

'Erm, we've already ascertained the abductors are Romanian...'

Nigels' stutter was all Jane needed to seize a moment of glory.

'Guv, with regard to the Romanian connection, I've done some work with the support staff and what do you know, Heather Ressler *has* been to Romania - about three years ago.'

'Is that so? Okay, Nigel, Jane, let's see what Heather has to say about that.'

Jane did not like the order in which the DI referred to them. *She* had introduced this important piece of information, not her colleague; *her* initial appeared first in the alphabet; and *she* was almost certain she had greater seniority.

'I'm not sure that's the right play, Guv,' DC Humfress responded, confidently and without hesitation. 'We've already pushed her quite hard and I fear she may just shut down. I need to spend some time rebuilding her trust before we can hope to squeeze anything else from her.'

'Okay, Jane, you know her best. I trust you. Do we know anything else about this trip? Did she fly alone, for example?'

'No, the booking was for six women. Could be a hen do.'

'Whatever the reason, it may have started innocently, but then given her an opportunity. If we can't put the pressure on Heather, I want Drake and Angela to speak with the other five women. I want confirmation as to why they were there. Did Heather meet anyone? What was her mood? Did it change? Has she kept in touch with anyone?'

'Good work, Jane. I've said it before and I'll say it again, I haven't liked Heather Ressler from day one, and I like her less and less with every passing day. She's a liar, she's unfaithful, she's vengeful, she's increased the life insurance, and now it turns out she has a connection with Romania, the very country from which our kidnappers herald. Let's get her.'

DI Bickley nodded repeatedly, his gaze sweeping the room, encouraging the team to commit their souls to the task.

'Right, Nigel, it looks as though you have more to share.'

'Yes, Guv. Nearly there.'

The detective once more referred to his notes.

'Jason believes the hospital must be in an isolated location, given that he is transferred from the van to the building naked, hidden only by the night.

'And one last thing; the surgeon might be a Buddhist. He told Jason he would be taught lessons so he could rise through various levels to reach Nirvana.'

As the constable spoke, Detective Sergeant Honeyman summarised each piece of evidence, displaying them on the smart board. Once Nigel had finished, each bullet point was then opened up for discussion.

With regard to motivation, if a member of the Ressler family had caused the woman to become disabled, and even though it seemed Jason Ressler had been transported a great distance, it was deemed a mistake to conclude the incident necessarily took place far away. It could just as easily be the case that the surgeon had been on holiday with his close female relative when the accident occurred. She might even have slipped on a grape at the store at which Jason Ressler worked, and then returned to Scotland.

With regard to Jason Ressler's stubborn refusal to go into hiding, DI Bickley concluded he had no choice but to accept the decision, taking the pragmatic view the victim would at least make a suitable lure.

He then turned to the one remaining bullet point, which caused most deliberation; the talk of Buddhism, learning lessons and reaching Nirvana.

A quick Google search informed the room that Nirvana is a stillness of mind - after fires of desire, aversion and delusion have been extinguished - attained by repeating the cycle of birth, life and death, over and over. The question was soon asked how removing bits of Jason's body might teach him anything. An ear might suggest the victim was not listening, but what was the lesson to be had from the loss of a testicle?

Jane spoke to be heard.

'As Nigel said, maybe the surgeon is himself a Buddhist, although I very much doubt it. They wouldn't hurt a fly.'

A voiced peeped up from the back of the room.

'Don't know about that. What about Kung Fu? David Carradine used to beat people up on a weekly basis.'

The reference might have got a greater titter had the majority of those in the room not been too young to have ever seen the cult TV series.

This was not a comedy store, as DI Bickley was quick to remind his colleagues.

'Right everybody, settle down. Before we go on to the next item on the agenda I'd like to point out there's every chance this talk of Buddhism is a load of tosh. We know these people like to use misdirection. Anna Richardson is a good example of that. If the surgeon is in league with Heather Ressler, what better way to put us off the trail than by making Jason believe the focus of the abductions is the woman in the wheelchair, not the victim himself, i.e. Jason Ressler. On that note, any news of our victim playing away?'

Angela Pace responded on behalf of herself and her partner, Drake Fallas.

'Sorry, Guv. So far he's squeaky clean, but we'll keep on it.'

'Thank you, Angela. Next on the agenda, I believe Mikala's team have had some success with regard to mobile phone usage.'

Overnight, the analyst had established all phone activity within the area of the supermarket, on each occasion the man identified in store had been seen staking out the premises. Several phones had dropped in that area, and at those times, but none had been the same.

'Our conclusion is that our man of interest used many different phones, or at least SIM cards, once only; perhaps from a pool. However, all is not lost. In the majority of cases, we have been able to identify an account address for each phone that dropped. All were local, consistent with use by local shoppers going about their legitimate business. For the remaining phones, to which no address can be associated, logs have been obtained. This exercise has produced a positive outcome. In a significant number of cases, the log indicated single use, but importantly they were to the same number. We have established the unique International Mobile Equipment Identity, IMEI, for the device common to each of these anonymous calls, which means, if it was used again, my team can trace it in real time, leading officers to his or her exact location.'

'Excellent work, Mikala. Thank you. I feel we're making solid progress. The net is closing in.'

DI Bickley then turned his attention to the author of the medical report.

'So Doc, why do you think he's chosen to remove the victim's ear and testicle?'

The consultant answered with authority, but without certainty, much of this case being guesswork.

'Minor surgery. My guess is he hasn't got the facilities to do anything more serious.'

Robert Bickley's eyes turned upwards and to the side, his head bobbing, his lips under pressure. During this moment, a new question was born, delivered at the speed of someone dipping their toe in the bath to test the temperature of the water.

'Is it feasible the surgeon might be harvesting these parts for the purpose of creating himself a new body, or replacing bits someone else is missing?'

On this the consultant's reply came close to being unequivocal.

'Creating some kind of human suit seems implausible as surely he would have taken a pair of good ears, et cetera. I would be more inclined to believe this was a case of spare parts surgery if he'd taken a kidney. They fetch big bucks on the international market, but ears and testes? Quite useless and easily replaceable with prosthetics. If he's not simply motivated by revenge, I can only guess he might be looking for the best example of each body part that he can find. Ressler's right ear and left testicle might have met some twisted criteria. Maybe he intends to farm his current patient for all the best bits before moving on to another victim.'

'Thanks Doc. Okay, remember why we are here. I know we have speculated the Resslers must be involved in something we do not yet know, but let me say this - regardless of what we believe to be the motive, concentrate on who did this. Jason Ressler does not deserve to have been tortured in this way, even if he has been unfaithful to his wife.

'It is of some benefit to our investigation, the perpetrator has been kind enough to stick with the same MO: Jason was abducted late on Friday evening and was returned in the early hours of the morning.'

The inspector had long, slender hands, the elongated index finger of his right bending back the digits of his left, in turn, as he worked through a list of similarities.

'A van of similar size was used on both occasions; it is believed there were three men involved in snatching and moving him; the journey seems to have been of the same or similar duration, although we only have the victim's perception of this; the destination, the surgeon, the figure in a wheelchair – all the same; and the victim has been subjected to another minor operation, conducted by someone trained in medicine. It is clear Jason Ressler is not a random victim, he has been specifically targeted and it looks likely he will be taken again. We may not be able to prevent that - Jason Ressler won't let us. We don't know when or from where he will be taken. It all seems pretty hopeless, but what we can do is try to find this madman before he strikes again. We have some solid leads. We're in a far better position than at any time during this investigation, so let's keep at it. No easing up.

'I will see you all here, the same time tomorrow.'

***

The morning briefings continued as regular as clockwork, but as there were no new breakthroughs, other cases began to grab priority. The identified phone had remained silent; the five friends of Heather Ressler confirmed they had indeed attended a hen do in Romania, had remained in each other's company throughout their stay, and all had thought it impossible for a liaison to have been had without their knowledge; the forensic report on the brick thrown through PC Billinge's living room window had drawn blank; and of the greatest significance, despite the fears of everyone involved, Jason had not been kidnapped for a third time. Once again, the Ressler case found itself on the back burner.

18

The evening had gone well. Jason had allowed himself to relax; to entertain friends; to put the children to bed, reading each of them a story. For once he had allowed the events that had disfigured him to remain dormant; the fear of being taken again to be put to one side.

Since his return, Jason had shied away from drink, no longer deriving pleasure from the numbing effects of alcohol; too similar to those induced by the surgeon's needle. But on this evening it felt right to share a bottle with his wife and guests. He had even managed a laugh; to smile without being prompted.

The evening ended with cheeks being kissed, hands shaken firmly, and promises to meet again soon.

Then to bed, Heather having prepared the room to perfection. The sheet and duvet cover were fresh; heavy lined curtains barred the light of a late autumn sky; the radiator maintained an ambient temperature several degrees below that of beneath the duvet.

'Can you rub my back?'

Husband and wife rolled onto their sides from which position Jason massaged firmly the muscles of Heather's upper shoulder; gently scratched the skin not covered by her vest top; rubbed her back through the material, from waist to the nape of her neck.

'Beneath my top,' Heather murmured.

Jason hoped Heather had in mind nothing more than a sleep-inducing massage, but after a short while she let out a gentle groan. Judging on past experience – before the things that had been done to Jason had been done – such sounds promised he would soon after be rewarded, her whimpers sparking life into his groin. But that was months ago. Since being forced under the knife, Jason had not once indicated any interest in making love, and Heather had not suggested it, believing he would let her know when the time was right. Was she testing the water? Did she hope this night would be the one when they restored the missing part of their relationship?

The answer was soon forthcoming, Heather's free arm reaching behind her, her hand taking hold of her husband through his pyjamas.

Jason pulled away. The pleasurable groans stopped in an instant, Heather's upper body twisting towards him, although she could not see him through the darkness.

'What's wrong? Does it hurt?'

'No.'

'What then? It's been ages. I thought you wanted to. Don't you fancy me anymore?'

'Don't be silly. I just don't feel like it. That's all.'

Heather turned on the bedside light and manoeuvred herself so the couple faced each other, their noses almost touching.

'Can you turn off the lamp, please?'

Heather looked into her husband's eyes. She could see he was not being awkward or dismissive. Perhaps he needed the anonymity of the darkness before he could talk about what was troubling him. Their very own confessional.

Having done as he asked, she took his hands in hers; soft and slender fingers gripping large, slightly hairy hands, almost twice the size of her own.

'Go on, what is it?'

She spoke gently.

As delicate as the subject was, Jason had never been able to keep a secret from his wife, other than her birthday and Christmas presents; that and his true appraisal of her bottom as it grew somewhat larger during her pregnancies.

'Okay, I know what you're going to say, but I just don't feel like a man anymore. There, I've said it.'

'Sweetheart, you know I would love you even if the whole lot was missing. I didn't marry you on the basis of how good your balls looked. Besides, I'm the only person who'll ever see you naked; at least I hope I am.'

Jason had no desire to discuss the attractiveness, or otherwise, of the male anatomy, subtly using his wife's second remark to steer their conversation in a new direction.

'I've never even thought about another woman. Even before I met you. I know for a fact you'd stray before I would, and even then I wouldn't.'

Finding it difficult to deliver the next statement, Jason paused for a moment, failing to notice that his wife made no effort to fill the gap.

'You know, I would understand if you wanted to be with someone else now – since all of this.'

The words bit deep into his wife's conscience, but somehow she managed to remain silent about her affair; the first and only time she had been unfaithful, to anyone.

'Don't be silly.'

If ever there was a chance, now their feelings had been aired, that Heather would suggest they might like to take it easy, canoodle, and see how things turned out, it had evaporated. Guilt was as much of a passion killer as was a stolen testicle.

'You're having the operation soon. Perhaps you'll feel more like it then.'

For the first time in many weeks, roles became reversed. While Jason slipped into a peaceful sleep, Heather's head remained sunken into her pillow, her eyes open to the dark.

***

The days following Jason's second return were spent in twice-weekly conversation with Natasha, seeking ways to cope with the physical trauma of amputation, and the mental trauma of not knowing – not knowing who was doing this to him; why; whether he would be snatched again; if he were to be, when, and what part of his body might be taken next.

The police had gone eerily quiet. The Family Liaison Officers still visited, but rarely had anything to report. However close they believed they were coming to an arrest, for all the assistance Jason had given them, in reality they were no nearer, and Jason was becoming increasingly concerned time was running out. Firstly, because the surgeon had led him to believe he would be taken again – to achieve new levels of understanding on the road to Nirvana. Secondly, the man who wielded the knife, and the gang who did his bidding, together had an established modus operandi. A month had elapsed between the first two abductions, leaving the victim overdue another visit from the Romanians.

Natasha had taught him that to sit and do nothing while he waited for the inevitable was to admit defeat. Consequently, Jason had used the time given him by the surgeon to think of opportunities for gathering evidence. To this end he had installed a dashcam in his car, cunningly not suckered to the windscreen, but hidden behind a carefully modified radiator grille, so it might capture images of his assailants without being discovered. Further, he had taken on board two specific pieces of advice – again Natasha's - to put effort into something he enjoyed doing and to keep a book of his emotions; a means of cleansing his mind, giving him something tangible to refer to when trying to make sense of his desperate situation. With regard to the first, Jason returned to his beloved dolls' houses with renewed vigour. However, as much as Charlie and Lily were excited to see their dream miniature house finished, populated by tiny Ressler replicas, they also wanted to make the most of their daddy being home from work; to sit at the table with them at mealtimes; to read to them at night. There was little hope that children of eight and six could be made to understand why he instead chose to avoid them. In fact, their father had become so focussed on his projects, concern grew he was not eating. He rarely joined them in the dining room and often forgot to finish what was delivered to him in the converted garage. Jason had never asked his wife to leave him alone, but then again, he never suggested she stay to keep him company. She took him food on a tray; always made a point of complimenting the progress her husband was making; and later collected the dishes, the food barely touched, even though it had been placed within Jason's easy reach. Something had to change.

Having spent several hours in the kitchen, Heather presented her husband his favourite meal, the aroma alone usually sufficient to prompt an 'mmm'; the first mouthful enough to cause him to place his cutlery down so he might give her a kiss in gratitude. However, on this occasion, Jason barely acknowledged his wife's presence.

'I've made your favourite.'

Her husband's head turned a degree or two to one side, but his eyes remained fixed on his work.

'Thanks, sweetheart, but I'm not really hungry.'

The presentation had gone much as anticipated and would have prompted most wives to drop the meal in their husband's lap before storming out, but Heather was the exception. She sat close by, prepared to have no conversation at all. She watched him work, he demonstrating the patience of a monk, as he fabricated the most realistic miniature conservatory a modeller could ever hope to achieve. It must have taken hours; it *had* taken hours. Heather had seen its painfully slow birth and progression over the course of several weeks; sheets of balsa wood and others of Perspex becoming an intricate structure to which Jason was in the process of applying individual brick slips, one at a time.

Despite the lack of interaction, Heather remained with her husband, hoping her company was appreciated, even if Jason did not feel like talking. Having nothing in particular to occupy her mind, she stole a thick-cut chip from his plate – already cooled from its once state of perfection - and looked about the room. Her eyes soon fell upon a book - A5, wire-bound - the pages of which bulged, the thickness of the book having expanded to many times its original. Heather took it in her hands. Her husband had to be aware she had done so, but chose to say nothing. This was all the permission she needed before examining the contents.

The book was the result of Natasha's second suggestion, but what had meant to be nothing more than a place to offload disturbing emotions, had instead become a place to download his every thought, all of which were connected to the abductions. The pages painted a vivid picture of one man's experience of hell. He had relived every moment of both kidnappings in his head, minute by excruciating minute, and had laid them upon the pages in writing, in the form of pictures, and with diagrams. It logged the before, during and after. It held details of conversations; answers to questions; notes about his surroundings; plans of those areas of the hospital that were known to him. It also revealed he had been sampling food, for example, many varieties of processed cheese from many different retailers, the packaging saved and stapled within the book, the pages annotated with comments pertaining to taste and texture.

As strange as this behaviour was, at least it explained why the author-come-food-critic was not as hungry as might have been expected.

'Sweetheart, what's the significance of the food?'

Surprisingly, Jason broke from what he was doing to deliver an answer.

'While I was away the surgeon fed me. At the time I was convinced he bought it at our store – at least from one of our stores. I'm sure he was taunting me; letting me know his knowledge of me is total; to the extent he feeds me the same food that you would.

I just wanted to test my theory; to check I'm not being paranoid.'

'And are you?'

'It's definitely ours. He could have taken it straight from our cupboards. It's not that the food he gave me includes some of the items we buy. Everything he gave me can be found on the shelves at our supermarket – everything – and I'm not talking big brands which could be bought anywhere, I'm talking about the value stuff, unique to us.'

'Didn't the police say he's probably been going through our bins?'

Heather did not receive a reply. She had lost her husband again to the intricacies of applying small bricks to a small surface, using small tools and delicate movements. The distraction she had caused had clearly affected his concentration, evidenced by his subsequent actions.

Although Jason had appeared calm throughout the period Heather had been with him in the workroom, and had spoken with the serenity of a psychiatrist, his levels of stress shot suddenly to the far end of the scale, one of the brick tiles slipping fractionally out of place, provoking him to smash his fist through the near-complete conservatory, before picking up the distorted ruins and tearing them apart, reducing each to ever smaller components. When he had finished, he showed no emotion, but started sweeping the fragments into a bin close to hand.

***

Heather met with her friend and colleague at the first opportunity, choosing their favourite coffee shop, the same one in which they had discussed Jason before.

Despite it being at Heather's request, Natasha footed the bill – her treat. Heather's pot of tea, cup, saucer and milk jug, Natasha's bucket of frothy coffee, and a three-tiered sharing platter of finger sandwiches and cakes took up almost every square inch of the table's surface.

'So much for me being on a diet,' Heather joked, gratefully.

'You certainly don't need to be on one of those. You're losing enough weight without it – all this stress you've been going through. Anyway, I thought you deserved it.'

'So, what do you want to talk about? You have my full attention.'

She coughed, partly because she had just managed to stop herself saying, 'I'm all ears', something she considered might have been inappropriate, given the circumstances.

To get herself into the right frame of mind, Heather first prepared a cup of tea, taking a sip to ensure it was exactly to her liking.

'When Jason lost his ear, it was bad enough. You probably remember me telling you how weird he became, removing the mirrors, et cetera. He would assess potential dangers wherever we went. Never let up for a minute.'

'So you're going to tell me it's got worse?'

'Not exactly. He's still happy to go out as long as he's wearing a hoody, but I'm worried. As I say, last time he constantly saw everything as a threat. Now it's as though he has prepared to be taken, or even wants to be taken.'

Natasha said nothing, but her face was focussed on her friend's every word.

'He's so difficult to live with. The kids and I rarely see him; he's become irritable; he's liable to outbursts of sudden and uncontrollable anger, although thankfully short-lived; and he's become an insomniac. He finds it hard to sleep because of the dreams, and won't take pills as it's too like him being back in that hospital. One minute he has total concentration; the next, on the rare occasion we sit down to watch TV together, I'll find him zoned out, staring out of the window into the darkness, fixated on nothing in particular.

'Despite all this, far from becoming a recluse, he's quite the opposite, remaining visible when he's out of the house, scared that if he cannot be found at the right time, we'll be taken in his place. I've even discovered him leaving a note on the front door, informing anyone who cares to read it where he can be found.

'Everyone thinks he's mad, but he's doing it to protect his family. Don't get me wrong, I still love him, but I don't know what to do.'

Natasha took her friend's hands in hers.

'Heather, you know as well as I do there's no quick fix. The real work begins once this is all over and they've caught these sick bastards. Until then, we have to support him – together – and I have to support you. That starts with you eating this cream cake and I'll speak with Jason during the week.'

Heather smiled for the first time in as long as she could remember and took half the slice of Victoria sponge in her mouth at once.

***

The day of the planned surgery finally arrived and by nine o'clock in the morning Jason found himself booked in and sitting in a side room ready for the surgeon's rounds. Although Mr Farnorth specialised in facial prosthetics and reconstruction, Jason was pleased to hear the consultant would also tackle his missing testicle at the same time.

'With regard to auricular reconstruction, we originally spoke about there being three options. Are you still happy to go ahead with the third technique, i.e. providing you with an auricular prosthesis, custom made to mirror your surviving ear?'

'Yes please.'

'The testicular prosthesis is a replica testicle made of silicone. It improves the cosmetic appearance of the scrotum and may also help improve your self-image. However, it is a personal decision and not everyone who has a missing testis wants a prosthesis. Would you like me to go ahead?'

'Yes, I would.'

'I have to warn you, all surgical procedures have a potential for complications. However, the majority of my patients who have these kinds of corrective surgery do not suffer any problems. Common side effects are…'

Jason feigned interest but inwardly wished the man would cease talking about the operation and just get on with it, but there seemed no stopping him.

'I usually perform the procedure under general anaesthetic. The testicular prosthesis is inserted into the scrotum through a small incision in the groin. The neck of the scrotum is then closed with stitches...'

The patient's eyes glazed over, life returning only on hearing a question directed at him.

'Okay so far?'

'I'm fine. Do whatever you have to, but can we get this done as quickly as possible. I've developed a bit of a phobia of places like this.'

Jason sounded exasperated.

'I can imagine you have. Nearly there...

'You may experience some discomfort following your surgery. While you are in hospital you will be given painkillers as you require them. When you go home, take your painkillers regularly and you should be fine. Things should settle down after a few days.'

'Shit, Doc. That's almost exactly what that psycho-fuck said. No need to tell me how to look after the wound; he's already done that. Twice.'

Instinctively, Heather reached out and placed a calming hand on her husband's knee, simultaneously locking her eyes with his, willing him to apologise for the outburst. Jason took heed.

'Sorry doctor, I didn't mean to be rude. I'm under a lot of stress at the moment.'

Mr Farnorth remained passive.

'Don't worry. I understand that you find this upsetting, but things will be slightly different, given this is a proper hospital, and remember, you will not only be looking after your wound, but the prosthetics too.'

Seeing his patient nod, the surgeon continued.

'One more thing and then I'm done. I promise.'

'Go on.'

The patient spoke on the wave of an involuntary sigh.

'We recommend that you gently pull the prosthesis in a downward direction on a daily basis to help set it in the correct position, but don't worry, we'll provide you with literature when you get back from theatre.'

The patient having no questions to ask, the consultant left the room to scrub up.

Despite his surroundings being a reminder of the rogue surgeon's home-spun version of a hospital, and despite the prolonged pre-operation chat from the eminent Mr Farnorth, Jason was excited that he had reached the moment of restoration without being snatched again. Clearly, he would continue to make his whereabouts known to all and sundry, post-op, but he would be able to carry out his business wearing decent clothes – not those of a delinquent youth, stricken with acne – and he could see himself returning to work as soon as the soreness had past and the dressings were off. Heather was pleased to note such a positive change in her husband; all the more reason to be disappointed then when, all of a sudden, Jason began shaking uncontrollably, a body-quake, affecting every muscle from top to toe. She was not to guess, but the trigger had been nothing more than a passing tea trolley, the cups chinking together in much the same way as had the jars intended for the long term storage of her husband's body parts.

Pre-op medication solved the problem.

***

A few days later, Heather discovered her husband standing naked before a full-length mirror; a sure sign things had improved, there being no blankets blocking his reflection in the event of an unintended glance.

'Do you think that if a stranger saw me right now, he'd know I'm part man, part rubber?'

'Firstly, I'd be worried if there was a strange man in our bedroom.'

At that, Heather realised what she had said, feeling as though a neon sign had was suddenly illuminating her guilty conscience, but the words had only significance for her, leaving her husband's expression unchanged. Without missing more than a couple of beats, she took up position beside her husband, looked to his reflection and offered her unbiased appraisal.

'Seriously though, that Mr Farnorth has done an amazing job. Really, you can't tell.'

Jason sighed.

'What's wrong?' Heather asked, taking gentle hold of her husband's upper arm.

'Nothing really, other than the kidnaps, the surgery and the living in constant fear.'

Heather's gentle grip became a soft massage.

'I know it's hard, but try not to dwell on it. Concentrate on the positives. You're on your way to getting your life back; we all are. Put some clothes on, the kids will be home soon. You never know, give it a few days and maybe we can take the new you for a test drive. I'll show you how good you look.'

Jason smiled.

'We'll have to be careful. I don't want it falling off just when we get to the good bit.'

'Do I detect a little joke? Have I got my old Jason back?'

'I don't know about that, but to be honest, I do feel the best I have in ages. I spoke with Martin Feller this morning. He's agreed to let me go in to work for an afternoon – to see how I get on.'

'That's brilliant news. I'm so pleased for you.'

19

Throughout the morning, Jason made himself ready for work, ironing his shirt, tie, socks and underpants.

In the days preceding, Heather had twice braved the bitter chill of the late November air, walking to and from the local parade of shops, dropping in and subsequently collecting Jason's work clothes from the dry cleaners.

The face that had hardened against the oncoming wind now showed it was capable of other things, softening to a curious smile.

'Why on Earth are you ironing your underwear?'

Her husband responded, adopting a coy demeanour.

'Don't laugh. I'm just being thorough.'

His response was a toned down version of the truth. Jason wanted to be as prepared as it was possible to be. So many things had been beyond his control of late, he was making the most of what he could influence, hoping to boost his confidence on what promised to be a big step along the path towards normality. To this end, everything he needed, or could possibly want, had been thought of, so that all was just as it should be, and better, including the expensive pen slipped into his inside pocket, and a small wad of virgin bank notes, withdrawn from the ATM, tucked within his wallet.

Whereas Heather had dressed in order to walk the children to school, Jason had chosen to remain in his pyjamas and bathrobe for the majority of the morning, eating lunch several hours too early, to avoid the possibility of contaminating his clean clothes with stray particles of food. He then took to showering, dressing and preening, timed to achieve perfection at the exact moment he was due to leave; a devised timetable with plenty of wriggle room, allowing for the addition of a few new subroutines.

Finally, Jason lowered himself into the driver's seat, closed his eyes and began performing an established set of breathing exercises, taught to him by the lovely Natasha Goodman, without whom his mental state would have collapsed many weeks before, bobbing beneath the waves for the third time, perhaps never to break surface again.

As he breathed he visualised his wife's smile, given freely in response to his quip about losing his ear during sex; the wet kiss, planted on his lips by Lily in gratitude for him having read her favourite story; and smiled fondly, recalling how Charlie had hugged him tightly and said innocently, 'Night, Daddy. I love you. I like your new ear.'

His eyes remained closed as the routine of starting the car commenced; his left foot pressing down on the clutch; the key plunging into the ignition barrel; twisting forward to bring life to the vehicle. He then performed one last, slow exhale, opened his eyes, and gave an almost imperceptible nod, encouraging his mind to believe he was ready.

Butterfly wings continued to churn the contents of his stomach for the duration of the journey, becoming ever more frantic as the supermarket came into view. Perhaps it had been foolish not to have his wife in the car for support, but he feared her being put in danger - should he be snatched again - more than he feared facing his boss; his colleagues; the customers. Besides, as she was not permitted to drive, and the store was far from her favourite shops, there would have been nothing more for her to do than remain in the car, abandoned like a dog by owners who had no thought for animal welfare.

Jason made his way through the staff entrance and directed his path towards Martin Feller's office, all the while hoping the weakness and shaking that had spread throughout his body was not visible to anyone who saw him. Close to his destination, he detoured into the men's toilet, where having checked the facilities were not in use, he tested his spoken voice. To his relief, as far as he could tell, it was normal; certainly if he consciously put his mind to sounding confident, suppressing the subtle underlying quaking of his vocal chords.

In the main corridor, Jason encountered several employees whose heads turned in his direction as he walked past them. Not sure how to react, some managed an awkward smile; none managed to say a word. At the end of the corridor, he knocked on his line-manager's door and entered, his head leading the way, checking he was not interrupting someone else's meeting. On seeing Jason's face appear around the door frame, Martin rose from behind his desk, enthusiastically, to greet his colleague with an outstretched arm and a firm handshake.

'Jason! Good to see you back. I knew you were made of strong stuff. Here, have a seat. I'll put the coffee on.'

Martin broke the ice with small talk, but soon found himself returning to the only subject he really knew anything of, or cared about – the business. Targets were the thing he lived by, Jason suspecting the man imposed his own set on his family. Rather than being dulled by such conversation, Jason found himself being sucked into the numbers; the hirings and firings; the latest promotions; and future plans for the store. The men could have spoken for the rest of the shift, but both knew there was never time to just sit and talk.

Martin placed a call, inviting Jason's team to the office, having previously given them no warning, in case their manager had experienced a last minute change of mind. The delay in their arrival was filled with further talk on the price of beans and where those products should be placed. By the time the double rap on the door came, Jason had forgotten his nerves and greeted his team with a self-assured smile.

'Well, I'm back...a flying visit this time, but I hope to return to my normal duties as soon as possible.'

Five of the six women, squeezed into what was a modest-sized room, managed to say the right thing, but no more, being overwhelmed by the elephant in the room. The sixth, Anna Richardson, was not so debilitated.

'Come here, let's have a look.'

Her soft, ageing hands grabbed her boss' cheeks, rotating his head to one side.

'That's amazing.'

Several times she turned his head from side to side, making comparison between the rubber ear and the genuine article.

'That's so clever.'

Her actions were wrong on so many levels, but her manager did not mind in the least, judging it better to have his head worked loose by an irreverent member of staff than to discover his appearance shocked her into silence.

Witnessing their co-worker's actions, the other five made their own examinations, showing restraint by politely shifting their positions, leaving their boss' head oriented to the front. Having done so, the team returned to work, filing out through the office door, each expressing how nice it was to see him. A short while later he joined them on the shop floor, performing his work in exactly the way he had always done, up until the fateful night of the first abduction. However, as previously agreed with Martin, Jason finished the shift early, leaving at the more sociable hour of five. In truth, he was grateful, having to admit quietly to himself he was feeling unusually fatigued.

Exiting through the staff entrance, he re-entered the store through the main doors, as a customer, picking from a bucket a bunch of flowers he thought would particularly appeal to his wife.

There was no need for Jason to exercise routine or sub-routine before setting off for home; the deed had been done; his personal battle won. Still reluctant to use the Old Felworth Road, along which he had first been kidnapped a little more than two months ago, he instead opted to take the dual carriageway; the longer route, but one that provided street lights and plenty of other road users to act as witness, so deterring any Romanian gang members who might otherwise be tempted to disrupt his journey. Although he was prepared to be taken again - indeed expected it - now was not the right moment. So much had gone his way these past few days, Jason wanted an opportunity to ride the wave; to be with Heather and the kids; to enjoy his wife's cooking; to read to Charlie and Lily, before kissing each good night; to go to bed early and perhaps reignite the intimate facet of his marriage. If he had to be taken again, his only request to whatever force it was that determined his life, was to be taken tomorrow.

Sticking to a modest sixty miles per hour, Jason remained in lane one – 'the slow lane'. This being rush hour, even the executive cars in lane two, with their imagined Fast Passes, barely managed to break the speed limit. Among their number were many commercial vehicles, the two classes of transport so close to each other that sleekly sculptured works of popular modern art melded with the slab-sided tradesmen's boxes. Any one of the latter might have belonged to his abductors, but for one of them to sweep across, forcing Jason off the road, would surely result in arrest. Hence, Jason dismissed the entire line of traffic as presenting little or no threat.

A Vauxhall Vectra estate car accelerated to leave a lay-by; a tricky manoeuvre for anyone wishing to re-join a busy carriageway on which most people drove too close to each other. Some thought it their job to prevent additional traffic merging with the flow, becoming angry when anyone had the audacity to attempt to slip in front of them. Whether by luck or by judgement, whether demonstrating bravery, or the driver's eyes were shut tight, the vehicle moved in to lane one, a few cars ahead. Having done so, it slowed; hardly the way to repay the thoughtfulness of whoever had inconvenienced themselves by letting him in. As soon as it was safe to do so – perhaps a little too soon – the two cars between Jason and the Vauxhall pulled over into lane two and overtook. Annoyingly, the Vauxhall then accelerated to the speed the traffic had been flowing at before it had pulled out. Jason shook his head, tutting in response to such erratic behaviour, but then settled down, continuing on his way at a comfortable distance, allowing a two second gap, providing a text book safe breaking distance.

A short while later, captured in his headlights, Jason noted movement in the back of the Vauxhall; a dog perhaps, but then a sheet of paper appeared, pressed against the rear window. Something was written upon it in bold letters, but being above the headlight beam, and at some distance, Jason could not make out what it said. As if the driver in front realised this was the case, the Vauxhall slowed, closing the gap. The manoeuvre was in no way violent, requiring no panicked reaction. However, the note that came into focus not only required such a response, it demanded one.

'FOLLOW'

Jason knew its meaning; knew who had written it; knew what was in store.

The sign disappeared, to be replaced a moment later with a banner, three sheets of paper joined together upon which were printed the words, *'FLASH TO CONFIRM.'*

Without need for a second's thought, Jason's thumb clung to the steering wheel as his fingertips pulled twice on the stalk.

The cars continued to travel in convoy, all the while Jason becoming ever more pressured by the gravity of his situation, trying desperately to boost his mood by the thought of the hidden camera beneath the bonnet, capturing every second of the emerging scenario: the make, colour and age of the vehicle; its model; the registration number; the hand written signs; and perhaps it was yet to capture clear images of the abductors, once they had stopped.

They had chosen a bold plan. Other drivers, passing in lane two, were bound to see the note displayed in the rear window and would be able to report this to the authorities when the police published a request for witnesses over the coming hours and days.

The vehicles indicated and pulled off. Jason continued to follow, each exit and turning taking them deeper into the countryside.

A sudden thought occurred, causing Jason to reach for his phone and activate the video camera. With the device lying on the passenger seat, he spoke up, ensuring the microphone would pick up his voice, knowing the lens could see nothing but the roof lining, lit dimly by the glow from the dash board and some accent lighting.

'It looks like I'm going away again. Charlie, Lily, make sure you are well behaved for Mummy. Heather, try not to worry. I'm sure I'll see you again soon. I love you all.'

The recording ended with a press of the red button, after which the phone was dropped into the door pocket, providing it a degree of anonymity.

To have added other information, useful to the police, was to run the risk of upsetting his kidnappers. Far safer then to keep the message short and hope it came to the ears of his wife and kids.

The convoy came to a secluded spot - a vast expanse of weed-infested concrete, in front of a derelict barn, outside which a featureless van waited. The number plate was probably false but its captured image might prove to be another nail in the surgeon's coffin.

As soon as the small convoy had come to a halt, Jason got out of his car and stood patiently and passively, waiting to be set upon. He left his headlights ablaze, assisting the camera within the grille to capture details as sharp as the device was able. He did not have to wait long. Three men approached, dressed in black, one gripping an automatic pistol in his right hand. Two gloved hands guided him closer to the van, where without protest, he succumbed to the indignity of having his clothes cut from him, only the dry-cleaned blazer surviving intact, it hanging from the hook in the rear of his abandoned car. The operation was as slick as the first, there being none of the mistakes of the second. His mouth was taped, his arms and legs bound, his head covered with the same, stinking hood as on previous occasions. Clearly, the speaking associate had either got his act together, or had been sacked. Strangely, Jason's only concern was for his prosthetic ear; that the roughly achieved placement of the hood might dislodge it, but it seemed to have stood the test.

As he was lifted into the rear of the van, his thoughts were not fearful, but pragmatic: hoping someone would switch off the headlights before they left, lest the battery went flat; that his car would be found before the bunch of flowers, nestled on the passenger seat, began to wilt, hoping they would somehow find their way to Heather; and that having told no one of the hidden dashcam, Crime Scene Investigators would discover it.

The rear doors shut. Jason's penis was fed into a proprietary urine collection bag. The van's engine sprang to life, immediately muffled by the return of the familiar soundtrack of random noises. The captive was surprised to find himself lying on top of a blanket, one doubled over, presumably for comfort. A second was placed over his naked body. Remembering the look of disapproval on the surgeon's face when last Jason arrived at the makeshift hospital, he suspected he knew who he had to thank for that little luxury, if thanks could be given to a man who continued to destroy his life, piece by piece.

Unbeknown to Jason, the man with the gun tucked the weapon inside the waistband of his trousers in order to free his hands to lift a can of petrol and gather the remnants of his victim's clothing. Dowsing one with the other, a sodden rag was placed on the driver's seat of Jason's Fiesta and another on that of the Romanian's abandoned Vauxhall. Doors, bonnet and rear hatches were quickly opened wide, the remaining petrol being distributed equally across the two interiors. A single match, cast from a safe distance, set the Vauxhall instantly ablaze, the dull whoosh failing to reach the captive's ears. Opening the rear door of Jason's car, the man in black discovered the pristine blazer, and within it a wallet from which he took several crisp bank notes, a credit card and a small slip of paper, the significance of which brought an unseen smile to his face. A further smile was generated through the callous act of discarding the last drops of fuel onto the bunch of brightly coloured, freshly cut flowers. A second match caused a second fireball that grew further than anticipated, singeing the masked man's eyebrows, exposed through the single aperture surrounding his eyes.

In a way many people would fail to understand, Jason felt relaxed, a deliberate state of mind that helped him draw sufficient oxygen to his lungs, given he relied upon his nostrils alone. By comparison to previous occasions, he had been made reasonably comfortable; there was no need for him to commit new evidence to memory; and by now the regime promised few surprises. His greatest concern was not knowing what piece of his body he would be returning home without. Other than that, he had endured before and he would endure again, and despite whatever the cross-dressing maniac promised him, surely the accumulated evidence from three abductions would be enough to prevent a fourth.

The routine on arrival at the bungalow was just that – routine. Both Jason's immediate wishes soon became fulfilled – to breathe fresh air and to feel a soft surface beneath his bones, softer than two layers of blanket, placed over a corrugated steel floor. The inevitable injection was welcomed too as it stole Jason's sadness at not being at home as planned, sharing with his family the best aspects of what had been, for the most part, a good day.

As he drifted from focussed reality, Jason felt the surgeon's gloved finger prod the area around his replacement ear, and then his scrotum, but he cared for none of it. The surgeon could examine whatever he wished; nothing would disturb the calmness of mind he now felt.

***

Jason woke the following morning to the smell of freshly made coffee and buttered toast. His bindings had been removed, leaving him the freedom of the steel tether, along which he had been given the freedom to walk, wearing the adapted clothes of previous abductions. Noticeable was the fact he had not yet been prepared for his next *procedure*, the reason for which was soon to be explained by a very tall man, dressed as an aging woman, holding a slender electronic notepad, his only means of communication with the man over whom he towered.

'I have decided not to rush things and to place less pressure on my associates. Hence, we will proceed tomorrow.'

No matter what was the content of the statement, it was always delivered in the same plummy British voice, never differentiating between good and evil. She was a slave to her master, doing his bidding without question. She lied about her personality. Those who might hear her issue road directions would think she was helpful, classy, sexy even. Little did they know she was capable of issuing threats of torture and death. Jason believed such a person deserved to be recognised for what she was. She hid behind a synthesiser because her voice was her greatest asset, while her features had to be grotesque. She deserved an ugly name appropriate to her looks - Gretchen; a name that conjured in his mind a woman in a man's body, laced with performance enhancing drugs; a shot-putter with large, hairy moles prominent on her chin.

As the surgeon slipped from the room, Jason spoke beneath his breath.

'So, Gretchen, since when did psychopaths start caring for the welfare of their henchmen?'

20

Nigel Chambley's index finger pressed the doorbell at 54 Russell Way. His colleague stood back a little, not wishing to be the person to confront Heather Ressler, to confirm her husband had been taken yet again. Surprisingly, it was Charlie, accompanied by his sister, Lily, who answered, both still wearing their pyjamas, despite it being close to eleven o'clock on a school morning.

'Oh, hello kids, we've come to talk with Mummy.'

'Daddy's gone away again, hasn't he? Why does Daddy keep going away?'

Nigel looked lost for words as he considered how he might answer his own children, given similar circumstances. They were so young; so innocent; so ignorant of the cruel things one man was capable of doing to another. Jane detected her partner's hesitation and stepped forward, walking between the two children, guiding them inside with a friendly hand on each of their shoulders. They stalled in the hallway. Jane dropped to her haunches, bringing her face level with those of the two children she now embraced.

'Every now and then your daddy has to go and see someone. Unfortunately, he never knows when he'll be needed, and he's never quite sure how long he'll be. We want to help all of you so he doesn't have to go away from you ever again.'

'What happened to Daddy's ear?' Charlie asked.

'That doesn't matter does it? He's got two again now, hasn't he?'

Charlie's face dropped, as children are wont to do when feeling upset.

'Some of the boys at school are nasty to me, saying my daddy's a monster because he's only got one ear.'

Jane placed her crooked index finger beneath his chin and raised it so the boy could no longer look towards the floor.

'Well, now you can tell them they're wrong, can't you.'

Jane could see this line of enquiry continuing for a long time, the questions becoming more probing and difficult to answer. Thankfully, a noise came from the lounge – a disturbed sound, as though someone was locked in a nightmare from which they could not wake, issuing moans and whimpers associated with fighting off an assailant, dreamt up by a troubled mind in a sleeping body.

'Okay, you two, what have you been doing this morning?' Jane asked with the serenity of a psychotherapist.

'We were drawing,' Lily answered, brightly.

'Then perhaps you can show Nigel here your drawings, while I talk with Mummy.'

A deal was struck, much to the horror of Jane's colleague.

Heather was to be found curled up at one end of the sofa, crying into one of what Jane imagined to be Jason's unwashed tee-shirts. The detective walked across the room and made to sit down next to her. Without lifting her head from the sodden piece of clothing that caught tears and mucus in abundance, Heather nonetheless acknowledged her guest by rotating in her seat, dropping her feet to the carpet, and in doing so made room for the detective's hips. Given Heather's physical appearance and display of emotional frailty, it was difficult to believe the woman had anything to do with her husband's abductions, despite the circumstantial evidence to the contrary – unless it was the case Heather had got into something she had not believed would go so far.

'I understand Jason has not returned since you rang us.'

Heather shook her head, her face still buried.

'We had a briefing this morning. We've already confirmed with Martin Feller that Jason left work at five. One of the cashiers recalls he popped back into the store to purchase a bunch of flowers. He said they were for you. The ANPR – sorry, the automatic number plate recognition – picked him up on the arterial road, but then we lost him. He must have chosen the busier route to make it more difficult for the kidnappers, there being so many other road users at that time. I suppose, with the nights drawing in so early at this time of year, whatever they did, they felt they didn't have to wait until later.'

Heather's fingers released the tee-shirt, letting it drop to her lap, allowing her instead to massage her temples, desperately trying to ease away whatever it was that filled her head. She had still not uttered a single word.

'Heather, what about the children? Have they had breakfast?....Would you like me to call their grandparents? The school?'

The massaging ceased but Heather's hand remained attached to her head, supporting its weight. She nodded, grizzled and began rocking from the waist. Prompted by the detective, she stopped to unlock her phone which she kept permanently close to her side in case she received news. The act of operating the screen to bring up her parents' contact details focussed her mind sufficiently to halt the downward spiral; at least temporarily. However, she was in no state to place the call herself.

Jane left the room, out of earshot of the children, who sat with Nigel at the kitchen table; out of earshot of Heather, without whom the detective felt she could speak more freely. The call was brief. In fact, the detective had only to mention to Mrs Truman that her son-in-law had not returned home for a third time, for her to begin shouting to her husband to get in the car.

Before returning to Heather, Jane checked to see how her colleague was faring. At least he had children; something Jane would like to have had herself by now, but had not yet found the right woman. Nigel had made the most of his task, getting the children to draw what came to mind, given suggested themes: their family; their school; what made them happy; what made them sad. The idea to do so had been prompted by one particular picture Charlie had put down on paper, showing his daddy with only one ear and a little boy – a stick man wearing shorts – with a downturned mouth. Charlie had drawn the Ressler family, all four of them holding hands, with a big sun in the sky, flowers, a tree, and the standard four-windowed house of his age group. Lily had drawn squares that she explained were books and that her daddy was reading them to her at bedtime. It was only then Nigel could make out what was supposed to be a bed. Lily – bless her – was no artist.

Nigel pointed to the image of Jason, minus an ear. The colours chosen were purple and black.

'Okay, Heather, your mum and dad are on their way to look after the kids. So that's that sorted. Now, what are we going to do with you?'

The suggestion she might benefit from a spell in a mental health unit acted as the psychological equivalent of rebooting a computer.

'I'll be fine. Once Mum and Dad have taken the kids, I'll have a shower and make something to eat and I'll feel a lot better. I'd be grateful if you could talk to the school. I don't want to start myself crying again.'

'Of course, but are you going to be okay on your own?'

'I can phone my Mum at any time, or I can always pop next door. Bob and Irene always have a jigsaw on the go, and they don't mind sharing.'

Angela took this to be tongue in cheek, a sign Heather was mentally stronger than she had given her credit for. At least the children were in no danger and so there was no need to involve Social Services.

The detectives remained at number 54 until Charlie and Lily had been whisked from the scene, excited to be spending time once again with their favourite grandparents. On leaving the house, Angela bumped into Irene Spillman who guessed something was wrong, given the length of time the detectives had been in attendance.

'Don't worry officer, Bob and I will make sure she's all right.'

***

True to her word, Heather freshened up, cooked a light meal for herself and ate at least some of it. She then spent the afternoon washing, ironing, vacuum cleaning, and finding places to return things to; toys that had found their way into the kitchen; plates, bowls and cups in the bedrooms that needed to go back downstairs. By the end of it, Heather was in need of another shower, but chose instead to open a bottle of wine, hoping it would see her through the evening; if not, she had more.

Slumped on the sofa, Heather settled down to not paying any attention to whatever was on TV. A book lay open next to her, one she had been meaning to read for several weeks now. She had managed the first paragraph but no more, and even that had made no sense, the words spoken internally but not translated into thought. She had scanned social media, hoping for news, but finding none; just the random jottings of people experiencing normal lives, posting trivial thoughts on trivial matters.

At eight o'clock, the doorbell sounded, cutting through the nothingness of the evening. Heather did not wish to speak to or see anyone, but she had never been one for hiding behind the settee. Besides, it might be news of her husband. The thought livened her pace, causing her to open the front door with purpose, but her enthusiasm died the moment her eyes fell upon her visitor.

'Oh, it's you. Are you here to help, or just hoping for another shag?'

John Ainsley looked hurt that she should say such a thing, but did nothing to retaliate.

'Actually, I was wondering if you'd heard anything about Jason.'

'Jason?'

'Yes, your mum said he'd gone missing again.'

'Well, yes, he has, but how come you've been speaking to her? You hoping to shag my mum as well as me?'

John's eyebrows rose, his head dipping, challenging her to consider whether she had the right to make such an accusation.

'No, but then I might have if she'd got me pissed and grabbed my balls.'

The tone of his voice was not aggressive. Instead it accepted the part he had played, but reminded Heather who had been the instigator. The sudden change in Heather's expression suggested his message had got through.

Not wishing for the situation to spiral downwards, he quickly addressed her first question, there being nothing controversial about it.

'Anyway, if you must know, I tiled your parents' bathroom a while back? Don't you remember? The other day I got a missed call from her. She left a message asking if I could go back and do the kitchen. I only got round to phoning her this afternoon and that's when she dropped into the conversation about Jason. I had to come round…to check you're okay.'

The pause was unnatural, prompting Heather to study her visitor's face intently.

'So, why are you really here? I know that look. You want to say something but you're scared.'

John peered back at Heather, knowing that in the time they had been together she had learned to read him like a book, and judged there was nothing to be gained by dancing around further, avoiding the true purpose of him calling.

'Okay, so here it is. I take it you haven't told Jason about us?'

'No.'

'Thought not.'

'And?'

'Well, it's just that I haven't seen you since the police interviewed me...thought you'd want me to tell you what they said.'

'Go on,' Heather responded, suspiciously.

'I confessed we'd had sex...'

'What!? You told them?'

'Yes, but I explained it was the first and last time; that we were an item a long before Jason...and that I was worried you might later cry rape, when you'd realised what a mistake it was...I told them about the video...I told them you had asked me to delete it soon after Jason came home.'

Heather eyed her visitor with even greater suspicion.

'And?'

'Heather, the police have seen the video; they took a copy of it.'

'What!'

'I know, but I was frightened. As it happened it's kept the police off my back. As far as I know they're no longer treating me as a suspect.'

'Bully for you, but what about me? They already think I have something to do with all this – you can tell – and now they've seen the grieving wife, drunk and naked, offering herself out to the first person who calls. Brilliant.'

'I know what you're saying and I'm sorry. Look, there's only one thing to do now. You have to tell Jason before they do....as soon as he returns home. I'm not saying it for my benefit - he'll probably want to kill me – I just think it's for the best.'

The ex-boyfriend and convenient lover left shortly afterwards, consigning Heather to a night alone and a second bottle of wine.

***

Later the same evening, DS Alan Honeyman knocked on his boss' door and entered without waiting to hear whether DI Bickley wanted him in the room or not.

'Guv, Jason Ressler's bank card has been used – a petrol station; about a two hour's drive from here. I've been on the phone to the manager there and they have CCTV. He's burning it to disk as we speak.'

The Detective Sergeant had done the right thing, lifting the DI's spirits more than he knew.

'Bloody excellent! They've made a mistake at last - a big one.'

DS Honeyman raised a cautionary hand.

'I don't want to piss on your fire, Guv, but couldn't this simply be another case of misdirection? They've done it before. Remember the holiday brochure and the love note from an old granny?'

Richard Bickley accepted the warning with a nod, but added a smile to indicate he was feeling lucky.

'Well, there's only one way to find out for certain. Put Fallas and Pace onto it, if you please.'

'I'm well ahead of you there, Guv, they're off to see the petrol station manager first thing in the morning.'

21

Having no recollection of being moved from one room to another, and there being prepared for an operation, the reluctant patient wondered at what point during the night the transfer had taken place. Tales of Father Christmas, repeated generation upon generation, convinced susceptible young minds of a fat old man coming down the chimney during the dead of night. In reality, parents all over the world waited until just moments after their children finally surrendered to the comfort of their pillows, before hastily filling festive stockings, then retiring to bed themselves, reserving energy for the big day ahead. It seemed logical the surgeon would act in a similar fashion, while the sedation was at its most effective and while his Romanian henchmen – the antithesis of Santa's little helpers – were still on site to assist.

Such a random thought tamed a fear that otherwise threatened to consume the patient entirely, but the distraction was all too brief. There being no other burning question to fill the void, Jason resorted to asking himself the day and date; a question not reserved for the occasion, but one he posed whenever he wished to divert his train of thought, or fill an empty moment. Ironically, the question, designed to break a loop, often became its own loop, causing him to fret whenever he found he could not stop asking it.

The answer to this simple question was Friday, 2nd December, as it would be later in the day when he asked it again, preferring his mind to think of something other than the loss of another piece of his body.

The calculation of day and date being nothing more than a frantic stopgap, Jason moved his foot to one side and looked down the length of his body to the far end of the room. The witness was there, just as before; just as she always was. Indeed, everything was as before, the only exception being the directional standard lamp, presumably meant for use during the operation. On this occasion it was lit, the beam inadvertently pointing towards the temporary studwork wall. Previous studies of his immediate environment had revealed vague outlines of furniture and wall paintings, left in situ when the room was converted for use as an operating theatre. Now, with the penetrating power of the lamp, shining through the heavy duty, green plastic sheeting, a new detail emerged - a picture frame, resting on a shallow shelf. Although Jason accepted he would not be able to pick out the subjects of the photograph in a police line-up, he could at least say, with confidence, they were an ageing man and woman – presumably a married couple - standing in front of a bungalow, itself set back on what appeared to be a gravel drive. A thought crossed his mind; a notion that this might actually be the very building in which he lay. If not, he was sure the two were at least connected. An excited mind told him he must study the image in as much detail as possible, but try as he might, Jason could not shift his bindings in order to close the distance. If the picture contained a house number, or a name, the photograph would keep its secret. Nevertheless, the property boasted other features that might lead to its identity. The bungalow was plain-rendered, painted canary yellow, and in the garden were three equally tall poplar trees, standing in line to the left of the building, having the proportions of cricket stumps, minus their bails.

As important as this discovery was, all interest in the frame, and the image it protected, was lost in an instant when the patient heard the key turn in the door. Hoping to fool the surgeon into thinking he had not yet returned to consciousness, Jason's head rolled away from the light source, his eyes closing - too tightly to be natural.

Noticing none of what his captive had seen, the surgeon repositioned the lamp, before rotating his captive's head towards the beam, giving Jason the perfect excuse to feign his wakening.

A single tap of the screen caused Gretchen to issue a short statement.

'Let us get this unpleasantness out of the way. Then, perhaps you will learn more about what both of you have done.'

By his actions, the surgeon was clearly not in the mood for engaging in conversation. Placing the iPad down, he set about making final preparations, allowing his patient a few moments to focus upon the words the device had spoken; to consider their precise meaning.

What both of you have done...both of you.

The statement suggested a strong link between Jason and whoever had wronged both the surgeon and the mysterious disabled lady who was always there to oversee proceedings. It also pointed to there being just one other person at fault. If this was his father, surely the surgeon would punish his mother, and vice versa. If one of Heather's parents, the innocent mother or father would now have a cannula in their vein, not Jason. Given the limited size of their combined families, that left only his wife. Of course, the deduction did not mean Heather was guilty; only that the surgeon believed her to be.

As much as Jason was keen to explore the notion further, for him the time had run out, the latest measured dose of Midazolam reducing his interest to that normally associated with watching a freshly painted surface lose its sheen.

On waking, the patient found himself in the recovery room, a beaker placed close to his head so he might draw water through a straw without shifting his body. Jason quenched his thirst, lubricating his parched throat in the process. Feeling no pain, he had no other option but to ask his tormentor a direct question, hoping it would not be met with summary punishment.

'What have you done to me?'

He need not have worried. His question being so predictable the surgeon already had his electronic notepad in hand, his stylus hovering over the play button, causing only a momentary delay before Gretchen oozed a response.

'You appear to be missing the point.'

The surgeon's eyes shifted towards the familiar collection of glass jars, standing upon the same chromed trolley of previous encounters. One in particular had been placed in the foreground, notable for its content – an index finger.

The reveal was always going to be a shock, but the way it was delivered doubled the effect. It was bad enough the crazed butcher should have taken Jason's finger, worse he had made a joke of it; worse still, it was no slip of the tongue – his comment had been typed; had taken effort; there had been an opportunity for him to think better of it, to delete the short sentence and compose something more sensitive to the situation.

Jason looked casually toward his bandaged right hand; a beaten man with insufficient fight left in him to feel or display anger.

'Please forgive me for that comment. I bring you here and treat you as I do to make others pay. You already suffer greatly for her sins yet you have always co-operated fully. You do not deserve such treatment.'

Jason thought nothing of this worthless apology. He had heard them before, yet still he was tortured; still his family was made to suffer. More significantly, Gretchen's shallow expression of regret had also been pre-prepared. For all the victim knew, the apology might have been written before the taunt.

The surgeon had prepared a third statement.

'Do you want to know why I chose to take it?'

The patient's ambivalence was clear, but still the recording continued to play. The victim could not help but listen, anticipating he would learn nothing. The surgeon, on the other hand, was more confident.

'If, on each occasion, I took a limb, our meetings would be too few. On the other hand, ten fingers; ten toes; feet; lower limbs: ears; nose; eyes. Then there are the internal organs: kidneys, one at a time; tonsils; appendix. I could take two thirds of your liver, let it regrow and harvest it again.

'Ultimately, this way we see one another many more times, offering you many more opportunities to learn what it is both of you have done.'

Gretchen's spoken passage was clear enough for even the most intellectually deprived village idiot to understand, the words striking helpless terror into the man it was intended to inform. Suffering three abductions – the loss of three pieces of his body – might be an episode in his life from which he could eventually hope to recover, albeit it given plenty of time and intensive one-to-one therapy, but there was not a man alive who could emerge from such proposed trauma with his mind, let alone his body, intact. This madman had to be caught, and before he could strike again, or Jason might as well be dead; an option to which he would give serious consideration if it were not for ensuring the continued welfare of his family. So desperate was he, his mind briefly found itself able to entertain a notion normally so abhorrent, it would be dismissed even before it was fully formed.

If Jason took his own life, his family would be taken instead, to suffer in his place, but if they all went together, the surgeon would be denied his perverted pleasures and their chronic suffering would end in an instant. The normally unthinkable remained a viable option for only the briefest passage of time before Jason came to his senses, his internal voice hurling abuse at him for displaying such weakness.

The surgeon was not finished tormenting him. Jason's eyes followed the madman's hands as they rearranged the jars, pushing to the front those that contained body parts from the two previous procedures.

'I have also removed those nasty replacements. I find it quite insulting you would seek to undo my work.'

A synthetic testicle – Jason's synthetic testicle - bobbed around, sharing a jar with the genuine article it sought to replace; similarly, two ears occupied another, one fake, one genuine. The titanium attachment screws had been removed from Jason's skull, and were resting on the bottom of the vessel, glinting through the preservative. Beyond this day there would be three wounds to tend to; three areas of his body that would remain covered; blankets would be reinstated over the mirrors; gloves, a hoodie and loose-fitting trousers would be worn at all times; or else he would simply choose to remain in a darkened room until the inevitable next visit from the Romanians.

The surgeon's stylus continued to tap the screen, causing Gretchen to make further comment; neither welcomed nor necessary.

'It would be difficult replacing your finger. In any event, I would advise against it; you would be wasting your time.'

At last the surgeon had finished saying his piece and exited the room, taking his chromed trolley with him. Soon after, the madman departed the premises to return the disabled witness to her usual place of abode.

Alone, Jason was left to lament the loss of his finger - the hand that caressed Heather's skin whenever they made love – and to come to terms with the fact that every forward step taken had been reversed, and more; and as if losing three pieces of his body were not enough, he now faced slow disintegration until the man he had been was no more than a memory and a series of pickled curios.

The surgeon's words replayed in his head, hearing them in the same plummy voice with which they had been delivered, 'You have already suffer for *her* sins.'

'*Her* sins.'

Jason repeated the abridged phrase aloud, emphasising the pronoun. Prior to hacking off his finger, his captor had given the strongest indication yet as to who was to blame. Here was another clue, so strong it made Jason wonder how it could take so many more operations to discover the truth. Perhaps the timetable was designed to facilitate him learning not only the who, but also the what, the why and the when.

'Christ, what has she done?'

Until now, Jason had refused to accept his wife might have any connection with his continuing ordeal. It was simply not in her makeup to cause pain to another; she worked to help those in trouble, not hurt them. However, the time had come to explore the idea and discount it, if at all possible.

He was no novice at re-living the abductions in minute detail. The memories he plucked from his head now filled an entire notebook; notes that included his wife's reaction when first setting eyes upon him in the hospital. It was understandable she would look shocked to see him, minus his right ear, but there had been something else – suspicion. Then the consultant had given evidence, supporting Jason's claims he had been taken and tortured. On hearing the news, Heather's expression changed. Jason could see it now – shock; not shock at what had happened, but shock to hear he was telling the truth.

Was it just possible she had arranged for him to be taught a lesson, but her wish had gone further than she had intended? At the time, Jason had put his wife's initial reaction down to the mistaken belief, common to both her and the police, that he had run off with Anna Richardson. If Heather had been so quick to accept this as truth, perhaps she had always harboured suspicions he had other women of interest. On the other hand, if any of this was true, how had it led to a woman being confined to a wheelchair, unable to speak for herself? For now, the jury was out.

***

While Jason spent his day in the company of a rogue surgeon, DCs Fallas and Pace raced to the forecourt of an unassuming petrol station, sited next to a single-lane A road, mid-way between two medium-sized towns.

Eric Campbell, the employed manager, remembered the man who claimed to be Jason Ressler, for being barely able to speak a word of English.

'Bloody foreigners. They should learn the language if they want to come over here.'

Drake Fallas remained professional, but could not let the comment die unnoticed, his family originating in Spain, the imputation being his own parents too were 'bloody foreigners.'

'Interesting, so what did this foreign chap buy?'

'Petrol and cigarettes.'

'And how many languages do you speak? For example, would you be able to ask for a tank of petrol and a packet of twenty Rothmans in Romanian?'

Unfortunately, Eric was too thick-skinned to realise the question was, in fact, a lesson.

'Wouldn't need to. English is the universal language. They all speak it – except this one, of course. Anyway, it wasn't twenty; more like two-hundred.'

Angela Pace made a note in her pocket book.

'Did he know the PIN?'

'Yes.'

Drake and Angela concluded their interview, taking into custody a DVD of the CCTV footage, provided by the bigoted Mr Campbell.

Back in their unmarked vehicle, Angela Pace ran the number plate of the car driven by Jason Ressler's imposter. It came back as registered to a motorcycle.

'Interesting.'

Drake was confused by his partner's reaction.

'Why do you say that? I'd have been more surprised if it *wasn't* a false plate.'

Angela offered her colleague a mint, gratefully received, and then took one for herself.

'Don't you see? You can't simply transfer a stolen plate from a bike to a car. For a start, it's the wrong shape and there's only one of them. It means our Romanian friends don't just nick the plates, they have the means to manufacture them. It's not much, but it helps paint a picture of who we're dealing with.'

Drake sucked on the mint, momentarily lost in contemplation.

'Nice one.'

It was then time for Angela to report their findings to DS Honeyman.

'Skipper, I've got a copy of the CCTV from the garage. It's definitely not Ressler. The man who used the card was a foreign national and looked to have been trying to get the most out of it before the card was stopped. If there was any doubt before, there isn't any more. Ressler's definitely been take again. Oh, and the gang aren't just stealing number plates, they're making them.'

By the time the brief update had been given, the detective's car was already en route back to base.

'Anything on tonight?' Drake asked casually.

Angela was grateful to have a partner with whom she could exchange small talk, the alternative being a long journey with only the radio for company, but now was not the right time, she having other matters to occupy her mind.

'So, how do you think the Romanian might have come to know Jason Ressler's PIN number.'

'PIN.'

'Sorry?'

'It's just PIN, not PIN number. Otherwise you're saying Personal Identification Number number.'

Angela's face produced a gentle grimace.

'Right, I'm glad we've sorted that one out. So, any idea how the Romanian came to have Ressler's *PIN*?'

Angela stressed the abbreviation, accepting her colleague's correction, hoping they could move on without further interruption.

Drake smiled, pleased to have scored a point in a game of which only he knew the nature, or the rules.

'Perhaps he was tortured,' he suggested.

'Maybe, but if that's the case, why now? Why not the first time, or the second? When he was taken from the lay-by, his cards were left in the car, untouched. The second time, his wallet was found on the hall table.'

DC Fallas, finding his thought processes hampered by the need to concentrate on the road, left his colleague to consider the conundrum.

'Okay, I take it we're agreed, Heather Ressler is not as innocent as she likes to make out.'

Drake responded with a dismissive 'yeh', spoken in a way that implied Angela's statement was both fact and common knowledge, and as such hardly worth mentioning.

His colleague continued, undeterred by Drake's sarcasm. In truth, he was merely a sounding board, his reaction being of little or no consequence.

'In which case, if Heather Ressler is behind all this, maybe giving the Romanians the PIN is some sort of sweetener.'

Drake gave an approving double nod, his lips puckered, his brow taut.

'Hmm, I like it. She pays the surgeon with something he can't get from his missus, and pays the Romanians in a way she doesn't think will implicate her.'

Angela produced a smug, contented smile which hung on her face for a moment, until her colleague added an afterthought.

'Nice, she gets her husband to pay for his own abduction.'

***

The day being remarkably quiet, Steven Billinge found himself despatched to an isolated location, next to an abandoned hay barn, responding to a report of two burnt out cars, received via a call to the police non-emergency line.

There was no expectation this would be anything more than stolen cars, used and abused by joy riders, before being burnt out in an effort to destroy forensic evidence. The only thing unusual was the fact there were two cars, apparently set alight at the same time. A quick check confirmed the absence of incinerated corpses, and gave up the identification numbers from both vehicles. A report would be filed; the owners would be given the news; insurance claims would be made; and the perpetrators would, in all likelihood, never be caught.

Satisfied he had fulfilled his duty, PC Billinge returned to base for a well-earned bite to eat in the canteen, and perhaps a chat with a fellow officer.

Sat alone at a table with a mug of tea and a packet of three individually wrapped shortbread biscuits, his attention focussed on the wall-mounted television, the officer anticipating the arrival of a familiar face in the room, or a friendly hand to drop gently onto his shoulder. He did not have to wait long.

'All right Steve?'

DCs Fallas and Pace were also of the opinion they had earned a snack and settled down beside their uniformed counterpart.

'Your guy's gone missing again.'

PC Billinge responded to Drake's comment with interest, guessing to whom he referred, this being the only case they had in common.

'Who? Jason Ressler?'

'That's him. Failed to come home again.'

'Where was he nobbled this time?'

'Don't know. ANPR picked up his vehicle eastbound on the arterial road, but then we lost him. Then we have his bank card being used two-hundred-and-fifty miles from here, and by the sounds of it, the person using the card was a Romanian.'

'The arterial? Shit, I responded to a callout near there, earlier this morning. Two cars burnt out. Do you think it might be connected?'

Drake looked completely nonplussed.

'Why is it always you?'

Steve Billinge shrugged his shoulders.

'Well, I've got a big patch and there's not many of us left since the cutbacks.'

22

Heather Ressler was grateful to witness the first light of dawn; relieved the ordeal of an almost sleepless night was nearing its end. Her thoughts were dull, her mouth dry, her pulse raised and loud. She felt dirty. She smelled unclean; the pores of her skin a factory of odours, bad bacteria, and alcohol. She felt simultaneously nauseous yet hungry.

This wife of a victim had temporarily lost her children to the care of her parents. Her husband had been snatched from her and *if* returned would, in all probability, be missing another piece of his body, cut from him with cruel finesse. Heather wondered how long she could continue to act as though none of it mattered; how she might react if her husband lost his nose; the nose that rested on her forehead when they stood and cuddled. The possibility of her returning to work was now just a distant possibility, Heather realising it would be impossible for her to mentor others while she found herself unable to cap her own desperation; to lift herself above the gloom. Her conclusion was stark. Soon she would be an alcoholic widow; her children in care; herself destitute. This was not the life she had dreamt of.

The not knowing was the worst: when and if Jason would return; how might he have been further mutilated; whether he would be taken again. Losing control over her destiny was almost as difficult to bear. The victim's wife was herself a victim.

Although worse for drink, Heather nevertheless felt defiant. It was time to take back control, though preparations would need to be made at a snail's pace, the disability of a hangover impairing her every movement. First something to calm the pain in her head; then something to calm her stomach – a greasy bacon sandwich; rehydration; a shower; her teeth; daywear; and finally makeup.

Heather made the bed, fluffing the duvet, plumping the pillows, smoothing the coverlet, intent on returning home at the end of the day, finally to sleep. At the same time she yearned to escape - to a destination she knew not where.

With a numbness of mind, Heather left the house, deliberately abandoning her phone on the hall table. Wherever she found herself, she knew she did not want to be found…unless she wished to be. Her body carried her to the railway station, transporting a mind that showed little interest in the path, or the environment through which it passed.

Waiting in the queue for a ticket, Heather reminded herself her children were being well looked after, and always would be, whatever the outcome.

'London please.'

From London she could go anywhere, or nowhere, or home.

She thanked the man for taking her money, smiled, took the rectangular piece of card in her fingers, fed it into one of the barriers, and passed through to the platform where she joined a heaving mass of power-dressed commuters. Among the hordes - each alone with their newspaper, or their phone - she was invisible. It being free of people, she chose to stand forward of the yellow line, in the textured danger zone. The regulars knew exactly where to wait, to line up perfectly with their favourite door when the train pulled in. All points in between were no man's land, extending to the very edge of the platform. Anyone who occupied these strips of real estate were destined to be disappointed when they discovered they were faced with a window. The irregulars were not a threat to the status quo. Because of this, barely a casual glance was given to this unfamiliar figure – a non-commuter – grey of skin, despite a generous application of foundation. As the minutes passed by, Heather's awareness of her surroundings faded, her thoughts turning inwards. There she heard her inner voice begin a slow chant.

'Nothing.'

She knew not why she kept saying this single, silent word, but repeated it over and over, regardless. Her tongue began to form the word, but still no sound escaped her mouth. Her eyes were blank; her face expressionless. Despite the trance, some part of her mind remained alert to the train entering the station. Her peripheral vision told her when to step out. Her subconscious mind had found a solution and decided to act. With her right foot extended into mid-air, her centre of gravity tilted forward, but at that moment a hand caught her shoulder and pulled her backwards, saving the train driver a lifetime of sleepless nights.

'Jesus!'

It was a man's voice, deep and bellowing.

Heather's saviour had folded his paper at just the right moment, leaving him time to observe and react.

Many tonnes of metal and glass, passing at speed so close to her face, brought Heather instantly to her senses.

Her intake of breath was audible.

'Oh God, thank you. I must have fainted.'

The event had not gone unnoticed, a member of the transport police being nearby to witness an apparent suicide attempt, gone wrong. He took control, took her arm, and guided the seemingly unstable woman away, back through the commuters whose minds were fixed on one thought – to claim their seat; the same seat as their unbreakable routine demanded. The man who had prevented her from delaying their departure caught her eye, asking if she was all right, but his concern was brief – shallow – years of conditioning causing him to fear the loss of his place on the train more than discovering why a fellow human might choose to take her own life.

The officer took Heather to a quiet room where he noted down her details. She claimed she had become light-headed, lost her balance and fallen forward. He did not look convinced. Heather explained she has been going through a lot of late and had not been eating or sleeping properly. The smell of alcohol continued to evaporate from her skin, offering its own explanation as to the cause of her dizziness.

'Is there someone who can come and fetch you? Your husband perhaps?'

Moments later, the officer would wish for the ground to open up and swallow him whole. He had heard of Jason Ressler; had read how the local supermarket raised funds to have his ear replaced. He was vaguely aware the man had been taken a second time, and was now to hear this woman's husband had been abducted again.

Understanding the woman's plight served only to increase the officer's concern. As a consequence, he insisted the taxi rank was not an option; nor was the suggestion she might simply retrace her steps on foot.

'My neighbour. Irene. She's always there for me.'

Surprised to discover Heather did not have a phone, a call was made on her behalf. The Spillmans did not need persuading, Irene's beckoning finger warning her husband to get his jacket, even before the conversation had ended.

Heather had promised the officer she would make an appointment to see her GP, but once home she no longer felt it necessary. Irene and a hot cup of tea were every bit as helpful as a packet of pills and a referral to a counsellor; someone just like herself.

Bob Spillman returned next door, to his jig-saw, which had reached the exciting stage when discoveries came with ever increasing frequency, building anticipation that the final piece would soon find its niche.

Meanwhile, Irene had become a counsellor of counsellors; an ear free to absorb whatever her neighbour found troubling.

'It's hard to explain how I feel, really. I exist, but I am not alive, if that makes any sense.'

'I can't say it does, dear. Perhaps you could try and explain it to me.'

Irene's client paused to gather her thoughts.

'At the station today, I felt nothing; as though I was nothing. I feel permanently uneasy, whether Jason's here or not; as though I'm waiting for the world to end. I feel so vulnerable. I can't concentrate on anything. My mind keeps wandering and all I have are negative thoughts, none of which have anything to do with my husband, or the kidnappers: memories of every embarrassing thing that has happened to me since I was a child.'

'Sounds like you need a chocolate Hobnob.'

Heather had directed her response to her fingers; interlocked and convulsing. Her neighbour's unexpected comment broke her stare.

'Do you know, Irene, I was going to say how I could probably describe a thousand different ways what it is like to be depressed, but...well, a biscuit...I mean, it's an improvement on me dwelling on the negatives, isn't it?'

Irene nodded.

'At least, when I'm better, I'll be more equipped to help my patients. I mean, if they need empathy, I'll have bags of it.'

The two women exchanged a weak smile.

'That's better. You have to admit, I've got you thinking about the positives now, not just the bad stuff, haven't I?'

Heather nodded; a subtle movement of the head, as though she was reluctant to admit her neighbour was right.'

'Heather, dear, I don't want to overstep the mark, but...you didn't really tell me what happened at the station. You weren't thinking of ending it, were you?'

The answer was not immediate, Heather's expression an indication she was not sure herself.

'I don't think so.'

'I don't think so? Either you were or you weren't. If you weren't then we'll say no more of it, but if you were, perhaps you need something more than a cup of tea and a biscuit. Let's face it, you've been through more than most people ever will, but you can't leave your children without a mother, and what about Jason? He needs you more than ever.'

'I'm not going to start popping pills if that's what you mean. It may sound odd, but I want to feel the pain. It heals me. I cry my tears; I cope; he comes home to me. That's when he needs me the most; that's when I need to be a strong wife – for Jason. When he's not here; that's the only time I get to release the real me.'

'And you need to be strong for Charlie and Lily too, don't forget that,' Irene reminded her patient.

'You're right, of course. Here's what I'll do. No more wine; no more self-pity; and I'll make sure I get a good night's sleep. I'm going to spend the rest of the day cleaning and then I'm going to ask my parents to bring the kids home. They can't keep missing school...Maybe tomorrow – to give me the day free.'

Irene had worked in offices all her life; had seen the evolution of technology; experienced customers paying in pounds, shillings and pence. She had witnessed the advent of word processors and then computers; printers taking over from photocopiers. Her career, though unexciting, had trained her for many things, but never how to read the minds of those with whom she interacted.

She stared into her neighbour's eyes, trying to fathom whether Heather was simply saying the things she believed Irene wanted to hear.

'Heather dear, I want to believe you...that a quick chat and a cuppa has made all the difference, but it terrifies me you're just saying it to get rid of me so you can do something stupid.'

For a moment, Heather contemplated responding with an indignant refrain, claiming that she would never – could never – take her own life and leave her children and her husband to the wolves, but she was an honest woman; too honest to lie to a friend.

'I'm not exaggerating when I say you have helped me immensely. And you're right in thinking my problems haven't been solved, but today has been a wake-up call and I'm never going to allow that to happen again. When Jason comes home, we'll deal with whatever they've done to him – together.'

'Irene listened carefully before making her judgement.

'Okay, but you know where we are if you need anything.'

Irene took her neighbour's hand in hers.

'I mean it, anything.'

***

Police Headquarters, Briefing Room, 09:00 hours, Saturday, 3 December:
Richard Bickley opened the briefing.

A new photo appeared on the smart board – a man, possibly of eastern European origin, with a close-cropped head of dark hair, his chiselled face sporting a trimmed beard.

'Okay, thanks to DCs Fallas and Pace, we now have this image of the person who has been using Jason Ressler's bank card. I take it we've published it in the usual places?'

DI Bickley looked about the room for confirmation and soon got it.

'Excellent. Right, Drake, I understand you've done some digging for us overnight.'

DC Fallas had waited patiently, quietly champing at the bit until given the green light.

'Yes Guv, firstly I should mention that the man using Jason Ressler's bank card, arrived at the petrol station driving a Volkswagen Golf GTi. However, the number plate, clearly visible in the CCTV footage, is associated with a motorcycle, registered to a Mr Benjamin Scott, resident in Lerwyn.'

DI Bickley nodded but did not interrupt the constable's flow.

'VIN numbers from both burnt-out vehicles have been retrieved. The first has been identified as Jason Ressler's Ford Fiesta. The second identifies a black Vauxhall estate, registered to one Mark Ancaster – also a resident of Lerwyn, getting on for three hundred miles from the farm where both vehicles were recovered.'

This time, the inspector could not help but pause proceedings to make comment.

'Now that is interesting. So, we have a clear connection to the north of England. Sorry, please, carry on.'

'The theft of Mr Ancaster's vehicle was reported three days ago. The ANPR that picked up Mr Ressler's vehicle on the arterial road did not pick up a Vauxhall bearing the index assigned to Mr Ancaster's vehicle, suggesting either it had been fitted with false plates, or it used an alternative route. Analysts have retrieved CCTV footage and have picked up a black Vauxhall estate, bearing a different index number, entering that stretch of the dual carriageway, approximately one hour before Jason Ressler is known to have left his place of work.'

DI Bickley's anticipation grew.

'Could it be the same vehicle?'

'Well, Sir, ANPR picked up the number plate of this vehicle at two points: the first, as I say, approximately one hour before Jason Ressler's Fiesta left the supermarket; the second, just over an hour later, only two seconds ahead of the Fiesta.'

The implications were immediately obvious to everyone in the room, but still the boss spelled it out.

'Well done Drake. Great piece of work.

'So, it looks like the abductors intercepted Jason's car along that stretch of road. Given the delay, they must have been parked in a lay-by. The occupants may have got bored and thrown something from the window, or it's possible other vehicles used the lay-by at the same time. I want the exact spot identified and searched, and I want signs deployed asking for witnesses. If necessary, pull people over and ask whether they saw anything.

'Right, we know where they made contact, but how did they persuade Mr Ressler to leave an A road and follow them to a secluded spot?'

Jane had a suggestion.

'A gun? Someone in the back, holding it up to the rear window. They were clearly driving close in front so it would have been visible in the headlights. We know they're armed?'

'Hmm, unlikely, given the number of potential witnesses, and the complete absence of calls made to the police. It would seem no one saw anything suspicious; at least nothing that bothered them sufficiently to consider reporting it. Oh well, if we're lucky we'll find a witness to give us the answer. If not, we may have to wait for Jason Ressler's explanation in person.

'In the meantime I have two other questions. The number plate of the Vauxhall captured on the arterial road; have we seen it before – at the supermarket?'

Mikala Braid, the analyst, raised a pen.

'No Sir, but the false plates used are registered to another black Vectra, so it seems they have been chosen carefully to avoid suspicion.'

'Thank you Mikala. The index number they cloned, I don't suppose that was registered in Lerwyn too, was it?'

'Liverpool, sir.'

'Okay, not far then. Strange that they should be so careful to use cloned plates from similar cars, but then use motorcycle plates on a Volkswagen. I'm thinking our man who used the bank card is a bit of a rogue elephant.'

Mikala could offer no comment, but made a note to work on her boss' theory.

DI Bickley's focus widened.

'Right, we have the theft of the burnt out Vectra from Lerwyn. We also have a cloned index number, connected to a motorcycle, registered in the very same town. We also have plates cloned to the burnt out Vectra, registered to another Vauxhall Vectra, registered in Liverpool, not far from Lerwyn. This must suggest the area in which these Romanians normally operate. The question is, does that give us a clue to the location of the bogus hospital?

'Right, search the lay-by; find me a witness or two; the local police can interview Mark Ancaster, Benjamin Scott and the owner of the Vectra from Liverpool; and get on to the Serious Organised Crime Authority and find if there is any connection between Romanian organised crime and Lerwyn, or the surrounding area.'

***

The surgeon brought breakfast, Gretchen resting on the tray, alongside toast and marmalade – thick cut Seville orange, just as Jason would buy it.

'I have given your position consideration. I should not have threatened you with an endless cycle of abduction, operation and return. Every man needs hope things will become better. I know what I said, but you have already cost me a lot in terms of both time and money. Perhaps you have learned your lesson. Perhaps I do not need to take you anymore. Do not leave town though...just in case.'

The victim considered this to be just another empty apology, to be taken with a pinch of salt. Of course there was a possibility the surgeon would not take Jason again, instead picking on someone else to feed his sick desires, but the evidence did not support the theory. The twisted sadist had all but stated he believed Jason and someone close to him – possibly his wife – had done something to cause the woman in the surgeon's care to be confined to a wheelchair. In which case, this was not about collecting body parts; it was purely about vengeance, and the only hope Jason had was that the surgeon considered three pieces enough. Again, the evidence did not stack up. The trolley transported many jars, enough to facilitate Jason being sliced and diced many times over. Not forgetting, just hours earlier, the surgeon had described how he might fill them all.

Jason's thought processes suddenly jarred to a halt – the only likely reason not to punish Jason anymore would be if the surgeon decided to punish someone else; someone he considered equally, or more responsible – Heather!

After breakfast, when the tray and disposables had been accounted for and removed, the surgeon withdrew to the room next door, and then to another part of the property.

Jason's routine, and his bladder, demanded he visit the bathroom, his wrist still attached to the steel cable by a leash. The trip was something to be cherished, not least because it removed him – at least temporarily – from the gaze of the silent, all-seeing CCTV cameras. It was also a chance to freshen up. However, as nice as it was to wipe away the stench from his armpits and to remove plaque from his teeth, this was no bath by candlelight, soothed by music carefully chosen to calm the soul. There was the leash to contend with; the damned, endless soundtrack of which Jason was now so familiar he could almost predict and imitate the next noise, whether it be a jack hammer, or a vixen barking. Also to contend with, unable to face his disfigurements, he washed without the benefits of a mirror; he had to urinate without touching his second wound; and could now use only his left hand for fear his mind would otherwise focus on the missing finger, the unnatural space hidden beneath a generous dressing.

To avoid seeing the latest amputation, Jason held his right hand behind his back, using only his left to squeeze paste onto the toothbrush as it rested on the tiled window sill; to operate the tap; to flush the toilet; and it would be a long time before he felt able to clean his left armpit, unless his wife was prepared to wash him like a baby.

His teeth clean, Jason placed the toothbrush back down on the tiles before picking up the tube of paste in order to snap the lid shut. His non-dominant hand, lacking coordination, caused the toothpaste to fall to the floor, the tube to tumble behind the basin pedestal. Out of sight, it required Jason to bend his knees; his one good hand to explore. The tips of his fingers fell upon an object, and brought it easily into the light. It was not the missing tube; rather a gas lighter, half full, flint present and working. The captive could think of no immediate use for it and was sure that if the surgeon had written such a thing as a list of prohibited items, a gas lighter would be on it. The solution was to tuck it back out of the way, behind the porcelain pedestal, where his fingers found what they had been searching for. With the toothpaste tube laying parallel to the brush, as neat as if placed by a man with OCD, Jason left the room, returning to his bed.

Lunch was presented and eaten; so too an evening meal. Then there came the sound of the Romanians returning, raising the captive's expectations.

Three of the surgeon's assistants entered the room where they brought their captive to his feet and immediately set about his body with electric trimmers, de-hairing his arms, back, head and chest. From there he was taken swiftly to the bathroom where a soapy sponge provided all the lubrication that was to be given. Razor blades smoothed every inch of his body, the Romanians being surprisingly careful not to draw blood. His body was then showered, a rough sponge being used to remove the top layer of skin, leaving the majority of Jason's body reddened. His eyes shut tight, he braced whenever the pad came close to one of his healing wounds. He need not have worried. Being in the employ of the surgeon they followed his instructions, which included proper care of the area surrounding the missing ear, testicle and finger.

Having been escorted back to the recovery room, naked, on paper towels, hair dryers evaporated any moisture that had not already dripped from his body. No towels were used.

Next, his foreskin was retracted; a bag taped to his groin; a torch shone into his mouth, ears and nostrils.

Jason accepted it all, assisting wherever he might. He acknowledged the gun and what it meant. He held his wrist out as the leash was unbolted.

Risking swift punishment, Jason nevertheless felt he must speak.

'Can I just ask, I'd be more than happy if you feel I have suffered enough, but if that means taking someone else, I urge you to continue taking me instead.'

He received no answer, but neither did he receive a penance.

The obliging captive donned a paper suit, following non-verbal instructions; accepted an injection without wincing; and allowed himself to be carried to the van, bracing against the bitterly cold winter air.

The sounds of the engine and soundtrack returned. Where he would be delivered to, and how long it would take to get there didn't matter; he was on his way home.

23

Heather had kept the promise she made to her neighbour. Following a spring clean – completed three months prematurely - during which she used every product under the sink, and every piece of equipment from the cleaning cupboard, she had retired to bed, exhausted and sober, anticipating the return of Charlie and Lily in the morning. She hoped the new day would also see the return of her husband. Such was the lack of sleep she had experienced since he was taken, Heather slept soundly; so soundly it took nearly a minute for her to respond to her mobile's ringtone and the loud vibration it caused against the surface of her beside cabinet. Disorientated, Heather rolled to one side, reached for her phone, and flopped onto her back, her head sinking into the soft, warm pillow, the device held at forearm's distance above her face. The emitted light was too much for eyes that by now had become well accustomed to the dark. It therefore took a fumbling thumb several seconds to dim the screen sufficiently for her eyelids to open. When they did, Heather's eyes registered the time - 03:07 - but in her confusion there was no telling whether this was the middle of the night, or mid-afternoon. Her brain continued to process the information, announcing its conclusion by authorising the release of adrenalin into her blood stream. A moment later she was wide awake and it was clear that any call received at such an hour was not meant to be social, unless it was from a relative in Australia, of which she had none. A call at this hour brought news – good or bad.

A hand reached out to switch on the bedside lamp. Heather's eyes bore the discomfort while her free arm raised her to the seated position. Her thumb found the missed call notification and tapped the screen, causing her mother's home phone to ring many miles away.

'Hello,' Heather said, her voice groggy but urgent.

It was Charlie who answered. So keen was her son to impart his news, there was no time for his mother to consider why an eight year old boy would wish to make a phone call in the middle of the night.

'Mummy, Daddy's back. He hasn't got his finger.'

Heather was not sure why she cried – with relief her husband was alive, in reaction to the confirmation he had been tortured further, or as an expression of gratitude it was not his nose.

***

The Family Liaison Officers made their way from the nine o'clock briefing, directly to the hospital at which Jason lay, freshly bandaged, recovering from the effects of the drugs in his blood stream and the cold to which he had been exposed, dumped naked outside Lynn and Mark Truman's comfortable, three bedroomed detached home.

Because the Trumans lived an hour from Heather's house, Jason had not been transported to his local Accident and Emergency department; rather one that lay closer to Heather's parents, an hour and a half from the Ressler residence.

Jason's Romanian couriers were not to know Charlie and Lily could sleep through anything, or that the children's grandfather took medication so potent, it rendered him unconscious for at least eight hours. Nor did they know Lynn Truman's normal reaction to mysterious noises in the middle of the night was to listen intently, convince herself she must have been dreaming, then bury her head in her pillow, swiftly returning to sleep. Had they known any of this, they might not have chosen to deposit their captive in such an exposed, life-threatening environment. As it was, Jason had been forced to adopt the foetal position, his body reacting instinctively to protect itself against the cold. The strategy had limitations and after his naked flesh had been pressed to the Truman's frost covered garden path for fifteen minutes he was close to succumbing to permanent sleep. Fortunately, as if an act of divine intervention, he was spotted by an insomniac who had braved the night, taking a brisk walk he hoped would eventually lead to at least a few hours of meaningful rest.

It was only when the blue flashing lights of an ambulance penetrated the curtained windows had Mrs Truman become aware of the drama unfolding right outside the front door.

***

Jane Humfress and her colleague were greeted by a man who looked very poorly, despite Jason's core body temperature having been restored to normal, the drugs having cleared his system, and his wounds having been re-dressed. A sheet covered his groin and the fresh wound to be found there, but in plain view was a bandage, wrapped round the patient's head - wadding substituting his ear - and a second dressing, wound round his right hand. In addition, the detectives could not help but notice the patient was now completely shaven – to the extent even his eyebrows were missing.

Jane placed a hand lightly on the patient's left forearm; the gentlest way she could think to gain his attention; to break the pitiful stare.

Jason's eyes moved towards her. They carried no emotion; in the same way his facial muscles remained almost superfluous, serving only to keep his mouth shut.

'The nurses tell me you haven't been left with a hair on your body.'

DC Humfress used her most sympathetic voice.

The fact that Jason replied at all was encouraging, even though he was close to tears.

'Look at me. I'm a supermarket manager. How am I going to face my customers, or my team? Forget the missing pieces and the bandages for a minute, I look like I'm undergoing chemo, or I've just been rescued from the Nazis. What I don't understand is why that psycho's checklist keeps getting longer. I mean, why did they have to do this to me?'

Jane squeezed his arm, unable to maintain her normal professional dispassion.

'They're thinking ahead. The first time you were taken was completely unexpected, so nothing could have been put in place to catch them out. Each time you're taken you've had another opportunity to think how you could gather evidence – forensics; a wire, for example.'

Her response triggered a memory, bringing life to the patient's face.

'That reminds me. Did you retrieve the dashcam footage?'

Both detectives' ears pricked simultaneously.

'What dashcam?' Jane asked, calmly.

'I installed one in my car – behind the radiator grille, so they wouldn't find it. It must have picked up their vehicles and probably images of the masked men too.'

Jane's rapidly changing expression prepared Jason for more bad news.

'I'm sorry, your clothes and your car were torched before you set off – as I say, they're thinking about forensics.'

Jason frowned.

'No! I loved that car. I'll never get the full value back on the insurance.'

His reaction was not what either detective would have expected, but knew from experience that people in extraordinary circumstances could act in extraordinary ways.

Jason took a moment to absorb the news, leading to another jolting memory.

'The flowers. She won't have got the flowers.'

Nigel Chambley issued an enquiring look.

'Before I left work, I bought Heather a bunch of carnations – her favourite. They were on the front passenger seat.'

He paused again to take stock. His head shook in disbelief.

'Everything was going so well. I'd had my operation; I looked normal; I felt better; I'd been at work for a few hours; and before I left I bought Heather the flowers to tell her I love her and to thank her for putting up with me.'

Believing Heather Ressler was somehow complicit in perpetuating her husband's ordeal, DC Chambley bit his lip. Although the police lacked hard evidence to prove a working theory, to him, the circumstantial evidence connecting Heather to the Romanians and their psychotic leader was overwhelming. For the victim not to see through his wife's lies – worse, for him to continue to treat her like Florence-bloody-Nightingale – was to witness the worst kind of emotional blindness.

Jane had some questions that needed to be asked. Mourning the loss of a bunch of flowers was not taking them forward.

'Is there anything you can tell us? For a start, how did he take you? Was there a gun?'

Jason found the question helpful, focussing his mind on what really mattered, enabling him to speak calmly.

'No, nothing like that. I was on the arterial road – thought I'd be safe in heavy traffic. A car pulled out of the lay-by, a bit ahead of me. I think it was a Vectra - an estate. His speed dropped, so the couple of cars in front of me overtook it. I was in no hurry so I stayed put. Then it sped up a bit. I was behind it for a while and I remember thinking it was in really good condition for an old car. Someone had looked after it – really clean and no dinks or scratches. Then someone in the back held up a sign at the window. It said *follow*. Then another one instructed me to flash my headlights to confirm I'd got the message.'

There, Jason paused to stifle a tear, his throat closing to prevent him crying like a disaster victim who had lost his entire family. Having patted his eyes with a fresh tissue - proffered by DC Humfress - and grunted against a closed fist, he was ready to resume.

'Sorry.'

Jane looked deep into his eyes.

'Don't be. You're doing really well.'

Always having found it difficult dealing with men who were crying, Nigel was glad his colleague was taking the lead.

'It's just that I knew what the instruction meant and what might happen to Heather and the kids if I didn't comply, so I did what it asked. Can you imagine how I felt? Being unexpectedly punched in the face is one thing, but being led away, knowing you are going to be punched is something entirely different.'

At that moment, Nigel understood what it meant to be Jason Ressler – a living, breathing family man, being destroyed, bit by bit, in the most horrendous circumstances.

'You'll be okay, fella. We're going to catch them and everything will be all right.'

Jane looked at her colleague, never having seen him melt like this before. Nevertheless, she still felt best placed to handle the victim, and she still had questions to ask.

'Anything else? Something that would help us find them?'

'Yes, there was a photo behind the false wall in the operating room – a bungalow – isolated – an old couple were standing outside. It was painted bright yellow and there were three poplar trees in the background. I think it was the hospital where they hold me – the previous owners' maybe.'

'Interesting. Anything else?'

'The surgeon said, and I quote, *You will learn more about what **both** of you have done.*'

'Are you sure that's what he said.'

'Positive. I've been repeating it over and over in my head all the time I was away because I knew it could be important. He also said I'd already suffered for *her* sins. He's got to think Heather's to blame, but we've both wracked our brains and neither of us can think what she might have done. He must have got us mixed up with someone else. You need to look for someone who looks like her, or someone close to her who might have done something wrong. A work colleague maybe. Natasha? They're often seen together.'

DC Chambley bit harder.

Jane saw her colleague's eyes narrowing, wondering what was troubling him.

'We'll speak with her again,' she responded, convincingly. 'Anything else?'

'Yes, well, he started off by making out he intends to take me over and over, listing all the pieces he might remove, internal organs and everything…'

Jane, wishing to clarify the situation as Jason saw it, interrupted before he had finished.

'Okay, so it's likely the surgeon intends to take you again…'

Jason looked uncertain.

'I thought so, but only the next day, when he brought me breakfast, he apologised and said I'd already cost him a lot of time and money and maybe I'd learned my lesson. He said he might not have to take me again, but not to leave town, *just in case*. I think he might have decided to move on to someone else. It was funny really. He'd typed in a dramatic pause, but Gretchen read out dot, dot, dot. Sort of ruined it really.'

'Gretchen?'

'Oh, that's just the name I give to the voice that comes out of that iPad. The bitch.'

'I see. Well, it's good that you can see the funny side, given the circumstances.'

Jane hoped he would respond with a smile, however small. He did not; rather his expression sank.

'Why the face? Surely it's good news if he's going to leave you alone.'

'Not really. The way I see it, he blames Heather and me for that woman being in the wheelchair - no one else. If he's finished with me, that might mean he intends to take her instead. I'd rather he continues to cut pieces off me than touch her – better one ruined body than two.'

Nigel Chambley could sit back and watch this man suffer for a guilty wife no more.

'Jason, I think we need to talk…There's some things about your wife that causes us concern. I know what you've said before, but let's go over it again.'

Jason looked confused, but indicated he was listening.

'Firstly, Heather has a driving conviction. We know your views, but that doesn't alter the fact she does have a conviction. Secondly, she lied to your neighbour, telling her she'd suffered a seizure rather than admit she'd been drunk driving. Thirdly – thanks to you – we know at least some of the kidnappers are Romanian, and what do you know, Heather's been there – without you. Who knows who she met out there, or what she did. We know she travelled with her friends on a hen do, but they can't vouch for her every move. Then there's the life insurance.'

'What about it?'

'Well, you recently increased your life insurance. Your wife told us it was to cover an additional mortgage, taken out for home improvements. Is that correct?'

'Sort of, I suppose. A friend of hers is a financial advisor. He said we don't have enough cover, especially with the additional loan. The new policy would provide money if I can't work due to serious illness, or if I die; less so in the case of my wife as I'm the main bread winner.'

'Jason, can you see how this looks? You say yourself you think the surgeon puts the blame on you and your wife, and you know you haven't done anything. Remember, she's the one who works for the NHS. If anyone has a connection with the surgeon, it's Heather.'

'You're mad. If Heather is working for the surgeon, why is he dropping her in it? And wasn't it you who said the surgeon gets his information about us from our bins? So what are you suggesting? It's really her who's passing it to him? And why would she do that? Do you really think she wants me bumped off for a few thousand quid? Even if she did, why would she go about it like this? If she hates me, she's hiding it very well, especially well if what she really wants is to see me hacked to pieces.'

DC Chambley was not going to let a man, blind to the facts, stay in his safe bubble any longer.

'I'm not suggesting any of that, but maybe she got involved in something which got out of hand.

Look, while you were gone, a man who we believe to be one of the kidnappers used your bank card. The fella at the petrol station recalls he knew your PIN. Jason, how did he know that if someone hadn't told him?'

Jason shook his head briefly, but violently, wild with frustration.

'That's just another case of you not getting your facts straight before you go hurling allegations around. As it happened, I recently managed to snap my debit card in two – God knows how – and sent off for a new one. It arrived with a new PIN – by separate post - a few days before I was kidnapped. I hadn't got round to changing it to my usual one at the cash machine and I had no intention of memorising it as I wasn't going to keep it. Hence I kept the slip in my wallet with the card. I know it's wrong, but that's the way it is. I suppose now I'm not going to be covered for any loss. Brilliant.'

Jane stepped in.

'Okay, Jason. We don't want to put you under any more pressure. We want you to get better. I'm sorry if all this seems a bit harsh, but we need to catch these people. Let's call it a day and find out where we get with this new information. If necessary, we'll come and see you at home and take down a few more details. In the meantime, write down anything that occurs to you. We'll be in touch.'

***

Jason was discharged the following morning, his father-in-law conveying him and the two children back home where Heather waited, filled with emotions and feelings, careful how she appeared to the outside world.

Charlie and Lily were excited to be reunited with their mother who came out of the house to meet them on the driveway. Heather had made every effort to look the normal housewife – mentally stable, sober and overly welcoming. Barely did she have time to give each of the kids a hug and a kiss before Charlie grabbed centre stage, bursting at the seams, eager to impart the most wonderful news.

'Nanny and Granddad got us an advent calendar. Lily got Barbie and I got Star Wars. Nanny said, when she was little they only had one between them and it didn't have chocolate; it had glitter on it instead, and they used it again every year. Lily's eaten hers, but you can have mine.'

Taking a breath, he held out the calendar, pointing to the correct door – number 5.

'Oh, have you saved it for me? That's lovely, Charlie.'

Heather extracted the chocolate from inside and watched her son's eyes follow it towards her mouth, clearly regretting his generosity.

'Don't worry, Charlie, you can have it.'

Charlie did not feign reluctance and popped it into his mouth, smiling.

Detecting his daughter might want a few moments alone with her husband, Heather's dad guided the grandchildren indoors.

Left on the doorstep, Jason suddenly looked more relaxed.

'Kids are hardy creatures, aren't they? All this going on and they still manage to take it in their stride. It's good. I'd hate to think of them being permanently scarred. They were fine in the car on the way down.'

Heather glanced down towards her husband's bandaged hand. Jason did not notice, his gaze being drawn through the front door, to granddad, and to the kids who were running rings around him.

Heather wore a smile, but there was little life in her voice.

'Yes, they seem happy enough, but I can't see it not having a lasting impact on them.'

Jason realised he had not given his wife a kiss. Pulling her close to him with his good hand, he touched his lips briefly against hers.

'I bought you flowers, but they were in the car. Have you heard, the bastards set fire to it – the car; my uniform; your flowers. Arseholes.'

'Never mind, they're all replaceable; you're not, and now I have you back, so that's all that matters.'

Before the couple went inside, Jason had a request.

'I know I've only just got back, but do you mind if I spend a bit of time by myself. I want to update my notes and I need peace and quiet in order to think.'

'Of course. I'll go and put the kettle on.'

Jason sat beside his dolls houses, notebook in hand, pen poised, his eyes closed so that he could re-live every moment; concentrate on every minute detail. Several cups of tea and a mid-morning snack had been consumed by the time his mind replayed the discovery of the lighter, hidden behind the sink pedestal. The memory warranted the addition of an illustration in the ever fattening book - an easy to find marker should he wish to refer back to the event in future. The act of sketching sparked two lines of thought; one positive, the other not so. Kicking himself, Jason realised he had not checked whether the body of the lighter bore a maker's name or mark that might have provided some small piece of evidence. He felt it likely he would have noticed if there had been, but he could not be certain. Given the heavy price he had to pay for every snippet of information, he knew he would lose sleep over such a lost opportunity. However, the second line of thought trumped the first, it sparking the memory of a life-hack, broadcast via the internet, many years previously. He had needed to gain access to the guts of an electronic device, but the manufacturer had used a tamper-resistant screw, designed to prevent amateur repairmen getting themselves killed. The advice given in the short video was to melt the top of a pen barrel, and press it against the screw head so that it took on its unique shape. A quick dip in cold water hardened the plastic, the end result of which was a pretty useful tool, suitable for the job in hand – at least on one occasion. Applying the hack to his current situation, the plastic picnic cutlery, supplied with his meals at the makeshift hospital, would be ideal. The life-hack filled another page, concisely translating the video into the written word. Eventually, the pen paused, providing a moment for Jason's thought processes to catch up; to consider the implications of what he had written. It was clear he could fabricate a screwdriver, but what good was that when any escape attempt would lead, inexorably, to the same problem at the heart of every plan he might devise – Jason's family would be placed in grave danger and that could never be allowed to happen.

The pen moved again; this time to strike two heavy diagonal lines across the hand written text.

Before he had the chance to begin making notes about the lunch provided by the surgeon, Heather entered the work room, bearing another hot drink and a plate of biscuits, and with the news her father and the children had popped out to buy something for lunch – after they had been to the park. Jason was pleased to see her; keen to tell her most of what he had recalled.

Referring to his notebook, he brought her quickly up to date, missing out DC Chambley's objectionable theories about his wife. Heather listened, feigning interest, awaiting her moment.

'What's wrong?'

'Nothing, I just need to tell you something.'

'Go on then.'

'It's not that easy.'

'What could be so difficult? Tell me.'

Heather took a deep breath and spread her fingers level with her waist. She exhaled, blowing through pursed lips. Her fingers then retracted, making loose fists.

'You're going to hear things. Things you shouldn't have to, especially after all you've been through.'

'Go on.'

Jason was pretty sure his wife was going to repeat the suspicions put to him earlier by the detectives. The reality was far worse.

'On the night you were first taken, I was frantic. The police seemed to share my concern, but then they found a holiday brochure in your car. It had a note stuck to the front. I will never forget those words - *Hi Sexy. Can't wait to be alone with you, love Anna.*'

Jason looked rightfully confused. Heather continued, knowing all would become clear.

'I rang your boss the next day to inform him you'd gone missing. I asked him if he knew an Anna. He told me she works under you, on your team. I asked to speak with her. Your boss told me she'd gone on holiday the night you were taken. You can imagine what I thought.'

'No, what did you think?'

Jason sounded suspicious.

'Don't make this harder than it already is. A holiday brochure is found in your car with a note from Anna stating she can't wait to be alone with you. She used the word love and added a kiss. Then I find the Anna you work with has gone on holiday at that exact same time…I thought you'd run off together.'

Jason's face formed an incredulous stare.

'You do realise Anna Richardson is coming up to retirement. She's well into her sixties. Are you suggesting I have a thing for old women?'

'No, I didn't know she was old at the time. That's just what the people who took you wanted me to think. The police said the kidnappers did it to put us off the scent, but that's only after you'd returned.'

'So, what are you trying to tell me?'

Heather shifted awkwardly.

'The day after you were first taken, people kept calling round. They all wanted to see if there was anything they could do. As the day wore on, the only thing I could do to calm down was to have a drink – a bit too much to drink if I'm honest. My parents took the kids because it wasn't healthy them seeing me so upset and not being able to explain where their daddy had gone. Then John popped round.'

'And?'

'Look, I was in pieces.'

'No, Heather, I was. Are you telling me you had sex with one of our best friends?'

Heather's head dropped, confirming he was correct in his belief.

'You couldn't wait fifty hours? Hell, you couldn't even wait a full day!'

'It wasn't like that. I wasn't gagging for sex. It was revenge. I phoned my mum. We all thought you'd run off with another woman – left me with the kids, without saying a word. Even the police thought so. When women cut up their husband's clothes, they don't wait a reasonable time do they?'

'No, but you didn't cut up my clothes. You shagged John! I can't believe I'm hearing this.'

'I know it sounds bad, but I was really hurt and I wanted to hurt you as much as you'd hurt me. I didn't know you'd been kidnapped. I didn't really have a plan, but it occurred to me you might return from your sordid love nest, whether to collect your things, or say sorry. My intention was to tell you how much better than you he was.'

'Firstly, there was no love nest, only an operating table. Anyway, was he better than me? Is he well hung? Did his dick make you hurt, it's so large?'

Heather was on the verge of tears. She knew this would be hard, but still it was difficult to remain strong.

'Don't. The reality is, I got no pleasure from it. It was like performing a task. I'm sure he didn't enjoy it either.'

'Well, that makes me feel a whole lot better. Anyway, why are you telling me now? I've been taken twice since then.'

Heather produced a tissue from her pocket.

'I didn't tell you before because I didn't want to add to your misery, but…'

'But what?'

'This time it all got too much…you being taken again; wondering what he was doing to you; me having not told you what I'd done. I wanted to stay, but I couldn't cope. I found myself at the station - bought a ticket to London – but then…well, as the train pulled in, I found myself stepping out. It was only because some man grabbed me that I'm still here.'

'You were going to kill yourself?!'

Heather nodded, her face too distorted to speak.

This was not an act designed to extract pity. Of the two revelations, the second trumped the first; in time, her infidelity might be forgiven; rather that than deny their children a mother.

24

The prison was on patrol state. B Wing was manned solely by Adam Sutherin, an officer with three years' service, making him one of the most experienced currently at the jail; a far cry from the old days, before austerity measures, when he would have been considered a young pup with bags of energy, but no advice to offer; perfect for doing the jobs traditionally reserved for the newbies. It being the evening, his duties included simply being there; answering cell bells – there for emergencies, but often misused, calling staff to the door to request toilet paper that should have been sought during the day; keeping a check on the suicidal maniacs; and waiting to be relieved by the night staff, due on duty any time after half eight. As always when he was alone, time passed slowly, relieved only by the pages of yesterday's newspaper and the football scores, available from the BBC's news website. While on the computer he found the energy to make entries about the behaviour of those prisoners assigned to him, using stock phrases that placated his manager, but who ideally wanted something more. Apparently it was not so useful to other justice agencies to know whether the men kept their cells clean and tidy, as it was to understand their personal circumstances, which would require talking to them on more than a superficial basis. That done, there was one more go-to site which promised to while away the odd fifteen minutes – The Police Gazette.

It was a fact that between periods of custody, ex-prisoners made themselves busy doing what they did best – spreading misery throughout the community on which they preyed. It therefore made sense for the police to publish wanted posters to prison officers, as much as to their own men and women, as there was every chance the criminal would be identified from images recovered from CCTV by prison staff, if the perpetrators had ever done time. The publication covered the whole country, making identification at one particular establishment rare, but it was still interesting to see what the underbelly of society was getting up to across the nation.

Adam scrolled through the pages, wondering how any of these men and women could ever be recognised from such fuzzy images, believing even their mothers would have difficulty. Moments later he had his answer. The poor quality, freeze-frame snapshots were not recognisable unless the viewer was familiar with the subject of those snapshots, and then it became easy.

The third image scrolled up the page. It showed a man in a small shop, the sort normally associated with a petrol station. The officer did not guess the figure - with a close-cropped head of dark hair, a chiselled face and a trimmed beard - was eastern European, because he knew it as fact.

Adam's eyes narrowed, his face drawing closer to the monitor.

'I know you, don't I?'

At that moment the officer's focus was disturbed by the sound of a key in the entrance door to the wing; a prisoner being escorted back to his cell, having been at court since early that morning. The offender, carrying a plastic bag of food – his packaged evening meal – was soon behind his door, denied his request to have a shower.

The escorting officer entered the office to book his charge back on and was grateful to find his friend and colleague had already done it for him.

Adam took the opportunity to seek a second opinion.

'Here, Mick, I know this geezer. You must remember him. What was his name?'

Mick confirmed the unknown man had been in their care within the last six months, but other than recalling he spoke no English and communicated through a bi-lingual fellow countryman, he was of no further use.

'You should give them a call.'

Mick took control of the mouse, repositioning the image towards the top of the screen, making room for text at the bottom.

'Here you go - DS Honeyman. There's a number.'

Adam followed his friend's advice, not immediately because it was late, and not the next day either because he was not on duty, but on the Wednesday morning he found an opportunity. The Detective Sergeant was grateful. Even though the prison officer could not put a name to the man in the image, it was at least a lead.

Alan Honeyman was quick to inform his boss, and then to place a call to the Police Intelligence Officer, embedded within the prison, located in the West Midlands, in excess of one hundred and thirty miles from the police HQ, at Furmington, the home of the Ressler investigation. While DCs Fallas and Pace made their way with haste, the PIO secured the necessary documentation, needed to grant them entry. Soon after their arrival, Officer Sutherin was requested to attend the PIO's office. When he arrived, the image in question was already up on the screen.

'So, you recognise this man?'

The officer was young, still only twenty-three, but he spoke with confidence, his experience after retail adding maturity to his age.

'Yes, but I can't remember his name. Sorry. All I can tell you is he's been here within the last six months and I seem to remember he was Romanian – couldn't speak a word of English. We tend to keep the foreign nationals together, so they have someone to talk to. Usually one of them can speak at least some English and translates for us, so it's not so much of a problem.'

'Can you remember anything that might help us identify him? It's very important.'

'Well, there is one way of finding out who he is.'

Angela Pace gave an encouraging, 'Go on.'

'Well, all the cells on B Wing are singles – that is, single occupancy. Most of the others around the jail hold two prisoners. Anyway, he was in the far, left corner of the ones, on Red Spur. That's B1-36. All you need to do is look on the computer for the history of that cell and it will give you the names of every con who's ever been in it. I know you can do it as I've done it before, but I can't remember how. Sorry.'

DC Fallas was at the same time excited, but frustrated; an emotion that lasted but a second, until the PIO let it be known he had used the facility on more than one occasion. As he spoke, the cursor navigated the program's hierarchy; the keyboard inputting the cell location. A list appeared.

'Do you recognise the name?'

Over the past year, the population of that particular cell had remained reasonably static, providing few names to choose from. However, Officer Sutherin would have been able to pick out the man if there had been twice the number.

'That's him – Andrei Lungu.'

'Are you sure?'

'Hundred percent. Bring up his photo and I'll prove it.'

One click produced a thumbnail. Several more produced an image that filled a quarter of the screen. It was definitely him.

'Is there a release address?'

Angela was salivating.

There followed another pause.

'There sure is, but it's not round these parts.'

***

DI Bickley received news of the breakthrough with excitement, easily detectable over the phone. The short conversation concluded with an instruction for DCs Fallas and Pace to follow the lead, and attempt to affect an arrest, the Inspector promising to call ahead to arrange for uniformed police, local to the target address, to be made available.

36 Hatton Gardens was a mid-terraced property in a down at heel part of Trefford, in the North of England. Not only was there no facility to park off-road, there was precious little room even for the assortment of refuse bins and recycling receptacles, cluttering the front. The absence of love and care shown for these small houses indicated a benefit street. Like the other properties in this particular row of eight, number 36 was a two-up, two down, fitted with the original wooden doors and windows, paint peeling from their every surface. The gutter leaked, staining the wall. A bill poster had shown the audacity to advertise an event, an A4 flier pasted on the skew, beneath the letter box. Given the date that DJ Mastodon was coming to town, it had been left there recently. No attempt had been made to remove it.

Local uniforms covered the rear of the property - reaching a minute garden space via a narrow alley, walled on both sides. DCs Fallas and Pace stood at the front door, accompanied by additional uniformed officers, one of whom chomped at the bit, he being in charge of a weighty battering ram, eager to put it to use.

A knock at the front door went unanswered. Drake Fallas peered through the letter box. His eyes saw no movement – nothing out of the ordinary – but his nose detected an odour that should not have been there. He stepped to one side and swung his hand forwards; an indication for the uniformed man to destroy the lock. Only one blow was needed, the door opening with such force it rebounded off the wall behind it, slamming back into its seat, the lock that had held it fast left lying on the hall floor. DC Fallas pushed the door inwards, immediately exposing himself and his colleagues to an atmosphere contaminated with a stench so strong it took his breath away – a mixture of decay, burned meat, the acrid aroma of burned plastic, and fuel. Its source was soon discovered, in the living room.

A man lay on his back, on the floor – a very dead man with a hole punched through his face, between his eyes, destroying the bridge of his nose. A cheap cushion lay nearby, its man-made fibre-filling ejected from the cover by the force of a single bullet passing through. The visible surface of the cushion was stained with incidental matter, the erstwhile contents of this man's head. But that was not where the punishment had ended. Examination would show the back of the man's head was missing, and by comparison, the entry wound was small and neat and should have been the only sign of execution. However, the lower part of the man's face had suffered too. Evidently, there was a high probability this was the man they were looking for; the man who had stolen Jason Ressler's debit card for his own use, straying from a strict protocol enforced by his employer. Once dead – or perhaps not – someone had filled his mouth with accelerant, his tongue preventing it draining to his lungs or stomach. A match had been thrown to him and into the flaming orifice, a plastic card had been inserted, now melted and blackened. Nevertheless, it was recognisable as a debit card.

The torch from Detective Constable Fallas' phone illuminated the charred interior of the victim's mouth, revealing, that although badly damaged, the embossed details on the card had partially survived.

Her phone issued an electronic click.

DC Fallas got to her feet, examined the image, enlarging it with an outward sweeping motion of finger and thumb.

'S, L, E, R. Ressler. This is Jason Ressler's all right. So this must be Andrei Lungu. Nice to meet you.'

Angela's words suggested she shared her colleague's black sense of humour, but her expression showed disgust and disappointment.

Drake, however, remained upbeat.

'Well, on the bad side, we've lost our witness and this lot have a murder on their hands. On a positive note, it's beginning to look as though the Romanians base themselves up here.'

Angela appreciated what her colleague was saying, but thought it right to put it in to perspective.

'Hmm, the whole of the north is still quite a big area, isn't it?'

While Scenes of Crime Officers went about their business, DCs Pace and Fallas went for something to eat, taking the opportunity to report back to DI Bickley.

As soon as the call came through that they could re-enter the property, both returned to Hatton Gardens as though responding to a bank robbery in progress. There they met DI Oliver, the newly appointed Senior Investigating Officer in the Andrei Lungu case, who had made a rare excursion from his office in order to fix in his mind an image of the murder scene.

The remains of the debit card had been removed from the victim's mouth and sealed in a clear plastic evidence bag, through which DI Pace took another image on her phone. If nothing else, while they waited for further news, she could at least confirm the card had been the property of their other victim – Jason Ressler.

Unfortunately, there was nothing else to make the trip worthwhile: no sign of any black Vauxhall Vectras; number plates; mobile phones; SIM cards; no incriminating photographs, documents or addresses - nothing.

Angela Pace and Drake Fallas returned to base, crestfallen, with an agreement for DI Oliver's team to work closely with his counterpart who would provide reports to each other as they came in.

***

Keen to show they were making progress, and to soothe bad feelings, the FLOs visited the Resslers the very next day.

Their reception was frostier than usual.

Jason went to the kitchen to make drinks. Heather remained in the lounge, encouraging her guests to sit themselves down on the sofa that was noticeably tidier than the last time they had seen it, as was the rest of the house.

'Don't mind him. I told him about me and John. He hasn't taken it well. Not surprising really.'

Once everyone was settled - the children temporarily banished to their rooms to watch cartoons - Nigel had the pleasure of breaking the good news, both detectives feeling he had more to make up for than Jane.

'We've found the man who we believe stole and fraudulently used your debit card.'

Jason and Heather moved to the front of their seats.

'His name is Andrei Lungu – or should I say, was. He's dead.'

'Good.'

Jason reacted without considering how much better for the investigation it would have been if they had taken him alive.

Heather was more interested in the detail.

'How did it happen?'

'We think he must have broken the rules and was executed by his associates.'

Jason could not help but interject for a second time.

'Good. I hope it wasn't quick either.'

For once he could enjoy the moment, having the satisfaction that one of his captors had met a grizzly end, without there being any comeback on him or his family. This was clearly an internal matter, and could not be interpreted as Jason avoiding being taken.

'Does the name mean anything to either of you?'

Both Mr and Mrs Ressler looked genuinely blank.

'We've also found links to Lerwyn and the Midlands. One of the cars that took you was registered to its owner in Lerwyn, and this Lungu fella committed some small time offences in and around Birmingham. I know it's a vast area, but can you think of any connection either of you might have with Lerwyn, Birmingham, or further up, to the North in general?'

The question served only to produce two shaking heads.

At last Jane could end their meeting on a positive note.

'Look, Jason – Heather.'

Jane's face directed towards each in turn.

'I really think we're closing in. We just need one more break and all this will be over.'

Heather smiled and clasped her husband's hand in hers. He responded by locking his thumb round her fingers - a sign, that despite their difficulties, their relationship somehow survived.

25

The arrival of Mikala Braid at the door of DI Bickley's office could not have come at a more opportune moment, certainly as far as the Inspector was concerned; not so Superintendent Ormsby, who was mid-way through subjecting his subordinate to a stern, one-sided conversation, reminding him the conclusion to the Ressler case was long overdue. Seeing the analyst's face at the small glazed door panel, the Inspector grasped the opportunity to cut short his grilling, beckoning her inside with a twitch of his fingers, much to the annoyance of the Superintendent.

Mikala looked at her superiors in turn, acknowledging them in order of their respective ranks.

'Sir, Guv.'

Both titles were accompanied by a subtle nod.

'Yes, Mikala?' DI Bickley asked, keen to discover what the analyst felt so important it justified interrupting such a high level scolding.

Mikala's response was spoken clearly but hurriedly, the excitement of her news being too great to contain.

'The common phone in the Ressler case has just become active at a town called Claydon Hills, not far from Trefford.'

To give the Superintendent his dues, although focussed more on procedures than the investigation itself, he had read the reports and absorbed even the finest details. Consequently, he knew instantly to which phone the analyst referred, and its significance.

'So we're talking in the general vicinity of the address where the body of Mr Lungu was discovered – interesting. Right, DI Bickley, I want you to get hold of your counterpart up there – DI Oliver as I recall - and ask him to make the arrest. Clearly, it will take time for our team to respond – it must be a three-and-a-half, four hour's drive – and we can't afford to wait.'

An internal phone call brought the office manager to the room. Being in the company of his superior, DI Bickley was unusually formal towards his friend.

'DS Honeyman, get hold of DI Oliver please. I need his team to make an arrest for us. And when you've done that, call the team back to the briefing room. Oh and assign a couple of DCs to Claydon Hills, we need someone up there post-haste.'

***

DI Oliver was more than happy to oblige, the arrest having the potential to progress his murder case - Andrei Lungu, the Romanian with a hole in his head and a crispy tongue. Besides, it was his turf.

Even before Oliver had acceded to his counterpart's request, DCs Drake Fallas and Angela Pace had been despatched to make the long drive north, with instructions to assist the interrogation, or at least sit in on it, if an arrest was made.

Back at base, the briefing room became full for the second time that morning, ready to hear DI Bickley deliver an unscheduled update. At his side, Superintendent Ormsby made a rare appearance.

'At 10:36 hours this morning, the phone linked to the person at the centre of the first abduction became active. Triangulation pinpoints the location of the phone to an executive car dealership at Claydon Hills, a small town to the south of Trefford, in the north of the country. As we speak, our counterparts there are attempting to apprehend the user. I have despatched DCs Fallas and Pace to assist, although they are unlikely to arrive in time for an arrest, should there be one. All we can do then is wait.

DCs Chambley and Humfress, I want you on standby to update the Resslers *if* an arrest is made. However, I don't want them knowing about any of this if we fail. Got that?'

The detectives nodded, keeping the pause in the briefing to a minimum.

'Mikala Braid and I have had a brief discussion as to why the perpetrator suddenly decided to use the same mobile again, when it has remained silent since the lead up to the first abduction of 23rd September. We have concluded it's either because they do not have an unlimited supply, and use a pool in rotation, or they've simply made a mistake. If it's the latter, let's hope it's the first of many.'

The briefing drew to a close. An excited murmur filled the room, the team torn between remaining together, awaiting news, and returning to their tasks, assigned at the first meeting of the morning. However, their minds were quickly swayed by a stirring pep talk from the Superintendent who stopped just short of ushering them from the room with two strikes of his hands and a 'Chop, chop.'

***

The salesmen at Geoffrey Howard Motors conducted business as usual, unaware of several unmarked police cars parked outside, covering the exits – as much as those exits could be identified. The premises, located in an industrial area on the outskirts of town, consisted of a central building, largely constructed of glass, surrounded by rows of cars, grouped by model, in a variety of colours. A rocky promontory had been fabricated in one corner, upon which a lone 4x4 vehicle demonstrated it was at home in such rugged terrain.

A man and woman entered the showroom, making their way directly to a cluster of desks at which salespeople sat, busying themselves at their computers. One such person – a woman in a power suit; the only woman on the team – was the first to see and react to the potential customers. She rose to her feet to greet them, her smile perfected over many years to be devastatingly effective. Although she was content to close a deal with a scruff in jeans, she still judged the customers by their attire. These were not the typical sort of people she expected to show an interest in the top of the range vehicles on offer, but certainly they did not look like time wasters.

In response to the production of a pair of ID cards, her expression changed to one of thinly disguised disappointment; the waning smile lingering on her face too long.

DC Jones made to address the salespeople's spokeswoman, but turned his head as the words left his mouth, scattering the question among the whole team.

'This may seem a strange question, but did any of you serve a foreign gentleman this morning, at around 10:30.'

'As a matter of fact, I did – a Romanian.'

The only female among them and she was clearly the most proactive of all. She had probably pounced on the earlier visitor in much the same way she had leapt from her chair to meet the detectives as they entered the showroom.

DC Jones looked at the woman's name badge.

'In which case, Judith, you may be able to help us. Could you give us a description?'

'I can do better than that; I have a copy of his passport.'

Both detectives' faces twitched with surprise.

'Really? How did that come about?'

'Well, he wanted a test drive, which is fine, but to satisfy the insurance company we have to have identification. He produced a passport. I photocopied it and gave it back. Unfortunately for him, we also need to see a valid driver's licence, and he couldn't produce one – said he didn't have it on him.'

'So what happened?'

'Well, I apologised, but insisted we have to have it. He made a call – presumably to get someone to fetch his licence along. I have…'

Mid-sentence, DC Jones gestured with his hand, keen to interrupt.

'He made a phone call?'

The detective's delivery put great emphasis on this part of Judith's evidence.

'Yes, although I can't be certain what he said because he spoke in a foreign language – Romanian I assume.'

'Please tell me this was at 10:36 hours.'

'I can't be sure from memory, but I could check the CCTV.'

The detectives' day was getting better and better.

'If you can do just that, if ever I need to buy an expensive new car, I'm coming straight to you.'

Judith's smile returned.

'Okay, it's a deal, but first I'll dig out that copy of the passport.'

In practice, the excavation she promised was merely the opening a folder on her desk.

'Can I keep this?'

Judith hesitated.

'You can, but I'll have to make a second copy as we'll need it when he returns.'

'Oh?'

'Yes, he's coming back this afternoon with his licence – four o'clock.'

'Forget buying a car, I might just marry you.'

Judith smiled again.

'No offence, but I'm already married and I need the commission more than a second husband.'

It was DC Jones' turn to widen his mouth.

'Okay then, let's go have a look at the CCTV. I haven't got access myself, but I know my manager does.'

Thankfully, the manager was adept at using the system, navigating to the requested time stamp with a few clicks of a mouse, controlling a master monitor, hidden away from general view in his office.

'There he is.'

The image on the screen was not much clearer than that of the facsimile passport, but as far as both detectives could tell, the suited man on the screen and the suspect captured in the travel document seemed to be one and the same person - and he was using his phone.

As the detectives looked on, they witnessed the suspect suddenly end the call and rip the battery from his phone. Even without sound, it was clear the man was not happy. The act was carried out in full view of the saleswoman who startled at the customer's unexpected reaction.

'What was going on?'

Judith shook her head gently, as though not sure herself.

'Well, as you can see, he was talking away in a foreign language and suddenly lost it. He must have seen the look on my face and felt he had to offer an explanation. He said the battery had died right in the middle of an important business call. He'd removed it from the case so he could get the right replacement. I have to say, I didn't believe him. Anyway, he tried to make light of it. Sort of 'typical - just when you need it' kind of thing.'

'So he did speak English then?'

'Oh yes, really well. Hardly had an accent.'

'Hmmm, did he say where he was going?'

'No, not really. He made the four o'clock appointment, then left. As he did he held the phone up and said he'd better get a new one. He had a lovely smile. A bit like yours.'

'You've been very helpful, Judith. My colleague and I will try to catch up with this gentleman later.'

***

On their arrival at the local police headquarters, DCs Fallas and Pace presented themselves to DI Oliver who had authorised his own Detective Constables to stake out the car dealership. Their arrival and the general situation was relayed back to DS Honeyman who managed logistics on behalf of DI Bickley.

'Okay Alan, what do you have for me?'

DS Honeyman made himself comfortable in the seat proffered to him.

'Well, DCs Fallas and Pace have arrived and been briefed by DI Oliver. CCTV from Geoffrey Howard Motors shows a Romanian using his mobile at the precise time our analyst stated the common phone was used. The man making the call has booked in a test drive this afternoon, at four. Assuming he finds his driver's licence, there's every chance he'll show. Even if he doesn't, we have copy of his passport; one Sebastian Gheata. DI Oliver has authorised a couple of his team to remain at the site, awaiting the Romanian's return. Oh, and he is more than happy for our men to sit in on the interview, if this Gheata fella is apprehended.'

'Okay, so we don't have an arrest, but this is still great news, don't you think? Thanks Alan.'

'No problem, Guv. So, what do we do now?'

Richard Bickley gripped the arms of his chair and pressed his weight backwards, causing the faux leather to creak.

'We wait, we hope, we think.'

'Think?'

DI Bickley was glad his office manager sought explanation as to his precise choice of words, providing the inspector a neat excuse to voice his current theory aloud.

'As it stands, nothing much has changed, other than we now have a location where the phone activated.'

'And we have a name,' DS Honeyman added, indicating his boss had his undivided attention.

As if party to their conversation, one of the team of fifty chose that moment to ring Richard Bickley's phone. The DI exchanged a few words before replacing the receiver. Alan Honeyman's eyebrows asked the obvious question, one which his boss was all too happy to answer.

'Sebastian Gheata entered the country six months ago. There's no trace of him having a criminal record, and no indication it is an alias – not yet, anyway. That means all we have is a Romanian man, with no criminal convictions, using a phone in a car showroom – hardly the breakthrough we were hoping for.'

'Yes, Guv, but if we assume he *is* our man, what does it all mean?'

A simple question, but one to which there seemed no easy answer. Consequently, Richard became still, his fingers gently tugging his lower face, his eyes focussing at random points across his desktop, none of which held his attention for more than a second. All the while, Alan sat patiently.

'Right, bear with me. I'm going to bounce something off you and you can tell me what you think.'

'Okay.'

'The burnt out car originated from Lerwyn – several hundred miles north of the Ressler's residence, school and places of work. A Romanian, believed to have been involved with the abduction of the 30th of November, was found executed at Trefford, again several hundreds of miles from here, and within striking distance of Lerwyn. That suggests at least part of the gang is active somewhere between the two. That ties in with the long journeys between all three snatch points and the makeshift hospital. And then today we have another Romanian, visiting a car dealership in much the same area, not far from Andrei Lungu's murder scene.

'So, it would be interesting to know this Sebastian Gheata's normal address and whether there is a trail leading to other locations – credit card transactions, for example.'

'Sorry, he didn't leave one; just the passport. I guess they meant to take the rest of his details this afternoon, when he returned.'

'Hmm, they have CCTV. Get them to check outside. As I understand it, the dealership is in the middle of an industrial estate. He's more than likely to have got there by car. See if they can retrieve an index number. If so, check with the DVLC for an associated address.'

'Yes Guv. And if we come up with an address which strengthens the connection with the Trefford and Lerwyn, what then?'

DI Bickley took another moment to consider the question and formulate his answer. Having done so, he rocked forward, resting his elbows on the desk, his eyes meeting those of his colleague.

'It is my opinion the surgeon is a highly trained professional who is capable of dissecting human anatomy without causing death.'

The Inspector's eyes diverted to his index finger which tapped the desk, indicating an imaginary identity.

'That sort of person is unlikely to have any sort of criminal knowledge.'

His finger performed a tight circle.

His mind continued to think as he spoke, his ideas forming only as they passed his lips.

'I'm trying to get my head round this. The two sides must have come together somehow. Jason Ressler has already concluded the kidnappers appear to be working for the surgeon, not the other way round. You have to ask yourself why? I can only think it would be because the arrangement is to their mutual advantage. My guess - whatever line of criminal activity the Romanians are involved with, they're likely to sustain injuries. What better solution than having a surgeon in your pocket, the only cost to them being the occasional abduction of a man the surgeon wishes to kidnap, but does not have the knowledge or wherewithal to carry out himself. If the Romanians and the surgeon have reached some kind of agreement, they must have come into contact.'

DS Honeyman's head nodded approvingly, and his boss was not yet finished.

'Thinking about it, I wouldn't be surprised if they approached him when one of their number got hurt. They may even have threatened him. Whatever the case, the Romanians would have gone to someone local to their operations. That means, find the centre of their empire, and the surgeon and his twisted little hospital will be close by. Find me an address, Alan. As soon as you can, please.'

'Okay, Guv, I'm on it.'

Without delay, DS Honeyman forwarded the request for further interrogation of the car showroom CCTV to DCs Fallas and Pace. It was too risky for them to act while their colleagues maintained a stakeout, but by five it would be safe to do so, whether or not Sebastian Gheata had showed. If he did not, at least they might yet find another route to his door.

At 16:15 hours, DI Bickley received a welcomed update from Geoffrey Howard Motors, passed from DC Jones to DI Oliver, to DCs Fallas and Pace.

'Guv, Sebastian Gheata showed up for the test drive and has been arrested. They're bringing him in as we speak.'

The very next phone call was to Superintendent Ormsby who received DI Bickley's news well. The next was to DS Honeyman with instructions to brief the Family Liaison Officers and despatch them to the Ressler's home. The next was a call to DI Oliver to thank him for his assistance; to request DI Fallas be allowed to attend the car showroom, assisting with the search of the suspect's address, when one was discovered, and the appropriate warrant had been served; and for DI Pace to attend the suspect's interview. The requests were received without any issues being raised.

***

Whatever the relationship between the Family Liaison Officers and the Ressler family had become, it was as though everything that had gone before now counted for nothing. Hatchets were not only buried; it was as if they had never been forged in the first place.

'Jason, good news. We've identified a person of interest. We're bringing him in.'

After the circumstances of the capture had been explained, to the surprise of both detectives, the three-time victim showed concern, not gratitude for a job well done, or excitement at the prospect his ordeal might be coming to an end. The reason for his reaction was soon made clear. If the police could not promise to capture the surgeon, his family would be at risk. In his mind, it would surely have been better to wait until the police were in a position to swoop, capturing the surgeon and his cronies all at once.

Given her colleague's previous brutal honesty, Jane Humfress was best placed to offer reassurance.

'Look Jason, as far as the surgeon is concerned, the Romanian is being arrested in connection with the murder of Andrei Lungu, someone we believe his associates killed for going off-piste. You've not tried to hide. There has been no raid on the hospital. The arrest is in response to their actions, not yours. The surgeon is not going to hold it against you. If anything, he'll be angry with the Romanians for drawing so much attention.'

Her words weakened Jason's protest, but it took for Jane to promise to contact her colleagues in the north, asking them to limit questioning to the murder inquiry, to put him once more at ease.

'Jason, this is good news. Really. We'll keep you informed.'

***

The man, travelling under the name Sebastian Gheata, arrived at the police station. There his fingerprints were scanned, and a DNA swab was taken. He was physically co-operative, but said nothing throughout the arrest, the journey to the police station, or during the booking process, preferring to maintain an assured expression, punctuated with an occasional disarming smile. Personal items were removed: wallet; keys; a mobile phone.

Surprisingly, when asked for the code to unlock the phone's home screen, the Romanian did so without fuss, although he remained resolutely mute.

As soon as the duty solicitor had arrived, the inevitable interview could commence.

The interrogation room was sparse; windowless, but well-lit; blank white walls presenting no distraction. Its most noticeable features were a small table with chairs on either side - enough to accommodate the suspect, his solicitor, and two detectives – and a desk-top recording device. CCTV captured both room-wide images and a close-up view of the Romanian.

Sebastian Gheata noted the counter had starting rolling, but continued to say nothing.

Jane had made her call as promised, changing the way the interview was conducted. DC Angela Pace had intended to sit in but she would have been required to provide the interviewee with her name, the name of the force for whom she worked and the reason for his arrest. In such circumstances there would be no doubt in the interviewee's mind, the murder of Andrei Lungu and the kidnap of Jason Ressler had been linked, increasing the risk of serious harm to the entire Ressler family. Consequently, DC Jones was accompanied by another Trefford constable, while DC Pace listened in from an adjacent room.

DC Jones opened the questioning.

'Before we get going, do you need an interpreter?'

'No comment.'

As noted by the car saleswoman, the suspect spoke with hardly an accent.

'I'll take that as a no then. So, Sebastian, can you confirm your name is Sebastian Gheata?'

'No comment.'

Can you tell us what nationality you are?'

'No comment.'

'We believe you are Romanian. Can you confirm this?'

'No comment.'

'You provided a copy of your passport to the salesperson at Geoffrey Howards Motors, at Claydon Hills, so there's no reason for you not to confirm your nationality for us, is there?'

'No comment.'

'Do you know a man called Andrei Lungu?'

The detective was sure he detected a slight tightening of the suspect's eyelids.

'No comment.'

'We believe Mr Lungu is also a Romanian national. Can you confirm this?'

The suspect was back in control, issuing no further tell-tales.

'No comment.'

'On your return to the car showroom, before you were arrested, you provided the salesperson with the address of your UK residence - is that correct?'

'No comment.'

'The address you provided is not far from 36 Hatton Gardens. Are you aware of this address?'

'No comment.'

'Sebastian, have you ever been to 36 Hatton Gardens?'

'No comment.'

'Tell me where you were between Thursday, first December and Thursday, eighth December.'

'No comment.'

'We've already obtained a warrant to search the address you gave to the saleswoman. Will we find anything at either of these locations linking you to any murders?'

'No comment.'

'Do you own a gun…a semi-automatic pistol?'

'No comment.'

'Or perhaps they belong to one of your associates.'

'No comment.'

The session would be recorded as a no comment interview.

The detectives left the room, leaving legal representative and client to talk in confidence.

DC Jones and his colleague were met by a frustrated Angela Pace, the local detective offering his Furmington counterpart a coffee by way of solace.

'Cool customer. Certainly doesn't seem worried we'll find anything.'

Sometime later, Drake Fallas joined Angela, having returned from a disappointing trip to their suspect's address.

'Nothing. Nothing to link Sebastian Gheata with the murder; nothing to link him to the kidnappings. Plenty of paperwork relating to the importation of fabrics and footwear, but even that all seems legit.'

DC Pace's response was similarly downbeat.

'Apart from a no comment interview, the phone he had in possession is not the one common to all the calls made during the stakeout of the supermarket.'

'What!?'

'You heard correctly. That's why he had no qualms about unlocking it for us.'

'Can we see from the CCTV whether he was using the clean one, or a different one this morning?'

'I doubt it, but I bet he wasn't using the clean one. My guess is that's why he became angry; he realised he'd used the wrong phone and put himself at risk of discovery. Hence he removed the battery. Then he dumped it while off getting his driving licence.'

Drake Fallas had to concede his colleague's theory was sound and added his own conclusions to the mix.

'Worryingly, if he only used that phone in connection with the first abduction, he may now suspect that's how we tracked him down, in which case he might connect his arrest, not with the murder of our man Lungu, but with the kidnap of Jason Ressler.'

Her colleague's hypothesis was sufficient to make DC Pace swear.

'Shit, that puts the Ressler family at even greater risk. I promised Jane we'd stick to the murder to avoid just this scenario happening.'

In an attempt to calm her anxiety, Drake pinned his hope on making charges stick and Sebastian Gheata singing like a canary to reduce his sentence. However, Angela was having none of it.

'Firstly, if he is involved, he's Mr Big, or at least someone high up the food chain. He's facing life imprisonment and no amount of Queen's Evidence is going to get him off it. Secondly, without the phone we have nothing. They're going to have to let him go.'

DCs Fallas and Pace witnessed the Romanian leave the police station in the company of his appointed solicitor. Sebastian Gheata turned to them.

'No hard feelings, eh?'

26

Since the bungled arrest and subsequent re-release of the Romanian, Sebastian Gheata, Jason had taken to sleeping on the sofa with the light on; not because he had suddenly become afraid of the dark, but if he were to receive uninvited night time visitors, they would have no difficulty locating their prey, without the need to go upstairs to where his wife and children lay in their beds. And as the surgeon's henchmen liked nothing more than for their targets to have an established routine, which they could exploit, Jason gave them one. Having once taken a pre-bedtime stroll around the neighbourhood to clear his head, he now continued to do so nightly, whether or not he wanted or needed one, regardless of the weather. And to make quite sure his routine was understood, he had printed and posted a notice beneath the external wall light, adjacent to his front door.

Gone for a walk 21:30- 22:00 hours
North on Russell Way
Left into Cherry Blossom Road
Left into Great Mill Road
Left onto Russell Way

Jason walked alone along Russell Way, an icy breeze snapping at his bare head. His coat had a hood, but it remained stowed as a padded collar, a deliberate act making him instantly recognisable to anyone who might be tracking him. A gloveless hand held tight a mobile phone, password protection deactivated.

Here, cars and other vehicles were sparse, especially at this time of night. Anything approaching from behind caused expectation, time and time again being dashed as they sped by, or pulled onto a neighbour's drive. Jason turned the corner into Cherry Blossom Road. Here the pavement ran parallel to the back garden of the last property in Russell Way. Any overlooking windows were substantially further away than those along the rest of the route – the perfect place; the spot Jason would choose himself if he were bent upon kidnapping a pedestrian. There came the sound of a diesel engine - the power plant of a van. It slowed. Once again, Jason's sense of expectation rose. His hand flipped his phone so that the screen rested beneath his thumb.

An arm protruded from the passenger window, signalling to the lone walker. The vehicle pulled over at a point several panels short of the end of the wooden fence. Jason tapped an icon, previously arranged to be the only one on the homepage. The app opened, revealing a pre-prepared message, sent at the further touch of his thumb. A glance at the screen confirmed it had been delivered, at which point the device was cast from his hand, sailing over the fence into the evergreen hedge beyond. Moments later, he surrendered to the waiting kidnappers. At that same moment, the screen of Heather's smart phone illuminated her bedroom. A small red circle alerted her to the arrival of a message from her husband.

I've been taken again. Such a relief as I've been terrified he'd take one of you after they arrested the Romanian. Hope to see you soon. Love you all. X

The snatch was met without resistance. The van moved off and continued some way while the victim undressed, placing his discarded clothing inside a carrier bag, as indicated by his lone companion for the journey. A liberal amount of lighter fluid was squirted from a tin; more than enough to achieve total destruction of the cloth. The vehicle pulled over. One of the guard's associates opened the rear doors, hooked a stick into the rabbit ears handles, put a match to the evaporating fluid, and tossed the flaming ball over a chain-link fence, onto waste ground. With the doors slammed shut, a torch illuminated Jason's mouth, ears and nostrils. A gloved finger was inserted into his anus, the reluctant owner of the digit pressing sufficient only to gain entry, secretly hoping if there was a tracking device there, it would reside just inside. Forced entry caused Jason to wince, but the pain was short lived. However, the unwanted stimulation had triggered something; a message transmitted to his brain, advocating the emptying of his bowels. At first, the regular gentle reminders were easily ignored, but over the course of time, suggestions became demands. Ignoring the problem worked for a while, but as the minutes and hours past, the auto system threaten to override conscious thought. Clenching buttocks held the inevitable at bay, but soon Jason had to accept it as a lost cause. The kidnapper had noted his charge's restless behaviour but had not considered its cause. Against established rules, Jason began to mumble and groan, his frantic voice stifled by the wide strip of tape sealing his mouth shut. The infringement earned the tormented man a slap, which in turn very nearly caused the prisoner to lose the fight. Far from Jason learning his lesson, the groans grew in frequency and amplitude. Only when additional acts of violence failed to bring order did the Romanian strip his captive of his hood and gag.

No sooner was Jason's mouth free, did he shout.

'I need a shit.'

The Romanian looked, at the same time, both disgusted and panicked. Knowing the van would not stop, whatever the circumstances, it was for him alone to discover a solution; one that would not cause delay; one that would not leave him inhaling foul odours for the rest of the journey. The guard quickly laid his hands upon a carrier bag, tipping its contents - tape and cable ties – to the floor. Fighting the vehicle's restless suspension, and the restrictions of movement caused by the bindings that held Jason's ankles and wrists firm, the captor helped his captive to the squat position, Jason's haunches overhanging the bag, its edges turned down. The manoeuvre was completed just in time, defecation happening as one massive ejection. The breath-stealing odour filled the small space in an instant. The Romanian pushed his charge back to the floor, hoping it caused him discomfort, commensurate with him having done such a foul act.

The bag was tied sufficient to close its neck. Gaffer tape and the hood were then replaced. Only then could a decision be made what to do with the package. Options were limited, but only one worked for the Romanian as it removed completely the source of the stench that scraped the inside of his nose.

Given that it was dark, and the van presented a wide load on a narrow lane, progress was sedate, presenting a solution that promised to be quick, easy and without repercussions. Bracing himself, Jason's personal guard cast open one of the rear doors, expecting to see nothing but the red glow of tail lights pooling on the road already travelled. Instead, the intense beam of a modern headlight poured into the space, emanating from a car that drove too close behind, its driver being increasingly frustrated that someone such as he should be held up by a white van with a missing number plate.

Panicked, the Romanian discharged the unwanted package into the brightly illuminated night and slammed the door shut, too scared of his employer to consider the consequences of him exposing the mission to a witness.

The driver of the Range Rover had paid a lot of money for the vehicle. The personalised number plate disguised its age, but it was virtually new. Designed to impress, it was almost too large for British roads, and the fuel economy paid scant regard to the threat of global warming; nevertheless, it demanded respect. Those who commanded lesser vehicles were meant to know to make way, and if they did not, they were supposed to heed immediately to the gentle reminder of flashing lights. On this occasion, not only had the dilapidated van not moved aside, someone had thought it acceptable to open the rear door to cast a bag of human excrement from it – a bag that collided with the Range Rover's windscreen and burst, the viscous content sliding down the glass in the driver's direct line of sight, triggering a degree of road rage rarely seen. Wipers made matters worse, smearing a brown slurry over a wide arc, temporarily delaying the reaction that was sure to come.

The driver's foot pressed down on the accelerator. The burble of a large, powerful engine, rose. Barely a glance was given to the road ahead; to the suitability of the conditions as an overtaking place. The vehicle swept past, the van's driver unaware this was anything more than an impatient snob who thought he owned the road. The Range Rover cut in close, as though squeezing in to avoid an unexpected oncoming car that was not there. The Romanian cussed beneath his breath; hit his brakes hard as the vehicle in front performed an emergency stop, only luck and lightning reactions preventing collision.

Aware of his cargo, the Romanian stayed in the cab, biting his lip, allowing the aggressor to come to him. The driver of the other vehicle, incandescent with rage, strode up to the driver's door, grabbing the handle, intent on tearing it open. It was locked. The Romanian wound down the window, wondering what he had done to cause this man to act so irrationally.

The stranger, dressed from head to foot in expensive attire, thinly disguising a well-toned physique, had every intention of explaining himself, but not necessarily in a calm and reasonable fashion.

'What the fuck!?'

The Romanian said nothing in response, but his body language challenged the man to explain his actions and the question he so forcefully spat from his lips.

'Do you think it's acceptable to throw shit all over my fucking car?'

The Romanian was truly dumbfounded.

'What you fucking talking about?'

He spoke with an accent, one which the bigoted driver seized upon.

'I should have known you'd be some fucking foreigner. Why don't you get out of the van and I'll show you exactly what I'm talking about.'

The angry man did not wait for a response, but instead went straight to the boot of his car, from which he produced a golf club, returning to the van, ready to do battle. Still the Romanian kept his door locked, and a hand on his passenger's knee, encouraging him to remain in the cab. Unable to control himself - red mist having fallen - the athletic golfer raised his club high above his head, to the full stretch of his arms, before bringing it down with force against the van's windscreen, producing a star-shaped crack in the laminated glass. The patient Romanian finally disengaged the lock, the assailant immediately grabbing at the door handle, pulling it wide open. Unable to consider the potential consequences of beating a man with a golf club – the injuries he might inflict – the man swung the club head behind his shoulder and prepared to strike. Then he saw the pistol. The nine iron, its shaft curved unnaturally from its impact with the windscreen, fell to the road; a declaration of unconditional surrender.

'Fuck you, English.'

A single crack filled the night air. The round passed through two hands and on into the man's head, who was dead before his body crumpled to the ground. The door of the van was pulled shut, the front of the vehicle manoeuvred around the stationary Range Rover, the rear off-side wheel of the van bumped over the dead man's legs.

***

The surgeon and Gretchen were on hand to meet the tortured patient. The host wore women's clothing, but no gown; an indication Jason would be left to rest before the surgeon took a scalpel in hand. The captor failed to acknowledge the marks Jason felt must be visible on his face – the blows heavy enough to have left the outline of fingers on his cheeks. The surgeon also failed to mention the unpleasant smell.

'I know you were hoping not to see me again, but I realised I have not tested you. I want you to tell me what you have learned and perhaps you can save your nipple.'

With every abduction, not knowing the intended piece to be removed was the worst part, although knowing it did very little to reduce the trauma. Jason breathed heavily, trying to steady himself, aware what was at stake.

'Okay, my wife and I have done something wrong...in connection with the woman who sits in the wheelchair. You place her so she can see that she is being avenged....'

The surgeon's stylus worked swiftly.

'Good. What else? I take it your nipple is dear to you, despite it having no purpose.'

Jason swallowed hard but silently.

'I think she's your wife.'

Neither the surgeon's body language nor Gretchen's synthetic voice chose to confirm or deny Jason's hypothesis. The penetrating stare said nothing, but encouraged his captive to continue; a feeling so great their minds might have been linked telepathically.

'I'm sorry if we've hurt you; your family. If you tell me what we've done I'm sure the guilt alone would add to the punishment. Won't you tell me, please?'

Gretchen waited patiently to receive her script.

'If you do not know what you have done, it is not for me to tell you.'

'I...I...I don't think I've done anything. I think you injure me to get at my wife, but I don't know what she's done. I wish I did. Really, I do.'

The surgeon's stare returned but it was short lived, his eyes diverting to the tablet.

'If you do know, but you deny liability, the lessons must continue. Take some time to relax. Have tomorrow to consider your position. Say goodbye to your nipple if you must. You may choose which one.'

The meeting was over.

Later in the day Jason's host provided lunch, and later still returned with an evening meal. However, it was only when he returned to collect the tray, was he accompanied by his ever faithful mouthpiece, Gretchen.

'Which is it to be? Choose one, or I will take both.'

In all the time he had been given, Jason had not once considered making a choice, his mind being close to overload. If he were to be asked what he had eaten, he would not know. If he were to be asked what was on his mind, he could not say, or begin to describe it. Even now, he had been asked a direct question, but struggled to process it. The unbroken stare of a madman helped bring his thoughts into focus. Putting his family, his career, his very survival aside, his turbulent maelstrom of thoughts temporarily calmed to mere choppy waters.

To decide which nipple he was prepared to forfeit was to accept responsibility. To deny the surgeon an answer was to cut off his nose - or a nipple - to spite his face. A choice had to be made, and quickly; the surgeon was not the kind of person to be left waiting. But which one? Did he have a favourite? Being right-handed, if ever there came a time in the future he wanted to stimulate one of his nipples, the left was most at hand. His fingers moved across his chest to check. He had an answer but then he hesitated, his mind warning him it might be a cruel trick – to give Jason a degree of control, only to whip it away to show he had none at all. The hesitation was not long, given Jason recognised either outcome represented loss with no more benefit than being given the choice of how he would prefer to die – he was still going to die.

'The right. Take the right…please.'

The surgeon nodded.

***

Having slept the night in the recovery room, the time approached when the operation to remove Jason's nipple was scheduled to commence. Although, without a time piece, and without knowing what was in the surgeon's mind, the schedule was more an informed guess.

The patient woke early, as might a condemned man, but found himself still in the recovery room. Time passed, sufficient for him to become drowsy and nap for several short periods. Each time he woke, he was still on the bed; still with the freedom to move the tether along its guide wire.

Noises could be heard above the perpetual loop of recorded sounds; noises suggesting the surgeon, or some other person, was up and about. Perhaps Jason's estimate of the time had been less accurate than he thought. It was possible the nightcap administered through his cannula was losing potency. Bearing in mind how much of it his body had absorbed these past months, it might have led him to regaining full consciousness sooner than expected.

The artificial light in the hall suddenly brightened; a bluer light, suggesting the opening of the front door; a notion strengthened by an increase in the sounds of human activity. Even the dullest of minds could correctly interpret the clues. Someone had been brought to the hospital; someone who needed immediate attention. That someone had to be one of the Romanian gang members. The fact he did not pass the recovery room door meant he had been taken straight into the operating theatre. The fact that a table was brought through from another area of the property meant there was serious work to be done. Several men, including the surgeon, took turns in using the bathroom, emerging wearing blue latex gloves – presumably the surgeon's seconded theatre assistants.

All the while, Jason pretended to sleep, his eyelids parted just enough to follow the drama unfolding outside his room. The theatre door clicked shut. Only then could Jason open his eyes fully and only then did he realise he was in need of the toilet.

Jason had no desire to soil himself, and had the means to prevent it. However, to slide along the cable risked being discovered in the hall; something that might easily be misinterpreted as him sticking his nose in where it was not wanted. The patient could see how such a situation might easily invite consequences, none of which would be pleasant. Given the circumstances, all that could be done was to tread the path between recovery room and bathroom as swiftly and as quietly as possible, and hope for the best. In his favour, the door to the operating theatre was shut; the procedure evidently under way. Whatever the condition of the patient, it was likely it would take far longer than it took a man to evacuate his bowels. That said, there was always the possibility the surgeon was without some vital piece of equipment and needed to fetch it from elsewhere, the emergency procedure having come without prior warning.

So far as the outward journey was concerned, Jason achieved his purpose without incident, other than accidentally forcing his finger through the two-ply paper. Were it not for this little accident, the patient would have made the return trip without washing his hands, saving vital seconds. As it was, he was forced to breach the shower curtain that divided the room, entering the clean zone. There he found something unexpected. On every other occasion, the clean zone had contained just four moveable items – a toothbrush, a tube of toothpaste, a bar of soap and a towel – but on this occasion the list was longer, bolstered by a box of surgical gloves, one of which lay torn, discarded by a man in a hurry; someone who had applied it without sufficient care. That someone had made a mistake. Attuned to every evidence gathering opportunity, Jason immediately realised its potential. Someone had worn it – albeit briefly – and would undoubtedly have left prints on the surface of the rubber; prints that might finally identify an individual, rather than merely a nationality. It had to be preserved. Jason pinched the rubber, minimising contact with it, and dropped it into the open neck of a fresh glove, pulled from the box. This he placed within his waistband. Then, having washed and dried his hands, he returned to the sanctuary of the recovery room, avoiding detection.

There, the first task was to preserve the evidence; easily achieved by tying the torn item within the fresh glove. The second was to hide it. Knowing he would be stripped - his orifices checked - there was no alternative but to swallow it. Soon, Jason knew what it was to be a drug mule, grateful he had only to force a single package down his throat.

Fear of being caught had caused the captive to act with speed, but he need not have been so hasty, the procedure taking longer than he could have imagined, no one emerging from the theatre until much later in the day.

The door could finally be heard to open. Shortly afterwards, a masked Romanian entered the recovery room to place the hood over Jason's head, facilitating the removal of the recovering Romanian patient to some other part of the property. The mood being good, Jason surmised the surgeon had been successful, or had at least postponed the man's demise.

This was good news, Jason correctly guessing the dust would be allowed to settle before any thought was given to him losing his nipple, the surgeon having no appetite to perform two operations in one day, or provide post-operative care to more than one patient at a time. However, what he had not guessed - what he could not know – was that the intended loss of his right nipple had been postponed beyond the foreseeable future, or that it had quickly been decided to return Jason home, no less a man than he had arrived. This news was revealed by actions alone, two Romanians performing the pre-journey checklist, free from the supervision of the surgeon.

There was something different in the way he was prepared for the journey, many stages of the surgeon's checklist being overlooked. There seemed only two explanations for this: either his couriers' work ethic suffered when it lacked scrutiny; or they had no intention of taking him home. After all, there was little point shaving his body if they meant to stop at some isolated spot, fire a round into his head, and then burn his remains. Fortunately for Jason, the latter would prove to be merely the fabrication of an overstressed mind. The driver and his team had received instructions to get rid of the Englishman. However, there was no stipulation they must deposit him close to his home, so the men had decided among themselves to do as little as possible, but Jason was not to know. He would depart the makeshift hospital, believing it to be his last ever journey, hoping that when it came to the end, it would be swift and painless. Everything he had endured had finally counted for nothing. The police had not found his torturer and he was none the wiser as to why the surgeon had chosen him. Given the hopelessness of his situation, he welcomed the sedation, forced through the cannula into his veins.

It was late, but not very late. A few hardy couples had finished their evening at the pub, had stopped for a bite to eat, braving the cold to purchase a burger from one of the many trailers parked in and around town, and then headed for the country park – by day frequented by dog walkers, by night, frequented by lustful couples, although not so many at this time of year, given the ambient evening temperature of Shropshire in the heart of winter. One such pair were aware of a van pulling in close by. A glance from the young man, cramped on top of his girlfriend in the back seat, confirmed it was not a police vehicle, there to ruin their evening. He was aware, but not particularly interested, that the van left again after only a short stay – perhaps the spot was not to the lady's liking.

After several minutes of energetic and ever more frantic movement, resulting in a mutually satisfying conclusion, the young couple tidied their clothes and climbed through to the front of the car, without opening either door. Having achieved his ultimate goal for the evening, the man was keen to depart. Switching on the engine, the windscreen cleared slowly, the side windows helped by the swipe of sleeved forearms. The young driver then switched on the headlights, selected reverse gear and, looking back over his shoulder, manoeuvred from the unmarked space. It was then the lights of his car caught, in their beam, large droplets of rain or sleet, and the stationary, naked body of a man.

***

Wadin Cojocaru arrived back at the makeshift hospital many hours ahead of schedule, a fact that did not go unnoticed by the man who ultimately paid his wages, and so called the shots – the surgeon.

'Why you are back so soon?'

The surgeon kept his sentences brief so as to be understood by the Romanian, who's English was, at best, poor.

'I no take him home, but I take him far.'

'Why?'

The single word conveyed much anger.

'You say get him away. I get him away – take him far.'

'How far?'

'One hundred kilometre.'

Unbeknownst to the surgeon, the Romanian was wont to exaggerate.

'What is that in miles?'

'Maybe sixty, I think. You want me move him?'

'No, leave him. You will only make matters worse, but you have practically brought the police to our doorstep. I will be speaking with Sebastian.'

The Romanian knew the man by another name, but nevertheless understood the person to whom the surgeon referred. His face tensed.

27

Police Headquarters, Briefing Room, 09:00 hours, Friday, 6 January:
'Okay everyone, quieten down, please.'
DI Bickley dominated his normal position, next to the smart board.
'Once again, Jason Ressler is back; at least he's no longer being held, but he's in Shropshire. It may be getting on for two hundred miles from here, and a lot closer to our friends up north, but this is to do with the kidnappings, not the murder, so it's our shout. DCs Fallas and Pace, you seem to like a long drive – St James' Hospital if you please. DS Honeyman will give you the address. I want Jason Ressler interviewed before he's discharged, or moved. I want to know when he's coming home. I want to know every detail of these past few days - from the moment our victim decided to advertise his whereabouts during his evening stroll, to the moment a couple of young lovers nearly ran him over in a country park.'

***

By the time the detectives had reached their destination, Jason Ressler was in a much better condition than when he had been found, naked, cold and confused.
Angela took the lead.
'Hello Jason, my name's DC Angela Pace and this is my colleague DC Drake Fallas. We're from Furmington Police station, the same place as the Family Liaison Officers you normally speak to. They'd have come instead of us but we thought it better if they stayed down south to look after Heather and the children.'
'Are they all right?'
'Yes, they're fine. When I say that, of course they're terribly worried about you, but nothing untoward has happened to them.'
'Thank God.'
To look at the patient's demeanour, no one would guess what he had so recently been put through. His eyes were bright, his body alive.
'Look, I've got so much to tell you. Can you get it down while it's still fresh?'
Angela's back muscles tightened, bringing her seated body to attention.
'Of course.'
Jason waited for an indication his interrogator was ready and then began, working his way through a mental check list.
'Firstly, he was going to take my nipple – he made me choose which one – but then he didn't perform the surgery.'
'Have you any idea why?'

'Well, there seemed to be some sort of emergency. One of the Romanians turned up wounded. I was getting in the way, so he had me removed. He must have been in a hurry as he didn't follow his normal routine. In fact he didn't have anything to do with my return at all. That may be why they didn't bring me all the way home.'

'Interesting. Maybe the driver was just too lazy to drive all that way back down to Hampshire. As it is, you're in Shropshire, just across the border from Cheshire, and that's not too far from where we found the murdered Romanian, and the car dealership where our colleagues picked up Sebastian Gheata. Be assured, Jason, we are closing in. Right, what else?'

'Well, when he asked me which nipple I preferred to lose, he suggested I might be able to keep it if I told him why he's doing this to me. I said the woman in the wheelchair was there to watch herself being avenged and he seemed to confirm that to be true. I suggested she was his wife. He didn't get angry like last time, so I think it is. I told him my wife and I are at fault, which seems to be correct, but when I told him I think it's more Heather, he neither confirmed nor denied it.'

Before continuing, Jason waited for the detectives to stop scribbling and for their faces to rise from their pocket books.

'Secondly, and probably more importantly, we stopped on the way to the hospital. I hadn't thought to go to the toilet before I went for my walk. If it had been number ones, there wouldn't have been a problem - I've said before, they provide a bag – but this time it was number twos. He made me go in a carrier bag, slapped me round my face and dumped me back on the floor of the van. 'Understandably, he didn't want to spend the rest of the journey with it stinking out the place, so I think he opened the rear door and lobbed it out.'

'What makes you think that?'

'Well, I couldn't see anything – I was still wearing the hood - but the sound changed and a bright light filled the inside of the van.'

'Okay, what then?'

'Well, even with the soundtrack playing full blast, I could still hear a car horn and some heavy acceleration. I guess it was a vehicle overtaking us. A few seconds later we came to a pretty violent stop. The engine was switched off and with it the soundtrack, so I could then hear everything. 'Whoever had pulled us over was shouting, asking if the driver of the van thought it okay to throw shit over his car. The other driver then told the van driver to get out of the vehicle. I don't think he did, but after a pause I heard something hit the bodywork. Then I heard the van driver say, 'Fuck you English', and what sounded like a gunshot. Not long after, we were off again. The van driver didn't seem in any particular hurry. We must have had to manoeuvre round something as I felt the wheels bump over an obstruction in the road.'

The detectives looked at each other, dumfounded.

Angela Pace thought it only right she should explain their reaction.

'Blimey, Jason, that's been all over the news. The driver of a Range Rover was shot in the head, not far from here, come to think of it. They put it down to road rage.'

Angela thought for a moment.

'Okay, I'll find out exactly where that happened. If we're lucky we'll pick up the van using ANPR. In the meantime, how much longer were you in the van before you arrived at the hospital – any idea?'

Jason's eyes narrowed, his lips tightened.

'I don't think I can give you a time, but we must have been three-quarters of our way when we stopped – that's only a guestimate, mind.'

'Okay, this is excellent. With each location we pinpoint, we're closing in on the hospital.'

Drake was keen not to leave without participating in the debrief.

'Anything else you want to excite us with?'

'One more thing, I may have retrieved a fingerprint.'

***

The initial wait for Jason to retrieve his swallowed package was followed by another, for the bag marked with biohazard tape to be transported to the forensics team and for them to work on the contents. However, the wait was worth it. Not only did the team recover a viable print, they were also able to identify a sample for DNA analysis. Further, the print was known to Interpol - one Vasile Ungur - a member of an organised Romanian gang, suspected to be involved with people trafficking, extortion, the supply of drugs, and prostitution. Not only did the database provide much useful information, it also held an electronic image of Mr Ungur, who bore more than a passing resemblance to Sebastian Gheata, the Romanian the police were forced to let go.

DI Oliver was quick to respond – sending a team to the Romanian's last known address - but was not surprised to discover the nest was empty. A call to the Border Agency confirmed the reason – Sebastian Gheata, also known as Vasile Ungur, had left the country, taking his false passport with him. If further confirmation was needed, CCTV footage from the airport left the investigators in no doubt the two Romanians were one and the same person, and that he had returned to his mother country within hours of his release from the police station.

28

Heather had not touched a drop of alcohol since her near miss with a train. Her husband, however, had come to rely on it to get him through the day. To make himself available to his kidnappers, twenty-four hours a day, required courage; courage that came from a mixture of moral fibre and deadened senses. There were side-effects to his bravery – wherever it heralded from. Jason's actions fell short of physical violence, but that did not mean he was easy to live with. The progress he had made on receiving a replacement ear and testicle had long since evaporated. The question of sex had not be broached since. Of course he still loved his children – he was prepared to sacrifice himself to save them – but sometimes he could not bear to be in the same household; their noise and bickering nipping at his patience. He was not easy to sleep with either: dressing and undressing in the dark; refusing to cuddle; and then there were the nightmares from which he sometimes refused to leave, even once he had been woken by a gentle rocking of his shoulders and the soothed tones of his worried but exasperated wife.

During the day, Heather longed for her husband to go out, but instead he chose to sit in front of worst kind of TV – cheap programmes about cheap lives and petty problems, easily sorted by a swift breakup, or a box of contraceptives. Although she was by no means match fit, she had persuaded her bosses to allow her to return to work, just so she could dilute her own problems with those of her patients who thought they had things to worry about, but did not. Then she would come home and be pleased Jason had not lifted a finger so she had plenty to keep her occupied, completing chores throughout the house, avoiding conversation about Jason's day. When he did speak, it was clear his glass was neither half full nor half empty – it had been smashed and he could not be bothered to buy a new one.

While tidying the master bedroom, heather discovered a box of laxatives on her husband's bedside cabinet. She had no idea he needed them, but understood why he did not base a conversation on their use. Nevertheless, there was no reason to leave the packet on display for anyone else to see – not that there had been anyone else in there, other than Heather and her husband, since her misdemeanour with John Ainsley, the uninvited appearance of two Romanian kidnappers, and the subsequent arrival of the entire Hampshire police service. She opened Jason's bedside drawer, her intention being to sweep the packet inside and forget about it. However, the task was not as simple as she had thought – if she had given it thought at all. Something prevented it moving forward more than a finger's width; something rising up to catch on the underside of the cabinet's frame. All it needed was a gentle prod of a fingertip – from a slender finger such as Heather's. It did the trick, the drawer opening fully. Nothing more would have been said on the matter, other than a suggestion Jason might want to do a spot of spring cleaning, if the offending content had not been at least another dozen boxes of laxatives.

The way Heather broached the subject was hardly subtle, she tossing several cartons of the purgative medication into his lap.

'Jason, please explain why you have a lifetime supply of this stuff in your bedside drawer.'

The reply was not immediate, there being some details of Jason's kidnappings he felt able to disclose only to the police; one of which was his need to shit in a bag in the back of a moving van, while steadied by his abductor; an act that had subjected him to new levels of shame and humiliation, and ultimately led to the death of an innocent man.

'Jason, I'm not having a go at you; I'm worried. If you take too much of this stuff, it limits your body's ability to absorb vitamin D and calcium; it can lead to decreased bowel function; it can mess with your bones, your kidneys, and your blood pressure. Whatever the reason you're taking it, there's got to be a better solution.'

Jason looked on, stoically.

'You don't know what I have to go through to keep you and the kids safe. Let's just say I've experienced things I am not prepared to experience again – ever. I love Charlie and Lily more than anything in the world and that means being prepared to tolerate things, but not when those things can be avoided.'

Heather failed to spot the clue to the reason her husband chose to keep his bowels empty, instead latching on to his claim he loved the children more than anything else.

'Well, sometimes you have a strange way of showing it.'

'What do you mean by that?'

'Look, Jason, I know you've been through a lot, but you have to admit, when it comes to us, you can be very unpredictable. When we come in the room we don't know whether you're going to cuddle us, or just shout. I know it's difficult, and I'm old enough to cope with your mood swings, but you can't take it out on the kids.'

'I don't blame the kids.'

Jason's response attacked his wife's train of thought, causing a momentary pause.

'What do you mean?'

Jason tried to back track, but he had created a hole and had nothing to fill it with.

'I'm not myself at the moment. I'll be fine once they've caught him.'

His answer was insufficient. He had declared his undying love for his children, but had omitted his wife's name from the list, and when given the opportunity to correct his faux pas, he had avoided doing so.

'You blame me.'

Jason tried not to respond, testing his words in his head before letting them pass his lips – what would be the consequences of telling his wife how he truly felt? His mind knew the answer to that question, but still he spoke.

'The surgeon made it pretty clear we are both to blame. I'm damned sure I haven't done anything. What about you?'

The statement; the question; the calm delivery – Heather felt bludgeoned, her senses temporarily knocked from her body, and yet her husband was not finished.

'I mean, can I even trust you? You told Irene you couldn't drive because of epilepsy. Kept it quiet about you being convicted of drink driving, didn't you? You shagged our best friend. You said it was a one off, but how can I be sure? You've been to Romania for Christ's sake. Is it a coincidence the people who take me come from that very place? You got me to increase the life insurance; a bit of lucky timing, wasn't it? Please, tell me, what in God's name have you done to this cross-dressing psychopath?'

Heather remained in shocked silence, unable to raise a finger, or a word, to prevent her husband storming from the house.

As spontaneous as his departure was, some part of him thought to first grab a pre-prepared note and pin it to the front door.

On his return, several hours later, Jason issued apologies, accepted unconditionally by his wife, as though they were not needed. She understood it was not him talking, but the damaged soul of a man who had been subjected to unspeakable atrocities. From then on he tried to modulate his mood; tried to be more of the father and husband he used to be, but still he could not deny himself the soothing effect of alcohol. Heather continued to run the household. She ran the children to school; she worked normal hours, cherishing her time away from home; she cooked and cleaned and shared the same bed as her husband, but they could not be intimate. Jason felt the rift between them. He tried to undo the damage by kissing his wife before they slept; by making her tea in her favourite pot; by forcing a smile and talking about the weather, but he could not dismiss from his mind the accusations he had aimed at her, not sure if he even wanted to.

The evening walks continued, but the notices pinned to the door showed they were taking him further afield.

Jason walked along York Road for a reason. He had urges that could no longer be met by his wife, but with certainty could be met in the alleyways branching off this well-known spot.

The woman lucky enough to secure his custom was in her late thirties and had probably never been a looker. The lifestyle into which she had fallen certainly did not help, but to Jason, her looks were irrelevant. It was dark and he had no desire to concentrate on her face while she performed the act - at a very reasonable price.

Lucy was used to all types of customer. She cared only about the money and getting it over and done with as quickly as possible, without coming to any physical harm. She cared not that her latest client wore a ski hat and a hoody. She did not notice he wore leather gloves, one of the fingers padded with cotton wool to prevent it flapping about.

Jason leant against a wall. Lucy fumbled with his belt and waistband before sliding his trousers to his ankles. She made to pull down his underwear.

'No, the boxers stay on.'

With that, he released himself, his flaccid penis being taken in hand by the woman who had already settled on her knees. Her hand began working her client into a state of readiness, the fingers of her free hand sliding up his thigh, ready to cup him – something appreciated and expected by her regulars and casual visitors alike. But not this man.

'Just concentrate on the shaft. You don't need to touch anywhere else.'

His words travelled on a breeze of air, tinged with the smell of alcohol.

Jason pulled out his phone, called up a particular website and began watching videos that quickly overrode the reluctance of parts of his body to grow.

Lucy paused to produce a condom from her bra. Her eyes met those of her customer, judging his reaction. If the use of such an item was going to be a problem, she wanted more money. She need not have worried. Even in his desperate state, Jason recognised a drug user when he saw one, imagining what interesting diseases coursed through her veins.

'Give it to me. I'll put it on.'

Jason returned to his videos as Lucy got to work. Despite the alcohol and the layer of rubber, he could feel it was not going to take very long. Why then did Lucy feel the need to disobey clear instructions and make to grab his scrotum? The customer reacted badly, pulling away as much as the wall would allow. Lucy's confused face had time to look up, wondering what she had done wrong, before her client's flattened hand came down upon her cheek. Lucy yelped with pain and ran from the alley to the safety of the company of another prostitute, standing beneath a streetlamp, advertising she was available for hire. Hardly in control of his own actions, Jason closed the phone, fumbled it back into a pocket, finished himself off with a few vigorous movements of his hand, discarded the condom over the wall, and pulled his trousers back up.

Lucy's scream had not gone unnoticed. Detectives Chambley and Humfress were by then in close proximity, having come looking for Jason at the behest of his concerned wife. They first encountered one prostitute comforting another, and then – following the pointing finger of the uninjured woman – found the man who had committed an assault, still trying to tighten his belt.

Not surprisingly, in the company of two detectives, Lucy became reluctant to accuse the stranger of anything – it was simply an unwelcome aspect of the job she experienced from time to time and would get over it. At least he had paid up front.

'Okay, Jason, I am not happy with this for many reasons. I believe you hit this woman and I should arrest you, but she is not willing to testify. Not only that, your wife sent us out looking for you as she is so worried about you, and this is how you repay her.'

'She shouldn't have worried. I couldn't have made it any clearer where I was going. You found me all right, didn't you?'

By the time Jason had been returned home, the children were both in bed and Heather was to be found lying on the sofa once more, crying into a cushion. When she heard her husband's voice, she leapt to her feet, desperate to check he was unharmed. He did not seem nearly so keen to see her, his head hung low, his eyes studying the floor. The reason for this was explained in a series of mumbles. Heather's hand leapt to her mouth, there to comfort a tortured face. Jane helped her to an armchair before her legs collapsed from beneath her. Jason was guided to the sofa.

Heather thanked the detectives, but asked them to leave. Only when DC Humfress had received several assurances Heather was going to be okay, did she and her colleague return to the station with another tale to tell.

The detectives had seen themselves out, the click of the front door setting a timer in motion, the seconds being passed in silence. Only when it reached nought did Heather feel able to speak.

'How could you, Jason? I want you to leave.'

Her husband's reaction was to respond with the dullness of motion of a drunk.

'No, it's you who has to leave. Unless you want Charlie to grow up with only one ear.'

She understood her husband's meaning; that he feared if he could not be found, one of their children would suffer in his place. It had an effect.

Heather rose from her seat, pulled a photograph album from the bookshelf and placed it on her husband's lap.

'I'm going to bed. Here, remember what's at stake.'

Jason said nothing but spent hours studying the images of a once happy family looking back at him. The photos taken so that in years to come each member of the family could recall all those moments that gave life purpose.

Since his latest return, Jason had almost admitted defeat. It had needed a crisis such as this to determine the next move on the chess board.

As quietly as possible, Jason made coffee and set about tidying the house without disturbing the family as they slept; some more soundly than others. Most significantly, he gathered together every bottle and can that declared alcoholic content on its label, and emptied each down the sink. He then found paper and pen and wrote a pledge to his family: a list of things he would and would not do, promising to be a better father and husband in future. He then slept on the sofa, rising early so he might shower and shave, that he might present himself in the best possible light when he entered the bedroom bearing a tray with breakfast upon it and a handmade card, the word 'sorry' dominating the front.

The truce was not immediate, but Jason's actions throughout the day spoke louder than the words he had written.

The children had not baked a cake with their Daddy – ever; had not watched a film with him for a long time; and rarely sampled his cooking, which was received to much acclaim, albeit potato waffles, burger and beans.

Later, having read Charlie and Lily each a bedtime story of their choice, Heather and Jason spent time together on the sofa, doing nothing more than watching TV, commenting to each other on the plot, Jason resorting to Google to answers questions about where they had seen certain actors before.

Once in bed, Jason was keen to know whether he had done enough.

'Heather, are we going to be okay?'

Heather took her husband's hand.

'Of course we are.'

29

Jason stood in the back garden, looking towards the bird feeders. Heather joined him, two mugs of tea in hand – one for him; one for her – their first of the day. He having just replenished the fat balls, it was reasonable for Heather to imagine he was waiting for the starlings to descend, and that anything he said would relate to wildlife, or the cold. Evidently, he had something else on his mind.

'Milestones'

'Sorry?'

'Milestones. We live by them: birthdays; Christmas; New Years; retirement; births, deaths and marriages. It's a time to reflect; to take stock.'

His wife responded with a lengthened 'Okay', suggesting she thought he might have gone mad, but was too polite to say. Whether it was a need to assure her he was not insane, or because he was rehearsing a theory, he continued unabated, never diverting his gaze from the feeders.

'I mean, here we are - Lily's seventh birthday - and I can't help but think of all that's gone on over the past year. I mean, on the twentieth of January last year she was unwrapping her new bike without a care in the world, and with a smile on her face. Who would have guessed by the same time next year I'd have been kidnapped multiple times and had several bits of my body hacked off by a cross-dressing serial nutter?'

His tone was matter of fact.

It was difficult to know how to respond. Heather judged it best simply to change the subject.

'As you say, it's Lily's birthday, so let's make it as special as possible. I've taken the day off so I'll walk her to school and once I get back we'll spend the day getting ready for the party. I've got some banners, so I'll need your help to put them up.'

Jason took a sip of tea.

'Twenty kids running round like a herd of springboks. We must be mad. I'm glad your parents are coming to help keep them under control.'

***

The party went well, each of the children arriving on time, showering Lily with generous presents. The hired entertainer was a Godsend; performing magic tricks; sculpting balloons; painting faces. As the children ate, Bilbo cleared away and was soon gone. After the party guests had eaten, the in-laws came into their own – in particular, Mark, who recreated the party games Heather had enjoyed as a child. With the children fully absorbed, Jason started the first clean, excess food being set aside for the fox and the green bin; paper plates and wrapping paper to the pink sacks. There would be a second clean later, once the young crowd had dispersed, Heather being unable to sleep and leave it to the morning. The final polish, to commence before breakfast, would restore the house to pre-party condition, leaving no evidence it had ever happened, save for the display pile of gifts and a long list of thank you letters to be written.

While Heather helped her parents in the lounge, Jason gathered together as many sacks as he could carry, drove his feet into a pair of open-back slippers, and struggled out through the back door into the garden, walking sideways, his load held away from each side of his body. Within three steps, he suspected something was wrong, the newly-installed security light failing to illuminate the patio and lawn. Confirmation he was not merely paranoid presented within a further few steps, a man, dressed in black, appearing from behind the wheelie bins, into the glow from the kitchen window. A finger was pressed to his lips; signalling a clear instruction – one that Jason chose to ignore.

'Really? Today of all days? Really? Can't you come back tomorrow?'

Jason remained calm but annoyed.

A second man appeared, similarly dressed. Together both uninvited guests took hold of their prey's upper arms, guiding him silently down the length of the back garden and through the gate at the end. An SUV was waiting in the cul-de-sac, on the other side of the fence. For once there was no sound track; for the first time he was not gagged, bound or hooded. There was no need – not for this stage of the journey. The vehicle continued along familiar roads, stopping on a remote area on concrete, the ground still blackened in two places – the spot on which two cars had been set alight; a spot next to an abandoned barn; one which Jason recognised from before. Within seconds of their arrival, security precautions commenced; clothes had been cut free; mouth inspected; tape, hood and bindings applied; fire started; and once on the floor of the awaiting van, Jason's companion for the journey took advantage of his captive's knees being curled to his chest, to thrust his finger deep inside Jason's rectum, the sweep being swift but thorough.

***

The surgeon was not interested in talking to his patient until both of them had been given the opportunity for a good night's sleep. When he woke, the captive was provided with breakfast and time to eat it at his leisure. All indications were that surgery was far from imminent.

The surgeon provided room service, clearing away the dishes to the kitchen before returning, Gretchen in hand.

'The police appear to have made headway, despite my precautions. I am interested to know just how much. I am guessing it is limited as I cannot believe they would put you in such danger if they were ready to pounce. So, before your surgery, I want you to bring me up to date. If I do not believe you, or I think you are holding back, I shall perform the latest procedure without anything for the pain. You will feel every cut and stitch. It will be agony. Then, if I am still not convinced, I shall replace you with one or both of your children; then your wife.'

In Jason's opinion, the surgeon could have saved the effort of writing such a lengthy threat. He need have simply stated what he wanted, both parties being fully aware of the potential consequences should the captive decide not to co-operate.

'Well, with regards to your identity, all I can say is I'm pretty sure you're a man, not a woman, and that you're a skilled surgeon – humans, not a vet. What else? Oh yes, I believe you use Romanian traffickers to do your dirty work. Erm, I don't believe you're a Buddhist. Erm, with regards to the person in the wheelchair, as I've said before, I believe she's your wife and she is at least part of your motive, being placed there to see her disability avenged. As to where we are, we have a few clues: one of the vehicles used by your henchmen was stolen from Lerwyn; the man who took it was found dead in Trefford; another one of the Romanians was picked up at a car dealership at Claydon Hills; of course, there's the road rage incident that made the headlines, pinpointing the exact spot we reached, about three-quarters along our way to get here; then there's the fact I was dropped off much closer to here on the return journey, probably taking me just across the county line. If you put a pin in a map for each of these, you get quite a cluster. I reckon we know the location of this place to within forty or fifty miles.'

With nothing more to confess, Jason looked to his captor for an indication how he was doing. The surgeon's stylus stabbed a short sentence.

'What road rage?'

Jason looked confused, but did not hesitate to answer.

'On the way here, last time. I had to shit in a carrier bag. The fella in the back of the van with me didn't like the idea of it stinking the place out so he threw it out the rear door. It must have hit another car. That led to an argument and your guy shot him in the face – it made all the papers.'

The surgeon's lack of reaction to the news led Jason to believe he was covering for the fact this was the first he had heard of it. He must have read of the case, or heard of it on the news, but probably did not realise the murderer was one of his own men.

'What else do you know?'

'Okay, I believe you are punishing my wife because of something you believe she has done to you. I believe you bring me here because it's probably a second home, although I don't think it's been occupied for some time – given the décor. We're in the middle of nowhere; either an isolated bungalow, or a small hamlet.'

There being nothing more Jason felt he could say, he waited expectantly to discover whether he had said enough, or too much.

'Good. You have come a long way. Tell me, how did you find out about my Romanian associates? Remember, I know what you have done. My associates may be goons, but they are experienced and well trained.'

Good was better than retribution, giving Jason the confidence to respond freely.

'One of them shouted at me in Romanian – just two words, but that was enough for the police.'

'Anything else?' Gretchen asked pleasantly, suggesting the man behind the words knew full well there was.

'I smuggled a fingerprint to the police. A glove within a glove; I swallowed it, but I suspect you already knew that.'

Despite the heavy disguise, a twitch of the surgeon's face told the captive he was wrong to have made that assumption.

The delay caused by the need for the surgeon to compose every letter and character of his response provided Jason time to regret his mistake.

'And whose fingerprint might that have been? I imagine if it had been mine, we would not be having this conversation.'

It was too late to be evasive, and there was a lot to fear if he was correctly judged to be withholding information. Reluctantly, Jason revealed the remainder of his hand.

'One of your Romanian friends – Vasile Ungur – here under the name Sebastian Gheata.'

The pause was agonising, Jason having no idea in what direction this stilted conversation would lead.

Finally, the surgeon tapped play, permitting Gretchen to respond on his behalf.

'Yes, he has had to leave the country because of you. Most inconvenient. In taking your nipple I am simply fulfilling unfinished business, but if it makes more sense to you, consider it payment for causing me complications. At least by your honesty, you have saved your family; your children.

The rest of the day and night past without incident or interest, and on the following morning Jason woke briefly in the operating theatre, long enough to experience sedatives and painkillers being forced into his bloodstream, returning him to a temporary state of carefree serenity. Thereafter, he woke in the recovery room, missing his nipple of choice, although the patient had only his captor's word for it, the generous dressing covering his chest to some depth. The sense of this latest loss was immediate. Although, on a man, a nipple served no purpose other than to add interest, nevertheless, it had been his since birth, and was now lost for no better reason than to satisfy the whim of a madman.

Following a brief exchange of words, the surgeon departed the property, presumably to return his wife home. The prisoner was left to dwell on his loss, strapped to the bed, remaining in much the same position until his captor's return, at which point the victim was given the freedom of his tether. From that point, Jason became confident of what was to come: the provision of familiar food; the return of the Romanians; the roughest kinds of pre-transfer preparations; an uncomfortable journey of indeterminable length; and finally the discovery of where he had been dumped, discarded in such a way as to keep him and the police guessing. He had every right to feel confident as it was indeed his captor's intended course of action. However, unbeknownst to both men, the surgeon's plans were about to be disrupted.

The doorbell rang, followed by frantic rapping on the front door. From the recovery room, Jason heard sounds of men with heavy East European accents. They having broken the golden rule of silence, the surgeon responded with a pronounced 'shhh!'

Still attached to his tether, Jason peered into the hall, hoping not to be spotted. His head cocked to one side, he caught a glimpse of four figures: two men dressed entirely in black, supporting a third, similarly dressed, but whose clothing had become heavily contaminated with fresh blood – seemingly his own; and the surgeon, indicating for the men to pass through to the *theatre*. Fearing discovery and retribution, Jason ducked back into the room, leaping onto the bed as though resting.

Such was the apparent emergency, all precautions appeared to fly from the window.

'Good God Nicu, this is the same man I patched up last time.'

This was the first occasion Jason had heard the surgeon's own voice, and knew it spelled trouble.

After a delay, his cross-dressing captor entered the recovery room with a needle, sedating his long-suffering victim, who in his half-waking state was aware of the surgeon moving through to the bathroom to scrub up.

30

The effects of the sedative wore off just as the stricken Romanian emerged from theatre. Evidently the procedure had taken far longer than those previously performed on Jason, who, while pretending to still be sleeping, heard other traffickers transferring their comrade through the kitchen, to the far end of the bungalow, presumably to a second makeshift recovery area. He heard this because, for whatever reason, some of the devices used to broadcast random noises to every corner of the property had been switched off. After a while, Jason's ears detected one of the kidnappers – possibly Nicu – speaking in a deep voice, carrying the length and breadth of the bungalow.

'Stay with him. If he dies we may be forced to reconsider our relationship. Boian will remain with you as your assistant. I must go.'

So now the captive knew the first names of two of the Romanians – Nicu and Boian. If the surgeon did not realise this immediately, he would undoubtedly come to suspect it; a situation that was not good for the prospects of Jason's continued survival.

The English-speaking Romanian departed. Jason waited for the coast to clear before making his way to the bathroom from where he opened his ears to any audible clue that might present itself. All was quiet. With no idea as to what he should do, the captive sat on the toilet. Now he had heard the surgeon speak – knew the names of his abductors – it would not be safe to release him in the usual way. If he simply escaped, the surgeon and his cronies would find him, placing his family in the utmost peril. The only hope was to alert the police and for them to stage a raid while his captor tended to his latest patient. That meant finding some way of communicating a distress signal, not only calling for assistance, but simultaneously and accurately pinpointing his location. To his mind, the only way of achieving such a goal was to find a mobile phone and hope it was not password protected. If there was one on the premises, and it was not kept on the person of the surgeon, the only other place it might be was the room adjacent to his own; a conclusion that was not derived at a snail's pace, but as rapidly as the actions that followed.

Reaching down, Jason retrieved the lighter from behind the sink pedestal. It lit, the flame heating the tip of his toothbrush handle, causing it to become a swollen ball of blackened, melted plastic. This he pressed firmly against one of two screw heads that held an anchor bracket to the tiled wall. Jason knew his makeshift tool would be no match for the coach bolts at the other end of the cable, secured fast into the timber studwork wall, but hoped it might at least cope with the less substantial screws, wound into a pair of brown plastic rawl plugs.

All eggs were now in one basket, there being no plan B.

The toothbrush, bearing an impression of the slotted screw head, was then tempered beneath water run from the cold tap. Content the plastic had cooled and would never become any harder, Jason put his creation to work. Placing it carefully, he applied forward pressure, twisting it in an anti-clockwise direction. He noted movement, but at first believed this to be the fragile moulding shearing under the applied torque. However, to his relief, he then witnessed a gap appear between the surface of the screw and the ceramic tile into which it was embedded. To save the tool, his thumbnail became a second screwdriver, teasing the slotted head round, a fraction at a time. Only once it was fully released did he repeat the process with the remaining screw. If anything, it gave up its home more easily than the first. The cable became free, its movement governed only by the second fixing at the far end. However, for all his ingenuity and effort, Jason had not won his freedom. It was apparent the small bolts securing the tether around his wrist, and to the cable, would never succumb to a spanner made from plastic; and that the tether's loop, which ran along the cable, was too small in diameter to pass over the anchor bracket still attached to the cable's free end. Nevertheless, the operation had given him unprecedented freedom to explore every corner of the bathroom, the recovery room, and most importantly, at least a portion of the surgeon's private quarters.

Buoyed by his success, Jason nevertheless paused to listen, ready to undo his work at a moment's notice. The reduction in ambient noise gave him confidence, sure he would detect footsteps if the surgeon or his men headed in his direction.

Fully aware the situation might change at any minute, and believing this to be his best and only option, the prisoner made his way along the hall, opened the door to the surgeon's quarters and entered, penetrating as far as the cable and tether would permit.

To his surprise, the first thing he noticed was the complete absence of CCTV monitors, suggesting the cameras in the recovery room were nothing more than dummies, raising the question, what else had merely been smoke and mirrors? Simultaneous to the discovery there were no TV screens, Jason could not help but notice the chromed trolley, parked out of reach at the far end of the room, the selection of jars sitting upon it reminding him what was at stake. However, there was no time to dwell on the matter. Jason had to find a phone, and quickly. Rifling through the accessible contents of the room, it appeared luck was not with him – no phone, and no charger to indicate the surgeon even had a phone. However, there were positive discoveries to be made: a thick lever-arch folder, full of plastic pockets, each containing documents salvaged from the Ressler's waste; and a diary, the sort of which would be owned by a school girl. Closer inspection revealed it belonged to someone called Charlotte, there being a strong possibility she was related to the surgeon – perhaps his daughter. Jason wanted desperately to read it and knew he would never get the chance if he were discovered out of bounds. Hoping to buy time, he quickly restored the appearance of the room as best he could, before returning to the recovery room to place the book beneath his mattress. Back in the bathroom, the screws were driven home once more, though not as tightly as he had found them; the lighter was returned to its place of hiding behind the sink; and the toothbrush handle was rubbed against a rough surface, going some way to restoring it to its original condition.

Next, confident the cameras would not reveal his secret, Jason lay on his bed and began reading, opening the book mid-point, hoping to build up a chronological picture that would reveal everything. The hand was pleasant and clear, enabling him to read quickly. The entries were literate, informative, and deeply personal.

Charlotte wrote of her mother and father – a surgeon. She appeared to be an only child. There was no mention of her surname. More importantly, over the course of many entries, spread across many pages, she laid down a brutally honest and open account of her life: how she had felt the pressure of school; how her grades had fallen short of expectation; how she had been having feelings for a fellow student – another girl; how she could not reveal this to the subject of her unrequited love for fear of rejection and ridicule; and how she could not, under any circumstances, relate any of this to her parents. She had been singled out by bullies and none of those she called her friends had rallied to her side. Charlotte had tried to speak with her parents, disguising her true difficulties, but found they lacked compassion, dismissing her problems as hormone-related; to be expected from someone her age. Far from demonstrating understanding, her father had demanded she try harder at school, reminding her how much her education had cost him. As for unrequited love; he felt a fourteen year old girl should not be chasing such a thing, and that was without him knowing her feelings were for someone of the same sex.

Clearly, Charlotte's parents had no idea how deeply she had been affected; that her mood was depressed; that she was tortured by anxiety. The only person she could turn to was her grandmother, but the pages recorded her passing away. They had been very close. Her grandmother had always been there for her, offering an open ear, and although she could not provide answers, she had at least been an effective pressure valve. Without that, Charlotte was left yearning for someone to ease her emotional pain. Respite came by way of a website, set up by a woman who herself had experienced the spitefulness of bullies and knew the effect such behaviour could have on young people. The ways the site helped her were revealed over many pages. Her descriptions seemed somehow familiar, but Jason was required to read on, through the entries of several weeks, before he was rewarded with the name of the site. When it was finally revealed, there could be no doubt the effort had been worth it.

'Oh my God! So that's it.'

Jason's eyes fell upon two words, *Heather Cares* - the name of a website Jason knew well, he having helped build and promote it, before having granted his wife full autonomy to run it. She had administered it with a passion, but its success had threatened its downfall. The site quickly became too big for her to handle, forcing his wife to hand over control to a charity that had run it successfully ever since. That was more than a year ago.

From memory, Jason recalled the website offered advice, and touched on the subject of suicide – how to spot the signs and how to prevent it. The site was relevant to all ages, but focussed on the young. As far as everyone could tell from feedback left on the forum pages, it was an enormous help to many in crisis; both parents and their children. Hence the charity was keen to take it on and make it grow. How then had such a good cause become a reason for hatred?

Over the months since Jason had first been taken, he had been skilfully led to believe his wife was somehow responsible for his predicament. It was clear now she had been, and continued to be, entirely innocent, filling Jason's mind and stomach with feelings of crushing guilt, and an overwhelming need to apologise for what he had said and done, made worse by the knowledge he might never get an opportunity to beg her forgiveness.

Somehow, Jason found the strength to carry on reading.

The pressures on Charlotte continued to build, and despite the website, without the grandmother's shoulder to cry on, the vulnerable young girl reached a state of hopelessness and helplessness, unable to bear the all-consuming emotional pain from which she could find no escape. Consequently, her mind turned to suicide and there she found her solution, raising her spirits to a degree of happiness she had not felt in a very long time. Her life was finally back in her control; albeit for a brief period.

The solution had required much soul searching and a degree of practical preparation, not normally associated with the abilities of a girl that age. She had considered the how, the where, and the when; she had weighed up the needs of the few – herself - against the needs of the many - her friends and family; and she had spent more time with her parents in the hope their last memories of her would be pleasant ones.

The picture was almost complete, the diary promising to reveal the final undiscovered pieces, but further examination was destined to be cut short.

So deep had Jason been drawn into the handwritten text, he missed the tell-tale sound of feet pressing on plastic sheeting; his peripheral vision failed to detect the figure of a man no longer in the disguise of a woman; a man who held an automatic pistol in his hand. He did not, however, miss the booming sound of a man's voice, freed from the constraint of speaking via an electronic tablet.

'How dare you? That is private.'

Caught red handed, Jason's only defence was to mount an offensive.

'That didn't stop you reading it, did it?'

'I am her father.'

Jason handed the diary to an outstretched hand, realising the lack of disguise could mean only one thing – they had reached the end.

'Anyway, what I am curious to know is how you came to be in possession of this.'

Jason thought quickly.

'I hooked it with my jumper. You were busy so I took the opportunity to investigate. I stretched my tether as far as I could, opened the door and saw the diary on the floor. I didn't know what it was at the time but I wanted to find out. I removed my top, made a loop and hooked it towards me. I'd say it was simple, but it wasn't.'

He sounded convincing, but not so much that an intelligent man would not be able to pick holes in his account.

Considering his initial outburst, the surgeon had lost his thunder, no longer seeming interested in the hows and whys.

'In a way I am glad it has come to this and we can end this little journey of discovery.

'Those Eastern Europeans are very efficient, but they are so difficult to work with. Besides, I am tired of expressing myself through the synthesised voice of a woman. Conversation becomes so stilted and unnatural.

'We will talk more, but first I must make preparations for your surgery. Mid-morning, tomorrow, I think.'

In an instant, Jason's thought processes were thrown into turmoil.

So, it was not over; not yet, anyway. And there were to be further procedures, but so soon? And there was no mention what piece of Jason's body his captor had in mind to remove.

After breakfast, the surgeon journeyed from the makeshift hospital and returned less than an hour later, at which point Boian was drafted in to remove the leash from Jason's wrist and then escort the captive, at gunpoint, to the equally makeshift operating theatre.

'Let me introduce you to my wife. If I had known you would be having another procedure so soon, I would not have troubled her the discomfort of an extra journey.'

The surgeon pulled off the burka, like a dust sheet from an old couch, to reveal a well-maintained, small-framed, middle-aged woman, her hair styled, makeup applied, but mouth dribbling.

The surgeon automatically took a tissue and dabbed the corner of her mouth, being gentle so as not to smudge her lipstick, or make her sore.

'I am sorry you have had to suffer, but you must understand, your wife DESTROYED my family. She killed my beautiful daughter and ultimately she is responsible for this...'

With that, the surgeon took his wife's hand in his and kissed it, the act of tenderness drawing no reaction from her.

Now normal conversation was possible, Jason felt free to use it.

'What are you on about? My wife is not a murderer, and I'd have known if she caused an accident.

I know I shouldn't have read your daughter's diary, but I did. I found mention of the website my wife used to run, but I still don't see the connection. Your daughter was a very troubled young lady, long before she found the site. If anything, it helped prolong her life.'

'Do not say another word!'

With the surgeon's finger on the trigger, the long torture threatened to come to an abrupt end, there and then, but after a struggle, the man with the gun finally regained control of his emotions.

'Nothing has changed. I am going to continue with my work, but I will not return you to your family between procedures. By the time I do return you, all my jars will be full, and you will not remember your wife's name, just as my dear Jennifer cannot remember mine.'

In a last ditch attempt to delay further surgery, Jason instinctively opted to beg some answers.

'In which case, you may as well explain to me why you blame Heather. I know your daughter took her own life. I read how Charlotte looked for help through my wife's website, but I cannot see why you are taking your loss out on me, or why you blame Heather.'

'Just because my identity is revealed, the rules have not changed. You will remain silent unless I instruct otherwise. In fact, nothing has changed. I will continue to operate on you, and after each procedure I will help you understand a little more. Do not worry, in the end you will have the full picture and it will have become clear why your darling wife deserves this. You are merely a means to an end. I want her to suffer the way I have suffered.'

Jason could not prevent himself talking, despite the clear warning.

'Is that why you took me on Lily's birthdays? A symbolic act. You have to tell me. I have to know why you take such pleasure in mutilating me.'

'I shall forgive your non-compliance, just this once, and I will allow you to ask me that same question again, once I have removed your foot.'

The surgeon's final word acted as a valve, releasing a surge of panic and despair that spread at the speed of sound to the extremities of Jason's damaged body.

'But, you said you were going to take only a little piece of me at a time – to give us more opportunity to talk.'

The captive had spoken without permission once too often, triggering a stern response.

'Do not take my patience as a sign of weakness.'

The surgeon offered his gun to the Romanian henchman who took the pistol and pressed it against the patient's temple, ceasing all conversation in an instant. Unburdened, the surgeon was then free to introduce yet another dose of sedative into Jason's bloodstream, years of practice overriding any desire to cause discomfort by way of punishment, the delivery being made with the utmost professionalism.

Jason's awareness returned. Sure enough, his left foot was missing. Tears came to his eyes as he cried for the hopelessness of the situation and for his needless loss.

The surgeon was with him in the recovery room, looking on impassively.

'You fuck!'

As usual, the recovering patient's voice was hoarse. Jason drank greedily from a beaker, offered to him by the surgeon, keen to rid his dryness of throat so he could continue his rant – unwise but unstoppable. One final gulp and he was ready.

'Before you started hacking away, there was nothing wrong with me. It would be bad enough if I'd had an accident, or had done something stupid, but there was nothing wrong with that foot – or my ear, or any of the other bits you cut off.'

Despite the ease with which he was now able to speak, the surgeon ignored his patient's words. Only when he had finished taking Jason's blood pressure did he respond.

'Before surgery, you had questions you wished to put to me. You may do so now.'

Not wishing to antagonise his captor, Jason took a moment to compose himself before asking what he hoped would be the first of many permitted questions.

'Why are you doing this to us?'

The surgeon took no time to consider his reply. As far as he was concerned, the reasons were clear and justifiable.

'My darling Charlotte took her own life. She was going through a bad patch and had a lot on her mind. Her grandmother knew, but she maintained confidentiality and so never told us. In fact, she said nothing to Jennifer or me, other than suggest I should not be so hard on her academically. Jennifer and I merely wanted to see our daughter reach her full potential.

'It was only when I read through Charlotte's journal - post-mortem - I realised how vulnerable my sweet daughter had become. Jennifer read the journal too and reacted very badly. She was racked with guilt for having missed the signs. We could not blame my mother because she had died a matter of weeks before Charlotte killed herself.

'The impact was so great that Jennifer tried to take her own life too. She failed and landed up in a near vegetative state. I do not know how much sinks in, but I have looked after her ever since and I do know she would want someone to pay. I knew she would want to see me avenge her and our darling daughter, Charlotte.

'Of course I too felt guilt, but I read Charlotte's journal with a clearer mind than my wife. I realised there was someone ultimately to blame; not me; not my wife; not my mother. In her writing, Charlotte mentioned your wife's website. I logged on to it. I studied every page and line of that site. Do you know how many times the word *suicide* was used? It asked readers if they felt they wanted to kill themselves. There were threads of people discussing their feelings, including Charlotte. How is that helpful? Quite the opposite. It planted a seed in my daughter's fragile mind that was not there before. So, you see, your wife was to blame and she had to suffer for her thoughtless actions.'

Overwhelmingly, Jason felt the need to interject, despite knowing it was probably not in his best interest to do so.

'You're mad! My wife's completely innocent. That site has helped hundreds of young men and women. It's supported them through times of crisis when parents like you have not been there for them.

'Look at you. You've damaged our relationship; you've planted doubt in our minds; Heather's had to live with false accusations and has been unable to prove them wrong? You've disfigured me, even though you've said yourself it was Heather you blame. What kind of crazed psychopath are you?'

The surgeon issued a knowing smile.

'Finally you begin to understand the point of my actions. I want your wife to suffer the way I have – to lose her loved one; to lose her relationship; to know pain as I have.'

With that, he paused for a moment, watching his message sink in, gloating as the anger on Jason's face subsided, the last vestiges of defiance and hope leaving him.

'One final thing. My daughter left this note.'

The surgeon held up and a piece of paper and read a portion of it aloud.

'I don't mean to upset anyone, but I can't live with the pain anymore...'

Having folded it carefully, he returned it to safe keeping.

'I have made a photocopy so that you can handwrite the same note, verbatim. Then you are going to kill yourself in the same manner as my darling Charlotte chose. If you do not, I am going to pick you apart and put each piece in a jar – and as you know, I have a lot of jars – and there will be no pain relief; no sedation.'

Hope had been lost, but desperation wanted to buy more time, causing Jason to fabricate further questions, delivering them at a pace.

'What about the Romanians? Where do they come in?'

The surgeon granted his patient a full answer.

'Happenstance...'

The surgeon spoke of his own kidnap; how his mind had festered for more than a year; having a plan – a desired outcome - but no means to enact it.

'I am still an atheist, but it was as if God had provided the solution. How many other surgeons can say they have been forced to work on a member of a gang at gunpoint? We came to an agreement. I patched them up. In return, they brought you to me. Hence our irregular meetings. Not only do I have my day job, my time off had to fit in with the Romanians' activities, and they get themselves into trouble more often than I could ever have imagined. They are not even as good as I made out. Do not get me wrong, they are part of a trans-European crime syndicate, but I very much doubt people at their level would have been able to track you down. If you and your family had simply left the scene, I would never have been able to find you. Now, as you know, I have a gun, and it is loaded, but I do not think I need to threaten you with it to make you do what I say. Thanks to you, your family remains easily available...'

Jason was beaten. In hindsight, he and his family could have gone into hiding – just as the police had tried to persuade him to do, avoiding nine-tenths of the mutilation; and levels of stress so high they caused his wife to consider taking her life. Instead, his life had become such a nightmare, at times he hoped it would end, and now he found himself copying a suicide note, to use as his own.

He handed the completed missive to his captor who studied it for accuracy. Satisfied, the surgeon spoke again.

'When I said *you are going to commit suicide*, I meant I am going to cut you and you are not going to stop yourself bleeding out. Luckily for you, my daughter numbed her skin with a spray before she carried out such an act, so that is something I am going to allow you.'

31

'Enough is enough.'

DI Bickley's fist slammed against his desk, indicating these were not empty words.

DS Honeyman rarely saw his boss so angry and wished it had been someone else's task to inform the inspector of the latest abduction.

DI Bickley's tone was authoritative.

'Alan, get hold of Mikala Braid and tell her to obtain Heather Ressler's phone data – everything – and when she's got it, I want her to pull it to pieces; work her magic. There's something that woman is keeping from us and I want to know what it is.'

***

Police Headquarters, Briefing Room, 09:00 hours, Monday, 22 January:

Richard Bickley took up his normal position at the front of the room, his face tense. There was a question to be asked, but he judged the response was unlikely to be positive. If it were, the Inspector assumed he would have been informed already, as soon as any breakthrough had been made.

'So, Mikala, what have we got from Heather Ressler's phone?'

Surprisingly, the analyst appeared pleased with herself.

'Well, Guv, I think I may have found something of significance. I would have told you sooner but it emerged only a short while ago and thought I'd better make sense of it first.'

'Go on.'

'Well, Heather Ressler has a number of e-mail addresses: a joint address with her husband that they seem to have had since they were married; her own, social address; an address she appears to reserve for business use as a counsellor…and one other.'

The pause caused the inspector's ears to prick.

'Initially I went through the first three as the fourth has been dormant for some time. To be honest, I wish I'd started the other way round.'

As keen as the inspector was to hear conclusions, Mikala was not to be hurried, there being files she needed to access to illustrate her findings.

'We've retrieved an e-mail, dating back two years, written by one Kenneth Gosling.'

She spoke the name with deliberate precision.

She had in her lap an electronic device. A swipe of her finger sent the document under discussion to the smart board for the entire Major Incident Team to see.

Hello, I am a great admirer of your website. You appear to be offering a very valuable service and because of this, I would like to meet with you to discuss the possibility of me making a substantial contribution to your cause. Kind regards, Kenneth Gosling.

'The references to a website, a substantial contribution, and to having a *cause* were all of interest to me. There's something about it that sounds coded.'

'Quite.'

Although not an analyst, DI Bickley had already drawn the same conclusion.

'Are you in a position to elaborate?'

'I am.'

Mikala's unseen hand swiped again. A second e-mail appeared on the smart board.

'Here we have Heather Ressler's reply, thanking her benefactor for his kindness and suggesting he might like to donate without them meeting. In response, Kenneth Gosling advised Mrs Ressler he would prefer to meet, to ensure he was making the right investment, given he was prepared to hand over £10,000.'

Several eyebrows raised in unison as fifty pairs of eyes read the short message. It was like watching a film with the subtitles turned on. Although the spoken word was clear and understandable, it was almost impossible not to read the text.

'Then we have Heather Ressler agreeing to them meeting...'

Another swipe published the corresponding mail.

'And finally we have a string of e-mails arranging a time, date and place for the meeting.'

'Interesting. So, do we know anything about this website, or Mr Gosling?'

'As yet, nothing about the website - as I say, we've only just unearthed the account – but we have, however, done a bit of work on Kenneth Gosling. These e-mails were all sent from a library at a place called Greychurch, located in the general vicinity of the Romanians' apparent field of operation, i.e., the north...'

DI Bickley's body straightened; his open right hand raised to chest height, his index finger slightly proud.

'So we have a man from the north of England, offering a sizeable sum of money to Heather Ressler...'

He addressed the room as if he were a teacher, pausing a video to highlight to the students a point of interest they might otherwise have missed, ripe for later discussion. Having fixed it in their minds, he returned his attention to the analyst.

'Sorry, Mikala, I can see I've interrupted you, mid-flow.'

The analyst made no effort to hide her irritation.

'Now, although he used an anonymous Hotmail account, he registered recovery options, in the event he locked himself out. The long and short of it, we have linked the account to an address – 'The Gables', Gentworth. If you are trying to find Mr Gosling, that would be a good place to start. In the meantime, he does not appear to have a criminal record and I cannot locate him on social media. He's either trying to hide, or he just likes to keep himself to himself.'

Her head raised from her laptop. To avoid further displeasure, DI Bickley allowed a moment to pass before he responded, lest Miss Braid was not quite finished.

'Thank you Mikala.'

DI Bickley widened his focus to encompass the entire forum.

'To my mind, this new evidence raises four matters of interest. Firstly, why has Heather Ressler never mentioned she has a website? Secondly, why has she made no mention of strangers offering her large sums of money? Thirdly, to what *cause* does this Kenneth Gosling refer? And, lastly, we have the greatest link yet between Heather Ressler and the activities in the north of England. So, what has she got to say about it? Right, FLOs, another job for you two. I want answers to each of these questions and I want them by close of play today. Thank you.'

***

Jane Humfress and Nigel Chambley made their way directly from the briefing to number 54, Russell Way. Heather Ressler had a lot of explaining to do. Thankfully, the children were at school and so would be spared their mother's grilling.

Heather suspected something was amiss when the detectives declined the opportunity for a hot drink and a chocolate digestive. Not only would it have delayed getting down to business, but it seemed improper to accept hospitality, only then to renew accusations their host was complicit in the repeated abduction and torture of her husband.

DC Humfress was in no mood to play games.

'Heather, a number of things have come to light this morning about which we need to have answers. For this reason, I'm going to come straight to the point.

'We have evidence that a man named Kenneth Gosling offered to give you £10,000 to support your cause. We need to know who this man is, why he wanted to give to you so much money, what exactly this cause is he refers to, and why have you never mentioned to us about you having a website?'

For a moment, Heather's ability to communicate left her; her mouth forming sounds but no words; her hands and fingers trying their best to mould gibberish into something coherent, but failing.

'How…how did you know about that? The only way would be if you'd read my e-mails.'

Jane's stony expression and absence of denial was enough to confirm Heather's suspicion.

'You have! I thought you had to have a warrant. That's what your PC Billinge said.'

Heather's outrage did nothing to alter the detective's expression.

'We do.'

'But surely to get one you have to have evidence that I'm something to do with all this.'

DC Humfress dropped her chin slightly, but retained unflinching eye contact; her head moved ever so slightly forward.

'The person who issued the warrant seems to thinks so.'

'But I haven't!'

The detective relaxed a little.

'Then convince us.'

It seemed an appropriate moment for all parties to sit down, Heather adopting the stature of a weak individual, her knees pressed together, elbows resting on her thighs, her hands interlocked, ever shifting.

Her eyes focussed on her accuser, but before she could speak, she first removed a crumpled tissue from her sleeve and dabbed her eyes.

'To be honest, I'd almost forgotten I ever had that website, or that e-mail address. It used to be a big part of my life, but it all got too much for me so I handed it over to a charity. I've had no dealings with it since.'

'But you can't have forgotten about it completely.'

'No, of course not.'

'Then tell me about it.'

Heather looked drawn; her response lacked vigour.

'Well, as you know, I've been a counsellor for many years now. Over that time I've seen so many young people at risk of suicide. Did you know, in the UK alone, one-thousand-six-hundred young people take their own life each year. I wanted to help them – make a difference. I looked around and found there was a lack of support aimed specifically at that age group. So I decided to start my own website – *Heather Cares*.'

'And you didn't think to mention this to us?'

'Why would I? I mean, it all got too much for me. I was a one-man band and the site was such a success, I just couldn't keep on top of it, so I got shot of it more than a year ago, long before any of this business started happening.'

'This man, Kenneth Gosling; do you know where he lives?'

'No. Should I?'

'It's our belief he resides in the general area your husband is taken to each time he is abducted. This website of yours could turn out to be the missing link.'

Heather rocked forward slightly, her eyes narrowing as though she was finding it difficult to see her interrogator.

'You're saying that my website is somehow responsible for what we've all been through over these past four months?'

'Could be.'

Heather fell silent, lost in the enormity of the suggestion. Jane's curative was a simple one.

'Perhaps we should have a cup of tea after all. Nigel, be a dear.'

Nigel Chambley was not used to his colleague talking to him as though they had been married for many years, but rose from the sofa to make his way to the kitchen, nonetheless.

Jane Humfress considered Heather had rested enough.

'Okay, I want you to tell me everything about it. If this *is* connected to your husband's abductions, I want to know how.'

Heather found her inner strength, fending off tears that had become her primary reaction of late.

'Well, I knew what I wanted, but had no idea how to go about it. Jason was great. He couldn't help me with the content, but he researched what we had to do. He bought the domain name through a web hosting company. We took all evening to decide what it should be called. In the end, I think it was Jason's idea. He said it sounded friendly, putting a woman's name to it. We chose the theme – what the background looked like. I added some articles and started a blog. Then I added a forum functionality. Those who wanted to write on it had to register. That way we hoped it wouldn't get bogged down with spam.'

'And did you get any trolls? Any threats?'

'No, far from it. The only messages we got were from parents thanking me for helping their son or daughter, and urging me to carry on the good work. And this guy – Kenneth Gosling - who contacted me with an offer to fund it, so we could reach more people - £10,000!'

'Very generous. Did he want anything in exchange?'

'No. His only stipulation was that we should first meet so he could make sure his donation was going to the right place.'

DI Humfress was pleased to hear that Heather was sticking to the facts, as Mikala Braid had presented them.

'How did he contact you?'

'Through the website. I used a PO Box and a separate e-mail address.'

'And did you meet?'

'Yes.'

'So he knows where you live?'

'No, not at all. I was careful to keep my website and my private life completely separate. We met at a tea room in town.'

'Tell me about this man.'

'I don't know really. I mean, I handed the site over more than a year ago, and I must have met him maybe a year before that.'

'Try.'

'He-he was a well-to-do man. You'd expect that from someone who was prepared to hand over such a large amount of money, wouldn't you?'

'And did he make the donation?'

'Yes, but he asked me a lot of questions first.'

'Such as?'

'Well, he wanted to know whether the site was effective. He was worried it might encourage young people to hurt themselves rather than save them. I told him of the feedback I received and he said he agreed with what I was doing.'

'Hmm, if this fella is our surgeon, it's an expensive way to discover where you live.'

'What do you mean? You think *he's* the one who's been doing all this?'

'I believe there's a strong possibility he is. If I'm right, consider this. Prior to meeting with you, he had no idea where you lived, or what you looked like. He offered you a large sum of money to help you with your very important work; a sum so large you couldn't resist meeting him in the flesh. All he had to do then was follow you home and he had access to you, Jason, the kids, and your bins. That's how we think he knows so much about all of you. He may even have sneaked a photo of you for his records.'

Heather looked sheepish.

'He didn't need to. I had some leaflets printed. My photograph was on them.'

The detective looked at her.

'You gave him a leaflet?'

'Yes, it seemed a reasonable thing to do. He was donating money and wanted to know about the work we did.'

'And have you had any contact with this man since.'

'No.'

'So having got what he wanted, he didn't need to see you anymore.'

'I see what you're saying, but if he is the surgeon, why would he wait several years before he started kidnapping my husband?'

'Well, my boss has a working theory about that. You have to remember, the man we're looking for is a surgeon – a professional. A man like that knows the workings of the human anatomy, inside out, but you wouldn't expect him to know anything about kidnapping, would you? Somehow, he's come into contact with an organised gang of Romanian traffickers. They probably found him, demanding he fix one of their men. It all makes sense. We know where your husband is taken to, within fifty or sixty miles – he's up north, about four hours from here. If you had upset someone locally, Jason would have been taken somewhere much closer – much more convenient. If the wrong you have done him has something to do with this website, the surgeon and his family could live just about anywhere. In fact, it would have been more of a surprise if they lived round the corner – think of the coincidence. Quite what you have done, I cannot say, but I'm sure *Heather Cares* has something to do with it. Now all we need to do is find this generous benefactor of yours.'

***

DCs Jane Humfress and Nigel Chambley, led by DS Alan Honeyman, crowded into DI Bickley's office. Feedback from the FLO's latest visit to the Ressler household was greeted far differently than had been the news of the latest abduction in the case. The desk once again received a blow from the inspector's hand, but this time it expressed excitement, not ire.

'Excellent. I'm tempted to ask DI Oliver's team to move in for us, but I don't want to show our hand too soon. If events continue as we anticipate, we're already too late to prevent the latest atrocity, and Jason Ressler is likely to be returned to us soon. In fact, he may already be in transit as we speak. 'Once he's returned, Fallas and Pace can debrief him and with any luck he'll have some new evidence for us. On the other hand, we can't afford to make assumptions and we can't delay following a lead as good as this. In reality, we probably have until the kidnappers decide to take him next time – whenever that is – to wrap this up. That gives us a little time; time enough for us to follow the leads, not hand it over to that lot up there to take all the glory. Agreed?'

Three heads nodded.

'Alan, you and I don't get out much these days, and you two, you seem to have been kept on the leash quite a bit of late. How do you fancy a bit of overtime?'

***

All four detectives set out for 'The Gables', sharing two cars in case the need arose for them to investigate more than one target simultaneously. On their arrival, four hours later, the men and woman decanted, the two DCs exploring the sides and rear of the property, ensuring no one made a bolt for freedom.

The detached house was large and of the type that did not receive visitors without nosey neighbours taking note. One such person found an excuse to come to the front of her property, putting out her bins two days prematurely.

Trying but failing to disguise her interest, she watched, from the corner of her eye, Richard Bickley activate the hand-pull entrance bell, wait a short while and then pound on the oaken door when a response was not forthcoming. Whoever this man was, he appeared to be in charge, and had the confidence not to run when he realised his presence had been detected.

The neighbour froze to the spot when she realised the suited man was making his way to her position. Unable to pretend she had not seen him, she averted her focus from the leaf she had chosen to cast into the green waste bin, and looked towards him, as though she had only just – at that very moment - noticed his presence. Her suspicion that he was up to no good was challenged by the pleasant expression the man wore on his face, and by the cut of his suit. She was further put at ease by the production of a warrant card from his inside pocket.

'Afternoon ma'am. Detective Inspector Richard Bickley. I was wondering whether Mr Kenneth Gosling still lives here.'

The lady, made wary by the publications of the local Neighbourhood Watch group, studied the Inspector's ID before she was prepared to answer, lest the group of neatly-presented men and woman were, in fact, burglars, casing the joint.

'I would say he is still here, but only on and off.'

'Oh?'

'Well, ever since the tragedy of his daughter taking her own life like that, and then his wife causing herself brain damage, you can never tell when he'll be in. Mind you, he being a surgeon – and a very important one at that – he's always been one for working long hours, but of course I was often seeing Jennifer and Charlotte back then, so the house didn't seem empty. Lovely people. Such an awful thing to happen.'

The inspector concentrated on her every word.

'Jennifer and Charlotte being Kenneth's wife and daughter, I take it?'

Just the one question was sufficient to trigger all the answers Richard Bickley might have wished for, DS Honeyman, standing beside him, filling the role of minute taker.

'Yes. Now I tend only to see Jennifer's carer, Madeline – lovely woman. Jennifer rarely goes out – unless it's to the respite home, every now and then. She's bed-bound most of the time, you see. Sometimes I see her in the garden, in her wheelchair, but she doesn't know who I am anymore. Still, I always like to say hello. I don't see much of Kenneth either. I only know when he's in because his car's there – a Lexus. Even when I do see him, he doesn't say anything. His mind seems permanently occupied these days. Such a tragedy.'

'So he's not here now?'

'No, he's got a lovely car – very expensive - but he never puts it away. He should, you know – makes it easier to steal, leaving it on the drive.'

'Quite. So the car not being here means he's not here?'

'Precisely.'

'And how long has it been gone?'

'Oh, I couldn't say, but if you're trying to track him down, you might like to try at the hospital – Longdale General. Or you could try the respite centre. I haven't seen Madeline of late, so Jennifer must be there – The Cherry Trees. I don't know the address, but you'll be able to look that up won't you?'

'Yes, thank you. You've been very helpful.'

'Oh, and there's his father. He's in an old people's home – The Beeches, at Sutton Cross. It's about thirty miles from here. I have to say, I've only visited there once – with Jennifer – but it looks very nice. If I have to go into a home one day, I wouldn't mind it being there.'

The inspector nodded and smiled, acknowledging the additional piece of information, wondering what else she might be able to shed light on if only he knew to ask. For now, though, three targets were enough for two teams.

While DS Honeyman took down the neighbour's details, DI Bickley turned to Google to determine the best route to the hospital and the nearby respite centre.

***

DI Bickley divided his resources, sending the constables to the hospital, in the hope of finding Kenneth Gosling, while he and Alan Honeyman took the respite home, in search of Jennifer. A short while later, both teams received further evidence they were on the right track.

The management at Longdale General spoke very highly of Kenneth Gosling's work, but said he was liable to taking time off at short notice – understandable in the light of what he and his family had suffered. A look at their records showed a clear pattern of absence coinciding with each and every time Jason Ressler had been taken, but that did not mean he was not simply seeing private patients whose insurance often drew him to the more exclusive facilities around the county.

The respite home also kept records. Jennifer Gosling went there often. Of note, she was delivered there a few days before every occasion Jason Ressler had been operated upon. The staff of The Cherry Trees thought it peculiar her husband left her there, giving him and Madeline a rest, only to then take her out for the day, within just a day or two of her arrival. Of far greater importance, their log recorded Jennifer Gosling had been taken by her husband early in the morning of the previous day, being returned during the afternoon. DI Bickley imagined this latest revelation pinpointed a narrow time frame in which Jason Ressler's latest surgery had taken place. It was then that the manager of the respite centre turned to the next page, in order to highlight a further entry, recording Jennifer Gosling's departure that very day, only hours before the detectives arrived – unusual, even by the Goslings' standards. One possibility came instantly to the minds of the two detectives. A knowing look confirmed they had both made the same conclusion. The surgeon had left the normal path he trod. Either there had been a postponement the previous day, or Jason Ressler was to be further mutilated, twice in as many days.

The staff at Longdale and The Cherry Trees had been most helpful, convincing all four detectives they were hot on the heels of the surgeon, but none of the witnesses could suggest where they might find him, other than places to which they had already been.

Having left one species of tree, DI Bickley's only remaining course of action was to head to another – The Beeches – first passing on instructions for DCs Humfress and Chambley to meet them there.

Official identification gave the Inspector and his sergeant passage into the premises and expedited a meeting with the facility's manager who was glad to introduce them to Vincent Gosling, a man in his mid-eighties with kind eyes and a damaged mind.

'I'm sorry, but Vincent has advanced dementia, so he'll be of little use to you, I'm afraid.'

DI Bickley resisted the urge to cuss and slap his forehead, instead allowing his eyes to scan the small but comfortable room, desperate to find something with which to turn his fortunes around. It smelled of old people, stale urine, and of moth balls that had never been there – the nose of a previous habitat, imported on the resident's clothing, into his new home. There were very few keepsakes. Nevertheless, one caught the inspector's eye. Walking over to a chest of drawers, he picked up a picture frame in his hands and studied closely the photograph it held – a man and a woman – probably a married couple – standing in front of a bungalow, three poplar trees clearly visible in the background.

The inspector turned immediately to the establishment's manager.

'Do you know where this is?'

'I'm sorry, I don't.'

Richard Bickley passed the item to his sergeant.

'I've read of this picture in one of the reports. Jason Ressler described seeing just such an image at the makeshift hospital. He had the feeling it depicted the place at which he was being held. This must be a copy. Find this bungalow and what's the betting we'll find Kenneth-bloody-Gosling.'

'Guv, how the hell are we going to find out where it is? Vincent can't help us. The home can't help us...'

For a moment it was as though the detectives had forgotten not everyone in the room was confused with dementia.

'You could always ask Vincent's daughter. She comes here quite often. I have her contact details as next of kin.'

Richard Bickley breathed a sigh of relief.

A phone call saved yet another car journey.

'Hello, is that Mrs Sophia Luty? I hope I've pronounced that correctly.'

'Yes. Is there something wrong?''

The recipient would not normally answer cold calls, but as DI Bickley had chosen to ring from the manager's office, the phone number on Sophia's screen was familiar to her. However, the tone of voice was more formal than usual, leading her to jump to conclusions about the welfare of her aged father.

'It's fine, there's nothing to worry about. My name is Detective Inspector Richard Bickley. I'm at the home with your father. Given his condition, I was told you might be able to answer a question I have about a certain photograph on display in his room. Can you do that?'

'Do you mean the one of my parents in front of their bungalow?'

'Yes, ma'am. Would you be able to provide me an address for that property?'

Sophia seemed confused as to why a detective might bother her with such a thing, but gave the answer he sought anyway.

'Yes, it's 'Abercrombie', Fitch Lane, Moss Green. Why do you ask?'

'Oh, it's just part of an ongoing investigation. Can you tell me, does anyone live there?'

'No, my father was admitted to the home early last year. Our mother had already passed away so it's been empty ever since. My brother can't bring himself to sell it – not while Daddy's still with us. Last time I drove past, it looked like he'd boarded the place up. Probably for the best. Don't want vagrants in there, do we?'

DI Bickley found a way of ending the call swiftly while maintaining the appropriate level of politeness.

The two detective constables arrived at The Beeches, just as their bosses were leaving. The briefing was short, before both cars drove away at pace.

***

A recce of the property revealed a Lexus motor vehicle, parked in a rustic lay-by to the rear, out of sight of the front door. The bungalow was in an isolated position, on the outskirts of a hamlet, so small, it barely qualified to have outskirts at all.

DI Bickley compared an image, snapped on his phone at the old people's home, with the real thing. Although the light was fading, the match was confirmed, the inspector finding the exact spot from which the original had been taken, many years before.

***

Jason had learned he was to die in the recovery room; more fittingly, now known to the victim as the mortuary. There was no question of his desire for survival causing him to flee the property, as his wrist remained tethered to the steel cable, strung between the room containing his death bed, and the bathroom. The only consolation was his freedom to wriggle and make himself comfortable in his last moments, the surgeon having decided there was no need for additional bindings – not while he had a pistol in his waistband.

Mrs Surgeon had been positioned so she could watch over proceedings, her disguise removed. She had no interest; her deadened eyes and the dribble about her mouth testified to that.

As though he was merely experiencing the withdrawal of blood for a routine test, Jason opted not to watch the procedure. Something felt cool to his skin – the application of anaesthetic. There was the sound of something being removed from its packaging – a scalpel, no doubt. Then there was the slightest of painless pressure on his arm.

'There, it is done. Of course, it would be far quicker if I were to open your artery up the length of your forearm, but it seems only fitting to mimic my darling Charlotte's actions. Consider yourself lucky. She died alone. At least you have me for company.'

Jason had expected it would be quick, or at least he would be unconscious in moments, but this was not to be. He knew enough about wounds from First Aid classes, that an arterial bleed would fire pulsing jets of blood across the room. The surgeon had opted for a vein, producing only a steady dribble. Nevertheless, over time, there were changes, whether imagined or real. His heart rate began to rise – not surprising considering the stress he was under. He was becoming paler, although his refusal to look at anything other than the ceiling meant he could not see it. His hands were becoming clammy, his entire being, lethargic.

The surgeon was a man of medicine to the last. The sound of a cuff inflating around the patient's upper arm could be heard – the bastard was checking his blood pressure.

'Good, you're coming along nicely.'

Jason began to feel faint; to experience shortening of breath.

'I am sorry this is taking so long. It is a misconception, taught by movie makers, that you will be here one minute; gone the next. It can take an hour or more.'

The surgeon spoke, but they were just words.

'From our point of view, I am pleased it is not over in an instant. Somehow I do not think that would bring us closure.'

The surgeon spoke for himself and his wife, who Jason suspected, was not even aware she was alive.

'Do you know, I am feeling quite thirsty and I am sure Jennifer could use a little fluid. It has been a long day for her too. Please excuse me for a moment while I go and put the kettle on. I shall be back in no time at all. Do not go dying on me while I am gone, will you?'

Jason paid no heed to the subtle laugh that accompanied the surgeon's rhetorical question.

The surgeon walked through to the kitchen, ran the kettle under the cold tap and looked lazily through the window into the back garden – lit only by the kitchen light - and beyond to the horizon, the darkness polluted by a thousand street lamps of the nearest town. Nothing filled his mind. But then something caught his attention; something much closer; the face of a man, lit by the screen of a mobile phone. Suddenly his mind was filled with thought. Rushing from room to room, peering through any window that had not been boarded up, he could see subtle movements; people who had no business to be in these parts, at this hour.

'Shit, they have found me!'

The surgeon ran back to the mortuary, considered for the briefest moment making quite sure his captive was dead, but there was no time. The surgeon having informed his wife of the sudden change of circumstance, Jennifer's wheelchair was swept from the room, through the kitchen, to far end of the bungalow. There he pulled back the duvet on a large double bed, scooped his wife in his arms, and placed her frail body gently on crisp, white sheets. There was just time to arrange her hair on the pillow, so she would look beautiful in sleep. Then there was the sound of anaesthetic spray being applied to her bared arm, followed by the sound of a package being torn open, taken from her husband's pocket.

'If there is a heaven, I doubt I will make it, but at least you will be restored. Know that I have always loved you and I shall continue to love you and our darling Charlotte for all eternity.'

Having said his piece, he made a deep, steady cut along the length of his wife's forearm, a jet of her blood hitting him on the cheek. The duvet was quickly pulled to her chin, containing further pulses that would otherwise shower the room.

The surgeon removed his shoes, lay beneath the duvet, applied the blade to himself, rolled to his side, and placed his arm across his wife, hugging her tightly. She did not react.

Jason's barely conscious mind took note of the sudden disappearance of his spectators and although *it* had nothing to say on the matter - content to drift into a comfortable sleep - his subconscious was programmed to live, seizing the opportunity to make one last-ditch attempt at survival.

The dying patient's eyes opened as much as his waning energy would allow. It took magnificent effort for him to scan his surroundings; to make sense of what he saw. On the surgeon's abandoned trolley, a dish contained a pile of blue rubber strips – tourniquets. Perhaps another ten minutes past before the wounded man managed to tie them about both his arms; another ten minutes closer to his final breath. The effort made him fainter still, causing him to fall back upon the bed to recover. The dying man knew there was no time to waste. He believed his rescuers were outside, but for whatever reason they seemed reluctant to come in, so it was for Jason to change their minds.

Experiencing weakness, the like of which he had never done before, Jason slid from the bed, the hardness of the impact with the floor barely registering in the pain centre of his oxygen-deficient brain. Uncoordinated crawling movements of limbs eventually brought him to the bathroom-end of the guide cable. There was no hope of retrieving the toothbrush from the shelf, way above his head. Even if he could, there was no question he would then be able to retrieve the lighter from behind the sink pedestal and use it to melt the toothbrush, to repurpose it as a screwdriver once more.

Although wishing he had not gone to such effort to restore the toothbrush to its original appearance, the dying man recognised there was still hope. In an attempt to avoid discovery, he had wound the screws back home, but had used no more force than his thumb nail was able to exert without snapping. Resting his ribcage on the rim of the bath, bracing himself with as deep an inward breath as he was able to draw, Jason applied pressure to nail which distorted horribly, but the screws finally gave.

His limited freedom would get him as far as the hall, but not to the front door. He looked about for inspiration and found it in the form of a floor mop, leaning against the wall, and a white towel, draped over a chromed rail. Unsure exactly what he intended to do with these items, he crawled along the hall passage, further hampered by the two items that he continually threw ahead of himself, and then caught up, continuing in this way until the guide wire and tether pulled taut. With his last reserves of energy, Jason swept the mop across the curtain that obscured the glass-panelled front door. The mop head tugged gently at the fabric. Twisting it caused the material to become tangled, enough to provide the gentlest pull. Thankfully, the curtain had been hung in haste – as a temporary means of denying line of sight into the property. The surgeon had been no expert, the gaffer tape fixing providing inadequate resistance. The thin curtain fell. Jason could see the darkness beyond the front door, but he could not know whether anyone in the dark would see him on the floor – if, indeed, there were anyone out there. Laying on his back, Jason took the white towel in his free hand, waving it feebly, determined to do so for as long as his heart would allow. His eyes closed but still he waved, although whatever vigour he started with soon waned until only his hand moved, resting on the floor.

Luckily for Jason, his efforts lasted long enough for two things to happen.

Firstly, fearing they were facing armed men, DI Bickley had called upon his colleague, DI Oliver, who had brought reinforcements, including armed officers from a tactical unit. Secondly, on their arrival, the tactical team had scoped the premises in order to gauge potential threats, before formulating a plan. One such spotter suddenly gained line of sight to the hall, lit by standard overhead domestic ceiling lights, bringing him a clear view of a motionless body on the floor, laying on his back, feet furthest away, one arm stretched above his head, resting on the floor. He relayed what he saw via his radio.

There was a pause.

'I see movement. A hand. It's holding something white and it just twitched.'

'Right, we're going in.'

The tactical unit were first to gain entry, quickly determining the bungalow held no threat, the only other inhabitants being a man and a woman, dead beneath a blood-soaked duvet. A semi-automatic pistol was found on the bedside cabinet, but was declared safe, it containing no ammunition.

Teams of paramedics were then free to do their work, only those who crouched over the motionless body of Jason Ressler having any hope of making a difference.

DI Bickley took the difficult decision not to go in, fearing the presence of his men at this critical stage might jeopardise Jason's chances of survival. He used the time effectively, instructing the resources at his disposal to set up a cordon. Bolt cutters were carried inside; a gurney was positioned just outside the front door; a yellow stretcher was taken to the patient's side.

Jason's unconscious body was transferred to the waiting ambulance, past DI Bickley who was desperate for news.

'I think we may have got to him in time, but he's lost a lot of blood. Only time will tell.'

32

Detective Inspector Bickley visited Jason briefly in the back of the ambulance, while paramedics stabilised their patient for the journey. He took some comfort in seeing the victim had regained consciousness and spoke directly to him.

'These people don't want me in here, but I just wanted to reassure you, it's over. You're safe.'

Jason appeared frantic, but it was not through fear for his own state of health.

'My wife, she's entirely innocent. The surgeon told me everything.'

'It's all right, we know.'

Jason's fingers gripped feebly the DI's sleeve, begging him to do his bidding.

'You must tell her that. If I don't make it, you must tell her I'm sorry for anything I said.'

At that moment Richard Bickley had no idea whether the victim would recover, or slip away, the outcome being in the hands of the paramedics and God. What Jason needed to hear was there would only be one conclusion and he would recover to tell his wife himself.

'As soon as I see Heather, I'll explain what's happened, to the best of my understanding. Then, when you're feeling better, you can fill her in on all the details yourself.'

'Can't you do it now? I want to tell her and the kids I'm okay. I want to tell them it's over.'

'It's best you get treatment first. I'm sure the paramedics here would agree with me.'

A nod showed both concurred wholeheartedly.

'Okay Jason, no more talking. We need to get you to hospital.'

Jason ignored them and responded only to the detective.

'And what if they can't save me? She'd live not knowing how sorry I am for doubting her.'

Even in his desperate state, the patient could tell DI Bickley was being evasive; in his words and expressions.

'Jason, I've just had word, Heather's gone missing. So have your children.'

The patient was stunned into silence, his eyes staring, his mind unable to take in the enormity of the news.

'Jason?'

The rescued man's eyes stared past the Inspector's shoulders. Richard Bickley placed the tips of his fingers gently of Jason's cheek, turning the man's face towards his own.

'Jason.'

The Detective spoke firmly, finally capturing the victim's line of sight.

'It's going to be okay. I promise you. The Romanians haven't taken them. As far as we can tell, Heather packed a bag for the journey. If the Romanians meant them any harm, they would have simply grabbed them, just like they did you.'

'Then where are they?'

'I'm afraid we don't know, but we are doing everything we can to find them.'

'Just like you found me.'

This was not meant as a compliment. It was true, the investigation had been complicated – lengthy. DI Bickley was prepared to take the implied criticism on the chin.

'Jason, is there anywhere you think they might have gone? Perhaps somewhere they might feel safe?'

Emotions, pain and paramedics made it hard to think clearly.

'Oh God!'

Hoping the patient had considered a lead, DI Bickley was keen for Jason to explain himself.

'What?'

Jason's eyes had become imploring.

'When it all became too much for her before, she was going to jump in front of a train. She would have done it if someone hadn't pulled her back. You don't think she's intending to try again do you, and take the kids with her?'

The detective's heart was suddenly filled with anguish, yet he remained calm, maintaining a professional outward appearance.

'Of course not. Heather loves the children. She would never do that.'

'But I've been taken twice more since then. I've been with a prostitute. I told Heather she must leave our home. Things have only got worse since last time. She said she wasn't contemplating suicide; it just happened. If that's the case, it could happen again. Oh God!'

The detective placed his hand on the patient's shoulder.

'Try to stay calm. It's my belief she's taken the kids somewhere she feels able to protect them. All we need to do is get the message to her that it's all over and she'll come out of the woodwork.'

'And how are you going to do that?'

'I'm going to put an appeal out as soon as I can get to a TV studio. In the meantime, you're going to hospital and get patched up so you're in the best possible condition for when they return.'

There the conversation ended abruptly, the patient slipping from consciousness.

As the ambulance pulled away, Richard Bickley found himself standing next to his old friend Alan Honeyman.

'Jesus Al, just when you think you've got the whole thing sewn up you get news like this.'

'I'm with you there. I'm due to retire in eighteen months. Solving a case like this tempts me to carry on. On the other hand, if we're too late to save the kids...I don't know...maybe I should go now.'

'Let's hope we find them then. I need you.'

***

Given the offences took place many miles apart, it made sense for the broadcast to be aired nationally. At the same time, a request for help was published to social media, the Ressler's family and friends being encouraged to share and re-share it.

***

George perched on his leather upholstered settee, watching the television; perched because the filling was so tightly packed, it was impossible to sink into it, or feel comfortable sitting upon it, the highly polished green hide demanding his feet remain on the floor to prevent his bottom sliding forward. The broad arms of carved, dark oak were not to everyone's taste either - reflecting the working man's aspirations of the 1980s, although this one was new – but George had confidence in his fashion sense. If it had been good then, it must be good now, especially as it did not come cheap. Still, he could afford it, having built up a very successful caravan park over the course of forty-five years. At the age of seventy-plus, he was pleased to tell anyone who would listen that he was a very successful man, had been with his wife for sixty years, and that they remained sexually active, although he often went too far, explaining she now had to 'thumb it in'. He never noticed the winces, or failed to tell the next person who was not quick enough to avoid him, especially when they had heard his revelations before.

January was out of season, a time to arrange for contractors to carry out site maintenance, and for him and his wife to holiday in Spain. Inexplicably, on this occasion, she had decided to go alone, refusing to leave contact details. He put a brave face on it, but if he was being honest with himself, he felt lost, the couple never having been apart for more than a couple of days in all the years they had been together.

At this time of year, a few hardy regulars stayed the weekend, installing decking and other features they thought improved their plots of land. Consequently, weekdays were the loneliest. Other than workmen who repaired roadways and improved the shower blocks, the only residents with whom he could converse were a woman and her two young children, but they tended to keep themselves very much to themselves. They had walked onto the camp, despite it being far from anywhere, and only ever walked to the nearby village when they could not purchase supplies through the site's sparsely stocked shop. She was friendly enough when she knocked on the door, but conversation rarely got beyond discussing the weather. The wealthy campsite owner concluded the woman must have experienced a bad relationship as she never engaged in talk of the children's father, and if the little boy, or the even smaller girl, ever tried to speak of him, the subject was changed in an instant. He had not even ascertained their names. Still, the mother had paid in full, in cash, and that was all that really mattered.

The television failed to keep his attention. However, George had embraced the development of modern technology and had grown a circle of friends across the country and beyond, accessible via all the different social media platforms; those that had come and gone, and those that remained. It was a good way to keep in touch, and also good for business.

Having settled down with a microwaved curry-for-one, and a stumpy bottle of French beer, George brought his computer to life, logged on to the internet and was soon scrolling down his Facebook page, showing particular interest to anything caravan-related. Someone was having a baby; several of his friends were holidaying in warmer climes - just where he ought to be; some dogs had been rescued; and some cats were doing funny things. Among these was an image of a woman who had gone missing. Relatives were worried for her welfare and for those of her two children, believed to be in her care. They were not the only ones to be concerned, if the number of times the post had been shared was anything to go by. George had seen a number of these requests before, usually started by someone loosely related to him, about someone who lived in a distant corner of the country, having no connection to him at all. They were local matters of little interest, for example a young man having gone missing after leaving the pub. Even if he was subsequently found murdered, it was unlikely he would be found far from home; almost certainly in the same county; almost certainly nowhere near George's camp site. However, in the case of the absent mother and her children, there was a significant difference. Although the woman – Heather Ressler - had disappeared many miles away, George recognised her face immediately.

He was now faced with a dilemma.

There was no suggestion Heather Ressler was a criminal, or was wanted for something she had done wrong, but she clearly did not want to be found. If he simply told her that the virtual world was trying to find her – at least confirm she and the children were all right – she might up sticks and move elsewhere. A man in his seventies – although healthy – could not hope to detain her against her will. That meant going to the police behind her back; something that made him uneasy, even though he had always been a law abiding citizen.

As coincidence would have it, the woman and her children walked past the window, heading from the shower block to their temporary accommodation. She looked sad, as though she bore the weight of the world. The children looked cared for - happy even - wearing warm dressing gowns and wellington boots, towels and wash bags in hand; everything designed to make readying for bed a fun experience for the young.

As much for Ms Ressler's sake as to ease his own conscience, George decided to make the call.

***

DS Alan Honeyman called DCs Chambley and Humfress to the DI's office where Richard Bickley waited impatiently to brief them.

'Right, Heather Ressler has gone south. We've received a call that she is holed up on a caravan site. She has the children with her and all three appear to be in good health. When you get there, hook up with the site owner, George Obray. Check they are in before you show your faces. I don't want her spooked. I've told Mr Obray not to tell Heather Ressler we're on our way, but if she shows signs of leaving to tell her it's all over, her husband is well and she should come home. Got all that?'

'Yes Guv.'

Nigel Chambley felt it his duty to be the first to break the good news to Heather; to makes amends, having planted doubt in her husband's mind, placing extra strain on their relationship, ultimately leading to Heather running away.

The journey took little more than an hour, largely thanks to flashing blue lights, normally concealed from view. Jane Humfress switched them off as they neared their destination, triggering a questioning sideways look from her colleague.

'It's always possible she has ventured into the village and I don't want to announce our arrival prematurely.'

DC Chambley nodded, acknowledging her decision was the correct one, but there was a caveat.

'I get to tell her, right?'

Jane Humfress had been convinced of Heather's complicity, every bit as much as her partner, but it was true she had never voiced her beliefs as openly as he had done. She shared his guilt equally, but recognised he had much more to be apologetic for.

'Yep, no problem.'

The vehicle slowed, adjusting to the speed limits of the local lanes. When it pulled onto the caravan site it did not venture far, choosing to stop adjacent to the owner's house, some distance from the guests' parking area.

George Obray confirmed the woman and her two children were at home and guided the detectives to the caravan, the only one displaying light among rows of near identical, temporarily abandoned aluminium boxes. There was no reason for the occupant to be startled by a knock on the door, but she was. Through the thinly insulated walls, Heather could be heard tucking her children out of sight, presumably fearing the Romanians had found them.

'Who is it?'

'Heather? It's Jane – Jane Humfress. I've got Nigel Chambley with me.'

She nodded to her partner, indicating this was the moment to make his announcement. Still the door remained shut.

'Heather, it's Nigel. We've got fantastic news for you. Open up, I want to give it to you face to face.'

A lock could be heard turning. The door swung outwards with little force. Heather stood back from the entrance, leaving a large kitchen knife on the work surface. She looked drained of life. Nigel Chambley stepped inside, approaching as though not wishing to frighten an injured animal that could not be told or understand he was trying to help.

'Heather, it's over. Jason's alive and the surgeon is dead. No more abductions. No more pain.'

Heather allowed herself to fall forward into the detective's arms.

'How about we get you home, get you changed and get you to the hospital? It's not local, so you'll probably want to take an overnight bag. The hospital have accommodation for families, so you can remain there until he's fully recovered. Does that sound good?'

It did.

***

The journeys home and then to the hospital were long, providing plenty of time for Heather to ask the many questions she had, but most could not leave her lips, her children occupying the back seat either side of her. The journey, therefore, became a breeding ground for the worst type of thoughts, grotesque images being painted of shredded limbs and disfigured features.

DC Humfress could see their passenger's anguish and did her best to comfort her at arm's length.

'It's okay. It's not as bad as you're probably thinking.'

***

Once again it was left to Nigel Chambley to entertain Charlie and Lily, while their mother, accompanied by Jane Humfress, entered the side room. Mutual smiles quickly turned to outpourings of tears as wife fell upon husband, paying no regard what injury she might be placing unwelcome pressure upon.

Outside the room, DC Chambley decided distraction was required, and so took both children's hands in his and led them to the hospital sweet shop with the promise they could have anything they wanted.

Jane waited outside the room, feeling awkward in situations of raw emotional display.

Jason mumbled words into his wife's neck.

'I thought you'd done something stupid.'

'I'd never hurt the kids. You know that. I just felt so scared. I've been having nightmares of what that maniac might do to Charlie and Lily. I just had to get away.'

Heather raised her body and sat down on a chair beside the bed, her hands holding her husband's.

'Sorry, your finger. I was forgetting. Are you okay?'

'I've lost a foot and a nipple, so no, not really.'

Her husband did not need, or deserve revulsion.

'A nipple? Men don't need them anyway. As for your foot, at least your socks will last twice as long.'

Heather's brave attempt at humour, and her husband's equally brave attempt at finding it funny, put a check on their wayward emotions, sufficiently that things which had to be said, could be said.

Jason felt the need to go first.

'Do you forgive me?'

'Forgive you? What have you got to apologise for?'

'Darling, I accused you of being responsible for all this; I paid a prostitute for a blow job.'

'That's nothing, I shagged our best friend.'

Both managed a forced laugh.

Heather's face once more became serious.

'Are we going to be okay – you and me, I mean?'

'Of course we are. Anyway, are the kids here?'

By now, Charlie and his sister had returned, and were right outside, already suffering a sugar rush. Given the go ahead, they barged through the doors, eager for reunion.

'Daddy, Daddy!'

Both children shouted in unison, before throwing themselves at the bed.

'Hi kids. I've missed you so much I've decided never to go away again. What do you think about that?'

'Are you going to get another ear?'

'Yes, Charlie. I'm going to get everything replaced and then I'll see about going back to work.'

He sounded not too certain about his last promise, but Heather was soon to put his mind at ease.

'I know it was a while ago now, but I spoke with your boss and they're keen to have you back, and they're prepared to make whatever adjustments are needed.'

'That's good. You see kids, everything is going to be just the way it used to be.'

Sensing it was the right time, Detective Constables Nigel Chambley and Jane Humfress entered the room to say goodbye.

'Don't think this is the last you'll see of us, but we'll wait until you're home. In the meantime, let us know if you need anything.'

Nigel Chambley accepted the thanks for all they had done, even if he felt guilty for receiving it.

Then, all of a sudden, the small Ressler family were alone.

'Are you hungry?'

'Hell yes. Have you seen what they feed you here?'

'Okay then, I'm taking the kids down to Marks and Spencer's. I saw it when we came in. I'm also going to pop into the newsagents. Is there anything you'd like?'

Jason thought for a moment.

'A puzzle book and some chocolate. Something the kids don't like, so I get the chance to have a bit.'

'Something with raisins in then.'

Heather gathered Charlie and Lily together.

'Don't be too long. Oh, and can you buy a card for the TV. It's cheaper if you get a few days' worth. I can't see them moving me before then. Anyway, I think you can get a refund.'

Heather smiled in acknowledgement and raised her hand as a temporary farewell.

A nurse could be seen passing by the door, a million things to be done, a ward full of patients to be cared for. Then another figure cast a silhouette on the small glass observation panel. It hovered for a moment before the door opened inwards. A man, dressed in black, wearing a ribbed pullover, combat trousers and a logo-free baseball cap, stepped into the room. The door shut behind him, creating barely a sound.

Jason did not know the man's identity, but knew what he was; what his presence meant. He had only one request.

'Please don't hurt my family.'

The man spoke English, but with a heavy accent – Eastern European; quite possibly Romanian.

'Just you,' he responded, his voice soothing.

'Thank you.'

Jason's final expression was one of sadness.

He did not have the strength to prevent the athletic Romanian extracting the pillow from beneath his head, nor did he try, trusting the rules had not changed – that co-operation spared his family harm. The nameless assassin was quick and efficient, using the silenced muzzle of his automatic pistol to trap the pillow against Jason's forehead, the stuffing acting as an additional baffle. The trigger was pulled twice in quick succession, the weapon was stowed, and then the man was gone.

The noise caused a number of people to wonder what they had heard, but none of them to check it out.

Only the silent cameras in the corridors witnessed the Romanian leave.

Printed in Great Britain
by Amazon